REBEL
COWBOY

NICOLE HELM

Published by Sourcebooks Casablanca, an imprint of Sourcebooks, Inc.
P.O. Box 4410, Naperville, Illinois 60567-4410
(630) 961-3900
Fax: (630) 961-2168
www.sourcebooks.com

Printed and bound in Canada.
MBP 10 9 8 7 6 5 4 3 2 1

For Maisey, who said, "Why not cowboys?"

Chapter 1

MEL SHAW REINED IN HER HORSE AT THE CREST OF THE familiar path that wound its way around the Shaw ranch.

She'd ridden this trail her entire life. On her eighteenth birthday, she'd ridden it with her father. On this very spot he'd told her, someday, what lay below would be hers. It had all been very *Lion King*, and in that moment, an amazing gift. This awe-inspiring tract of land in the shadow of barely snow-peaked mountains would someday be entrusted to *her*.

Someday had turned out to mean five years, almost to the day, when a freak accident had put her in charge... of a barely surviving ranch, a delinquent brother determined to burn every Shaw bridge, an injured and withdrawn father, thousands of dollars in medical bills, and livestock that needed to be cared for and tended daily.

These days it felt more like a noose than a gift. But it was a noose she *loved*.

Mel took a deep breath, squaring her shoulders and squinting into the blue sky. All this was for nothing. She wasn't giving up leadership here for very long—three months at most. And Caleb...Caleb could handle this.

Maybe if she repeated that to herself enough, she'd actually believe it. Her younger brother had gotten his act together in the past few years. When they thought Dad would die, he'd changed. She could trust him to take the reins now.

Regardless, she didn't have a choice. The Shaw ranch stretched before her, like her heart laid out on display along the edge of Blue Valley, Montana. Every barn, work building, even the old house, was looking weary in the early summer morning light. Spring had not been kind.

The years had not been kind.

But she would turn them around. Some idiot hockey player wanting to drop twenty grand on a consultant was just the financial stopgap she needed to get things really going again. They could start to rebuild some of those partnerships that debt, and Caleb, had compromised, to rebuild the cattle herd that had diminished to next to nothing. They could be *Shaw* again.

The clopping sound of another horse on the trail behind her interrupted the quiet. She didn't bother turning around—it could only be one person.

"It'll be okay."

"I know." She'd gotten a lot better at lying to Caleb since Dad's accident. *Everything will be okay. I'm not even tired. Who needs a foreman?*

"I won't disappoint you."

"I know that too." She offered him a smile as he brought his horse to a stop next to hers. He looked impossibly young to her, even though she was only two years older. Before the accident, Dad had always joked she'd been *born* older, like George Bailey in *It's a Wonderful Life*. Apparently destined to be on the hook for a failing business.

Only she didn't have hero Harry to rescue her. She had a brother who'd alienated everyone in town, finishing the job Mom had started before she abandoned them twenty-some years ago.

Mel swore she could feel the noose tightening,

making it harder to breathe. Harder to lie. She tried to shake it off—all the memories, all the doubts, all the responsibilities piling up against her.

She was taking the reins, taking this summer job away from the ranch. She was going to save them. She *was*, and Caleb was going to help. He'd found a constructive way to deal with whatever demons had plagued him. Demons she'd never understood—demons he'd never *let* her understand.

She had to believe in him. Trust him. Unclench a little. *Ha*.

"Will you get me his autograph?"

"Sure." She paused for effect, then gave Caleb her best big-sister glare. "On my paycheck."

Caleb laughed. "Had to ask." He cleared his throat, staring hard at the ranch below. "I know I've said it before—"

"Then don't say it again. The situation is what it is. I'm done with apologies. All that matters is we're doing what's best for Shaw." That's all that would ever matter.

"What about what's best for you?"

She clicked her tongue, turning the horse around so she could head back to the main house. "Shaw *is* me, Caleb." The thing she could count on no matter what. Each peak in the distance, each slightly leaning building, every blade of grass that came back year after year. It was her center, her core. It was her; she was it. Always.

Everyone around her might let her down, but this place couldn't.

———⁓⁓⁓———

Dan Sharpe rolled off the most uncomfortable mattress he could remember ever spending a night on. The twinge in his back as he stood reminded him of the indisputable fact that he was getting old.

Thirty-five meant he was no longer the young phenom on his team.

The sad fact of the matter was, his teammates looked at him like he was as old as his famous father.

That's not the only way they look at you.

What did it matter? Technically they were no longer his teammates. His contract was up, and after screwing the pooch in two Stanley Cups, rumors were starting to swirl that his complete cave under playoff pressure wasn't so much psychological as it was criminal. His agent thought there'd even be an investigation.

Dan scrubbed his hands over his face and walked over bowed floorboards to a tiny en suite bathroom that had seen better days. Probably twenty years ago, before Grandma and Grandpa had moved south and rented the old Paulle place out.

Apparently rented it out to people who didn't care much for comfort or things of this century.

Which was fine. Part of this self-exile was about pushing himself out of his comfort zone and doing some hard work that had nothing to do with hockey. Far away from any rumors that he was some game-throwing asshole. Let the NHL investigate. In fact, he hoped they did, because he'd be proven innocent. Sure, he was still an asshole, but he was not a cheater.

The pounding coming from the front of the house was muffled enough that Dan thought about ignoring it, but then he remembered his consultant was supposed to be showing up today.

He had no idea what time it was. *Crap*. He grabbed a

T-shirt out of his suitcase and pulled it on as he walked through the old hallway he just barely remembered from his childhood, through the kitchen decorated in blue ducks, of all things, and to the front door.

Buck, the guy who'd been doing maintenance for his grandparents the past few years, stood on the porch next to a young woman. They were both smiling...until they looked at him.

Then those smiles died. While he was pretty sure it had nothing to do with hockey, he'd been on the end of that change enough times to fall back into old habits. Because if people weren't going to be happy to see you, why not make them *really* unhappy?

"Howdy, partners," he said.

The woman's cool expression went to pure ice, jaw setting, dark eyes not even bothering to meet his. "Mr. Sharpe, I assume."

"And you are?"

She stuck out her hand, grudgingly it seemed. Like she didn't want to touch him. Or even be here. Not the normal reaction from women who sought him out. "Mel Shaw."

He tried to keep the shock from showing on his face, but he couldn't manage it. When Buck had suggested Mel for the job, he'd never mentioned she was a woman. A young woman. A young, *attractive* woman, even under all the cowgirl garb she had going on.

She was tall, her hair a rich brunette. She had a pert nose dusted with freckles, and a lush mouth that didn't match the sharp angles of the rest of her. Her hand wasn't soft as it shook his, but she had long, delicate fingers.

Not at all the picture of *Mel Shaw* he'd had in his head when Buck said he'd arrange for a summer consultant.

Mel glared at Buck as she dropped his hand. "You didn't tell him?"

"Sorry, too fun."

"You're a jerk, Buck."

"Anyway, I'll leave you two to get acquainted." The man tipped his hat, and if Dan wasn't mistaken, laughed himself all the way back to his truck.

Dan's Harley looked out of place sandwiched between two old, huge pickup trucks. He looked back to the woman on his porch to find that nothing about her irritated expression had changed.

"I don't care that you're a woman." He didn't. Really. She was wearing a cowboy hat, cowboy boots, jeans streaked with dirt and dust, and a plaid button-up shirt. In every respect, she appeared to be the real deal. It didn't matter that she also had breasts.

Which she then crossed her arms over, because apparently he'd been staring. *Crap*.

"And I don't care that you're some hotshot hockey player, so I guess we're even."

"Well, calling me a hot anything kind of says otherwise."

She looked to the sky and took a deep breath. "Mr. Sharpe, I think we're getting off on the wrong foot."

"You're right. Come on in."

She furrowed her brow at him. "You're not even dressed."

Dan looked down at his T-shirt and ratty gym shorts. "Well, I'm not naked."

Her cheeks went a little pink, and he couldn't stop

himself from grinning. Of course, the grin that usually caused women to bat their lashes or slip him their number just caused Cowgirl to roll her eyes.

"I bet you expect women to drop their clothes when you smirk like that."

He wasn't sure why her disdain struck him as funny, but it did. Maybe because it had nothing to do with the rumors, nothing to do with him booting the puck more times than a reasonable person could think was an accident.

"Well, Mel, can't say I'd mind that."

The pink in her cheeks went darker, but she fixed him with a glare. "Watch it, buddy. I may need the money, but you try to sexually harass me and your balls will be in some serious danger."

He held up his hands in mock surrender. "Let me point out that you were the one who brought up taking off your clothes, not me. Still, I apologize. I'm not really known for saying the right thing at the right time." No, Dan Sharpe had a habit of always doing the wrong thing at the wrong time. Funny, none of his teammates had cared until last year. Probably because until then, hockey was the only thing he'd never screwed up.

Guess there was a first time for everything.

Which was why he was here. Hiding out. Couldn't say the wrong thing to the press if they weren't around. Couldn't mess it up more, make everyone's life harder if he was far, far away.

That was the hope anyway. His hope, his agent's hope, and though Dad hadn't been anything but encouraging, Dan had a feeling he was really hoping his son didn't screw up his chances at a front office promotion.

Besides, Grandpa had once said this place had

meaning. Dan might be needing some of that *meaning* in his life if hockey evaporated.

Damn, but he needed to get his shit together. He turned back into the kitchen, leaving the door open for Mel. "Coffee?"

"Please tell me you didn't just roll out of bed." She stepped inside, eyes immediately assessing the kitchen as she took off her hat and placed it on the counter. She looked even younger without the hat, with freckles, a fresh face, and her dark hair pulled back into a serviceable braid.

But his eyes kept falling to her mouth. It made him think of a different kind of servicing.

Which was super douchey, even for him.

"I'm still working on the time change," he offered by way of sad excuse. Bottom line, he had no idea what time it was. The clocks in this place were all wrong. His phone had died last night, and he hadn't felt much like charging it—not when all the calls seemed to be more bad news.

"Yeah, that one-hour difference must be a real bitch."

He snorted in surprise. Mel Shaw was an interesting development. He'd been expecting some crusty old stodger to yell orders at him while he slaved over menial tasks. Truthfully, there had been some appeal in that.

There was some appeal in Mel doing the same, though. Anything to keep his mind occupied was A-OK in his book. Since he couldn't skate to clear his thoughts like he usually did, this was the only other thing he could think to do.

"All right. First, you need to get dressed. Into clothes you can actually do some serious work in. You're also going to need a different vehicle. I'm assuming money's no object for you, and you'll need something with hauling capabilities. Besides, that bike will get eaten up driving around out here."

She said it with such obvious disdain, like he hadn't worked hard for his money. Sure, he wasn't saving the world one blown Stanley Cup game at a time, but he *was* sacrificing his body and possibly a healthy old age for the fans' enjoyment. He wasn't exactly sitting on his ass having gold coins thrown at him.

"You're giving a lot of orders to a guy who's your boss."

She kept her arms crossed over her chest. "You're not my boss. Consultant means my job is telling *you* what to do."

"I'm paying you."

"You're paying me to teach you how to run this place. That means I'm in charge and you listen to what I say. Basically, you're paying me to be *your* boss. Keep that in mind. Now, go get dressed so we can actually get some work done around here." She gestured to the back of the house. "I'll make the coffee."

He didn't move or say anything at first—just watched her. She certainly looked like Ms. Tough Guy, but she also didn't meet his gaze, and she looked uncomfortable, maybe even restless. Like this job was the last thing she wanted to be doing with her time.

Interesting.

So, he gave a little nod. "Can't say no to that. I like mine with cream."

She snorted, turning to the coffeepot. "Of course you do," she muttered.

He had to chuckle. Three months of going toe-to-toe with some cowgirl with an attitude problem sounded a hell of a lot better than flashbulbs, veiled and not-so-veiled accusations.

And who knew? It could even be fun.

Chapter 2

MEL STARED AT THE COFFEEPOT, WATCHING DARK liquid trickle into the glass carafe. She didn't like the jittery feeling in her gut. Nerves. But not quite like the nerves she got when she had to go talk to the bank or miss a payment on something. These were different nerves.

Crap-he's-hot nerves. She'd googled the guy. She'd seen some pictures of magazine shoots he'd done, but she figured Photoshop had gone a long way toward making him look like some kind of hot celebrity.

Unless he had Photoshop done on his actual face, he just looked like that. And that smile? That was a *smile*. Smiling was rare in her world lately. So rare it seemed almost like a mirage.

When Dan reappeared, he was wearing jeans. The dark-wash kind that looked like they'd never seen a day of work. A little too tight around the thigh to make riding a horse comfortable.

A little too tight around muscular, yummy thigh to make *her* comfortable.

"Maybe we should start over," he said, sounding sincere for the first time since he'd opened his door. No condescending drawl of *partner*, and no lame sexual innuendo.

"Yeah. We should." She turned back to the coffeepot. She was definitely not thinking about sexual anything right now. She most certainly wasn't blushing.

Liar, liar, pants on so much fire.

She hated him for this. The good-looking thing, the weird-sexy-charm thing. Things she didn't know what to do with. Hockey players were supposed to be all toothless lunkheads, right? Instead, he looked like fiction. Black hair long enough to run fingers through, green eyes the color of mountain sage, sharp nose and cheekbones, strong jaw, all his teeth.

Plus, an incredible body. Yes, he was obviously a professional athlete with that body. The T-shirt he was wearing was practically a screaming invitation to ogle his shoulders. Broad and muscly and...

No. She was not this girl. Even before, when she'd had the time and inclination for that sort of thing, tongue-tied and blushy had never been her MO.

Everything with her one and only romantic entanglement had been easy and sweet and not...confusing. She did not do confusing.

So, yes, they needed to start over.

She took a deep breath, trying to push the nerves away. "The first thing we should do is take a ride around. Get the lay of the land. Then I can help you draw up an overall ranch plan, a daily schedule." She handed him his coffee—black, because he hadn't *had* any cream in his old, whirring, rusty refrigerator.

She'd been surprised to find the house in about the same shape as that refrigerator. Old, poorly running, heavy with disuse. Every part of the place she'd seen was kind of a dump, really. She'd expected a famous hockey player who could drop a bunch of money on a *consultant* would also drop a lot of money on fixing up a place before he stayed in it.

"You'll also want to go grocery shopping, if you have any hope of eating today. Have you spent any time getting acquainted with Blue Valley?"

"Is there much to get acquainted with?"

She shook her head. While she hadn't expected the disrepair, she wasn't surprised to find Dan Sharpe was kind of useless. She pulled the little notebook and pen that she used for taking notes around the ranch out of her front pocket.

"You eaten breakfast?" she asked.

"Nope. Just crawled out of bed, remember?"

"What were you planning on eating?"

He glanced around the kitchen with a thoughtful look on his face. "You know, I hadn't given it much thought. McDonald's nearby? I haven't had one of their hash browns in years."

She stared. And stared. And stared a little more.

Dan grimaced. "No McDonald's, huh?"

"Buck said this was your family place. They didn't clue you in to anything?"

"My grandparents moved to Florida over twenty-five years ago, and they aren't in the best shape to clue me in."

She scratched her pen across the top of the page until the ink gave, then she started her list. "We'll go to town first. We should go ahead and pick up some fencing supplies—from the looks of it, that'll be your first order of business. Then we can do a grocery run before coming back."

"Fencing?"

Jeez. He really was clueless. As much as she'd expected him to be spoiled by money and fame, she thought if he wanted to run this place, he'd actually know *something*.

"Maybe, before we do anything, we should figure out just what you're wanting to do here."

"I want to start a ranch."

"In your mind, what does that entail?"

He shrugged, starting to paw through cabinets. "I dunno. Riding a horse. Humming the *Bonanza* theme song."

She swore under her breath, but when he lifted one eyebrow, she knew he'd heard her. "I need the twenty grand, don't get me wrong, but I'm not here to get your ranch going only to have you screw it six ways to Sunday once I'm gone. Or once you are."

He found a tin of crackers and pulled it out, lifting the lid and sniffing before slapping it back shut and tossing the whole thing into the garbage can.

The garbage can that didn't have a garbage bag in it. This guy was a serious mess. *Twenty grand. Twenty grand.* She needed to repeat that over and over. Nothing mattered. Nothing but getting to the end of this three-month job and getting that paycheck.

He closed one cabinet and opened another, but it was empty. So he turned to her, leaning against the counter. He had a habit, already, of looking directly at her when he spoke. All charm and smiles and green eyes and… stuff. But this was different. No smiling. He wasn't even making eye contact.

"Look, I get it. I don't know a thing about anything. That's why I hired you. I haven't the first clue what I'm doing. All I know is my grandpa always made it sound like… He made it sound like ranching meant something.

Gave him a purpose or whatever. He said this place was his heart. And, the fact of the matter is, my entire life's purpose is hockey, and whether or not I'm going to be involved in hockey in any capacity for much longer is questionable right now, so I want something. I want something that's going to matter if the one thing that *does* gets taken away from me. Grandpa suggested this—his heart—so here I am."

She didn't dare move, or speak. She absorbed those words. The honesty in them. "Why not ask your grandpa for the advice, the help? If he loved it so much, why did they move away?"

Dan stared hard out the dusty, filmy window. "He's not doing so hot these days. Neither of them are, actually, and it's been a long, slow road to not really being all there. They moved to a warmer climate for Grandma's health, and it killed him a little bit. Never been the same. In fact, his suggestion for me to take this on probably wasn't even a rational one, but it stuck with me."

She could feel the sadness coming off him in waves. Or was that her own sadness? Dad might still be mentally there, but that was about it. He mainly wheeled around the house like a ghost, barely speaking, never getting involved. So, she was pretty familiar with that heavy bleakness of not knowing how to fix someone you loved.

Then his eyes did meet hers, that cocky grin back in place. The only hint he had just spilled his guts was the fact that his hands were gripping the counter. Which made his biceps stand out, and those shoulders...

"I'm at your mercy, Cowgirl," he drawled. It didn't matter that the drawl was fake, or the words were goofy, she could very much imagine him being at her mercy. Or her being at *his* as he pushed off the counter and walked toward her.

"It's no accident I'm dropping a pretty penny on you. Just about anyone I talked to brought up your name. Told me to get Mel Shaw, not Caleb. So, here I am, having Mel."

If he hadn't brought up Caleb's name, she might have dissolved into a pathetic puddle of lust. But the mention of her brother—and people warning Dan away from him—undercut any fantasies Dan *having her* might have brought up. All that was left was determination.

She'd done a lot in the way of mending her brother's burned bridges, but the fact of the matter was, every time Caleb had stolen from one of the businesses in town, every time he'd crashed his pickup into someone's fence, the people of Blue Valley put a little black mark against the Shaw name. People might like her, respect her, but none of them would give an inch when it came to helping with the ranch, because Caleb was a part of it. No matter what Caleb had done to try to make amends.

At least the town respected what she'd done enough to give her this. She couldn't ignore that it was something.

So, she'd do this. She'd do a hell of a job helping Mr. Hockey Player become Mr. Awesome Rancher. Or at least Mr. Doesn't Embarrass Himself Rancher.

She slid the notebook and pen back into her pocket, fixing Dan with her best I'm-the-boss glare. "Grab your wallet, moneybags. We've got some errands to run."

His grin changed, from that cocky "I'll get the best of you" quirk to something softer and more genuine. "You're really going to do this?"

"Paying me, aren't you?"

"I figured when you heard how much work teaching me a thing or two was going to be, you might bail."

"That's one thing you'll learn about me pretty damn quick, Sharpe—I don't bail." She grabbed her Stetson off the counter and pulled it low on her head. Then she marched out the door to her truck.

She was here for the money, and she wouldn't leave without that, but at least she had enough insight into Dan's motivations to care. Care that he got off his feet and running, care that as oblivious as he seemed, he was in it for the heart of the ranch. She knew how much that could mean.

So, nope, she wouldn't bail. And maybe it wouldn't be the worst thing in the world to get a deserted ranch back and running again.

―――

Dan watched Mel from his seat in an uncomfortable vinyl booth while she chatted with two sheriff's deputies at the diner counter.

She smiled at these guys. Laughed at their lame jokes. Not that he could hear their jokes, but they were cops. How funny could they be?

Even after his rather personal revelation of why he was here, and her dragging him around all morning, spending his money on all means of supplies, she didn't smile or chat with *him* like that. She gave orders. She muttered under her breath.

She didn't laugh at one of his jokes.

It took him a few minutes to realize he was jealous. It was a foreign emotion for him. He hadn't had a lot to be jealous of over the years. Sure, there'd been a few times in his younger days he wished he hadn't been the son of a famous hockey player, because of the way people sometimes treated him, but he was also smart enough to know his dad's name had paved a few bumpy roads for him.

It also helped that his dad wasn't a prick—that he was, in fact, an all-around decent guy. So any jealousy on the "famous hockey player dad" front had faded.

This? This was new—and almost kind of nice. Knowing Mel was something he couldn't have. Like he was practicing for all the other things he couldn't have.

Are you really sure you can't have her?

He ignored that asshole thought as she made her way back to the table with two glasses of water. She slapped one on the table then slid into the booth across from him.

"No waiters in Blue Valley?"

"Georgia's understaffed right now, and I was already up there talking to Garret and Al."

"Yes, I noticed. Talking, chatting, laughing."

She gave him a "what the hell are you talking about" kind of look, but he kept his gaze on the counter and those two cops as he took a sip of the water.

"I think we're good on fencing supplies and basic tools." She got her little notebook out of her pocket— such a nerdy move, but it always drew his gaze to her breasts, which made him wonder about her breasts… which probably wasn't okay.

Luckily a harried-looking woman set two plates down in front of them before disappearing behind the counter again, distracting him from that dangerous line of thought. His mouth watered at the plate piled high with fatty food.

"I'm thinking we get the place looking better, then make a plan where to go forward. So, menial stuff first. And since you have no food, we hit the grocery store next." Mel unrolled her silverware from the paper napkin. "Then it's back to your place. I'll help you unload, we'll check out the storage situation. That will probably finish up today. There's a lot of work ahead of us, but I'm not putting in overtime unless you pay overtime, got it?"

"Yes, ma'am. You're the boss, ma'am. Anything you say, ma'am."

"It's good you think so much of yourself. It must make up for all the people who want to smack you upside the head."

He stiffened, because that hit close to home. A home she didn't know about. Or, if she did, at least didn't feel the need to point out. Thank goodness for that. He forced a smile and a flip comment in return. "Doesn't it just."

He picked up the burger, stomach rumbling. The breakfast apple pie snack cake thing from the convenience store had been lackluster at best. This burger was huge, thick slices of bacon and cheese hanging off the sides. At least he wouldn't starve thanks to his lack of cooking skills. "This is not on my diet."

She looked from her burger, eyebrows raised. "Your diet?"

"So to speak. When I'm not skating every day, I tend to have to be a little more careful about what I eat. Thank you turning thirty."

"You're only thirty?"

"Only? How old do you think I am?"

"I thought I read that you were—" She cut herself off, immediately taking a too-large bite of hamburger.

"Oh, you read about me? Do tell."

She shook her head, chewing, then swallowed it all down with a gulp of water. "I just wanted to make sure you were who you were supposed to be and all that."

"Right. So, what did you read?"

He had to admit, he enjoyed watching her squirm. It was a nice dinner show to go along with his hamburger. Which was delicious.

He would need to find some kind of workout regimen for when he was here. Once they proved him innocent, some team would sign him. They'd have to, and he couldn't have gained twenty pounds in the off-season.

She popped a fry into her mouth and took another bite of burger, stalling for as long as she could, but he wasn't giving in. He kept eating, watching her, waiting for an answer.

"Look, I read a few articles about…the game, and that article in *Bright Lights*. Which said you were thirty-five, by the way."

He let the first part slide off his shoulders. She looked more embarrassed by it than accusatory, and he didn't feel like dwelling on the bad. Not when she'd also looked at his *Bright Lights* spread. "Okay, so I'm thirty-five. *Bright Lights*, though—I was shirtless in some of those pictures. Were you reading *only* for the articles?" He popped the last bite of hamburger in his mouth. Would it be wrong to order another?

"No wonder you're in such great shape. Carrying around that ego must be hard work."

He leaned back in the booth, crossing his arms

behind his head. "There you go, complimenting my body again. Maybe *I* should be concerned about sexual harassment."

"I kind of hate you."

He grinned. He wasn't all that convinced of that. She might not laugh at his jokes like she did with Barney Fife and Andy Griffith over there, but she'd worked relentlessly to help him out this morning. Being honest about Grandpa and everything had softened her up. "I think you hate that you *don't* hate me."

"Can we go, or are you going to lick the grease off your plate too?"

He looked down at his completely demolished plate. Licking the grease off didn't seem half bad, but she was already scooting out of the booth. She slapped the bill to his chest when he stood. "Lunch is on you." She pointed to the cash register and then walked to the door.

Though not before smiling at Cop 1 and Cop 2, of course.

Scowling, he reached into his pocket and pulled out his wallet. He handed a credit card and the bill to the harried woman who'd dropped their plates off. Well, he'd make sure to leave her a nice tip.

She smiled, shaking her head. "Sorry. We don't take credit cards."

"Wait. *What?*" She couldn't be serious. Everywhere took credit cards. Even Nowhere, Montana, had to take credit cards.

The lady laughed, and so did the cops sitting at the counter, one tapping something into his phone. "Mel said you'd about die over that." She took his outstretched card and ran it through the machine, still chuckling to herself.

She handed him the receipt, dimple winking as she smiled. "Welcome to town, Mr. Sharpe."

"Yeah, gee, thanks." He signed the receipt, leaving her a more than generous tip in hopes she'd help him get Mel back at some point. Never underestimate the power of money.

He nodded to the cops. "Good to see you fellas hard at work."

"Told you he was an asshole," one of them muttered as Dan walked away…realizing a little belatedly that pissing off the local police probably wasn't in his best interest.

When he stepped outside, Mel was leaning against the building, arms across her chest as they almost always were, but she was smirking.

"Some joke," he said.

Mel laughed, the sound surprising him. She had a good laugh. Low and genuine. And her smile softened her face. She wasn't intimidating when she smiled. "Man, you should have seen the look on your face."

"How could you—"

She held up her phone—a pathetic old flip phone— and he had to squint at the screen to see the picture of him with mouth slightly ajar, eyes a little bugged out.

"Where the hell—"

"Garret." She laughed again. "You deserved that one, Sharpe. Now, let's go. We've got food to buy and shit to do."

He snatched the phone out of her hands, but she only shrugged and started walking to the truck. He followed, trying to figure out how to delete the picture on her relic. He finally figured it out, only to run into someone in the process.

When he looked up, a kid and a bike were on the ground.

"Aw, shit, kid, I'm sorry." He went to help him up, but the boy was already popping to his feet, brushing his knees off and retrieving his baseball hat.

"It's okay." The kid grinned at him like he'd found a pot of gold instead of fallen off his bike. "You're Dan Sharpe, aren't you?"

Dan used to love this stuff. Kids recognizing him, idolizing him. Now he was always a little worried they'd call him a cheater or spit in his face.

Instead, the kid kept smiling and started digging in his bag. "Hey, if I can find a marker, will you sign my backpack?"

"Yeah, no problem."

"Sweet." The kid pulled out a Sharpie and handed it to him. Dan went through the requisite "do you play hockey" and "who's your favorite team" spiel.

Then he helped the kid with the bike and handed the kid's backpack to him. "See ya round."

When he finally joined Mel at the truck, she was scowling at him.

"What? I was being nice."

"I know. That's the problem," she muttered, climbing into the driver's seat.

"How is that a problem?" he asked once he was settled into the passenger's seat.

"I want you to be a bad guy."

"Why?"

"So I can laugh at you when you fail," she said

in all seriousness, pulling the truck out of the diner parking lot.

"Are you saying you *won't* laugh at me if I fail?"

She sighed. "Yes, that's what I'm saying. Although I'm disappointed in myself for having that kind of heart." She drove in silence out of Blue Valley and the fifteen minutes to a bigger town and a grocery store.

"You'll want to stock up. Felicity's General Store back in Blue Valley has a lot of the basics, but the hours and selection are limited," she advised, all business again. Any hint at that momentary softening or camaraderie gone. She was the boss man—or woman, as the case may be. He was the lowly serf, paying her a chunk of change to tell him what to do.

They got to the grocery store, and she told him to get what he wanted while she looked around. They separated and Dan searched for all means of easy-to-prepare foods. Easy Mac. Frozen pizza. Yeah, he was really going to need some kind of workout plan if this was going to be his diet.

Maybe he could hire a cook. Maybe he could hire Mel to cook for him.

He happened down the personal hygiene aisle, the condom display catching his eye. It wasn't like he was so certain he was going to sleep with anyone up here, but it couldn't hurt to have some on hand. Especially if he hired a cook. Although that would probably be wrong.

If he was thinking a little bit about Mel, well, he was a guy.

"What the hell do you think you're doing?"

"Buying condoms." He plucked a box off the shelf and grinned at her.

She made a kind of squeaking noise as her face went pink.

"Don't worry, I don't plan on using them with you. Unless you ask nicely."

"Fuck off, Sharpe."

"I'll take that as a no. I'm good at reading signals like that."

"You're...you're..." She took a deep breath, doing that "look up at the sky" thing she did when he really irritated her. Then she glared. A lesser man might slump down, shrink away, apologize, but he was not a lesser man.

"You're trying to piss me off," she finally said. "Possibly your natural state is trying to piss people off."

"Possibly."

"One of these days, it's going to kick you in the ass."

He could tell her it already had, because if he was the type of guy who hadn't gotten a rise out of pissing people off, he'd probably have a few more teammates jumping to defend him.

Instead, he was on his own. His agent fought for him because, well, money, and Dad was mostly trying to avoid the situation, keep his nose clean. As he should. Dad didn't deserve to be dragged into his crap. No one did.

"Can we *go*? It's going to be dark by the time we get home at this rate."

Home. Funny. He couldn't remember the last time he'd thought of somewhere as home. But this very well could be his home now. A nice concept. A silver lining to all the other shit.

So, he smiled at Mel, dropping the condoms into the cart. "Sure thing, honey."

"I'm waiting in the car," she grumbled, stomping away.

Yeah, this potentially-being-home thing was a bit of a silver lining after all.

Chapter 3

MEL PULLED HER TRUCK INTO THE GARAGE AND SAT there for a few minutes. She was starving, but the chances of Dad or Caleb having made something for dinner were slim. She was exhausted, but she'd have to double-check all of Caleb's work today or she wouldn't sleep.

Today had not gone at all like she'd anticipated. She couldn't pin Dan down. Parts of him were exactly what she'd expected of a spoiled professional athlete. But parts…well, she could admit in the solitude of her truck cab that parts of him definitely got to her.

In not totally unpleasant ways. Luckily, she wasn't stupid enough to go down that road. Just because something wasn't unpleasant didn't mean it was worth going after. Because nothing as shiny and loaded as Dan Sharpe stuck around Blue Valley for very long.

She hopped out of the truck, willing those thoughts away. Right now she needed to focus on food, chores, Dad, and then, if she was lucky, sleep.

Color was creeping into the valley even as it disappeared from the sky. A slow turn to green, hints of pinks and blues, riots of yellow, a big burst, and then gone again.

Usually it was her favorite time of year. The promise of warmth and life and color. Today she missed winter a little bit. The harsh reality of it. The grays, the biting cold.

"You are one sick puppy," she muttered, pushing into the main house through the back door. She pulled her boots off and dropped them on the mat, trying not to cringe over the fact that Caleb's weren't there, which probably meant he'd tracked.

She stepped into the kitchen, where Caleb stood at the counter, still wearing his boots. But he smiled at her, and hey, he was the only one most days, so she gave him a smile back.

Dan smiles at you quite a lot.

"Pizza," Caleb offered, a plate full of crumbs in front of him. "There's one of those bag salad things you hate in the fridge."

"You know, having a penis doesn't make you incapable of making actual food."

"Oh, and here I thought it was always flopping around, getting in the way."

She shook her head and pulled open the fridge. A lot nicer fridge than Dan's. Probably the only nicer thing she had than him—till he replaced it. "Men are pigs."

"Beer in the fridge too."

"Hallelujah. I'll consider you a little less of one." Mel rummaged around in the fridge until she'd gotten everything she wanted. "Dad eat?"

"I made him up a plate, but I haven't checked in."

"Fiona have any problems?" Mel asked. The nurse that came in three times a week to help Dad was a saint and rarely complained if Dad was rude, but occasionally…

"She didn't say anything."

Mel put the beer and salad down on the counter, then stared at it, trying to work through all the exhaustion that made her feel so damn helpless.

"I can fix you the salad."

"Don't baby me, I might cry."

"Don't cry, I might run." He was smiling when she looked at him, but she knew he was exhausted too.

"Maybe…maybe if this money pulls through, we can hire someone on." She unscrewed the cap of the bottle of dressing and poured some into the bag, shaking it a little before grabbing a fork.

"*If* the money pulls through? Bad first day?"

"No, just weird." She popped the top to her beer and guzzled the first drink.

"Weird how?"

"I don't know. The guy is hard to make sense of. He's a cocky bastard."

"Well, you were expecting that, right?"

"Yeah, but…" She couldn't explain to Caleb that she didn't hate him for it. She didn't know how to explain that to herself. He was arrogant and way too flirty, but he took everything in such easygoing stride.

Maybe that was it. He could look at life and see easy, and she had never known people like that. Shaws were so bound and determined to make everything damn hard.

"I'm just tired. Tell me how things went here."

"I checked off every chore on your list, madam taskmaster."

"I only meant—"

"I know what you meant, and I'm not going to get pissy about it. I did what you wanted me to do. You want to grill me or check my work, you can, but you've got enough shit on your plate, Mel. Trust me to handle it, please. If you keel over, I'm really screwed."

She took a deep breath, then tossed the bag onto the

counter and grabbed a pizza off the little cardboard circle it rested on. Nearly cold, but better than slightly browning bagged lettuce.

"But you'll…" She tried to rein in all the emotions exhaustion was letting free. "You promise me if there's a problem you can't handle, you'll bring it to me. Even with everything on my plate. I need to know—"

"We're not losing this place. I promised you that when Dad was in the hospital, and I'm not going back on it."

She swallowed the lump in her throat and nodded.

"I'm sorry that I ever made you doubt—"

She waved it away. "We've had our apologies and our tears and our come-to-Jesus moment. I don't want to rehash it. Things are fine. We're getting there." She popped the last bite of unsatisfying pizza in her mouth. "I'm going to go check on Dad."

"I'll come with. Maybe we can talk him into watching some TV in the same room as us or something."

She wasn't sure she was feeling sturdy enough to be rebuffed by Dad right now, but Caleb was so determined. She couldn't argue with him.

But when she stepped into the living room, they were greeted by Dad's snoring, soft and even. "Well, so much for family togetherness," she whispered, going over to grab his—thankfully empty—dinner plate.

She noticed the half-empty bottle of Jack Daniel's that had most definitely not been half-empty this morning peeking out from a blanket lying on the ground.

Dad had never been much of a drinker, even these few years after the accident, but occasionally…

Yup, when she pulled back the blanket, there was the

old family album. She didn't know where he kept it. It always disappeared after one of these episodes.

The fact that it was opened to a picture of her mother, the mother she looked more and more like with every passing year—made her feel cold all over. Why did she have to look like that woman?

"It doesn't mean anything, Mel." Caleb nudged her arm. "He was over it a long time ago. All his stuff now is about the wheelchair, not her."

Mel wondered if Caleb believed it, because she sure as hell didn't. Not that she could change any of it. There was no going back. Only forward.

She dropped the blanket back in place, letting it hide Dad's sins, so to speak. "I'm going to go to bed. I'll see you in the morning."

"Mel…"

When she stopped in the doorway, Caleb didn't say anything for a long time. Then he said, "It's going to be okay. We're going to make it okay."

"I know," she lied. Then she let a little bit of the truth slide. "But what about him?"

She didn't wait for Caleb's answer. Couldn't. She needed to crawl into bed and sleep away the tears burning behind her eyes.

Dan hiked toward the aging barn. Surely he could find some cell service somewhere in this godforsaken wasteland.

Okay, that was harsh. The place was pretty awesome-looking, especially with the sun rising over the mountains. The hills were green, and the sky seemed impossibly blue. In the early morning light, the barns and older, ramshackle buildings didn't look so much like they were out of a horror movie. And, hey, the trek around the property was getting him a little cardio.

He reached the top of the swell of land. To his right was an old barn-type thing. There seemed to be little enclosures for animals inside. If he had to guess, he'd say it had been used for horses.

He held up his phone, but a strange noise made him jump and drop the thing. "Shit," he muttered, bending to pick it up. When he straightened, he let out a yelp of surprise.

There was a thing. A not-small furry animal thing standing at the fence, staring at him expectantly.

He stared back at the animal, then helplessly at his phone. Hey, cell service. He googled random animal names he thought the thing could be until he found a picture that looked mostly right.

A llama.

How did he have a llama on his property? How had Buck not mentioned he had a llama, period? Surely the guy had been taking care of it. Llamas didn't take care of themselves, did they? There weren't packs of wild llamas running about Montana.

Were there?

"So, hi." The llama didn't respond at all. It stood there and stared at him. The thing was probably hungry. Maybe he should find it something to eat. "I don't suppose you'd like to tell me what you'd want to eat?"

The llama stared. Didn't move. Dan gingerly held out his hand, but when the creature nipped toward him, he pulled back. "Okay, so either you're very unfriendly or you're very hungry. We have a word for that in human speak—hangry."

He needed to feed it, and he needed to stop talking to it like it was going to talk back, because he was sounding crazy even to himself.

He backed away, then jogged down to the house. Of course when he got to his kitchen, he had no cell service to look up what llamas ate. Shit. When was Mel supposed to get here?

He poked around in his fridge before pulling out a container of lunch-meat ham. Grabbed a few pieces of bread and a bottle of water and a bowl.

Worst he could do was offer random food it wouldn't eat. Surely he couldn't kill a llama with a sandwich.

He trudged back out to the barn where the llama still stood against the fence. Watching him. Still. Dan slowed his pace. That thing was motherfucking creepy.

"Hey, fella, want some ham?"

It moved around, and he figured that was sign enough. He peeled back a few pieces of the lunch meat and tossed them in the llama's direction.

"What the hell is that?"

Dan glanced to where Mel was hiking up the hill. Thank Christ she was here. "According to my research, it's a llama."

"Why do you have a llama?" She approached, hands on her hips, wrinkling her nose at the creature before them.

"I don't know. It was just here."

"What are you feeding it?"

"Ham."

"Ham? *Ham?* You can't feed a llama ham."

"Well, then what do I feed it?"

"Hell if I know, but not ham!" She made her way to the fence, then gingerly pulled the pieces of ham out of the grass at the llama's feet. "Grain. Straw. Bread. Something remotely sensible."

"I maybe panicked a little bit."

"I see that."

"I know you're a genius cowgirl and all, but tell me you wouldn't panic if you got the crap scared out of you by a llama."

"My panic rarely involves ham," she said drily.

"Fair enough."

She stared at the creature, and Dan couldn't help noticing she looked a little more haggard than she had yesterday. Her hat was pulled down low, but he could see circles under her eyes, and she looked pale. Even the way she stood was different. Slumpy instead of that ramrod straight "I've got this shit covered" posture she'd walked around with *all* day yesterday.

"You okay?"

She gave him an are-you-crazy look, all scrunched-up nose and drawn-together eyebrows. She seemed to give him that look a lot for only knowing each other about twenty-four hours.

"You look…" He tried to think of a diplomatic way of telling her she looked like death warmed over. But he didn't have much practice being diplomatic, so he came up empty.

"I look what?"

"I don't know. Like you had a crappy night of sleep."

"Perceptive for a man with his head so far up his ass he feeds a llama processed meat."

"It wasn't because of me, was it?" He didn't like the

sudden guilty weight in his gut. Sure, he was paying her a shitload of money to be here, but he didn't want to be making her life miserable in the process.

"Don't flatter yourself, wannabe cowboy."

"I meant because you hate me, not because you were up all night fantasizing about me—but if we want to pretend it was the latter, I'm all for it."

She let out a gusty sigh. "Believe it or not, I have bigger problems in my life than you."

"Like what?"

"What do you care?"

He shrugged. "I don't know. We're going to be spending a lot of time together. Maybe we should be friends."

She snorted. "You don't need me to be your friend. You need someone to kick your ass every morning. And you need someone to figure out what the hell to do with your llama."

"That almost sounds dirty."

"Buck didn't tell you about this?"

Dan shook his head. "Didn't mention it to you either?"

"No."

"No chance it's a wild llama?"

"Yes, Sharpe. It's a wild llama that hopped a fence, went into a stall, and is desperate to eat your ham."

"That *also* sounds dirty."

"You are giving me a headache." She pinched the bridge of her nose. Her plaid shirt was green and blue today, and while the serviceable work shirts she wore didn't do much to show off her figure, the jeans did admirable things for her—

"Stop staring at my ass, Sharpe."

"Sorry." Sort of.

"Let's figure out how to take care of this llama, huh?"

"You can't tell me taking care of llama problems together *isn't* friendship."

She glanced at him. "Don't have a lot of friends, do you?"

"Not really." Which he'd never spent much time thinking about, but it was true. Once upon a time he'd counted his teammates as friends, but he'd always been a little bit apart. Not quite one of the group. Probably because he was a jerk, and his dad was a legend. Probably because at the first threat of any complex relationship, he bolted. "What about you?"

She shrugged. "Haven't had much time for friends the past few years. Besides, not many people stick around Blue Valley."

"So, how do you have time for this?"

"Twenty grand, Dan. I have a lot of time for twenty grand."

"Hey look, we're becoming friends already."

"Because you're paying me?"

"Because you called me Dan. Not Sharpe or asshole or moron. You called me *Dan*." He smirked. "We'll be best friends before you know it."

"You sure do like your delusions."

"They aren't half-bad." Besides, she was almost smiling instead of looking sad. He'd managed to cheer her up, maybe. That was new. Kind of a nice feeling.

"You'll leave too, you know." And all at once, her smile was gone. She didn't look at him; instead, she looked out at the sky. It was a gorgeous blue, interrupted only by distant mountains.

"I'm not sure it's permanent, but I'm not building this place to never come back to."

"You'll leave," she said with such certainty it was hard not to believe her. "People like you don't belong here."

He was used to people having zero faith in him outside of a hockey rink, so he wasn't sure why that struck him as a personal insult. That he didn't—couldn't—belong. But it hit, and it hit deep. "What does that—"

"I'm going to call Buck and see if he knows anything about the llama." She walked away before he could argue with her, before he could demand to know what *people like you* meant.

Well, he'd find out one way or another.

Chapter 4

Mel was not curious. She refused to be. In fact, she was angry. Angry she was sitting here fixing Dan's damn fence while he paced the hill, phone to his ear.

Except she couldn't even muster *angry*, because for the first time since she'd met him, Dan was not smiling or joking or even looking a little sad and wistful.

He was *furious*. Every step he took seemed to be a personal attack on the ground beneath him. She was all the way down the hill, but she could occasionally hear a sharp curse reverberate in the air.

The call was important. She couldn't argue that fact away. She couldn't sit here not doing anything either, even if this was his responsibility. If she didn't do anything, she'd start thinking again, and she was tired of thinking.

Thinking about Dad. Mom. The stupid dream she'd had last night that had left her feeling lonely and a little achy. The conversation with Dan about friendships didn't exactly help.

Especially since he'd been *very* friendly in her dream.

It had been a while, on that front. Which she could deal with. Did deal with, quite fine actually. It wasn't like sex was some kind of magical experience, no matter what fantasies dreams might offer.

The friendship thing was harder to roll with. The fact of the matter was, she *was* alone, because even though her brother provided a certain amount of company, she kept a lot from him. As much as they told each other everything was going to be okay, she was pretty sure neither of them believed it.

It would be nice to have someone hug her, tell her that, and somehow convince her that it was true. Like Tyler had been able to when things were easy. But things weren't easy anymore. So, someone to care might be nice, but that was not in the cards.

She was an island, and while it was better that way, sometimes the loneliness was a bit much. It made Dan enticing. More so than he should be.

Forgetting that he would ultimately leave risked more than she had to lose.

It took a certain something to stay here, in this dying town, surrounded by so many people with sob stories, struggling to get by. It was not for cheerful people who liked to flirt and laugh. People who were used to a certain way of life, who could throw their money around and have all their problems vanish.

Blue Valley was for people who were either too stubborn to leave or didn't have a choice. She was little bit of both.

Dan was neither of those things.

So, whatever achy feelings she harbored for a guy she'd known all of twenty-four hours, they were stupid. A friendship with him would be stupid. There were too many holes in her heart to willfully add another.

After a few minutes of almost complete silence, Dan made his way down the hill. It was like seeing a completely different side of him—every muscle in his body tense, a scowl so deep it dug grooves in his face, making him look more his age.

Thirty-five. That was totally way too old for her anyway.

"Everything okay?" The words slipped out despite her knowing better. She should not be getting involved in his non-ranch business. Not asking if he was all right. They weren't friends. He was her meal ticket. The end.

The anger all but waved off him, and whoever had pissed him off should be glad they weren't here. She was pretty sure if Dan had the source of his anger in front of him, it'd be bruised and bloody.

He didn't answer her question, thank goodness, but he looked at his phone, then out in the distance. Pulling his arm back, he hurled it into the overgrown brush on the other side of the falling-apart fence. It landed with a thump far away.

Mel looked at the field, then at him. "Feel better?"

He sighed. "Fuck no. I need that damn phone." He scrubbed his hands over his face and uttered about every curse word known to man.

Then he stomped into the field, cursing all the while, looking for his phone. It took him a few minutes, but he found it and shoved it deep into his pocket. Mel moved her focus to removing the rotted fence post from its hole, biting her tongue so she wouldn't ask. She didn't need to know. It was none of her business.

Screw it; she had to ask.

"Okay, so what's the deal? Why are you suddenly full of rage? Next thing I know you'll get all big and green and start smashing things."

He snorted. "The NHL doesn't want to conduct a formal investigation into whether or not I took bribes to screw up the game, which screws me, because I'm damn innocent, and now I can't prove it. And no team will take me. And…" He took a deep breath, but it didn't loosen any of the tension in his face. If anything, it only centered it. "I need to pound something into dust."

"Here." She handed him a post and a mallet, pointing at the hole in the ground where the old rotting fence post had been. "Pound away."

He stared at the tools, then shrugged. "What the hell." He wedged the post into the ground, then took the mallet. On a deep breath, he lifted it over his head.

She didn't think she'd fallen into that *Thor* movie, but she'd keep watching just to be sure.

The fitted T-shirts he always seemed to wear weren't practical for ranch work, as she'd tried to tell him, but she was a little glad he hadn't listened, as the thin cotton clung to the line of his back, his muscles an almost graceful wave of tension and then release.

When the mallet came down, biceps and forearms absorbing the impact of rubber on wood, he barely even paused before he was swinging the mallet back up and bringing it down again.

It was all done with a mesmerizing grace…and was it suddenly really hot? The temperature must have jumped ten degrees at least.

Once he'd pounded the post way farther into the ground than it needed to go, she cleared her throat. "That's probably enough."

He looked at the post, slowly dropped the mallet from its cocked position behind his shoulder to the ground. "Guess I got carried away."

"A bit." So had she, watching him. Shoulder and arm muscles bunching as he'd lifted the mallet and then brought it down hard. Oh, hard. Muscles. *Crud*.

"Feel better?" She hoped he did, because she sure as hell didn't.

"Yeah, I do." He took a ragged breath, let it out.

"Can I ask?"

He sighed with a tiredness she recognized, because she felt it almost daily. The kind of exhaustion that wasn't so much physical as emotional, because you knew you had to keep fighting, but you didn't think you'd ever get to stop.

"Ask away," he said with a grand hand gesture, leaning against one of the sturdier fence posts.

"What *did* happen?" None of her business, and knowing probably made all her attempts at not befriending him useless, but, oh damn well.

"I… I don't know. Two years ago it was a fluke. I was thinking too much about the next play, about how this would be it, the thing that put me over the top, and I lost sight of the puck. Never done that, but I wanted that Cup. I wanted it so bad, and I was an idiot."

"And last time?"

He kicked at the ground. "I had that moment stuck in my head. Playing like a loop. All I could think was *don't fuck it up again*, but I did. They're not lying when they say professional sports is more mental than physical, Mel. Some guys have all the physical talent in the world, but they can't handle the pressure. I didn't think that was me, but one mistake and I can't move past it. I'm not any good at fixing my mistakes, never have been."

Oh, crud, crud, crud. He just *had* to make her feel sorry for him.

"Well, if that's true, why would anyone think it's criminal?"

"I'm too good to be that bad only when it matters."
He shrugged like it was indisputable fact. "I don't really
want to talk about this anymore. Can we just pound shit?"

"Right, yeah." She looked back at the mangled fence,
the supplies they'd bought yesterday. They needed to
get a few more posts in, pour the quick-set concrete.

"Out of curiosity, do you believe me?" he asked.

He was staring at her earnestly. Like her answer
mattered, even though they both had to know it
shouldn't. "I don't have any reason not to believe
you," she said carefully.

"Well, I guess that's something. Thanks." He gave
her shoulder an awkward pat, and she tried to ignore the
fact that he was close. Kind of sweaty. *So hot.*

Cruddy crud crud.

―――∽∼∿―――

"Well, no one I've found is interested in taking the llama
off your hands, but the straw we left will do for tonight.
I'll do some more searching tomorrow."

Dan stood on his porch, watching Mel tick things
off her list. There was an unfamiliar panic jumping
around in his gut at the prospect of being left alone in
this tiny old house in the shadow of imposing mountains. "Yeah, sure."

"We'll set her up some grazing space tomorrow. If no
one wants her, I guess that makes you the lucky owner.
Just leave the ham for your own dinner."

Dan looked at the house behind him. Though the
kitchen was now well stocked after yesterday's grocery store outing, the thought of making dinner…
dinner alone…

"You want to stay for dinner?" It was a pathetic invitation, but he was feeling pathetic. Lonely. If he didn't distract himself, he might do something stupid. He had no idea what kind of trouble he could get up to in the middle of nowhere, but he didn't trust himself.

"No, thanks."

"Ouch. No conscience over leaving me here by my lonesome night after night?"

"Two nights and no conscience at all." But the way she studied him, frowning, undercut the words. She did care, or she'd already be out the door. He worked on his best pathetic look, until she sighed.

"Look, if you really want a decent dinner and some company, you can come with me."

"Come with you?"

"To Shaw. I was planning on cooking for my brother and dad."

"You're inviting me to your house for dinner? For dinner cooked by *you*?" Now he felt really pathetic. Mel Shaw was pity-inviting him to dinner.

"If I have to cook for two assholes, I might as well cook for three. Do *not* tell my dad or brother I called them assholes, but it really gets my goat that I'm expected to cook just because I have breasts and don't want to eat pizza every night."

"Gets your goat, huh?"

"You want a decent meal, you shut up and get in the truck."

He wasn't going to argue with that, and it might be interesting to see her operation. He hadn't thought much about her living situation. He figured she'd sprouted from the ground, snarky cowgirl fully formed. No father involved.

But he climbed into her truck, and she drove away from his grandparents' ranch and toward Blue Valley's sad little Main Street. It was only seven, but almost every establishment was closed except the diner and what appeared to be some hole-in-the-wall bar.

Back outside of Blue Valley, driving toward the mountains that always seemed to be just out of reach, he glanced at Mel. She had her hands tight on the wheel as she navigated bumpy country roads.

She'd thrown her hat in the backseat, and the braid she usually wore was falling out of its band at the bottom. It had done that yesterday too, strands unraveling from the rigid line of hair she showed up with each morning.

He'd probably never spent so much time wondering about someone before. At least someone who wasn't himself or an opponent on the ice. But Mel was like no one he'd ever known. Or maybe he'd just never started paying attention until hockey was out of the picture. Until everything was out of the picture.

She turned onto a dirt road that curved up and around a hill. In the valley below, a few buildings seemed to nestle into the earth, like they were sunk there, not built on top. If his place looked old, this place looked ancient. Deserted versus well-used, but both with the heavy weight of the mountains settled on top.

"Here she is," Mel said, driving onto gravel and winding down toward a cabin-type house. It was bigger than his place, two stories. There was a porch in the front and one above on the second story. A little saggy, a little worn, but it looked cozy. Inviting. A *family's* home.

Mel pulled in front of a detached garage. She paused

as if she was going to say something, but then shook her head and got out of the truck, so he followed suit.

She led him to a side door and stepped into the type of room Mom had always made him throw his gear into. A mudroom, she'd called it, though hockey had never had anything to do with mud.

Obviously ranching did, if the muddy rubber mat on the floor was any indication.

"Lose the shoes, Sharpe," Mel ordered, pulling her own off.

"But I'm not wearing boots."

"You should be. I don't mop, so we don't do shoes in the house. Lose them. And while we're on the subject, you really need to get a working wardrobe."

"Are you going to *Pretty Woman* rancher me?"

"Are you a hooker with a heart of gold?"

He laughed and followed her farther inside, reminding himself not to stare at her ass while in her family's house. Even he had manners sometimes.

They stepped into a dim, spacious kitchen that looked much more up-to-date than the one back at his ranch, although not nearly as modern as his place in Chicago.

A young man walked in from another entrance. "Hey, Mel. Oh…"

"Caleb, this is Dan. Dan, my brother Caleb." She gave Caleb a nudge when he walked over to her. "Do not feed his ego. I have enough problems with this one," she muttered.

Dan shook the man's outstretched hand. "Nice to meet you."

"Big fan," Caleb said in a low voice, glancing at Mel over his shoulder.

She scowled, but went to the refrigerator and started pulling out ingredients. "I'm going to get the food started. Caleb, be useful and make Dan be useful with you."

"Aye, aye, Captain."

While Mel made dinner, Dan helped Caleb set the table. It was all very homey and weird. He'd never really had homey, that he could remember. Before his life had been hockey, hockey, and more hockey…well, he didn't remember that time—didn't particularly want to. The months leading up to his parents' decision to get divorced had been…not good for him, but when Dad had put him on the ice and told him his troubles didn't matter there, his whole life had become hockey. And since it had saved him, even Mom hadn't been able to argue.

There hadn't been home-cooked meals and tables set. More like a sandwich and a piece of fruit from Mom when she was on the go, and being taken out to restaurants when he'd been with Dad.

"So, um, this is a nice place." Dan had never considered himself bad at small talk. But he was quickly realizing he'd never sat around in silence, because people usually wanted to talk to him, ask him questions. He'd never been counted on to be the conversation starter.

"I'm sure you're used to a lot nicer."

"Well, my grandparents' place isn't exactly the Ritz."

"The old Paulle place, right?"

"Yeah, you know it?"

Caleb shrugged, glancing back at the kitchen. "Back in high school, no one was living out there. It was put to use, you could say."

"Know anything about a llama?"

"Huh?"

"Never mind. So, teenagers were out there making out a decade ago?"

"Among other things." Out of nowhere, Caleb seemed incredibly stiff and uncomfortable. "Hey, you want a beer?"

"Sure."

"Be back." Caleb disappeared and suddenly Dan was standing in the middle of a decent-sized dining room alone. The furniture was nice. Old, sure, but the kind that looked like family heirlooms.

He didn't belong here. The intensity of that feeling struck him hard, a panic that squeezed at his lungs. This was all old and real and it belonged. It had grown from this earth and been here for centuries, and who the hell was he?

Taking on his grandparents' ranch had been more of a whim, an escape, and it hadn't come with a heavy sense of responsibility. After all, his grandparents weren't likely to ever make it back to Montana, and what little memories Dan had of the place weren't those of lifelong love and devotion. Mom had certainly never been eager to make the trek up here. She'd escaped the minute she'd been old enough.

But the Shaw house? It screamed all those things, and for some reasons he couldn't—or wouldn't—define, it scared the bejesus out of him.

He had to get out of here.

He ditched the set table and the old furniture and the discomfort banding around his lungs, and headed for the kitchen, for Mel. She gave him a lot of conflicting feelings, but at least the verbal sparring with her didn't induce panic.

Her forehead was scrunched up in concentration, eyes on the cookbook while she twisted a can opener around a can of vegetables.

"Do they not have electric can openers in Montana?"

She jumped, some of the liquid from the can sloshing over her fingers. She swore and then plopped the lump of vegetables into a pot on the stovetop. "Where'd Caleb go?"

"Beer."

She pursed her lips and stared hard at the cookbook. "Everything should be ready in about ten minutes."

"Domesticity. It's a good look for you."

"F—"

"You don't have to say it." He held up his hands, pretended not to be highly amused. "That look tells me everything I need to know."

"*I hate you.*"

He put his elbows on the counter, resting his chin in his hands as he grinned at her. "You don't hate me. I don't doubt you *want* to hate me, but you don't."

She let out a gusty sigh. "Why, oh why did I think it was a good idea to bring you here?"

"Handsome. Charming. Excellent company."

"Pathetic. Lonely. Friendless." She stirred the vegetables in the pot absently. "Apparently my pity kicked in for a few seconds there. Very rare. That's how pitiful you are, Dan."

He shrugged. "Got you cooking me dinner. I'll take it."

Caleb reappeared. "Ready yet? I'm starving. Frozen pizza leftovers are shit for lunch."

"Sandwich, Caleb. Two pieces of bread. Ham. Maybe a little mustard. Voilà."

"I—" He shook his head. "Never mind."

Mel stiffened. Dan didn't have much experience reading family dynamics. He didn't have siblings. He barely remembered a time his parents had been in the same room, let alone discussed each other. The divorce and his subsequent…issues had ended all that. So, he understood people in isolation, when he put his mind to it, but the weird sibling thing here was beyond his scope.

He could only guess there was some history there. Some not exactly nice history.

Mel bent over, pulled something out of the oven. Which gave Dan a rather up close view of her ass. At least, until Caleb cleared his throat.

When Dan looked his way, there was a threatening look on Caleb's face.

Yeah, Dan really, really should not have come here.

"It's not gourmet, but you'll both pretend like it's the best damn thing you've ever eaten." Oblivious to Dan and Caleb's nonverbal exchange, Mel continued handing out orders. "Caleb, grab the green beans." She plopped the casserole dish—a sad version of possibly pork chops—into some kind of holder thing and marched to the dining room.

Caleb got the green beans, and Dan followed him. At least until Caleb stopped.

"I may be the younger brother, and you may be famous, but don't think I won't kick your ass to next Friday if you do one thing to hurt her."

Before Dan could formulate a response to *that*, Caleb was walking into the dining room…and asking Mel something about cow testicles?

Dan glanced longingly at the door, but he'd been

foolish enough to let Mel drive him over here. He was stuck. Stuck in crazy Shaw-ville. Population two, apparently.

He hoped he'd have a chance to escape.

He settled down in a chair next to Mel. The wood was uncomfortable, heavy and encompassing. Reiterating that feeling of being trapped.

Well, Dan had learned his first important Montana lesson today. Never, under any circumstances, let loneliness lead you to accepting a pretty woman's dinner invitation. Unless there was guarantee of a whole lot more than food, and a whole lot less family.

An older man wheeled into the dining room. It had to be Mel and Caleb's father, and yet they looked surprised to see him.

"Noisy," he muttered. Then his eyes rested on Dan. "Who the hell are you?"

"Um. Dan. Dan Sharpe?"

The man grunted, then turned his wheelchair around and disappeared. When Dan looked back at the table, Caleb and Mel had their eyes on their plates. After a few seconds, Caleb pushed back. "I need another beer. Anybody else?"

"Uh, no thanks."

Mel shook her head.

Then they were alone in her dining room, the silence heavy and uncomfortable. Dan had no words to interrupt it, no way of diffusing the tension in that silence. Caleb reappeared with a beer, sat down with a heavy sigh, and then they all ate. Not saying anything.

Dan wished he'd stayed home. Alone. Far away from complicated families.

Chapter 5

"YOU READY TO GO?"

Dan nodded, looking more than ready. Why hadn't she thought to have him drive his damn self?

Because she hadn't been thinking. Not even for a second. He'd looked lonely and lost, and she'd been an idiot.

Dan had a way of tugging on that little softhearted underbelly she tried to ignore at all costs.

Damn, damn, damn. She needed to nip that in the bud quick.

She stepped onto the porch and paused, taking a deep breath of the summer evening. The sun had set, but the sky was still light to the west. Not for long. Stars already twinkled in the east. It was enough to settle some of the pain stirring around in her gut.

Until Dan stepped out behind her.

She should move for the truck. Get away from him as fast as possible. But she needed this view. For a couple more seconds. To feel okay again. Strong again. Like she could handle...everything.

"So, what happened to your dad?"

She should have known it'd never be that easy. "Horse spooked and threw him. He's pretty much paralyzed from the waist down." She ran her hands over the smooth wood of the railing. "Happened a few years ago. Can't say any of us are used to it."

"That's tough."

Tough. Yes. But it wasn't a tragedy. Just halfway there, or something. "You know, it's not so bad." She kept thinking if she said it often enough, out loud, to Caleb, to whomever, someday it would start being true. *Not so bad.* "We thought he was going to die. So, we're lucky really. It knocked Caleb out of his rebellious stage." But Caleb had already had a third beer to his lips when she'd asked Dan if he was ready to go. Rebellious stages weren't so easy to break. Not when they were rooted in a pain he refused to share with anyone else. A pain she'd never been able to reach or understand.

And if Caleb went back to the way he'd been…

He'd promised he wouldn't. She had to believe in that promise, even if she'd long ago learned promises were bullshit in the face of reality. "It could all be a lot worse," she forced herself to say. Because she wasn't breaking down in front of Dan. She wasn't breaking down, period.

"It could be a lot better though."

Her throat closed up, but she wouldn't let her emotions have that kind of power over her. So, she went with the truth. "Yeah, it could."

"Things seem bad."

"Not bad, though we're kind of robbing Peter to pay Paul. Medical bills, part-time nurse, making the house accessible, on top of ranch stuff. But we'll get through. That's why I had to…"

"That's why you had to take the job with me even though you'd rather be here fixing this."

She shrugged. It felt weird having him know that, but it wasn't necessarily a bad weird. Just odd. "Anyway, it

won't affect how much time and effort I put into you.
Don't worry about that."

"Trust me, I'm not worried about that." He was silent
for a few seconds, his hands only a few inches from hers
on the railing.

For the briefest of moments she wished he'd put his
hand over hers. Offer some physical comfort. Because
that would be pretty nice right about now. Someone
offering something simple. To care, or at least pretend to.

That told her everything she needed to know about
her current mind-set.

"I…if you need money…"

The offer snapped away the self-pity, the fear,
because *fuck* his pity. She was doing this. It was hard as
hell, but she was doing it. "How long have you known
me, Dan?"

"Uh, two days."

"You don't offer money to someone you've known for
two days. I don't care how much you have." She made
a move for the truck, but his hand rested on her elbow.

He didn't grab or hold her there, but the touch was
enough to make her freeze. To try to hold in everything
touch might elicit. Sparks. Attraction. Want.

Fear.

This wasn't the comfortable touch she'd yearned for
a few minutes ago—this was something bigger. And she
wanted nothing to do with it. She had more than enough
on her plate.

"Let me pay you weekly. I thought monthly would
work, because it'd keep you around longer if you
decided I blew, but let me do it weekly. And I'll up it,
a bit."

Again, the pity allowed her to break free. Step away from his fingertips against her skin. Even if that stupid touch would remain burned into her memory, *she* was the one who broke it. "I don't want your charity." But it was tempting. Necessary. Charity or not, more money... more frequently...the things she could do with that.

"You'll take it, though, won't you?"

The "no" was on her lips. The "fuck you." The "I quit." But she was too smart to let any of those come out. "Yes. Not much of a choice."

"You can teach me how to cook."

"Huh?" She frowned back at him. What was he talking about?

"For the added money, you can teach me how to cook." He smiled, and as charming as that smile was, it was more dangerous than his innuendo, than his body, than everything. Because that smile was kind. Like when he'd signed that kid's backpack outside the diner. She had to admit that *he* was kind, and that was dangerous.

Tyler had been kind, but he'd never made her heat from the inside out. That had been the appeal, why she'd agreed to marry him. He'd never leave and ruin her.

Funny, that.

"You want to pay *me* to teach you how to cook? You ate those tough-as-nails pork chops, right?"

"I don't need to know how to make five-course meals. I just need to know how to put a few things together that might, on occasion, taste better than some crap I put in the microwave. Maybe the pork chops were a little chewy, but it was still better than 'Budget Frozen Meals for One.'"

She should tell him to talk to Georgia. Or find some

old ranch wife who was lonely and bored. But instead, because his smile was kind and she was tired and felt things she didn't want to feel, the truth slipped out. "I'm not sure we should be spending extra time together."

His kind smile morphed into that "I'm Dan Sharpe sexy and I know it" smirk, and suddenly she felt less mushy toward him. A lot less mushy.

"Oh really? Why is that?"

She smiled sweetly, batting her eyelashes. "I might be forced to murder you, and Shaw will *really* be in trouble if I'm in prison."

He chuckled, but then his expression loosened, grew serious again. He looked at her, right in the eye, and whatever toughness or humor she thought she'd grabbed faded away. Her heart hammered, her breath came faster, and before she could think better of it, her eyes dropped to his mouth.

If he kissed her…she would smack him. Push him. Kick him in the balls and ream him out good.

Or you could kiss him back and enjoy something for once in your sad, pathetic adulthood.

"I know I don't know jack shit *about* jack shit, but I can't image anything you run could ever fail, Mel."

His sincerity might have broken a lesser woman, but for her—tough, sturdy, responsible Mel—it was a reminder.

She didn't have time for Dan Sharpe. For enjoying herself. She had a ranch to save. For her father, and for Caleb, but most of all for herself. It was the one thing that could not leave her. So, nothing was more important than Shaw. Nothing ever had been, and nothing ever would be.

"You ready to go?"

He nodded, and surprise of all surprises, Dan finally shut the hell up and did what she wanted.

~~~

Dan woke up to pounding on his door. He rolled over and pulled the pillow on top of his head, trying to drown out the sound.

But it didn't stop. It got louder and pounded into his bed. Cursing, Dan gave up and rolled off the mattress, trudging to the door.

Halfway down the hall, his brain engaged enough to know it was Mel. But he was too tired to care, or put a shirt on, or muster up the required apology.

He swung the door open. "Go away. I'm tired."

Her jaw dropped, then firmed. "I'll remind you this is a business relationship, and you should be *clothed* at all times, but first, learn this and accept it: you don't get to run a ranch *and* sleep in." She pushed past him, and though he supposed she tried to keep enough distance so they didn't touch, her hip kind of grazed his…underthings.

So *so* not what he needed with her right now. Not after last night. Not this morning when exhaustion would undermine any attempt to be easygoing and charming.

Unfortunately, erections didn't seem to understand the word *exhaustion*.

"Surely, once in a while, even if you're running a ranch, you can sleep in. Being your own boss has to have some perks, right?"

"You are so clueless it breaks my brain. Animals don't give a crap who's the boss. They need to be cared for every morning. So, no, no perks."

"I don't have animals."

"You have a llama! And if you want to be profitable, you'll have more than that."

He took in the dark circles under her eyes, the way her hair wasn't pulled back quite as tight as it normally was. In fact, her shirt was even buttoned crooked. "You look like you could use a sleep-in."

"I could. I could use a sleep-in every damn day for the rest of my damn life, but I do not have that luxury, and, this summer, neither do you." She slammed a hand onto the counter next to the coffeepot. "You could *at least* have coffee going at this point."

"Well, you're pleasant this morning," he muttered. He'd drum up some sympathy for her later, but right now he needed coffee. Even if what he really wanted was sleep.

He'd stayed up way too late being an idiot. Sitting next to that damn llama pen in the pitch dark and reading article after article online about his future.

The picture the media painted wasn't pretty. The picture his agent painted wasn't pretty.

Forced retirement.

When he was still as good as he'd been when he'd led his team to the Stanley Cup the first time. *He'd* done that. Practically on his own. No one had picked them to make the playoffs, but he'd been the best damn player in the league, and he'd motivated the rest of the team to step up and follow his lead.

Everyone had said so. He'd been the reason they got there.

And then the reason they'd lost in game seven.

Shit, he really hated thinking about this. He'd come

out here to *not* think about this, about how the one thing that had helped him escape when he didn't know what to do—and Lord knew he never knew what to do—was evaporating, and there was nothing he could do to fix it.

The word *retirement* was being bandied about in a way it never had been before. If no one in the NHL was going to absolve him, he was screwed. And now Mel was barging in, telling him he was failing this too.

That temper he tried to ignore, joke his way out of, stirred, and he didn't have any reserves left to swallow it down.

"Get dressed."

Mel's sharp order cut through the crap in his brain, but it didn't make him feel any better. "Like what you see?"

"Oh, yes, I can hardly keep my hands to myself," she said. She was mocking him, and maybe if he'd had more sleep, he'd have the wherewithal not to care, but it pissed him the hell off when he was so close to seeing the end of something he loved.

And she just kept talking.

"Your world must be so nice, Dan. Walk around with more money than you know what to do with, think every woman should fall at your feet. You screwed up, but no one gives a real shit about it, because it's a damn *game*." She gave his bare chest a poke at the word *game*, and it was just about the last straw.

He grasped her wrist before she could keep poking or pushing him or whatever the hell it was she was aiming for. But it didn't help the frustrated, edgy feeling in his bloodstream. Her wrist was somehow dainty and soft, small compared to his big hand encircling it.

He stared at it, and when he glanced up, found she

was staring at it too. And damn if that lick of attraction didn't twist and twirl with anger and frustration, creating a potent desire that had absolutely no place here.

So, he focused on her furious gaze. "You're in a pissy mood this morning, and I hate to break it to you, but so am I. So let's agree to step back before we both say a whole bunch of things we don't really mean."

She tried to wriggle her hand free, but he held firm.

"I'm pretty sure I'd mean every last one of them," she said.

"Not going to be satisfied until you have a good fight, huh?"

Finally, she wrenched her hand from his. "I'm not going to be satisfied until you give me an inch."

It was on the tip of his tongue to tell her he had quite a few inches he wouldn't mind giving her, but she kept on.

"Not being ready when I get here is insulting, Dan. Especially, *especially*, after…last night." Some of that anger disappeared or lowered into a hurt he didn't know what to do with. That was the kind of hurt he skated his ass away from.

"You know I'd rather be at my own damn ranch," she continued. "And I can't be. The least you could do is make my time here worthwhile."

Since that made him feel about two inches tall, and since he was tired of her ability to do that—because, sweet damn, the past two years had done plenty to make him feel like that—he forced a smile. Probably more of a nasty smirk.

"Define worthwhile, partner."

"I know this is all a big joke to you—a fun lark while you wait for other people to get your real life back on track—but you could pretend to care every once in a while."

It struck a nerve, an exposed one. Struck it hard enough he didn't have the reserves to laugh it off or pretend it didn't exist. Not care? He always cared too damn much, so damn much he couldn't handle it, couldn't deal with the things he couldn't fix, so he escaped.

Only there was nowhere left to escape to, so he went on the offensive instead. "Watch it, Mel. I may be trying to be a nice guy these days, but it's not my first instinct by a long shot."

"Oh, yeah, and what are you going to do to me, Mr. Not-So-Nice-Guy?"

He didn't take a second to think about it, just went with what had been his instinct since she'd blushed on his porch a few days ago. Gave into the lust mixing in with all those unpleasant feelings.

He crushed his mouth to hers. Not gently, like he'd wanted to do last night. Last night, he'd wanted to comfort her somehow. Offer some kind of commiseration, and while he realized a kiss wasn't the best way to do that, it had been the only thing he could think of.

This was not a comforting, commiserating kiss. This was "I will show you what's what." She was apparently finding out *what's what*, because she kissed him back. Actually, it was more passive than that. She allowed him to kiss her, to scrape his teeth across her bottom lip, to cage her against the counter.

But passive wasn't what Dan wanted from Mel, and in the end, that's what had him stepping back.

He hated himself in that moment. She looked like she wanted to give up, give in, but not to him—to the overwhelming demands that seemed to be dragging her down. She looked like she wanted to dissolve, disappear, never return.

That, *that* he hated himself for.

"Don't ever, and I mean *ever*, do that again." She straightened her shoulders, took a deep breath, and let go of the counter behind her. Though he supposed she was trying to look tough, she looked about as menacing as a peewee hockey player who hadn't learned how to handle a stick yet.

He might hate himself for pushing her there, but he wasn't going to let her see his regret, his guilt. "I'm an easygoing guy, Mel, but if you keep pushing my buttons, I will damn well keep pushing back."

"Yeah, well, unbutton my buttons and prepare to lose some anatomy you hold dear."

He hated to lose his temper, didn't like to feel all that rushing regret after he went off the handle or did or said something stupid. Because there was a voice inside his head telling him to step back, cool off, but the anger and frustration pumping through his veins made listening to that voice impossible.

So he stood toe to toe with her, and purposefully touched the top button of her shirt. He brushed his thumb across the hollow of her throat. "That so?"

Her eyes held his. She didn't shiver under his touch, didn't melt, didn't slump or cower and make him feel like a total dick. She stood there. Still, yes, but like some untouchable thing. Like some goddess trying to decide if she'd deign to let him continue to think he could touch her.

"You know what?" she said, not moving, not

looking away, not anything, her eyes boring into his. "This is stupid."

"I agree." Except he had no idea what he was agreeing to. He only knew she wasn't swatting his hands off her, and she wasn't stepping back. She was standing there and any insecurities or weaknesses from earlier had disappeared.

The woman in front of him right now looked like she could knock him flat with one blow. One word.

Instead, she knocked him flat with one kiss.

Chapter 6

MEL HAD NEVER IN HER LIFE MADE A MISTAKE THAT felt so good. A shocking punch of melted heat centered at her core. The rough bristle of his chin scraped her skin, causing her to shiver, but the heat made her insides feel like liquid.

No kiss had ever made her feel this good. So good, she couldn't even regret it. Because it meant Dan's mouth was on hers, his big hands gripping her hips with all the strength and precision of someone very used to being in charge.

She would let him be in charge. She wouldn't even question it, because his hands held her exactly where she needed to be for his mouth to explore hers.

Her palms flattened down his smooth, bare back with a mind of their own, and something growly escaped his mouth as he pushed her back against the counter until she couldn't go any farther.

She was a woman who rode horses and faced down cows and clomped through all manner of labor-intensive chores every single day. So much so that she never felt small or fragile or *dainty*, but somehow, being pressed to the counter, feeling the definite outline of Dan's erection against her stomach, she felt…

Like a siren or a seductress. Someone soft and curvy and beautiful who could bring a man to his knees with a whisper instead of a blow.

She had never in her life wished so desperately for a man to take off her clothes. To feel big hands stroke over her skin. She had never felt an ache this sharp, this *needy*. Never in her life considered making a mistake so...enthusiastically.

She wanted this mistake like she wanted survival. The thrill. The release. Something that wasn't weighty. That didn't squeeze around her lungs and her heart.

Here it was. In her reach, against her mouth, pressing up against her entire body. Here was the mistake she'd never allowed herself to make. There was no responsible, sensible part of her brain surviving this.

So she accepted it. The heat. The desire. Even the desperation. The way her blood throbbed in time with need. She let his tongue explore, take. She let *go*.

She ran her hands up over his shoulders and then down his chest, letting her fingertips absorb every shock of attraction, every exciting inch of his warm skin, but he caught her wrists halfway down, stopping her before she got to his stomach. "I'm a little soft these days," he said against her mouth, interrupting the kissing.

She blinked at him, her mouth still all but pressed to his. Her body *definitely* pressed to his. Which was not soft. At all.

He was famous and had money coming out of his ears. He was *gorgeous*, and that little flicker of self-consciousness over his not one hundred percent in shape hockey body—even though in her book he had to be sitting at a 99.9 percent—undid her. She didn't want to dwell on what it said about her that his weaknesses were the things she couldn't fight.

Self-consciousness. Not knowing what to do without hockey. This miserable ranch.

So she loosened her wrists out of his grasp and did something even more nonsensical and unreasonable than kissing him. She pressed her palm to the bulge in his pants, absorbed the heat of him, the length of him. "You are decidedly *not* soft."

He huffed out a laugh, but his fingers curled around her wrists again, pulling them away from his body, but not letting them go once he did. "I don't want you to have sex with me out of anger."

Some of the exciting, forget-all-her-troubles warmth cooled, the throbbing dulled, leaving an unsatisfied ache. "I think you might be out of luck any other way." Because this certainly wasn't born of anything except basic physical attraction and frustration. Period.

He dropped her wrists, looking ridiculously sheepish for someone who'd initiated this whole thing. "Maybe we should be out of luck then."

She scooted sideways so he wouldn't be right in front of her, so she could escape. The rejection stung more, because she never should have let this happen in the first place. It was supposed to be wrong and stupid and feel good, and he was saying no.

No.

Didn't that figure? "I should go."

"Mel, you can't go. We have…"

"Work to do?" She arched an eyebrow at him, because she was determined to be tough and unaffected, on the outside at the very least. She gestured toward his very obvious erection. "I think you might be busy."

"Don't go. Don't make this—"

"Don't tell me what to do, Sharpe." She would not be told how to live her life. There were already too many factors taking away her choices. "I'm going to go feed the llama. You get dressed and…do what you need to do. Then we're going to Bozeman to get you a damn truck."

"Mel."

"End of story." Because she was in charge, and the point here was not Dan. It was to get his neglected ranch off the ground. Dan was an inconsequential part of this whole thing. "Make some coffee and bring me a mug when you're finished."

She tried to walk out of his house with a normal, purposeful stride, but she wasn't delusional enough to believe she accomplished it. This was a stomp, a storm out.

What was wrong with her right now? She needed to get it together. So she walked and walked until she came to the fence around the stables. And the llama.

She stared at the llama, and it stared back.

She took a deep breath and slowly let it out. She was fine. This was fine. She was strong and in charge, and just because she'd been feeling a little beat down lately didn't mean she couldn't handle this.

She should thank Dan for rejecting her. It was the best damn thing to happen today.

"Oh, that asshole." Because as much as she *should* be grateful, there were certain parts of her not getting the message.

She squeezed her eyes shut and pushed away from the fence. She couldn't keep losing it with Dan. Even if he felt sorry enough for her not to fire her, she had her pride and her name.

She would not let him think she was a flake, or worse, that she would ever be one of the many women who dropped their panties for him.

She took another deep, centering breath. That thought helped. Imagining hordes of women tossing their—probably much lacier and more expensive—underwear at him helped. She was not made for Dan Sharpe.

She was made for these mountains.

Hard, craggy, but impressive. Standing the test of time, century after century. Maybe she wouldn't be around for centuries, but things she worked for would.

Mr. Hockey Player could not move mountains, even if he could get her blood pumping.

The llama made some creepy llama noise, like a sheep on steroids. They were really going to have to do something about this thing. How on earth had it survived without anyone even knowing it existed?

Mel faced down the beast. It didn't move, didn't blink. She had the sudden desire to somehow win. To show this animal what was what. She was immovable; *it* was an animal.

She stared it down to no avail, and when it didn't move, she decided to take matters into her own hands. She put one foot on the bottom of rung of the fence, ready to leverage herself up and over, but Dan's voice stopped her.

"What are you doing?"

"Next time, llama," she muttered, putting her foot back on the ground. She turned to Dan. "Just trying to feed him."

"Shouldn't you go through the indoor part? You know, so he doesn't eat you or pulverize you with his demon eyes." He handed her a mug of coffee. Just as she'd asked.

Which made her feel soft, and when she felt soft—attack. "Well, I'm not a wimp, Dan."

He scratched a hand through his hair, which looked kind of wet. He'd taken a shower. *What had he done in there?*

Her eyes were halfway to his crotch before she remembered she was a mountain and all that. A mountain unmoved by erections, too-tight-for-work jeans, and T-shirts that strained against the bulge of biceps.

Oh, for fuck's sake.

"Mel, I'm sor—"

"If you apologize, I will punch you." The last thing she needed was his pity on top of his rejection. Just the thought made her skin crawl and her overheated body cool.

"The normal response to an apology is, 'that's okay' or—"

"There is nothing for you to apologize for. We had a momentary lapse in sanity. It's over." And because she was tough and strong, she'd swallow her pride and keep going. "But I am sorry for how I barged in here this morning. Taking my foul mood out on you was not fair or conducive."

"Conducive."

"Yes. Conducive."

"Did I…break you? Because apologies and talk of being *conducive* is really strange coming from you."

"No. I'm unbreakable." Or at the very least, she hid her breaks until they went away. "Now, are you ready to go buy a truck or what?"

He was silent, that green gaze steady on her face,

dark eyebrows drawn together as if she were some equation he was trying to figure out. She didn't budge, didn't blink—much like the llama, she merely accepted his scrutiny. Until his features smoothed out and he nodded.

"Sure. Let's go buy a truck."

The llama method worked. She'd have to employ it more often.

Dan was not in the habit of not knowing what the hell to do. At first, it had seemed like a novelty. Hey, something to learn, something to challenge him. Make him forget all the shit he'd left behind. A new escape.

But not knowing what the hell to do about *everything* sucked. His career, ranching, Mel—not one thing made sense.

He was lost. And he was being carted around by this woman—who didn't make any sense to him. Not because she was irrational, or hard to read, but because he didn't know how anyone could possibly be as mentally tough as she was.

She had *not* been happy that he'd put the kibosh on angry sex. Hell, he hadn't been happy about it, but instead of getting upset, instead of giving him a piece of her mind, she'd shut it down. Hadn't let him apologize.

She'd apologized.

Gone on as if that kiss was simply a stumble on an otherwise narrow and forward-moving path. But only she knew where the path was going. and he didn't have a clue.

He glanced at her profile: jaw set, eyes squinting at the road, hands tight around the steering wheel. How could she be wound so tight all the time and not ever break? Mel considered herself unbreakable, and maybe she was. Maybe she was made from sterner stuff than he'd ever known. Like those damn mountains, beautiful and distant.

"What's your full name?"

Her "what the hell is your deal" looks were almost comical at this point. The way her head jerked back, as if she was allergic to his questions.

But maybe if he could know her better, he could understand how she did it. Handled all this. Maybe he could emulate it. Maybe he could find a way not to cave or run away when the hard stuff came.

"What do you mean my full name?" she demanded as the landscape transitioned from wild and stark to a city. It still wasn't a city like he was used to. But Chicago and Minnesota boasted no mountains.

"What's Mel short for? Melanie? Melissa? Mel... Melicent? Melhard-ass?"

She rolled her eyes, and he noticed that her hands on the wheel loosened. He grinned.

He might not have it all figured out, but his general ridiculousness relaxed her...when it didn't piss her off.

"It's just Mel."

"Mel isn't short for anything?"

"No." She stared hard at the red light. Always staring so hard at everything. Concentrating. Working. She made him tired. "I was named after my great-great-great-grandpa who started the ranch. I'm the oldest. I was going to be Mel Shaw regardless of the outcome."

"Not even Mellie?"

Any humor at the question was gone. Her tone was

flat. "Sorry to disappoint. There is no secret feminine side of me."

"Now, on that, I beg to differ."

"I've castrated cows, Sharpe—think about that before you differ too much."

"You've castrated cows, you probably pack a mean punch, but you sighed when I kissed you, sweetheart."

"*I* kissed you, meathead. About took you out in the process too."

"Can't argue that." He waited a beat until she snuck a glance at him, then grinned. "But you still sighed."

"It's best if we don't talk about it."

"Is it?" he mused. He kind of liked how her cheeks got a little pink.

"Yes."

"Hmm."

She leveled him with a sharp look, or as much of one as she could muster before returning her gaze to the road. "Are you rescinding your moratorium on angry sex?"

"Rescinding my *what*?"

She huffed. "You know what I mean."

"Fine, and no."

"Then kiss talk is off-limits." She pulled the E-brake a little soon and the truck jerked to a stop. "Look at that. Here we are."

He broke his gaze from her profile—pretty and feminine whether she wanted it to be or not—and took in the sea of cars and trucks, shiny and new. He didn't want to do this.

Maybe he should have done the angry-sex thing after all.

She got out of her truck, all business and determination, and he sat in the passenger seat, sulking. He wasn't proud of himself, but not embarrassed enough to get out. *She* wanted him to get a damn truck, *she* could do all the work.

You hired her, you fucking moron.

Right.

There was nothing wrong with getting a truck. After all, it would make him feel all rancher-like, driving around in one of these big-ass things, and that's what he was here for. To figure out how to be a rancher. The motorcycle wasn't practical for ranch life. It was a spur-of-the-moment response to not being under contract.

So, he had no idea why this was a thing. A thing he didn't want to do. A thing that made him feel antsy and pissy.

He supposed it was like a promise. Trucks had to be taken care of. Like llamas. And women. Needing him for things he'd never been able to give.

A man in khakis and a shiny red polo shirt came out, all bright smiles and arm gestures. Nodding and scanning the lot when Mel spoke. She smiled. Her posture was relaxed. He hated how she could be two people. This light, breezy, *friendly* woman to everyone but him.

Which was enough to knock him out of her truck, ready to take some of the power here. He sauntered over to where Mel stood with the salesman, resisted the urge to scowl when Mel chuckled at something the guy said.

"What's the word, darling?" he asked cheerfully.

Mel's look could have probably set his face on fire, but the slick salesman smiled broadly, holding out a hand. "Good morning! So, we're looking for a truck?"

He shook Dan's hand earnestly, cocking his head. "You look really familiar, sir. Have you bought with us before?"

Dan slung his arm around Mel's shoulder, which tensed underneath his arm. Which, yes, increased his pissed-off desire to act on his innate douchiness. "Sure haven't. You mind giving us some space to look around? The lady here sure does like to—" He brought his fingers together to mimic incessant talking.

"Absolutely. We are *not* one of those pushy, in-your-face dealerships. Take all the time you need, and just find me when you're ready to test drive." The guy gave an overly wide smile, then did the creepy "shake your hand too long and look you in the eye" thing before finally heading back into the pristine-looking office.

The breath whooshed out of him as Mel knocked a fist into his gut before he had a chance to block it.

"Hey!"

"I pulled it, bastard. What is your problem? Why on earth would you send him away? We're trying to buy you a necessary tool for your ranch."

"I don't want to hear some spiel from some asshole. I just want to get this over with."

Mel sighed, all world-weary and "you're so stupid, Sharpe." "The spiel is important. You have to figure out the best truck for your needs. You have to be friendly so he gives you a deal. Oh wait, I forgot who I'm talking to. Do I need to explain what deal and negotiate mean to you, moneybags?"

The irritable, sexually frustrated part of him wanted to be offended, but it was hard to argue. Money had never been a concern, an issue. It was there, like air and hockey and pretty women who usually fell all over him.

In the face of Mel's life, her struggle, her complete disgust with him—except for that kiss—he couldn't argue that he didn't give a shit about deals or negotiations.

All he wanted to do was skate. Lace up and feel the air breeze by, a man in control and on top of the damn world. *All your problems float away, don't they, son?*

They did. When he was playing hockey, they fucking did.

He did not want to have to ask Mel for advice, and he did not want to have to question why he'd turned her down when it was not at all what he *wanted* to do.

He couldn't remember too many times he'd done the right thing, the good thing, when it hadn't given him something he'd wanted.

Standing in a warm parking lot, he wanted to take a stick to every last windshield. So, he did his best to not give a crap. "Pick one."

She blinked at him like he'd asked her to strip.

"What do you mean 'pick one'?"

"You're the expert. You know my ranch. You know trucks. I know jack." He waved an arm to encompass the whole stupid lot, his whole stupid lack of knowledge. "So, tell me which one to buy. That's your job. If you were me, which would you choose?"

She looked around the lines of trucks, something slackening her jaw. Her expression was...horrified. He couldn't work that out. She loved making decisions—especially decisions for him—but she all but recoiled from the suggestion.

"I'm *not* you. I don't have your money. I don't have

your ranch. I don't…" She cleared her throat, swallowed. "I don't have these kinds of choices, Dan."

She had a way of saying things that jabbed somewhere in his chest—a dull, aching pain right in his center. Things he didn't think she fully understood the weight of.

Because in some strange twist of fate, the things she said hit him like a ton of bricks. He had no way of fighting her words, escaping the emotions in them. And he knew, like he'd always known, at some point he would be unable to escape.

Making things too hard on Mom so she'd left Dad, walking away when Grandpa had wanted to tell him the story of the ranch that was his heart. When he hadn't recognized Dan for the first time. The mess with his team. And here, there was nowhere to go. Nowhere to run away to.

"You're the one who said I needed a truck," he snapped.

"Yes. But, you should pick it!"

It was not the way she usually yelled at him. It was the way she'd yelled at him this morning, like yelling was the only thing that was keeping her from crying. That…that he couldn't be irritated by or pissed about. This woman had some serious stress on her plate, and while he was in no way up to the challenge of dealing with it, the least he could do was offer a distraction. "Let's go eat."

"What?"

"You're about to break, Cowgirl. Let's take a lunch break." He rested his hand on her arm in an attempt to guide her toward her truck.

She jerked her arm away from him. "I told you I'm—"

"You're human, Mel, whether you want to be or not." A human who needed something to give, and it didn't take a genius to realize the give wasn't going to come from her. "I'm hungry. We'll do the truck some other day." A day when they could both handle it. So, maybe never.

She opened her mouth, presumably to argue more, because God knew the woman didn't breathe without arguing, but then her eyes took in the trucks again, the lot, and her hands shook as she pressed fingers to her temples.

"You're such a pain in the ass," she said in a wobbly whisper.

"Yup, that's me. We gonna go eat?"

"Yes. Yes, food. That's what we need. Food."

He didn't think that was what they needed at all, but he wasn't about to argue. Not until her hands stopped shaking. Not until something around here started to make sense.

So, maybe that was just never going to happen.

Chapter 7

MEL DID NOT LIKE BEING STEERED.

Scratch that. She liked it. She did not like the fact that she liked it.

But sometimes it was nice to be the one following instead of leading, acting out the decision without having to have made it. She let Dan drag her along, grumbling about Montana and its lack of fine dining.

Fine. Dining.

Bozeman had never felt like an alternate reality until she'd stepped into it with Dan Sharpe at her side.

"Here we go."

Dan pushed her into some restaurant that immediately made her feel out of place. The lighting was dim, and the strains of some classical song played somewhere over the hostess podium. There was a couple at a table facing them—the man in a suit, the woman in a pencil skirt and blazer—and it was clear they did *not* approve of her and Dan's jeans and T-shirts.

"I don't think we—" But before she could whisper her suggestion that they didn't belong, Dan was greeting the hostess, a pretty young blond in black slacks and a white button-up shirt. Bright red lipstick and some fancy eye makeup.

She hated herself for thinking it, for feeling it, but she immediately scowled. *That* was Dan Sharpe's type of woman. Someone who knew how to put makeup on and flirt as if she had the key to the damn world hidden in her smile, and it was the guy's job to find it.

Dan would have *no* trouble finding it.

She tried again. "We really shouldn't—"

He waved a dismissive hand at her, and if she weren't so out of her element, she might have punched him for that too.

"I know we're a little underdressed," he said to the hostess, leaning on her podium, oozing that self-assured charm. *Ugh.* "But do you think we could get a table? I'd really appreciate it." He smiled and extended a hand to the woman.

She took it eagerly, and then smiled, looking up at Dan from under her lashes. "It'd be my pleasure," she said in a husky voice.

Mel knew it was small of her, but she wanted to sucker punch the girl, much like she'd sucker punched Dan in the dealership parking lot, except harder.

A lot harder.

Which…seriously, she'd never been the jealous type. Tyler had actually gotten irritated that she hadn't been angry when she'd found him cozied up to Kyrie Watson at some stupid party senior year.

But she hadn't cared. Not really.

Why did she keep comparing Dan to Tyler? First of all, Tyler was ancient history, her ex-fiancé for almost five years. Second of all, Dan was *not* her boyfriend or fiancé or anything. And he wasn't going to be.

So, she seriously needed to get her brain on a track that made any lick of sense.

It was only as the woman grabbed two menus and slipped something into her pocket that Mel realized Dan hadn't just charmed his way into the too-nice restaurant.

He'd paid her.

"You gave her money!" she hissed, hopefully quietly enough that the hostess a few strides in front of them didn't hear.

"I did indeed. Is that against some cowgirl code of yours?"

"Here we are. Your server will be with you shortly." The hostess seemed to be waiting for something, hovering over the table, but Mel didn't have a clue as to what. Finally, she plopped the menus on the table and left.

"You're supposed to sit down so they can place the menu in front of you," Dan explained to her as she might have explained fence-building to him. He slid into his seat, picked up the discarded menus, and began to read.

"You bribed her to give us a table." She didn't know why she was stuck on that, maybe because this place gave her the creeps. All white linens and dark woods and people in suits.

He rolled his eyes. "Yes, this has been established."

"Why?" Mel demanded. She didn't want to eat here. People were staring. Everything was weird, and she already felt weird enough with all the almost-breaking-down she kept doing around Dan.

"I'm hungry."

"We passed a diner, a café, a—"

He looked up from the menu, fixing her with a glare—which was surprisingly effective, since he rarely glared. "Shut up and sit down, Cowgirl. And hurry up and decide what you want to order. I'm starved."

She wanted to argue, but she had nothing in her left to argue. No strength, no fortitude. Maybe she *was* breaking. So she sat and poked through the menu. "I... Everything on here is over twenty bucks."

Dan laughed, the jackass. "It's on me."

"That doesn't excuse overpriced food. I could buy, like, three steaks at Felicity's store for the price of that prime rib."

"Go for the filet. I insist."

"Sharpe—"

But the waiter approached, went into some spiel about specials and wine lists, and Jesus H., this *was* an alternate reality.

Dan asked a few questions, and it took the waiter disappearing into the kitchen for her to realize— "Hey! You ordered for me."

"You were sitting there staring at me like I'd grown another head. Besides, payer's prerogative."

"You can't keep...buying my meals."

"Why not? You wouldn't eat here if I hadn't pushed you inside. I should pay. Besides, you had no problem with me paying at Georgia's."

"It cost twenty *total*. Not per person."

"It's all the same to me." He watched her carefully when he said it, as if he expected her to have another almost-meltdown.

So she swallowed all the words down. Because she was tired of him seeing through her—or more accurately, tired of being so transparent.

Helping him pick out a truck had seemed fine, good even, no different than telling him what to do at his ranch. But the way he'd put it: "if you were me." That had shaken her, because for a second there, she'd allowed herself to think about what it might feel like. If she had all the money in the world, what would she do?

She wasn't one for being materialistic, but this wasn't about buying a fancy car or a new house. She just wanted to feel…safe. Like she had enough to take care of everyone she needed to take care of.

And disappear. You want to disappear.

She blinked at the stinging in her eyes, and Dan pried her hands off the menu she hadn't realized she was still clutching. Then, even worse, he enclosed her hands in his.

"If you're thinking I expect you, with all you have to deal with, to be perfect, to always be in control, then you're wrong. I would not think less of you if you cracked every once in a while. Trust me. I'm the king of cracking."

"I don't care what you think," she said, precisely, carefully, so she didn't give any emotion away. Why would she care about what he thought? He was little more than a stranger. Just an employer.

Except for the part where you threw yourself at him this morning. And he rejected you.

She didn't dare look at him, didn't dare look at his hands over hers. So she looked at the table, the dark wood in contrast to the blinding white of the napkin underneath the gleaming silverware.

He removed his hands, slowly, the tips of his fingers all but trailing along the length of hers.

"Look, if acting like you've got it all together gets you through the day, by all means, keep pretending. But I do see through it, and if it's a bit much, for what it's worth, you don't have to pretend with me."

She swallowed the lump in her throat and straightened her shoulders. It wasn't pretending—it was surviving. He wouldn't have a clue about that.

Not a damn clue.

She met his gaze. "I appreciate the offer, but it's unnecessary."

He held her stare, unblinking, like he could see through everything. She wouldn't allow herself to believe that. Some rich-as-sin hockey player didn't have any insight into her life, no matter how much he knew, or would know. No matter how much she pretended or didn't pretend. He did not have the life capable of understanding hers.

"Consider it an open invitation."

Maybe if things were different—if he wasn't handsome and charming and everything she knew better than to trust—maybe that would be comforting. But much like that night at Shaw, Dan's kindness was more threat than invitation. Kindness never stuck, and beauty and charm were an illusion.

"You know, if you're set on keeping your motorcycle, you could consider getting a Gator instead of a truck."

He was quiet for a few humming seconds—nothing but the murmur of fancy-businesspeople conversations and the faint notes of some string instrument and his green eyes zoned in on her face, assessing, unlocking.

Well, she just had to make it two months, three and a half weeks without being unlocked. She could do that. She *would* do that.

Let Dan buy her this too-expensive lunch, let him think he'd gotten to her. Meanwhile, she'd erase this morning from her memory. She'd start over—God knew she was good at that. She'd underestimated Dan, and how close she was to her breaking point.

She wouldn't again.

"I'm going to go out on a limb and guess when you say *Gator*, you mean some kind of vehicle, not an actual alligator."

"Astute, Sharpe."

"Thought we'd moved to Dan."

"You're whatever I want you to be whenever I want you to be."

"That so?"

"I'm the boss, remember?"

"Oh, I remember." He leaned forward and opened his mouth, but before he could say some undoubtedly smart-ass comment, his phone rang. He frowned and pulled it out of his pocket. His frown deepened to a scowl. "My agent," he muttered, already getting out of his seat. "Be right back."

He disappeared out of the front, leaving Mel alone, in this place she did not belong, with a very expensive meal being put before her.

A rather meaningful symbol, all in all.

—◦◦◦—

Dan glared at the red brick of the building across the street, the faded sign that stuck out from what appeared to be a shoe store. Beyond the buildings were more fucking mountains. He didn't know why they pissed him off—they just did.

"Can't we do an independent investigation?" he interrupted as his agent yammered on about possibly interested teams that sounded completely one hundred percent *not* interested.

"Listen, Dan, you *could*..."

He could all but see Scott pinching the bridge of his nose and rolling his eyes. And the use of "you" instead of "we" was...well, purposeful.

"I'm not saying I don't believe you, because of course I do. I'm your number one supporter here, but is a private investigation worth the media circus? What about the possibility—"

"The possibility of *what*?" Dan demanded, fingers clutched around the phone so tight it began to hurt.

"Look, you don't know what they'll find. Not that you're guilty. Just, you can't trust anyone. You know, man? If someone in an investigative role even hints at you even talking to someone shady—shit, Dan, your career is *over*. I've got Phoenix *this* close to giving you a tryout."

"A *tryout*? A *tryout*? I..." He stopped himself before he said *I am Dan Sharpe, damn it*. Because that sounded a little too dickish even to his ears. But he *was* Dan Sharpe, damn it. He'd outgrown the need for a tryout fifteen years ago.

"We gotta play the game, Dan."

"If we had an investigation—"

"Look, I'm not going to stop you if that's what you want to do. I'm advising against it, but I can't stop you. I just think working your way back up the hard way is ultimately going to be a better way to end your career on a high note."

End your career.

"Let me work my magic. You just lay low in Idaho—"

"Montana," Dan said through gritted teeth.

"Right, yeah, hang out there. Keep in shape. See if you can find somewhere to skate. But, you know, take a break. Chill. I'm working things out. You know I want you to play next year as much as you want to."

Of course he did. That's how he got paid, but that didn't make Dan any happier with sitting around *waiting*. He wanted to act. He wanted *something* to be in his control.

He took a step down the sidewalk, to where he could make out Mel at the table. Their food had been served, and she was attacking the steak like it had mortally offended her.

He didn't doubt she was picturing his face as she hacked it to pieces. He didn't doubt she was working on all the ways she was going to control the rest of the summer. Trucks and Gators and llama care and fuck all.

He didn't mind taking a backseat when it came to that stuff. He let Mom take care of his money and investments, and Scott handle endorsement deals. He paid a lot of people to take care of every part of his life that wasn't hockey.

But hockey had always been this thing he'd controlled, been good at, been a king at. He had made it his escape, his everything. He hadn't felt the loss of that so acutely until this moment, talking about tryouts and working his way up the hard way, and knowing that it didn't matter.

He was always going to be labeled a cheat. Hockey was already lost to him.

"Dan?"

Dan hit End and shoved the phone in his pocket. He

wanted to toss it into a field again and not retrieve it this time, but there were only old, weary-looking brick buildings and huge trucks driving up and down the main drag.

He marched into the restaurant instead. This morning had been full of…weirdness, but he was going to put a stop to it. He was going to find some grasp of control, and if he had to ask Mel to teach him how—so be it.

He slid into his seat and leaned across the table, close enough to Mel's face to notice the freckles, the way her eyelashes went from dark to almost gold, eyes that edged from dark brown to nearly hazel.

Not feminine his ass. "Okay, Cowgirl, add one more thing to the list of things you're going to teach me."

She furrowed her eyebrows at him. "You must have had a pleasant phone call."

"First of all, you don't eat the bacon off a filet, like that." He pointed to the plate, all of the bacon gone, only half the steak left. "Aren't you supposed to be cow people out here? Don't you know a thing about steak?"

"I know if it's Montana beef, it's superior. And if it's set in front of me, I'm going to eat it however I want." She pointed her fork at him, leaning in, though she stopped abruptly—perhaps realizing how close their faces were.

How similar this was to this morning.

She moderately leaned back, back rigid and chin in the air. "So, what the hell is on my list of things to teach you?"

"This control thing you've got going on. The unbreakable shit. I want to know how to do that." How she had made herself her own escape. He desperately needed to learn that.

She shook her head. "That's not a…teachable thing. That's just me. It's in my bones. You have to struggle and…learn how to survive. You've never had to survive a day in your life."

He bristled at her assessment, but he certainly couldn't *argue* with her. So he leaned back and attacked his steak, much like she'd attacked hers.

"You just have to…decide. That it won't break you," she said after minutes of silent chewing. "I don't know how to teach that. It's a decision I make."

When he glanced up at her, she was staring at her plate. She wasn't frowning, exactly, though her lips were downturned. It was more sad than angry.

"I make it every day," she said in a quiet voice. "If hockey means that much to you, you decide to find a way to get back to it. Considering the fact that you're famous or whatever, I doubt it'll be that much of a struggle."

"Don't go feeling too sorry for me," he said dryly.

"Sorry, I don't feel sorry for millionaires. I feel sorry only for people with actual problems."

"You think people with money can't have problems?"

"I think people with money can solve a lot of problems that crop up. I think money smooths a lot of problems away. I also think *you* personally don't have too many problems, aside from sucking when it counts."

Sucking when it counts. Not a pleasant way of putting it, but accurate. Dan Sharpe sucked when it counted. Mel might not see that as much of a problem, but Dan certainly did. It was the kind of problem you didn't just decide to endure, to survive. It was an inherent piece of himself.

Like Mel's hard-assness or Dad's quiet calm, Mom's intense focus.

Only, sucking when it counted wasn't a positive. Not even close.

"You'll land on your feet," she said sharply, like she was irritated with herself. "I wouldn't worry about it."

Which was part of the problem—he'd worried about very little in his life before this had happened. He didn't like worrying, didn't like being uncertain or lost. He was in over his head with this ranch stuff, and it didn't bother him too much because it was supposed to be a distraction.

But what if come fall it was more than that? What if it was all he had? He had considered that, but not in a real way. In the fairy-tale way where ranching would be easy and fun. It didn't even take a full week here to realize rebuilding his grandfather's place wasn't just throwing some money around and pounding a few posts.

It was hard. It would endure.

Would he? *Could* he?

He cleared his throat. "Hockey is the only thing I've ever been any good at." It was oddly uncomfortable to admit that weakness to Mel. Usually he had no problems admitting weakness in everything that wasn't hockey. Call him foolish or stupid or selfish—he'd agree with it all easy enough.

But something about admitting the whole of what he was worth to Mel seemed a stupid thing to do. He wished the words back into his mouth as he pushed the green beans around on his plate. "How can I not worry about that?" he grumbled, irritated with himself, with Scott, with her, with fucking Montana and its damn mountains everywhere.

"I doubt hockey is the *only* thing you're good at."

The weak compliment was enough to smooth some of the edges of his frustration. If Mel was complimenting him, surely all wasn't lost. "Well, sure." He took a bite of his steak, chewed thoughtfully. Remembering the way she'd kissed him this morning, remembering the fact that *he'd* said no. *He* had been in charge there. "You know, I'm pretty good at sex too."

She choked on her water, then glared at him. "That's an off-limits topic."

"Off-limits, huh? I don't know. I was thinking maybe we should revisit the…uh…what did you call it? Some kind of moratorium." Yeah, maybe they should revisit that after all.

"Too late."

"Is it?"

"Yes. It is." She pulled the napkin out of her lap and wiped her mouth. "Now, if you'd hurry up? We've wasted an entire morning on nothing, and you have a limited use of my services. You want to be good at something, Dan? You're going to have to try. You're going to have to care. And you're going to have to not get on my bad side."

Try. Care. Two things he stayed away from outside of an ice rink. Hell, even inside a rink sometimes.

"I can't promise the last one," he said. She made an exasperated sound. "But let's try the first two. I'm going to need a book store."

"You need to *work*, not read."

"Knowledge is power, Mel."

She rolled her eyes. "You'll be lucky to get a fence in come August at this rate."

He didn't say anything, instead focusing on finishing

his steak. When he'd decided he wanted to go pro like Dad, he'd followed his father's footsteps inch by inch, so he hadn't had to come up with a plan of his own—there had been a route already laid out to follow.

Wouldn't Mel be surprised when he came up with his own road map? Okay, he'd probably be a little surprised too, and he might even fuck it up.

But if he was going to *care*, why not try?

Chapter 8

"I'M GOING TO START A LLAMA RANCH."

Mel blinked. She had barely gotten out of her truck when Dan blasted her with...*what?* "It's a little early to be drinking." The past three days had been relatively normal after their little blip a few mornings ago.

Dan had been quiet, a good worker, doing whatever she told him to do. No flirting, no sex talk. He had been the perfect gentleman.

It had been weird, actually, but she figured he'd just set his mind to trying to be good at this ranching thing. She'd been thankful that he was over being all...purposefully charming and crap.

But apparently he hadn't been focusing on getting the more dilapidated parts of his ranch in working order. Instead, he'd been thinking about llamas.

Possibly he'd been abducted by aliens, or hippies.

"I'm not drinking. I've been researching."

"Researching llamas?" She squinted at him in the early morning light, confused that he was carrying a book. Even more confused that he was wearing glasses. "Researching llamas and wearing glasses. Are you okay? There's this thing called the mountain crazies around here—I think you've come down with it."

"I do not have the mountain crazies." When she kept staring at his glasses, he yanked them off his face. "So, I don't see well close up. I don't see what the big deal is."

"Oh my God, you're so old you need cheaters." It was such a hilariously un-super-hot Dan thing, she all but giggled. "You have old-guy eyes."

"I do *not* have old-guy eyes. I have astigmatism. Kind of."

This time she couldn't help herself—she did giggle. Not the sound of an in-control, take-charge kind of woman, but he was so flustered by his "kind-of" astigmatism. "Sure you do, *Dad*."

The baffled indignation on his face morphed into one of those sharp, sexy looks that made her completely forget the glasses in his hands. He smirked. "Look, I'm all for pet names, but let's not get weird."

She rolled her eyes. "So, we're back to that."

"Back to what?"

"All your lame sexual innuendo."

"Hey, my sexual innuendo is not lame."

"Can we get back to the point?" When he only looked bewildered, she pointed at the book he was carrying. "Your llama ranch."

"Right. So I was researching the mystery-llama problem—which would make an excellent band name by the way—and I found some websites for llama ranches. One in Oregon. One in Idaho. There's a bunch more, but these places raise llamas to sell, or to use as pack animals. Some people even shear them for yarn. I mean, the possibilities are endless."

She closed her eyes tight, counted to ten. Honestly, she had to be dreaming. One of the biggest hockey players in the NHL was not standing here telling her he wanted to start a llama ranch. It just wasn't possible.

But when she opened her eyes, he was still there,

glasses in one hand, *Llamas for Dummies* in the other. As serious as could be.

Llama ranching.

She blew out a breath and tried to figure out how to handle this bizarre turn of events. Even when she thought she had Dan pegged or beaten or something, he found a way to be…completely unpredictable.

Like she needed another complex, unpredictable relationship in her life. Even if it was only a working relationship, it still meant some give and take. Per usual, she was in the all-give position. Though she had to admit that Dan took much less than the rest of the people in her life.

Oh, she was so sick of feeling sorry for herself.

"You know, normal ranch herds include cattle, horses. The end."

"Well, exactly. It's been done a million times. Why not do something different?"

"So, are you looking for the consultant who tells you you're an idiot or the consultant who helps you despite being an idiot?"

He seemed to consider, looking over at the barn/llama stable on the hill. "Let's go with the latter."

"I don't know anything about llamas."

He grinned, all dazzle and spark. "Then we can learn together."

She supposed it was that dazzle, that *smile* and the way it radiated fun and ease and just a touch of "why the hell not" kind of attitude that got under her skin so much. That made her lips curve upward in a return smile. That could all but see his ridiculous plan working out.

It was a dangerous dazzle, because it made her want.

She could see this different life, this different path, where things weren't so hard, where she wasn't tied to this land she loved with balls and chains.

And as always, that want, that brief flash of different, was like being punched in the gut. A light she'd never be able to enjoy. So her smile died, and she frowned at his book. "You'll need more than that to get started."

"Yeah, I know. I've got more inside. This isn't a whim."

"Isn't it?"

He shook his head and started marching for his dilapidated old house, marching with a kind of purpose she'd never seen from him. She would not be swayed by that purpose, or drowned in it. She had her own purpose.

Twenty grand.

So she walked after him, determined to be as helpful as she could for the duration she had to put up with his crazy scheme to start a llama ranch. *Llamas.*

She had to admit, she was still surprised that he hadn't brought in a bunch of people to make this place more habitable yet. It was still old, dusty, and creaky, but it didn't seem to bother him.

He had papers and books all over the old, filmy kitchen table. A laptop sat in the middle of it, all shiny and expensive and way nicer than her and Caleb's shared desktop that whirred and offered the blue screen of death more often than actually booting up.

"Where did you get all this?"

"Library."

"The library closes at four. We work until after five every day. How did you—"

"I emailed, um, what's her name, Jenny? She had someone drop off a bunch of stuff for me last night. I got my Internet set up too, though it's so damn slow I want to throw my laptop out of the window half the time."

"And you…"

He picked up a stack of stapled-together papers, and waved them at her. "Examples. Of other llama ranches."

She took the outstretched papers and began to flip through them. Printouts of llama ranch websites. She knew next to nothing about it, but other than the type of care the animals got, the setup couldn't be all that different from her cattle.

What was left of their herd anyway.

"This guy has a mullet," she said, knowing it was unkind and beside the point.

"So?"

She flipped to another stapled-together packet. "*This* site says llamas are addictive."

"Okay, it's a little strange, but still. It's not dependent on cattle prices, or a "horse having the right kind of baby" thing. Llama yarn is llama yarn. Pack animals are pack animals. It's a low-risk investment."

Oh, God, he was making *sense*? That was cruel and unusual. How could she argue with him when he was making sense, making his own plans, thinking things through? The fact was, no matter how crazy the idea, she couldn't. She could not argue with sense and someone else making a decision on their own.

"It also gives me room to do a lot of things if these tryouts my agent is working on come through. There are a couple of resorts around here—I can rent the llamas out for pack animals for hikes in the mountains. Which gives me the income that could offset needing to hire someone to handle ranch stuff when I'm not here."

When I'm not here. So much for wanting the ranch to be his heart and crap like that. He was already planning on not being here, already planning on going back to hockey.

It was not a shock—she'd known that all along—but something deeply uncomfortable lodged itself in her chest at the thought of him not being around.

Which wouldn't do. Not at all. "All right. Then, let's make a plan of what we need to do to get you ready for a llama invasion."

He grinned, and she looked away. She would not get sucked into that grin.

"Llama invasion. Also an excellent band name."

"Unless you're ready to move on to making emo punk music, let's focus on what kind of buildings you'll need. Any of your books tell you that?"

He pawed around on the desk. "Here we go, captain. Lead the way."

She sighed. Leading was getting damn exhausting.

—∾∾∾—

Dan loaded the last bundle of lumber into the back of Mel's truck. After drawing up plans and to-do lists all day yesterday, he'd finally convinced her they could actually start on a project—repairing and expanding the fence around the enclosure his current llama was already in.

He grinned. Couldn't help it. This *doing* something—like an actual something with a goal in place, and a plan in mind—was…almost as good as being on the ice again. He felt invigorated, ready to take on the world.

Or maybe just one of Georgia's bacon cheeseburgers. "Lunch at Georgia's?"

She wrinkled her nose. "Thought you were determined to do your protein-shake crap this week."

Right. Staying in shape for possible tryouts. But he glanced down the street toward Georgia's little diner. "I'll get a salad."

"I'm pretty sure their salad dressing has as many calories as a burger."

"Okay, then I'll get a burger. I've been hauling lumber all morning. I can cheat a little." Because he knew it would irritate her, he curled his arm up, flexing his bicep. "Muscles still in fine shape."

She rolled her eyes so far up in her head it was a wonder they didn't get stuck there. "Work on your humility muscle."

He lifted shut the truck-bed door and hooked his arm with hers. "Come on, Cowgirl, I'm hungry."

"You know, if anything, you should be calling me cow woman. Though I prefer Mel. Or rancher. Ms. Shaw if you're feeling particularly proper."

He grinned down at her, not letting her pull her arm away. "*Ms. Shaw*," he drawled. "That does have an interesting ring to it."

"It's my name," she grumbled, struggling to get out of his grip as they crossed the street.

"Right, but Ms. Shaw…well, it brings to mind a teacher. Hair in a bun. Glasses."

"Sorry, I don't have old-guy eyes like you."

"I'm not old. You need to get over my reading glasses."

"*You* brought up glasses. And you're seven years older than me. That means, when you were graduating high school, I was still in elementary school."

He scowled. Having reading glasses did not make

him *old*. And if he was a little touchy about being seen as old, it was only because his whole livelihood was a young man's game, and even he had to admit he wasn't *young* anymore.

But he *wasn't* old, and if she was going to try and irritate him, he was going to return the favor. "Well, you're not in elementary school anymore, Ms. Shaw, are you?"

She glared at him, but in that under-the-eyelashes way that tended to remind him of the morning he'd kissed her. That hard-assed gaze she'd leveled him with before initiating that kiss. *Kiss*. What a lame word for the ass-kicking it had been.

He might have ended that possibility, but it didn't mean he didn't regret it. It didn't mean he wouldn't mind repeating—

"He bothering you, Mel?"

Dan scowled at one of the cops who'd been in the diner with them the other day. The one who'd made the asshole comment.

Fucker.

"Nothing I can't handle, Al."

Before Dan could get a word in edgewise, he felt a sharp rap to the back of his knee, so he buckled mid-step and stumbled. Mel pulled her arm out of his and sauntered ahead of him, that low, husky laugh enveloping the air.

"See?" she said, patting Al on the back as she stepped inside the diner.

"Watching you, buddy. Mess with her, you mess with me."

"You're not my type," Dan muttered, following Mel in the diner, half expecting the asshole to follow and start a fight.

But he didn't, and Mel waved him over to a booth while she talked to Georgia at the counter. There were a few customers, mostly older men wearing overalls or coveralls. All covered in dirt and grease, even on the ones who looked too old to do much of anything with either.

Mel slid into the booth, a glass of water in each hand. "Did you order for me, Ms. Shaw?"

"Yup. A spinach salad with a super-healthy balsamic dressing. On the side. No cheese."

That sounded about as appealing as eating cardboard, especially when Georgia hurried by carrying two greasy-looking hamburgers.

"Stop lusting after the beef, Sharpe. I got you a damn hamburger."

"Thank God." He might have cried if he'd actually had to eat a spinach salad. Or sneak-ordered a hamburger and somehow snuck it back to his place in his pocket or something.

Before he could say more, a tall guy stopped in front of their table. "Mel," he said, sounding surprised.

Her whole body stiffened, and her face went completely blank, like a switch had been flipped. The only sign of any kind of emotional reaction was that she swallowed before she looked up, and put her hands very carefully in her lap. "Tyler."

Her lips curved, but Dan wouldn't call it a smile. It lacked any of the warmth or even sarcastic edge her smiles always had.

"Hey. How are you?"

Dan looked from Mel and then to the guy. He couldn't get a read on the relationship here. The guy seemed both pleased and…weirded out to see her. Mel just seemed to shut down.

"I'm good," she said, her eyes never once glancing Dan's way, as if he weren't even there. She looked at the guy, but if she felt anything for *Tyler*, she didn't show it. "You're back in town for a bit?" she asked, sounding as bland as Dan had ever heard her.

Tyler glanced at Dan before smiling down at Mel again. "Possibly more than a bit. Dad's…up to something. We'll see." Another look back at him. Dan affected his best famous-athlete smile.

Mel's whole blank expression tightened, but he couldn't read whatever emotion was behind it. "Tyler, this is my consulting client, Dan Sharpe. Dan, this is Tyler Parker."

Tyler held out his hand, something both friendly and sad in his smile. "Nice to meet you, Dan. I recognize you, right? You play for the Blackhawks."

"I did."

"Right." The guy looked sheepish, making Dan want to punch him. He'd prefer the overt assholery of Al the cop to that.

"Anyway, it's good to see you, Mel. Maybe we can catch up some time."

"Absolutely," she replied, sounding the opposite of absolute. "You know where to find me."

His friendly cheer dimmed at that. "I do. I do. Well. I won't keep you. It was nice to meet you, Dan." His hand reached out like he was going to touch Mel, but then it fell, and Dan did not like that *at all*. "Take care," he said in a quiet voice before moving away from their booth.

She nodded, the empty curved-mouth expression not leaving her face until *Tyler* exited the diner.

She didn't say anything. Not one offer to explain who he was or what Dan had just witnessed. She sat there, blank expression, hands in her lap, silent.

He shouldn't let that piss him off. After all, she'd made clear she had no intention of being friends. Still, he thought they'd been building a kind of almost-friendship. He knew some of the harder pieces of her life, and the things he'd told her about Grandpa and the ranch he'd told no one else.

So, whether she wanted to admit it or not, there was a foundation of a relationship here, and her keeping tight-lipped about the tall guy with the fucking sad smiles pissed him off.

"So, ex-boyfriend, I'm assuming."

Her expression didn't change. She didn't move. Mel Shaw, Queen of the Nonresponse. He hated her a little bit for that talent, probably because he was jealous of it. Sometimes he could hide his pissed off, his hurt, but he had to mask it with other things. Jokes, teasing, being an asshole. He couldn't just be...blank. All that emotion, reaction—always wrong place, wrong time—folding in on any noble intentions.

"You could say that," she said, her voice quiet and distant as she looked over her shoulder at the counter. "Man, I'm starving."

"So, you're not going to tell me about him."

"No, I'm not."

"Why not?"

She finally glanced his way, irritation flickering in her eyes. "Because it's none of your business."

"Why? Because you wouldn't want him to know you threw yourself at me a few days ago?"

It wasn't a shock something shitty would come out of his mouth. Not a shock the look of hurt on her face made him wince. No, nothing about the way he was handling this all wrong was a shock.

"No, Dan, because it's ancient history that—and I know this will be hard for you to accept—has nothing to do with you. Now, if you'll excuse me, I have to go to the bathroom."

He didn't say anything, the hard weight of guilt and self-disgust lodging itself tight in his chest.

Georgia hurried up to the booth, sliding the plates onto the table in her harried manner. For the first time since he'd been here, not one ounce of that burger looked or smelled appetizing.

Hell, maybe he'd found his diet after all. All he'd needed was a little bad behavior and a few dashes of self-loathing.

Chapter 9

THEY ATE LUNCH IN SILENCE. NO MATTER HOW WEIRD things were, no matter how irritated she got with him, or vice versa, they'd never sat in silence for this long. Dan always broke and said some stupid joke or something.

Anything.

· But he ate his burger in silence, leaving half of it on his plate as he got up to pay the bill.

Mel had no idea what she'd done wrong. She didn't spill her sad Tyler history and wasn't going to. No reason for him to be bent out of shape.

But…

Damn buts.

She could have been more forthcoming. She probably should have been. Not because she owed him exactly, but because seeing Tyler should not have been a big deal. Talking about Tyler should not mean anything, or be something she avoided.

It was ancient history. The ancient-est. She should have explained he was an ex, and there were no hard feelings, and this was nothing. Certainly nothing for her and Dan to be fighting over, or whatever it was they were doing.

But it hurt. Tyler being nice hurt. Wanting to catch up.

She wished she could blame him for everything that had happened, but in the long line of people who'd turned their backs on her, Tyler was the most justified.

"Ready?"

She glanced up at Dan, standing next to the table in almost the exact same spot Tyler had stood. Back in town. Possibly not for a short while. Meaning she'd likely run into him a billion and one times.

Have to deal with that low-level guilt, that insidious line of thought that told her something was wrong with her for not making it work, not giving a little when he'd wanted something so simple, so fundamental.

You don't…you don't love me? You'll marry me, but you don't love me?

She shoved out of the booth and forced herself out of the diner, trying to leave that uncomfortable memory behind. The look of shock and horror on Tyler's face when he'd faced her with that impossible question. She'd been too stressed and worried and sick with everything going on with Dad to lie, to pretend she wasn't unworthy of all that devotion.

She didn't love him. Had never really loved him. He'd just been a perfectly serviceable choice. Reliable. Wouldn't leave. Was good with letting her take the reins. Never pushed.

Never gave you an orgasm.

That thought was all Dan's fault, because she had a really bad feeling he'd be quite the expert on that front.

Good Lord.

She climbed into her truck, and they drove the entire way back to Dan's ranch in silence. More silence. She pulled her truck up Dan's drive, around the house, and up to the llama enclosure. He hopped out without a word.

Fine. That was great. Maybe that could last the whole day. By the time she forced herself out of the truck,

Dan already had the back opened and was collecting an armful of posts.

She swallowed at the lump in her throat, irritated that emotion was clogged there. Words were clogged there, and they wanted to escape.

He walked over to the enclosure. Stomped, more like. Pissed, like he'd been when he had talked to his agent on the phone outside the restaurant in Bozeman.

Yeah, when you promised yourself you wouldn't let him get to you anymore.

He was making her really bad at keeping promises to herself, because the words were pushing out her throat. The explanations—she couldn't keep them in. "We were engaged."

He stopped mid-stride, a hitch in his step before he dumped the pieces of wood in an unceremonious pile next to where they'd decided to expand. Slowly, he turned, eyebrows drawn together as he studied her. "You were *engaged* to that guy?"

"Yes." Why was she telling him this? He had no right to know her personal life, and yet he made her feel like a jerk for keeping it to herself.

Or you're that desperate to talk to someone about it. Which was beyond pathetic. Everything with Tyler had blown up years ago. She couldn't even remember the last time she'd thought of it. She'd moved on, or at the least buried it. There had been more important things on her plate to deal with. Dad. Caleb. And now Dan. Dan's ranch, anyway.

Yeah, like Dan isn't on your plate too.

She whirled back to the lumber. They needed to focus on work. She'd explained and—

"So what happened? He broke your heart and deserves a punch in the face? Because I'd happily offer my services in that department."

She swallowed at the lump in her throat. It was such a stupid macho offer she shouldn't be touched by, because Lord knew if someone deserved a punch in the face, she could certainly deliver it herself.

But somehow it was touching. It was nice. Someone offering to do something for her, or in her name.

But Tyler hadn't broken her heart, not in the way Dan meant, and he certainly didn't deserve a punch in the face. She might, but not Tyler. "No, that won't be necessary," she managed evenly.

"I'm not talking about necessary. I'm talking about a little repayment for being an asshole."

"He wasn't an asshole. He didn't break my heart. In fact, it was more the opposite." She stood there, hand on a piece of lumber, trying to work out all the conflicting emotions going on. Emotions she'd never dealt with because everything with Tyler had gone down when she'd still been drowning in surviving Dad's paralysis, and those emotions had taken precedence.

Yeah, because you've really dealt with all those emotions.

"Look, can we get to work? I—"

"*You* broke *his* heart?"

She let out a breath. Of course Dan wouldn't let it go. He was not the let-go, move-on type. He pestered. And she relented. She didn't want to know what that said about her. "Yes."

"How?"

"He wanted to marry someone who was going to love

him, and that wasn't me." *I don't have that kind of thing in me.*

"Why the hell were you engaged to a guy you didn't love?"

Yes, she supposed to someone like Dan, that would sound insane. Crazy. But the last thing she wanted out of this life was love. Love was fleeting. Love was painful. Love disappeared in the middle of the night, leaving people confused, hurt.

Scarred.

All she wanted was stability. She didn't want to worry she couldn't measure up to someone's expectations. She didn't want passion or dazzle. Those things got eviscerated in Blue Valley. She wanted someone to take half the work, hold half the reins.

She didn't want to be left again. It wasn't wrong to want that, to protect herself. It was smart. And worse, so much worse, she didn't want to be put in the position where *she* might leave, she might hurt that person who cared for her.

She didn't want her truest, ugliest self to come out, so she kept it locked away far from anything like emotion.

"Mel."

She cleared her throat. Keeping it in didn't exactly work—she had too much to keep in—but that didn't mean she had to spill her guts. "He was a nice guy. I liked him just fine. I wanted something stable, and Tyler was…that."

"Well, sure, for a friend, but isn't marriage supposed to be love and…stuff?"

"You ever been married?"

"No."

"Engaged?"

"No."

"Your parents a shining example of lifelong love and monogamy?" she demanded.

"Well, no."

"Exactly. I've never been a fairy-tale girl, Dan. We started dating in high school. It was comfortable. He proposed right before Dad's accident. It seemed like the thing to do." Never have to be afraid or hurt. "Someone to build a life with who wouldn't hightail it to California when he got the urge." Or, maybe, more the fact she wouldn't be devastated if he did.

"Why would hightailing it to California even be an option?"

She wasn't going there. Nope. She'd gone far enough. "Are we going to expand this damn fence or not?"

"Who hightailed it to California?"

"No one."

"Look, I'm not the sharpest skate on the ice, I'll give you that, but I'm not dumb."

And that was her breaking point, though God knew why. There had been far more poignant breaking points in her life, but those had all been fought through. Somehow.

"God, Dan. I don't... Fine, you really want to know? When I was seven, my mom walked out. Disappeared. Never heard from her again. I saw my dad struggle to deal with that heartbreak, that betrayal, and still manage to be a decent father and rancher and member of this damn community, and what does he get for it? Paralyzed. A shitty son who undermined everything he worked for until it was too damn late."

And a daughter who couldn't reach him. Couldn't find a way to unlock that cage he'd put himself in. She had to somehow wake up every morning and convince herself it was him, not her. Mom, not her.

It wasn't that she was unlovable, so easy to leave or shut out. It wasn't that her father could see that deep down all she wanted to do was run, just like the mother she despised.

She swallowed at the lump now fizzling, a hard wedge in her esophagus. Her normal rationalizations seemed so brittle and weak, and she wasn't sure why. "With Tyler, I just wanted someone I could depend on, and he wanted more. I don't have more. So. There. That's it. No big tragedy."

And it *wasn't* a tragedy. So why did she have tears in her eyes, threatening to fall? She kept her eyes wide, refusing to let them win. She would not cry in front of him. She would not.

I am unbreakable.

Remembering telling Dan that not so many days ago was the last straw. The tears became too many to contain, falling onto her cheeks. Unbreakable Mel, what a laugh. She *was* broken.

Even knowing she should fight him off, get in her truck and go, when Dan's arms hesitantly wound around her, she didn't push away, or stiffen—she leaned into him. She just wanted to lean for a little while. Was that so wrong?

She didn't sob or wail—no, she wouldn't let herself do that—but she didn't fight the tears. She let them fall and soak into Dan's T-shirt. She let Dan's arms hold her close. It was odd to take comfort from a man she didn't understand in the least. But he held her until she was done, and who had ever done that?

She couldn't ever remember crying until she was spent. The few times she allowed herself to cry, it was usually a quick thing. Get it out and over with. She didn't have time for long fits of self-pity.

But she had officially cried her eyes out. On Dan.

The embarrassment climbed deep, made it impossible to pull away from the hard, comforting safety of his chest. Because, if she pulled away, she'd have to face him.

She'd rather stay in the cocoon of warm, sturdy comfort that smelled like sawdust and pine. That felt like heaven.

Because she couldn't remember the last time anyone had hugged her. Not since Dad's hospital room. Caleb had hugged her then—they'd hugged each other, but that had been the last time.

She felt that loss acutely, so acutely she could almost tell herself she didn't care who was offering it now. Strong arms holding the weight of her, holding the weight of everything.

How long had she wanted that? Too bad it was from the guy who was going to disappear in a few months.

Actually, that was good, because this way she couldn't forget that this offering of…whatever…was a temporary thing. Not something she could depend on or get used to.

Dan would leave, like Mom had. Like Tyler had when she hadn't been able to give him everything. It was an inevitability. She wasn't cut out for…people's love.

Which meant she couldn't be hurt by it.

Comforting in a way, but problematic in another.

Because if she knew it was temporary, if she knew she couldn't be hurt by it, why would she resist it?

Oh, so dangerous to think such a thing. Dangerous enough that she pulled away from the hug and the comfort. From Dan.

Dan, who you don't have to resist.

But she did. She didn't know why; she only knew in some part of her that he was dangerous and needed to be resisted, no matter what that dark, quiet voice in the back of her head said.

"We should go unload your lumber," she managed, her voice rusty.

"That sounds like a euphemism." There was humor in his tone, but it was tempered with something. Something that made her chest ache.

Not pity. Pity was too gross of a word, and this wasn't gross. It was sweet. Sympathy or commiseration or, God forbid, care.

"We have to work."

But his hand reached out and touched her face, brushing tears off her cheeks. Dan stepped closer, like he was going to hug her again. She would stand firm against it this time, she would—

His hands cupped her jaw, green eyes fixed on her face. On *her*, the cool of his calloused palms a welcome relief from all the heat in her cheeks. From the crying, from the embarrassment.

"You know, the other day, when I said I wanted you to teach me to be such a hard-ass?" he asked.

"Yeah, you changing your mind?" She tried to step away, but his gentle hands tightened on her, keeping her in place.

"I didn't even have a clue how deep it goes, how strong you are, and I thought you were pretty damn strong."

She didn't know what to do with words like that. Like he *admired* her, respected her.

She'd had respect before. Respect for her work was not a problem, but someone being impressed by *her* was…well, most people looked at her with half respect, half pity.

That feeling rushed into all the aching breaks in her armor, slipping through the cracks. Dangerous, she knew. She should not let anything he felt for her do anything, be anything. Except, she was weak. Vulnerable. And she wanted the danger, the hard edge of this wrong feeling, the wild heartbeat that came with him standing too close, his hands cupping her face, strong and sturdy like he could take on everything that was on her shoulders.

An illusion, and she'd never been one for believing in illusions, but she saw their appeal now. The appeal of losing herself in it, in him.

"Mel."

She may have closed some of the distance between them, but she wasn't the only one. She had promised herself to be strong, to resist, but Dan's mouth on hers, his hands on her face, it was so much better than resisting.

No one had ever kissed her like they couldn't help themselves. Like it was all that mattered. This was the second time he'd done it, but it still wasn't the same. This wasn't angry, frustrated kissing that burst into heat and flame.

It was soft. His tongue traced her bottom lip, swept inside her mouth with a languorous ease that matched the way the heat and ache spread through her. Slow, steady, until she was all but humming with it. With the word *more*.

The ripple of fear settled somewhere underneath desire. She felt it, but she didn't act on it—couldn't. She was drowning in a sea of want. She wanted him to touch her, to follow the spiral of electricity that wound through her body. Every time his mouth touched hers, it was all she could think about. His hands on her skin. Her skin on his skin.

Until a bleating cracked through the peace of a quiet mountain afternoon.

Mel jerked back, eyes falling to where Mystery Llama was standing at the edge of the fence. Staring. Judging.

Not judging, wacko.

"He's hungry," she said, pointing to the llama even though Dan's hands were still on her face, even though she could feel his body heat through her clothes and feel his breath on her temple. Even though everything inside of her was still reeling from confusion mixed with desire.

"The llama will keep."

It would. It probably would, and as much as she wanted to throw up her hands and say *sure, why the hell not*, it was the middle of the day. They were in the middle of a project. You did not just leave something undone because you wanted connection. Wanted sex.

Oh, but I bet it will be really awesome sex.

She shook her head, stepping away from Dan and the idea that she could ever forget a responsibility. That she could let a few aches and desperate fantasies change the fact of her reality. She raised her chin, determined. "We have work to do. And you're paying me. So, that makes this weird."

'He was quiet for a few beats, eyes steady on hers. "One of these days, you're going to run out of excuses."

She wanted it to feel like a threat, something she could fight against, be angry about. But it didn't feel like that at all. *One of these days* sounded like a gift.

A gift she could have if she ever wanted it.

Not for you.

Why did that keep getting lost in all this…whatever it was? Dan was not for her. She knew that. But she also knew she *could* have him, however briefly, and she wasn't sure she was strong enough to resist that forever.

Dan put every last ounce of energy into work. He wasn't going to push Mel. The way he saw it, she had enough people trying to take things from her, and he was determined not to be that guy.

Even if it gave him blue balls in the process.

Every time he thought he got to the bottom of all of Mel's stress, everything that made her so rigid and careful and tough, he fell down some other chasm.

He couldn't say he was surprised that her mother had abandoned her family. She obviously had issues with people leaving, and she'd never mentioned a mother. What he was still working his way through was the anger, the absolute disgust in the way she'd explained what happened.

Then she'd cried. As if the anger had just been hiding this vulnerable hurt underneath, as if that's what her tough-girl attitude was *always* hiding.

Seeing that filled him with an unease he didn't know how to fight. Hurt was not something he liked to deal with. Was not something he'd ever had any skill at dealing with.

He had cracked under all the emotion of his parents' crumbling marriage. Fallen apart, trouble and tears and too much. *Too much for me to handle with an absent husband*, Mom had said when she'd thought he hadn't been listening. He had been her last straw.

Then Dad had taught him to skate, and he'd skated away from all feelings since then. From his own, from his mother's. His grandparents'. He'd used hockey as an excuse not to visit. Grandma's decline had been much worse, much sharper than Grandpa's, and the way that broke Grandpa's heart was written all over his face.

Always.

Dan's chest ached, a deep, helpless pain he didn't know what to do with. That pain he always chose to escape. So he didn't do any more damage, like he had done with his parents. Except there was no skating, no escape in his immediate future. Just...fence building and llamas.

Well, at least it was something.

"It's seven. I need to head out." Mel yanked off work gloves and slapped them against her knee. "Think you can handle getting it closed up?"

He looked at the two posts they had left, which would bring the enclosure to a new, expanded rectangle.

"Yup."

She nodded once then turned on a heel and headed for her truck. No good-bye. No "thanks for letting me cry on you." No "hey, now that it's quitting time, how about some sex?"

Which was good, really. This afternoon had given him this feeling of being strong and a take-care kind of guy, but he couldn't let that feeling go to his head. Hugging someone while they cried did not equal being capable of handling much of anything.

When was the last time you tried?

She got to her truck, pulling open her door without a pause. He should not say something. He should focus on the fence and just…leave things as they were.

But he could remember what it had felt like holding her while she cried, wiping away the tears and kissing her with the salt of them still on her lips, and even knowing it was false, fake, and would probably come back to bite him in the ass, he felt like maybe—just maybe—he could be of some help to her. Be some kind of white knight, even if he'd always sucked at it.

"Mel?"

She paused, one foot on the step of her truck, hands braced on either side of the door frame. She cleared her throat, shoulders straightening, always bracing for the next blow.

He was *not* going to be the one to deliver it. If he could promise himself one thing this summer, it was that he was not going to be someone who added to the load she had to carry.

Even *he* could manage that.

"What, Dan?"

"My door is always open."

She looked over her shoulder at him, eyebrows scrunched together in that whole "I do not get you" expression she wore more than occasionally, but then she smoothed out her features and nodded, pulling her cowboy hat down a little on her head, like a tip of the hat. "I'll keep it in mind," she said quietly.

That was enough that he found himself smiling as she drove away.

Because something about vulnerability on Mel drew him. The fear and the discomfort didn't disappear, but stronger than both those things was this strange and powerful urge to help. In whatever lame way he could.

So, he would. Being in Blue Valley was all about learning new things, after all, so that's just what he'd do.

Chapter 10

MEL PEELED OFF HER BOOTS AND DUMPED THEM ONTO the mat. The empty mat, because Caleb was in here somewhere with his damn boots on. Tracking dirt. Not giving a damn.

He's trying as much as you are.

Oh, she didn't have the energy for this. She didn't have the energy for anything. She was wrung out—from crying, from working her ass off on a damn llama fence, all so she didn't have to think about that crying, that kiss.

Was it too much to ask to come home to boots on the mat and dinner on the table? Yes, too much to ask. Everything was too much to ask. That was her life.

Except for the times Dan made her forget. The hug, the kiss, the door-always-being-open thing. It wasn't real, but it was there. Possible.

The kitchen was dark, as was the living room. Everything was quiet and heavy, and she wanted to scream. Scream and scream and scream until something changed, something clicked.

But she didn't. She walked through the house, finally going out to the back porch. Caleb was sitting in one of the old rocking chairs, staring moodily at the mountains.

There was a glass next to him, the kind of glass that made her stomach clench. Except, she'd give him the benefit of the doubt, because aside from too many beers the night Dan had come over for dinner, he hadn't been drinking.

It was just pop. Not a drop of Dad's whiskey in it.

But when she wrenched her gaze away from the glass, Caleb's gaze was on her. He didn't bother to hide the scowl, and she tried to hold on to that last glimmer of hope. She needed him not to have done this.

"Fiona quit," he said into the dark silence.

"What?" Those weren't the words she'd been expecting. "Why?" It had to be some misunderstanding, something she could fix. Maybe with the extra money Dan was giving her, she could offer a raise...

"Dad did something, she wouldn't tell me what." Caleb waved an arm. "She only said it was too hard, and she couldn't do it anymore."

"What are we going to do?" Fiona had been a godsend. Mel hated the thought of going through the process of finding a new nurse who would come out here.

"You could run an ad, I guess."

"*I* could?" Under the exhaustion and the sadness and the fear, a lick of anger flamed to life, and there was just enough kindling to make it blaze.

"My hands are kind of full, Mel."

"So are mine," she replied through gritted teeth.

"Yeah, having that guy buy you lunch every day at Georgia's must be rough." He pushed out of the chair, taking an angry step toward her. "You know I don't hear much gossip, but I'm hearing plenty about you and Dan gallivanting around town."

"Gallivanting?" She was so angry, the repeated word barely exited her throat. He thought she was *gallivanting*.

"I don't know if you noticed, but I'm kind of carrying this ranch on my back right now."

"And what the fuck am I doing, Caleb?" He had been drinking. She could tell, because he hadn't been like this in a long time. Belligerent. "What have I been doing the past five damn years?"

"I need a drink," he muttered, pushing past her. "You want me to have this conversation, I need a lot more booze in my system."

"You've had enough," she said firmly, following him into the kitchen.

"Easy, Mom."

He'd never laid a hand on her, but he may as well have with that. "Don't you ever, ever say that to me."

His shoulders slumped, hand resting on the outside of the cabinet she thought to be empty. But he must have more alcohol in there.

He rested his forehead on the door of the cabinet next to his hand. "I'm sorry for that. I am."

"You need to tell me what this is. Why you keep doing this." They couldn't keep dancing around this, and she couldn't keep ignoring what was happening. Not if he was drinking. Not if he was lashing out. She couldn't do this again.

He straightened and seemed to use great effort to remove his hand from the door. But when he turned to face her, his expression was completely blank. "I don't know what you're talking about."

Bullshit.

It was all too much, and his apology was worthless without an explanation behind it. So damn worthless. All of this. What was she fighting so hard for? When he couldn't just explain himself. When he had to turn anywhere but to her. "Fuck you, Caleb." She had to get out of here. Go somewhere…

She knew where she shouldn't go, but everyone else got to do what they shouldn't do, so why not her?

"Mel."

But she didn't stop, not for a second. She was going to leave. She was going to go be selfish and stupid, and Caleb could deal with that for once in his life. She grabbed her boots, pulled the first on.

"Where are you going?"

"Out." She jammed her foot into the other boot. "Don't wait up."

"What are we supposed to do?"

She turned to face him, and the anger was so big and bright and glowing, she didn't care what she said, or what they did. "Grow some balls. The pair of you."

"Nice. Real nice. After all the shit I've dealt with today—"

She didn't listen. She looked down at her boots. No, she couldn't go in boots and work clothes. So she stomped upstairs to her room. She could still hear Caleb grumbling, but she was done, and nothing he could say could change that.

She pawed through her closet, trying to find something that wasn't denim or flannel or plaid. She had nothing. Not one scrap of feminine, seductive clothing.

Damn it.

So she did what any smart, resourceful woman would do. She grabbed a pair of scissors from her sorely neglected mending box and cut a pair of jeans into shorts.

Short shorts.

She changed into her nicest underwear—which was black cotton instead of nude cotton, but hey, it was something. She shimmied into the short shorts, and found a red tank top she usually wore under another shirt.

Yanking her hair out of her braid, she stalked to the bathroom. It was all kinky and weird, so there went that idea. But instead of re-braiding, she just pulled it back into a ponytail.

It took about five minutes of searching through her bathroom cabinets to find her makeup. She couldn't remember the last time she'd had occasion to wear it, and the nail polish in there had long since separated, the lip gloss tube all dried out and cracky.

But she had eyeliner and mascara, though not the best hand at putting it on. She frowned at her reflection. The eyes were okay, dark and dangerous, but she needed lipstick.

She looked around the bathroom, then finally got a Q-tip wet and shoved it into the lip gloss tube. She managed to create enough color on her lips that, as long as she didn't chew it off, should stay for at least a little while.

She gave herself a once-over. It wasn't perfect, but it would do. *Story of your life*. Well, so be it.

She stomped downstairs, seeing Caleb was gone, presumably to drink himself to death on the porch again. Dad shouldn't need any help getting to bed, but if he had any problems, he could call Fiona and apologize. Mel had spent a fortune on making the house as accessible as possible for him.

At the cost of everything.

For once, *he* could face that. For once she didn't have
to stand there and pretend all the hard work she put in
wasn't a big deal. She was leaving because it was a big
deal. Everything she'd done going completely unrecog-
nized was a *big* damn deal.

She wouldn't use liquor or a shitty attitude to make
herself feel better. What she needed was something that
would feel so good, so encompassing, that she didn't
have to think about anything else.

Dan was the answer. He'd rejected her once, and
she'd rejected him once. So they were even—on even
ground, and neither of them would make that stupid
mistake again.

And if he did? Well, if Dan Sharpe wasn't up to the
challenge, she'd damn well find someone who was.

—◆◆◆—

Dan stood under the hot spray of his shower. He was
starving and would kill for a beer, but he couldn't quite
make the move to get out.

It had been a day. A day that had kicked his ass as
well as any high-intensity playoff game might.

Funny how the water seemed to cool at just the
moment his brain turned to hockey. Seemed about right.
He wrenched the water off and grabbed the towel from
the hook.

They still smelled a little musty, and he had to assume
they always would after all the washings he'd done. He
could get new towels, of course, just like he could get
someone to fix this place up, but just like with the truck,
something stopped him.

Maybe he should stop letting it. He had a plan now. A

plan in place even if he left. He was building something for…something. Someday. Even if he got back in the league, he sure as hell couldn't play hockey forever.

Much as he'd like to.

He dried off, pulled on his boxers, and ran a hand through his wet hair. He needed a haircut, and to do some laundry that wasn't towels. He was out of clean pants, and he doubted the T-shirt situation was much better.

But first, he absolutely needed food.

He hadn't conned Mel into teaching him to cook anything yet, and while he could probably search the Internet for a few tips and tricks to making something with the chicken in his fridge, he was too hungry to fiddle around.

Scrambled eggs would have to do, along with a little light llama reading, then some laundry.

Life had gotten weird.

He went through the prep, cracking a few eggs into the skillet, tossing some cheese in for good measure. He'd get back on the "protein shake, vegetables, and lean meats" thing tomorrow.

Drawing the spatula through the raw eggs, he squinted at the pages of his book. Then he cursed and went to retrieve his glasses. "Old-man eyes, my ass," he grumbled, sliding the thick frames onto his nose.

He glanced from the book to the eggs, stirring occasionally. When a knock sounded at the door, he paused. Why was someone at his door at nearly eight thirty at night?

Shit, his life hadn't just gotten weird—it had gotten lame.

The eggs were about done, so he took the pan with him. Buck and Mel and the kid who'd dropped off his library books the other day were the only people who ever came out here, and he wasn't expecting anyone.

He opened the door and about dropped the pan. Mel stood on his doorstep looking…not at all like Mel.

She stared at his chest, and he acutely felt the fact that he was basically standing here in his underwear holding a pan of eggs. And she wasn't exactly fully dressed herself.

She stepped inside. "Take off the glasses. Put the pan down."

They were words, and perhaps at another time they might make sense strung together, but he could see her legs, her arms, the tops of her breasts. He could see more of her than he could *not* see of her.

"I'm sorry, did you…say things?"

She closed the door and crossed her arms under her breasts, which…um…what was happening? She had makeup on. And sexy clothes. With cowboy boots.

He was dreaming probably. Yes, this was an unconscious fantasy.

"I said, take off the glasses and put the pan down," she said in a careful, measured tone.

"Could I possibly then get dressed?"

"No." She shook her head emphatically, the loose ends of her ponytail swinging back and forth as she stared him down. "That will not be necessary."

"Um." He'd never considered himself shy before, and he'd certainly had his fair share of brazen sexual proposals thrown his way. He'd even taken up most of those women.

But those women weren't Mel.

Her eyes met his, cool and determined, but there was a flash of something underneath. He couldn't read it, she kept it so well hidden. "Glasses. Pan. Now."

"Can you maybe fill me in on what's going on, and why?" Carefully, watching her, he set down the pan, flicked off the burner, and then—because, eh, why not—he took off the glasses and placed them on top of his book.

She took a deep breath and straightened her shoulders. She pushed out her chest, which meant he could see down the front of her shirt enough to see the tops of a black bra.

She looked so…soft. Which was not a word he'd ever associated with her, but his fingers itched to touch, to run along the delicate curve of her breasts, the sloping angle of her collarbone.

And then follow it with his mouth.

"We're going to have sex."

His gaze jerked from her breasts to her face. "Right now?"

"Yes."

"And I don't suppose I have any say in the matter?"

Her expression flickered briefly, like a quick flash of uncertainty before she banished it. "You want to, don't you?"

He scratched fingers through his hair, trying to work out the right way to deal with this. Because, something about being a good guy for Mel, when he'd never been much of one before, held some strange appeal. He wanted to try this new good-guy thing. "Well, that's not a straight yes or no question."

"Yes, it is. Either you want to get me naked or you don't."

Oh, he wished it were that straightforward. That they were back in Chicago, his place, a hotel room, anything easy. But nothing about Blue Valley, Mel, or this ranch was simple or easy. "I would like that, but there are… ramifications to that. Complicated ones."

"No, there aren't. Not really. I need…" She took a deep breath. There was hurt and pain all over her face, but she didn't slump in the face of it. She looked at him straight on. "I want to forget about everything. You can make that happen, can't you?"

"Well, not permanently."

"I don't need permanent. I just need right now. I just need you."

He let out a breath. This whole "be the good guy" thing was proving difficult, because he didn't know what the good-guy thing to do here was. He felt like good guys probably said no to emotional pleas for forget-everything sex.

But it was what she wanted, and Christ, that getup was killing him. So…

He was at a loss.

"I am going to say this once, and only once." She swallowed, her palm pressing against his bare chest. Warm, soft, small. He could almost forget those hands were capable of ripping a post out of the ground or—as she'd once warned him—castrating a cow.

"Please."

Then, like she had the other morning, she let her hand trail down his chest, across his abdomen, to the waistband of his boxers, and he sucked in a breath. He'd said "no" once, and it hadn't done much of anything.

Was it really such a bad-guy thing to do to say yes? To give her what she asked for? What she'd said "please" for? He was pretty certain he could give her exactly what she wanted, and what he wanted in the process.

So…how could that be wrong?

Chapter 11

THERE WAS A WHOLE WORLD OF EMOTIONS GOING ON deep in her gut, but Mel breathed through them. She wouldn't analyze it—downright refused to—but the warmth of Dan's chest under her palm was like this center point, a calming force in a sea of frustration, hurt, and anger.

She wanted more of that, more of him. The way simply touching his bare skin made every part of her buzz to attention. She wanted his mouth on hers, his body on hers. She wanted to find the end to this perpetual ache.

She took a deep breath before lifting her gaze to his. He had to say yes, he just had to—

He placed his hand over hers, and for one horrible second, she thought he was going to peel it away and try to be all noble and crap again.

Instead, he lifted her hand to his mouth and pressed a kiss to her palm, his eyes never leaving hers.

The bolt of heat and giddy excitement was sharp, quick—a kind of jolt Tyler had never given her in kisses on the actual mouth. Which wasn't a fair comparison. They'd been young and inexperienced and, well, she hadn't allowed herself to be attracted to much more than his stability.

It was the way she worked.

Until Dan.

Involuntarily, she jerked her arm back, feeling that this was maybe just a bit too much, but Dan's grasp on her wrist was firm. His thumb brushed over the inside of her arm, and she shivered. She honest to God shivered from the simplest touch.

"You can stop me anytime," he said levelly, those eyes of his seeing too much, understanding far too much.

But she didn't care, not if simple touches could do this. Not if he could erase all the crap in her head, even for just a few minutes. "I don't want to stop," she snapped. She'd put on these ridiculous clothes and this ridiculous makeup and told him to take those *ridiculous* glasses off and stay in his underwear.

They were doing this.

"Okay, but I'm putting it out there anyway."

"Okay, sure." Whatever. Whatever it took to get him to stop talking and start doing. So she could stop feeling like her nerves were going to cause her to bolt. No. Way.

His grip on her wrist tightened, and he pulled her to him, still keeping space between them, but not much, and it seemed to jump with electricity, like the air during a thunderstorm. Sparking with danger and an unpredictable force of nature.

"You're going to have to come a little closer, baby," he said in a low, gravelly voice that was…new. New. No slick lines, no easy jokes. There was a thread of serious intent in his voice, and that was…well, almost hot enough to pretend like he hadn't called her baby.

But she didn't like that, even when parts of her did. "Don't call me baby," she managed, her voice coming out…breathless. Strange to her own ears.

"Darling? Sugar? Honey?"

She swallowed as his hand traveled up her arm, leaving a trail of goose bumps in its wake. She stared hard at the column of his throat, the way it curved into those strong, broad shoulders. Muscled. Athletic. Real. This man who didn't seem totally real was touching her, looking at her like she was something edible.

Which almost made her forget they were talking, but then his hand stopped at her shoulder, and she remembered. "None of that endearment crap. Mel."

"Mel."

She forced herself to look at him, to be brave and strong and enjoy the *hell* out of this. "I'm not interchangeable."

His mouth curved, the sexy smirk of a man who... was going to make her forget. Yes. That.

"No, you're not interchangeable. You, Mel Shaw, are one heck of a unique woman."

"Damn straight."

His palm cupped her neck, thumb brushing the underside of her jaw. The touch shivered through her, gentle, so gentle, but with a hint of a promise for more. Her eyes wanted to flutter closed, but that seemed weak somehow. To not be able to look him dead on when he made her stomach flip to her toes.

He leaned forward, mouth brushing across her temple. "It's okay to close your eyes."

"I don't need to—" Her words stuttered to a stop, her eyes fluttering closed as he pressed his mouth to the spot just beneath her ear, just above her jaw. Everything inside of her seemed to sigh when his mouth lingered there.

"There we are," he said softly against her ear, the rush of breath making her shiver again. Or was that his other hand on her hip, pushing up her shirt, fingers brushing her side?

She couldn't decide, mouth or fingers—and then he took her earlobe between his teeth and scraped. Her knees honest-to-God felt weak. It was not just a saying—they all but buckled.

"Oh *God*." She hadn't meant to say that out loud, but Dan didn't give her a chance to be embarrassed over it, his mouth crushed to hers. One minute it was all lazy seduction, and now she was being pressed up against a wall.

And, *oh God*, seriously. There was no other phrase that did this justice—the possessive way his hands cradled her face, the hard press of his chest, his erection, the near-growl as he used his tongue, his teeth against her lips.

The desperate excitement, the building heat, it was all new and exactly what she'd been after. She hadn't been overstating the current that ran between them. There was something here. Something bigger than simple attraction.

No. Not more. Just…different.

His hands moved from her face, down her sides, and then without removing his mouth from hers, he pushed her shirt slowly up her rib cage, then over her breasts. She felt his fingers at the top of the bra cup, and then the cool air against her. Exposed. Exposed to him so that every nerve ending in her body was bracing for impact, all but vibrating with the desperate need to be touched.

When he brushed a finger across her nipple she nearly jumped, a noise escaping her. She couldn't believe that was a sound coming out of her own mouth, but the little squeak popped out, and it *was* her.

He finally broke the kiss, but his eyes were still so close to hers, his mouth all smiling and amused and sexy.

"Hm." He brushed his finger against her nipple again, and she tried valiantly not to squeak and shudder, but it was no use. The feeling was too much. The jolt. The pleasure. The way it centered at her breast and sank lower.

When was the last time something had ever felt this good?

"I like that," he murmured, his eyes rapt on where his hands cupped her breasts. Then his head bent, and her throat caught.

He was going to…

The soft friction of his tongue was so electric, so erotic, her head fell back and hit the wall. She didn't even care. His mouth on her like that felt so good she didn't care about anything anymore. This was all she needed, the heat of his tongue, the press of his palms.

Perfect.

"We can just do it here," she said, her breath coming out in little bursts. Almost panting. Stupid, but she couldn't help it. The aching edge of desire was so tight, so needy, she couldn't help anything. And she'd never done anything like that. Just…spur of the moment, let's do it in the kitchen. Against a wall. That could be done, right?

He paused, straightening to his full height as if he was considering it, then he shook his head. "Maybe next time. Tonight, I am going to see all of you, Mel."

All of her? Oh, that sounded…scary, actually. Some of the tight spiral of arousal faded. She felt cramped. She didn't want that. She just wanted some sex. Explosive, actually orgasmic sex.

But he was pulling her through the little hallway to his bedroom, one cup of her bra still askew, her shirt bunched at her armpits. It was hard to think about any of that when his firm, tight athlete's butt was right in front of her in thin blue cotton boxer shorts.

She wanted her hands on it. Which was so *weird*. She couldn't ever remember being desperate to have her hands on someone's ass and—

He stopped, and she all but ran into him. He laughed, low and husky, a strangely light and feathery sensation moving down her spine. When she lifted her eyes, she recognized the expression on his face.

Pleased-with-himself arrogance at catching her ogling.

That might usually irritate the crap out of her, but she found with her hand in his and him all but naked, it was a good look. A yummy look.

"You have a nice ass," she blurted, trying to play it off as something she ever normally said to *anyone*.

The rumble of his laugh would have made her smile, except he seemed surprised, not just amused. She felt kind of bad for…well, she didn't feel bad for being hard on him or whatever, but maybe she had a little tiny bit of guilt over one or two of the not-so-nice things she'd said to him out of irritation.

"This isn't angry sex," she said.

"Yeah, I put a moratorium on that, remember?" He grinned, tugging her shirt all the way over her head. "Teaching me how to ranch, expanding my vocabulary— this is quite a learning experience."

Which was fine, but not the point. "I think you're hot."

His grin went sly, and he tossed the shirt into the recesses of his messy room. "I know."

Of course he did. How could he not see the way she wanted to melt into him? The way she all but disintegrated with every illicit touch. "Right, but, what I mean is, it's not just... I'm not using you, exactly. You are...a person who I don't... I know I can sometimes come off..."

He gave her ponytail a tug, then cupped the back of her neck, fingertips brushing against every sensitive part. "Spit it out, sweetheart."

She'd like to, but he kept touching her and looking at her, sending the sparks of attraction and lust so deep, so hot, so intense she had a hard time forming words or thoughts. "I like you, okay?" she said, exasperated and itchy. "You're not a bad guy."

His hands stilled, and she realized he was doing all the touching, and she was doing all the letting him touch. She needed to stop that, stop being so passive. Passive was not in her vocabulary. She wanted to touch. She wanted to take as much as she wanted him to take, to give.

"Not a bad guy, huh?"

She forced herself to look him in the eye despite the fact that he was slowly edging the straps of her bra off her shoulders. But she was surprised to find some serious concentration on his face. "I just didn't want you to think... I mean...you're not just some random guy." She'd come here specifically, for him, and yes, it was just temporary, something to do because she wanted to do something on a whim, but it was still... She wasn't at the Pioneer Spirit getting drunk and hitting on the first guy to cross her path.

"I think I get that."

"Okay then. I mean, I just, I'm not here to—I..."

He took a step toward her, so his knees pressed to

hers, her breasts brushed the front of his chest setting off an electric current that almost made her knees buckle again. "You want to forget," he said, hands reaching around to unclasp the back of her bra.

"Yes." Which he was helping her do. All this touching, and she was already forgetting what had brought her here. Because everywhere his fingers touched, she felt revered, she felt things she normally didn't. Soft and feminine and special.

"Then let's do that."

Dan was trying to take it slow. Not because he thought she particularly needed that, but because he wanted to enjoy this. All of it. For all her "you're not a bad guy" sentiment, he wasn't stupid enough to assume there'd be more of this.

This might be a onetime deal, and he was going to make the most of it.

Except, she kept making these noises that made him forget about the slow thing. Like the way she inhaled sharply once he'd gotten rid of her bra, and the way she'd sighed when he palmed each breast.

He wanted to make her sigh a million times, to feel her give, relent. There was nothing he did that wasn't met with some kind of response, and all those thoughts of going slow dissolved. Dissolved into him nudging her onto the bed and immediately beginning to fumble with the snap and zipper of her shorts.

He wanted all of her. All. Mel, laid out on his bed, wanting him as badly as he had been wanting her. He would find some patience for that. Somewhere.

"Here." She pushed his hands away, undoing the zipper herself and pushing them down her hips. This time he pushed her hands away, hooking fingers in the waistband of her panties and flattening his palms all the way down her legs until the shorts and panties dropped to the ground.

He kneeled above her, reminding himself to take this in, to remember, and to make it count.

Maybe if he took care, found some way to, it *would* count, at least for a while.

"Mel Shaw naked on my bed." Not a terrible thing to feel satisfied over, pride in. Even if she wasn't really here for him, she was here for something he could give her. She could have gone to one of those dumb cops she always laughed with, to the ex she hadn't loved but had been willing to marry.

So, yeah, this was an accomplishment.

"Yes, are you going to stare all day, or are you going to do something about it?" Her cheeks flushed, but she kept that chin jutted, as if he needed any more proof she was tough and fearless.

But he didn't say or do anything. Because for a few seconds he wanted to commit to memory the curves of her body, the way the parts of her that saw sun were darker and more freckled than the pale skin of her breasts, her abdomen. The pink tips of her nipples, the white scar on her shoulder.

Every inch.

"What?" she said into the quiet. He supposed she was trying to be demanding, but she came off unsure.

Like there was one inch of her she should be embarrassed over.

"Christ, Mel, do you have any idea…" *He* didn't have any idea. She was just…like no one else. Not ever.

He pressed a kiss to the spot underneath her belly button, feeling the muscles of her stomach jerk in response. He savored the places she was soft, delicate. Her stomach, the inside of her elbows. He dragged the pads of his fingertips over her rib cage and then repeated the process with his tongue, savoring each intake of breath, each dreamy sigh.

She gasped when his mouth covered her nipple, his tongue circling it until she all but whimpered his name. He'd been meaning to keep his hands in place, centered on her hips so he didn't forget to go slow, but it was no use.

One hand held him leveraged above her, and he was doing anything with his tongue that made her gasp again. A flick across her nipple, a swipe under her ear. But the other hand…wandered.

Over the soft skin of firm thighs, down to her knee-cap and back up again. He inched his finger closer and closer, torturing himself, torturing her.

He thought he heard her whisper "please," but it might have been his own imagination. It might have been his own desperation echoing in his ears. He slid his finger inside of her and groaned in time with her.

"Dan."

When he glanced up, he found her watching him, bottom lip between her teeth, eyes slightly wide. It took her a moment to meet his gaze, and when she did, he slid his finger deeper, soaking up every moan.

"You're beautiful," he said earnestly—possibly the most earnest thing he'd ever said.

Her eyes fluttered closed, the blush on her cheeks going deeper. "You don't have to sweet-talk me. I'm already naked."

"I'm not sweet-talking. Wouldn't work if I did. You'd see right through it. So don't be stupid. I think you're beautiful. Believe it."

Her lips curved, and for the first time since the kitchen, she reached out, touched him. First lightly on the chest, then moving up to his shoulders, her hands rough from all the work she put in day after day. There was something so…enticing, that she could be so many different things—shy, bold, rough, smooth.

Her fingertips traced the curve of his shoulder blades, the length of his spine. He forgot everything except the warmth of her, the weight of her hands on him, the steady rhythm of his hand, of her breathing.

And when her hands traveled to the inside of his boxers, he was the one watching intently, the one whose verbal response couldn't be helped.

She closed her hand around him, and he swore roughly, unable to keep his own eyes open. She stroked, the friction welcome and too much all at once.

When he managed to open his eyes and look at her, her mouth was curved. "You're smiling smugly," he accused.

Her hand traveled the length of his erection again, and he whistled out a breath, but two could play her game. He kept pace with her, and each time she stroked, he did the same.

"I am not smug."

"You're so smug. Trust me, I know smug when I"— she stroked again, and he had to give himself a minute for fear his voice would crack—"see it."

"Okay, so what if I am smug?"

He added another finger, sliding over the spot that made her squeak.

"Just wait. I'm going to give you a whole hell of a lot more to be smug over."

"There's going to need to be less talking and more… actual penetrating."

He huffed out a laugh, pained to have to leave her in order to paw through the nightstand drawer for the box of condoms he'd bought the other day.

Making her blush.

He sat on the edge of the bed, opening the box of condoms, retrieving one square from the row. "I lied, you know."

"About what?"

He turned to her, standing so he could push the boxers off. "When I said I wasn't buying these for you."

She rolled her eyes, but even so, her gaze was glued to him as he rolled the condom on.

He wasn't sure what to say, even if she did want less talking and more…penetration. Shit. Maybe there *was* nothing to say. They'd certainly done their fair share of talking.

He leveraged himself over her. No, he didn't have the words for this thing, because it was big, and for all her hard-ass proclamations, it required some level of care. Sure, he was bad at that, but he could learn. He wasn't an overwhelmed kid anymore. Like any skill, it just took practice and the desire to do it.

He certainly had the desire, and he was very willing to practice.

So he lowered his mouth to hers, something gentle,

careful, but she grabbed him, guiding him to the hot center of her.

Okay, careful evaporated. He took her bottom lip between his teeth, scraping as he braced himself on one elbow and closed his hand over her breast, brushing his thumb back and forth across her nipple until she made that squeaking noise again…and then he slid inside her and kissed her as she moaned.

He felt like he was being swallowed alive by something he'd never truly understand. Everything about being inside of her, everything about her under him, everything…

"Honey. Mel," he corrected. Even though she reminded him of the jar of honey he'd bought off that roadside stand on a whim. Warm and smooth, a decadent sweetness brought on by a whole hell of a lot of work.

Her fingertips dug into the backs of his shoulders, her body arching to take him deeper.

He'd ignore the little flicker of an idea that this was somehow different than his norm. That every feeling, every sensation coiled deeper, stronger, longer than it ever had. That this wasn't just a physical thing, or even just a vague affection-type deal. Something about being with Mel was…

More.

He did not want that. So he focused on her underneath him. The way her palms were rough, but the skin of her arms was smooth. The way the breath of her sigh drifted across his ear like a whisper. A secret just between them. The tight, wet heat of her as he entered and withdrew, keeping his own release at bay as best he could.

Something changed. He had no idea what. Suddenly she was tense, and when he glanced down at her face, she had her eyes squeezed tight like she was bracing herself for a hit she couldn't avoid.

He stopped, still inside her, trying to figure out what kind of mistake he'd made, what cue he'd misread. "What's wrong?"

She shook her head, eyes still squeezed tight. "Nothing."

"Nothing my ass. What is it?"

"Nothing. Really. This is great. I just…can't. Or something. I don't know. It's me." She made a waving gesture with her hand. "You go ahead and finish."

It took him a few seconds to get through the shock of *I just can't* in this context, and to see past it. "Um, no."

"No, really, it's fine. This was great. I just can't."

She still had her eyes all screwed shut, and this was… what the hell? No, he was not going to accept that. "Mel, open your eyes."

She shook her head emphatically. "It's too embarrassing."

"Oh, honey." He brushed the hair off her forehead, fingertips lingering on her cheek when she just barely opened one eye. "You know what you have to do?"

The other eye squinted open. "If I knew, I wouldn't have this problem."

"You're going to have to let go."

Her eyebrows drew together, truly perplexed, maybe a little irritated. "Let go of *what*?"

But it seemed pretty obvious to him. She carried everything, every second of every day, on her back like a million individual weights. Clouding up her mind, her heart. Even when she wasn't thinking about it, it was there.

Which meant there was only one answer to her question. "Everything."

Chapter 12

SHE COULD ONLY GAPE AT HIM. LET GO OF *EVERYTHING*? What did that even mean? She was here, wasn't she? Ignoring all her responsibilities and saying "screw you" to the people she was supposed to be watching over? He was *inside* her.

This was letting go. Orgasming was like that mystery llama—she had no idea where that would even come from. And she'd probably never find out. She thought she'd been so close. The way he'd touched her, kissed her, the way he'd *explored* her…it was like nothing she'd ever experienced.

Feeling him, taking him, it had been everything she'd hoped for, and she'd been so close. But something about that moment just before letting go…it was like every other time. She tensed, she froze, and she just knew…it wasn't going to happen.

"Look, I… I just don't think this is going to happen, okay? You should at least get something out of the deal." Because she wasn't selfish enough to walk away. He'd tried, so he deserved a reward.

"Something out of the… Look, Mel, you don't get something out of the deal, neither do I. Those are the rules."

She moved up onto her elbows and glared at him. "There are no sex rules."

"There are. A whole book of them. Dan Sharpe's Rules for Sex. Rule number one: her first."

"I *can't*," she replied through gritted teeth. She refused to be amused by him. This wasn't funny. He was still inside her! He just needed to understand this was *her* issue. End of story. And she wasn't going to lay here under him and *talk* about it.

"Okay," he finally said, and she could tell he wasn't going to let this go. He had something up his sleeve. "Tell me one thing."

She sighed and let her head sink back into the pillow. Of course *this* he would apply himself to. Forget getting a truck, but sex, let's make sure that happens. "Sure, but—"

Before she could finish, his mouth closed over her nipple. "Oh God." Everything in her mind fizzled to a stop when he did that. The way his tongue teased, tasted. It bowed that need sharp again, and she arched her back to meet him, even knowing how pointless it was.

"Tell me what you want, Mel."

A different kind of heat filled her face, but not the sexual excitement kind of heat. The deeply ingrained "oh my God, don't say those kind of words" kind of heat.

Tell him what she wanted? How could she do that? She didn't know.

Okay, that wasn't altogether true. She knew, she just…couldn't say that. Out loud. She couldn't… Nope. She couldn't even say no, so she managed a childish nod.

She closed her eyes, because this was supposed to be fun or easy or anything but another hard thing, another thing that didn't go right. Futility coursed through her, disappointment, and most stupid of all, tears threatened.

Still Dan didn't move. But he swept the disheveled

hair off her forehead and kissed her there, and then her temple. She didn't want to open her eyes, but he kissed her cheek, her lips. He kept kissing and touching, and the embarrassment and the self-pitying pain got a little lost in the warm, affectionate touches.

She could tell everyone and herself, too, that she'd learned to live without easy affection. She didn't need it. It was foolish and probably dangerous, the kind of thing that led to relying on someone or believing in someone wholeheartedly.

The kind of thing that led to heartbreak.

That thought alone forced her eyes open, but Dan's gaze was intent on hers, and she lost her train of thought.

"How about this," he said, his thumb rubbing circles over her shoulder, green eyes holding hers. Soothing, relaxing. "I'll guess, and you at least give me an idea if I'm on the right track."

"I don't—"

He took her nipple in his mouth again. This time the pressure was more intense, the sensation zinged through her enough she had to grab onto the sheet. How did he *do* that?

"You were saying?"

And he claimed she'd been smiling smugly.

"O-okay, I like that," she managed, and it wasn't so bad admitting that. So, she liked it? She was supposed to, wasn't she? Or he wouldn't have done it. Or it wouldn't feel good. So, no, saying "I like that" wasn't a big deal at all.

"What about this?"

His hand that had been on her shoulder traveled down her side, over her abdomen, tracing her hip bones, and then it dipped to where they met. He withdrew, then slowly thrust deep again, his fingers gently brushing.

It was intense, like nothing else, not even anything she'd ever done to herself. And the orgasm she'd been trying so hard to chase earlier built again. He touched her, listened when she sighed or said "there." He never made her feel foolish—he stroked each desire, each word with hands, with his mouth on hers.

She was so close to that precipice that always seemed so elusive, but here, with Dan, she could say what she wanted. She could *enjoy* what she wanted. Every time he slid into her, he touched every sensitive spot he could reach, lighting a fire that wouldn't simply die. Not this time.

There was a brief flash of panic, but he surged deep, and she forgot what she was supposed to be panicking about. Forgot everything except the way the pleasure went sharp, and then warm and luxurious as sudden orgasm pulsated through her.

God, the way he moved, every muscle taut as he seemed to keep his own pleasure at bay, watching their bodies meet as he teased out the last flashes of hers...

She'd never felt this way before. She'd never thought she could.

His mouth curved into a cocky smile at her breathless noise, but then it softened, and he rested his forehead on hers, groaning as he moved deep one last time.

He held her there, and it took a while for things to work around in her brain enough for the reality of the situation to really sink in.

She'd done it. Well, he'd had a lot to do with that, so maybe *they'd* done it.

Ill-advised, sweaty, *orgasmic* sex. And Dan's arms were around her, holding her close as he shifted to his side. She didn't burrow in exactly, but neither did she pull away. It couldn't be too dangerous to enjoy it for a few seconds. The aftershocks of pleasure, the simple fulfillment of someone holding her close.

He kissed the tip of her nose and eased away. "Be right back." He disappeared into the hall, and she heard the squeak of what she assumed was his bathroom door.

She stared up at the ceiling, trying to pull together a thought through the hazy, lazy warmth enveloping her. She should get out of bed, but the sheets smelled like Dan, and that was kind of nice. To curl up here and wait for him to come back.

And then what?

Her drooping eyes popped open. Yeah, she was not dozing the night away in Dan's bed. Geez, what was wrong with her? She scrambled out of the bed to find her clothes, except he had piles of crap everywhere, and she didn't see them in the dim light.

She had to get out of here. This was… Oh, damn it, it had been so much bigger than anything she had begun to anticipate.

She wanted to chalk that up to orgasm, but it was more than that. Some warm, gooey emotion centering in her chest. The kind of emotion that wanted to snuggle into his bed, and breathe the smell of him, and all the things she couldn't allow herself, because that was not what this was about.

Forgetting not wanting. Doing something irresponsible. Certainly not letting herself dwell.

She'd gotten what she'd come for, no pun intended, and now it was time to get the heck out.

When he returned, unabashedly naked and just so damn gorgeous, it was not fair. Not fair that he could look like that and her brain would grind to a halt.

"Clothes. I can't find my…clothes," she said lamely. He might stand there having no qualms about his nakedness, but she felt…weird. Exposed. Like he could see through to that gooey center.

He wrinkled his nose and looked around, then grabbed a lump of fabric from one of his half-opened drawers. "Here, this'll do for bed."

He pulled the T-shirt over her head, dressing her as though she were incapable. It should be insulting, but all it did was make the warmth spread, a completely non-sexual ache centering in her chest. It was such a *sweet* gesture. Why did he have to go and be sweet?

She looked down at the logo on the shirt. Some athletic company in Chicago. So far away. The place he'd return to.

She had no doubts about that.

He pulled the band that had already lost half her hair all the way out, raking his fingers through released strands.

"Oh, don't," she said, pushing his hands away. "It's all crinkly from my braid earlier."

He chuckled, smiling down at her like…something special. "I like it."

She needed to get out. There were all kinds of alarm bells going off in her head, but they were drowned out by that special feeling.

Had she ever felt special? *You're not.*

Before she could begin to analyze the complications

that went along with that thought, he was cupping her face—he did that a lot here, so easily, like his palms belonged on her cheeks, his fingertips belonged in her hair.

He kissed her, light and sweet. No deep, dark meaning, no demanding—it was just nice and comfortable.

Every kiss from Tyler had come to mean something, weighted with something. Always like he was searching for something, and she could never find whatever it was within herself to give to him.

It had become smothering, something to avoid or soldier through because he was a stable partner—and that was what she'd wanted. Kissing had become a chore.

But kissing Dan was like a treat, and maybe that meant affection was okay. Light and easy couldn't be a sign of something more. Relationships were hard and painful, so the weird feelings weren't something to worry about, probably, because they came with ease and felt good.

Maybe this meant nothing. Wouldn't that be nice? Something light and fun and, overall, meaningless. Nothing in her life was all of those things.

So she kissed him back and let him lead her to bed. If this was her rebellion, why not rebel to the fullest?

He couldn't imagine any scenario in which Mel would be happy with him for letting her sleep in. After all her lecturing about ranching being something you didn't get a break from, et cetera, et cetera, she'd probably be pretty pissed he let her sleep while he went to feed and water Mystery Llama.

But he also remembered how desperately she'd said she needed a sleep in, how that would be so damn nice.

So he'd give it to her and incur whatever wrath that provoked. He was pretty sure that was taking care of someone, and it kind of shocked the hell out of him how good that felt. How much more he wanted to do for her. It didn't feel weighty or complicated, like everything with his family. It felt right.

She deserved that, someone to take care. Lord knew she didn't let anyone do that if she could help it, so he'd press his advantage while he could.

He jogged up the hill to the llama enclosure—his strange morning routine that he was beginning to enjoy. It wasn't all that different than getting up and going to the gym, the rink, or for a run.

Prettier view. Fresher air. He missed the ice, the smell of it, the feel of that cool air on his face, but even late June mornings in Montana weren't too hot.

He walked inside of the enclosure, still not quite trusting this llama's humor. It'd stopped biting at him, but there was still a off-putting staring thing, the occasional spit. Usually the thing didn't spit while Dan was trying to feed it, though.

He pitchforked some new hay into the space. Possibly the grass in the newly opened enclosure would be enough food for one, but he still felt like making sure there was new hay each morning.

He pumped new water into the multiple buckets, placing them around the edge of the fence, all the while chattering along. He found the more he talked, the more the llama kept away from him, and despite wanting to grow one llama into a pack of llamas, the thing still unnerved him.

"Wonder if you'll be nicer if I get you some friends." He'd read that llamas were herd animals and liked company. The vet who'd come by to check her out had confirmed that. Dan still needed to work a few things out first, but he had a to-do list, some potential breeders, and everything.

He was not a one-trick pony. He could do more than hockey, and if he missed the skating and the thrill of competition, well…

Yeah, he didn't know what to do about that *well*, so he finished up his chores and headed back to the house. If Mel was still asleep—and he kind of hoped she was— he would make her breakfast.

When he stepped into the house, he was met with silence. He paused for a few seconds to see if he heard any movement, but not a peep.

Pleased, he went to the kitchen and found the pan of eggs he'd forgotten all about last night. Pleased did not begin to cover it.

He wouldn't wonder what had brought her here, what little thread of control had snapped in her.

Okay, so maybe he wondered a little bit, but it didn't have to matter. Maybe she'd tell him. Maybe she wouldn't.

She probably won't.

He ignored that voice in his head. Maybe if he focused on this whole taking-care thing enough, she'd tell him. Maybe if he got really good at it…

What? What do you hope would come of that?

He wasn't sure. A mix of unease and hopefulness

centered in his gut. He wasn't sure if the unease was caused by the hopefulness or if they were just dual feelings fighting for prominence.

Either way…he didn't like it. Didn't like conflict or indecision or any of it. He wasn't a five-year-old kid anymore, making it too hard on his parents to stay together. He wasn't a teenager avoiding his grandparents. He was an adult, and he was going to learn how to do this taking-care thing.

One step at a time.

He focused on washing out the skillet, making a new batch of scrambled eggs, making toast.

When he heard movement in the hallway, he didn't bother to turn around. "Good morning," he greeted, forcing himself to sound cheerful. Forcing himself to *feel* the cheer instead of the weirdness in his head.

"What time is it?" she asked through a yawn.

He glanced back at her, standing in the entrance of his kitchen, the hem of his T-shirt skimming the pale skin of her thighs. He liked her legs, the long, muscular length her sturdy work jeans never gave him a glimpse at.

"If I tell you that, you're going to kill me."

She looked around the kitchen, presumably for a clock that was set to the right time. She scowled when her perusal came up empty. "The time, Sharpe."

"Eight thirty."

"Eight…" She blinked like she'd never heard such a thing before, as if this was impossible, to wake up at eight thirty. "How could you let me—"

"Before you blow any important gaskets, I already fed and watered the llama, called the lumber company to make sure they had those extra few things we

needed—which they'll have ready for us around noon—
and"—with a grand flourish, he presented the skillet of
eggs—"I made breakfast. After I threw away the eggs
you made me forget about last night and cleaned this
pan, since I only have one."

The shock on her face didn't dissipate, though some
of the irritation did. She looked at the eggs, then back at
him. "No one…" She cleared her throat. "Well, anyway,
thank you, I guess."

"You could rephrase that so there's no 'I guess.'"
He grinned at her before scooping the eggs onto a
plate. The toaster popped and he slid the piece of bread
onto her plate. "I have peanut butter or…well, I have
peanut butter."

"I can—"

"Sit down and tell me what you want on your toast.
I'm waiting on you."

"*Why* are you waiting on me?"

"I've never done it before. Nice change of pace." And
it was. Probably because she was so damn baffled by
it, and probably because he'd felt ineffectual and useless since he'd come here. Well, scratch that, since he'd
screwed The Game—so being effectual and useful had
its appeal.

"What do you want on your toast?"

"I guess peanut butter."

He slathered it on the toast for both of them, then
puttered around getting everything on the table in front
of her. A big plate of food and a full cup of coffee. He
could feel her watching him, but, much like he had with
Mystery Llama, he chattered and worked and pretended
like he didn't notice.

And because he knew at least a thing or two about women, he didn't mention that he was comparing her to a llama in his head.

"You're…shockingly good at this."

He slid into the chair next to her, trying to ignore the warmth the compliment offered. It was no big deal. Who couldn't make eggs and toast and serve it to a beautiful woman he'd had sex with last night?

Twice.

She rolled her eyes. "Smug smile, Sharpe."

"Just…remembering."

"Oh jeez," she muttered, focusing on eating her food, drinking her coffee. He liked the way the messed-up hair and his T-shirt made her look more…human, less like the machine that usually steamrolled into his life.

He liked that too, in a weird way, but he couldn't deny seeing the softer side of her, this, last night, made her less…intimidating.

Not that he'd ever admit to being intimidated.

"Can I ask you a serious question?" she asked.

"Sure."

"Why llamas? Really? I mean…that thing is so creepy."

He chuckled. "You don't believe all the reasons I gave you the other day?"

"Cattle or horses or, hell, crops would be more sensible."

"Dan Sharpe is not known for being sensible."

She screwed up her face in mock disgust. "Oh God, you just spoke about yourself in the third person."

He donned his best hockey-announcer voice. "Dan Sharpe does that sometimes. Dan Sharpe is a pretty important person, and the third person emphasizes that."

He was more than a little rewarded when she laughed—a full-bodied, cheerful laugh he didn't think he'd ever heard come out of her mouth.

He would do a million goofy things to have that happen again.

But she stood, her plate and mug empty. "Well, enough of this leisurely morning. There is work to be done."

"No rush."

She placed the dishes in his sink, her eyes caught on something outside the window. "Not true, Dan. It's nearly nine a.m. I haven't started a day this late in… ever. Even when I have the flu, I get out of bed and do chores before nine."

"Well, that's just sad, darlin'."

She shook her head, shoulders back, and fixed him with an I'm-the-boss glare. "We have work to do, and it's long past work hours." Some of her surety faded and she smoothed a hand over her hair. "I'm going to need to go home for a little bit. I don't have…work clothes." Her cheeks were pink as she fiddled with the hem of the shirt, pulling it down. "I'll work overtime."

"You know that's hardly necessary."

"It's very necessary. You're paying me to do a job, and I intend to do it. Otherwise…" She looked off at some point past his shoulder, expression pained. "Paying me and having sex is weird without work."

He pushed away from the table, irritated at what she was insinuating. He wasn't sure what the odd mix of discomfort and twisting in his stomach was, but he didn't like it. "I'm not so hard up I have to lure women to sleep with me."

She didn't even falter when he stood toe to toe with her.

"I'm sure you're not, but nevertheless…"

"Honey, your nevertheless always wants to make me beat my head against the wall."

"I wish you wouldn't call me that."

"Mel," he said, cupping her face. He liked that for some reason, the feel of her cheeks under his palms, the way she looked up at him when he did it. She always felt warm and real and…alive, with a kind of current that seeped into him, something akin to the feeling he got when he was on the ice. Like there was some untold source of energy there.

"Mel," he repeated. He'd lost his train of thought on what they'd been talking, er, arguing about. So, he kissed her instead.

He had been braced for an argument, but she didn't give it. She sighed against his mouth, and he wanted her again. Again and again.

"I need guidelines. For me," she said against his mouth, not pulling away, not uncurling her fingers from his forearms.

"All right. Name them."

"I need eight hours of every day that are spent on working your ranch. No touching, no flirting, and definitely no sexing."

How she said that with a straight face was beyond him. "Sexing," he said with a snort. "You are something else, Mel Shaw."

"Deal, then?"

"One question."

"Yeah," she said warily, but remained still against him, still not backing away or putting distance between them.

"Do they have to be eight straight hours, or can there be…breaks?"

The slight pink to her cheeks went darker, but her eyes just drifted down to his mouth. "Um, well, I guess. As long as the breaks were specifically delineated."

"All right. Specifically delineate." He backed her into his bedroom, more than gratified at the sound of her laugh, the wideness of her smile.

Yeah, taking care wasn't half bad.

Chapter 13

THE STARS WERE OUT IN FULL FORCE, AND MEL KNEW she needed to head home. She had snuck home after Break #1, managed to avoid Caleb and Dad, and had returned to Dan—no, Dan's ranch—and put in eight full hours of work on preparing his stables for llamas.

Okay, and two breaks.

Really awesome breaks.

How much longer could she let that go on?

Worry about it later. Yeah, much later.

"Did it ever freak you out as a kid?" he asked.

She glanced back at Dan, who was sitting on the fence they'd just expanded, the llama not too far to his right. The damn thing still tried to bite her if she got that close to it, but it seemed to understand Dan was its meal ticket.

"Did whatever freak me out?" she asked, patting down her pockets to make sure she had her keys and wallet. She couldn't deny she didn't want to head home any more than she could deny she needed to go check in on things.

He motioned his chin toward the sky. "Look at all that. So big and vast and bright and we're just…these little blips. Gives me the creeps. Like aliens are watching me."

She snorted. "City boy. Just wait till you see the Northern Lights." Oh, wait, he probably wouldn't be here *to* see those, would he? She turned her gaze back to the sky. It *was* vast, with bright dots and trails of stars and cosmos and whatever else was up there, the world around them completely dark.

It had never been her favorite part of the day. Darkness had always meant too much time for thinking. The fuzzy reminder of something she wasn't sure was a dream or reality.

Mom whispering good-bye in the dark.

"I have to go."

"You could stay."

"Unfortunately, I really can't. Dad's nurse quit yesterday, and…" She had never mentioned Caleb's issues to Dan, not in detail, and she wasn't sure she wanted to now. "I just need to make sure he's okay, start trying to make some alternate arrangements."

"Anything I can do to help?"

Tempting, but she needed to be careful about where she let Dan help. Distractions, yes. Family stuff, that had to be a no. Because it was her family, and she would always be bound to them. She would not always be bound to Dan. She wasn't bound to Dan, period.

She might do good to remind him of that as well as herself. "Not unless you can find some pretty nurse to charm into working for me three days a week."

"I'm only interested in charming one pretty rancher at the moment."

She did not like the little flip in her stomach one bit. That little flip, a hop of hope, a burst of excitement, that was the kind of thing that was going to get her in to trouble if she trusted it too much.

"Then, I guess I'm out of luck." She pulled her keys

out of her pocket and jangled them from her fingers. "I'll be back tomorrow."

Though she could just barely make out his form in the dark, she could tell he hopped off the fence and advanced on her. The kind of advance she should retreat from, but she was not a woman who believed in retreat.

Especially if standing her ground meant a kiss. Which it did. His mouth on hers, soft and warm against the cool of the evening. Strong arms around her, capable when they wanted to be. Sturdy.

Quite a dangerous illusion.

"You know, if you want to think of me tonight while you're drifting off to sleep," he said against her mouth, bodies still pressed together, "I wouldn't be offended."

"Ha." Only she was already getting a little squirmy thinking of him and the things he'd done to make her feel good. Really, really good. "I'll see you tomorrow, Dan."

"Yes, ma'am." After a pause he released her and she pulled her hat back down after the kiss had knocked it precariously up.

"Come by early tomorrow. I'll make you breakfast again."

She stopped her backward retreat, that annoying flip taking a few extra turns this time. "You don't have to feed me."

"Maybe I'm not one hundred percent innocent in my motivations," he said, and, oh hey, there were all those squirmy feelings again.

Worse, there were other feelings. Those things he made her want that she'd spent so much of her adult life trying not to ever consider. Someone to take care of something so she didn't have to. Someone to care.

But he didn't care. Not in that way. This was about attraction and sex and maybe some mutual fondness, but not *care*. "You know, there are plenty of women in town who'd sleep with you." She meant it as a flip comment, a reminder that sex was all this had been.

It didn't even take the whole sentence getting out of her mouth for her to realize it didn't sound flip. It sounded nasty and mean, and he didn't deserve that.

"I thought I'd been clear. I'm well aware that I could talk quite a few women into my bed, but I choose to talk you into it," he said in that tone that oozed ease, but underneath…underneath something dangerous and cutting was hiding.

She should apologize or make light or something other than dig herself deeper, so of course she went ahead and dug herself deeper. "You didn't talk me into it. I showed up at your doorstep."

"Yeah, you really forced my hand." She could barely make out the shadow of him advancing on her, and again there was her mind telling her to retreat and stubbornness telling her to stand her ground.

It wasn't a shock which one won, and it wasn't a shock that her body wasn't braced for a blow—no, her traitorous body was leaning in for another kiss. Another moment of heat and power and forgetting all the ways she was failing.

But he didn't kiss her. He gave her ponytail a tug, much like he had last night when she'd been tongue-tied. She couldn't decide if she liked it or not. On the surface, it seemed like some strange power play, but her lady bits…well, they seemed to like the little tug just fine.

"I can't promise you much, *Ms. Shaw*," he fake drawled, "but I will promise you this." His tone grew serious, his palm cradling her cheek. She had to repeatedly remind herself not to snuggle in like a cat desperate for a pet.

He was so quiet for so long, his hand resting against her face, her heart absorbing that painful, bittersweet ache she refused to give name to. She couldn't wait any longer for him to finish. "You promise me what?" It shouldn't matter. She didn't believe in promises. At least not from the likes of him. Okay, anyone.

"I promise that I won't make your life any harder than it already is. I'm not going to add to your load, Mel. I will do everything in my power to make sure of it."

Her heart was beating harder, her chest tighter, making it difficult to take a full breath. *You don't believe in promises. You don't believe in promises.*

But no matter how much she repeated that to herself, his promise wrapped around her heart and squeezed, painful and sweet at the same time. She had to clear her throat before she could speak, had to blink a few times to make sure the burning in her eyes was just the air… or something.

"Thank you," she said—a whisper, but in the quiet of the mountain valley evening, the whisper held weight.

His thumb brushed across her cheekbone, then his lips brushed against hers, so light and quick she didn't even have a chance to reciprocate.

Which was good. She was way too shaky for reciprocation to be a good idea. "Good night, Dan. I'll…be by…early."

She couldn't see his mouth in the dark, but she could

only figure he had on one of those cocky-ass grins she wanted to equally smack and kiss off his face.

"Night, Cowgirl."

"Good night." This time she forced herself to her truck, no backing away, no dawdling. She needed to get home, not just to check on things, but to distance herself from all this…feeling. Danger.

Who knew danger could feel so good? Make her feel alive and giddy. It was better than anything.

Is that how Caleb feels when he's drunk?

Well, good-bye giddy, hello responsibility. Would Caleb be sober today? Apologetic? Pretend nothing had happened?

She drove home along dark streets, the only interruption her headlights cutting through the thick black of night. The dread at going home wasn't new. It was hard not to dread all the things she had to deal with, especially in those early days of Dad's paralysis.

What *was* new was the wishing she was somewhere else. Wishing she'd stayed with Dan. That was new and not particularly comforting. Was that what Mom had felt before she'd left? Wishing for anything but home?

Mel pulled into the garage shed and took a deep breath. She had worked her ass off for years. She was not her mother, no matter how many times she entertained thoughts that might be similar.

Mel climbed out of her truck. She would not be shaken by any choices she made, because she had made them with her eyes wide open. If Dan made her *feel*, well, she wasn't stupid enough to think that might last.

The house was dark, and Mel didn't know what that

could mean. If she should be happy or scared. What would be waiting for her?

You do not have to be responsible for it all. Caleb is supposed to be stepping up.

But Caleb had been drinking last night, drowning whatever pain he wouldn't share, and she didn't know how to face that without crumbling.

She stepped into the mudroom, the empty boot mat all but mocking her. She should know better than to even look at this point. She pulled off her own boots, carefully placed them upright with room for the other pair of boots that *should* be there.

She stepped into the kitchen and stood there in the darkness, trying to decide what to do. She should check on Caleb, on Dad, but she couldn't force herself to do either of those things.

What she didn't have a choice in was making sure Dad had a part-time nurse. No one had been happy when she'd attempted to take on that role back in the beginning.

The floorboard creaked, and Caleb appeared. "Where have you been?"

She straightened, looking him directly in the eye. If he'd been drinking, he hadn't drank very much. "None of your business."

"Look, I'm sorry about last night, but—"

"No buts. I am not interested in your buts. Did you do any work to get Fiona to come back or find a new nurse?"

"No, I—"

"Then get out of my way, because I have things to do." She wasn't ready to forgive Caleb yet. She wasn't ready to give him that chance, and she wasn't ready to face that him drinking as much as he had last night meant...

Yeah, she couldn't stand to think about what it meant right now.

Dan was a man who thrived on routine, and luckily he'd forced himself into one the past few days. It made a remarkable difference on his attitude. Probably having a plan in place helped too.

Then there was Mel in his bed. Okay, possibly that had the most to do with his newfound good mood that even texts from Scott about *still* being "this close" to tryout possibilities couldn't dim.

Especially with the fact that the sun was rising over the mountain, he'd gotten a hell of a run in, and Mel Shaw was driving up the gravel a full thirty minutes earlier than usual.

Oh, there was a lot he could do with those thirty minutes.

First, Mystery needed to be watered and fed. It was a chore Dan would gladly speed through.

By the time Mel made it up to the top of the hill, he had almost filled and moved all the water barrels and added a bit of hay to the pile. He felt like a right and proper rancher, all things considered, even in the face of Mel's infinitely ranchier appearance.

Flannel shirt, heavy-duty work pants, boots, but he could clearly picture everything that was beneath now, and he looked forward to undoing all those buttons, shedding all those layers she guarded herself with.

"Perfect timing. I was about to go take a shower. You can join me." He flashed her a grin as he moved the last barrel of water over to where she stood on the other side of the fence. He definitely didn't miss how her eyes dropped to his arms as he hefted the weight of the full barrel.

When she looked up at him, caught in her shameless appreciation of his muscles, her cheeks tinged pink.

"I already took a shower, Dan," she said firmly, though he was pretty sure her mouth had curved at the corners just a teeny bit.

"Are there laws against two showers in a day? Some kind of drought? Because I'm pretty sure sharing means—"

She clapped her hand over his mouth, and he grinned against it. Too bad there was a fence between them, because he was pretty sure if there wasn't—

"You need a hose so you don't have to heft those barrels around." She dropped her hand from his mouth and pointed to the barrel of water he'd just moved. "Add it to your to-acquire list."

"Don't pretend like you didn't enjoy the show."

"Ugh." But now she really *was* smiling, regardless of how hard she tried to press her lips together.

Something about that, that happiness that *he* put there filled him with a kind of…he couldn't even put words to it. His chest felt full and tight and like if he didn't act, it would all burst beyond any control he had in this strange place.

So he did the only thing he could think of. He hopped the fence and did the first thing that came to mind.

Tackled her to the ground.

She pushed at his chest, but she was laughing. "Lord, you really do have the mountain crazies."

"If that's what I have, it's not half bad."

She shook her head, but there was a loosening in her muscles, not quite pushing against his chest as hard. The crisp grass under his palms, the coolness at his knees from where they pressed in the ground, even the warmth of the morning sun on his back all faded away as he looked down at her…and that overflowing-chest feeling was back. It didn't hurt, but it didn't feel right, and underneath it was a kind of excitement, like being in one of those playoff games.

The pressure. The thrill. Knowing it mattered.

You screwing it up.

Something deflated, went cold, and Mel was just staring at him, underneath him, and this was stupid. Thinking about anything to do with hockey was stupid when Mel Shaw was on the ground beneath him.

He dipped his head lower to press his mouth to hers and forget all that other junk, but she spoke first.

"Your phone is ringing," she said quietly, her eyes steady on his, searching for something—he wished he knew what. He wished this not-knowing crap would go away already.

Or maybe he really didn't want to know.

But his phone *was* ringing in his back pocket, a strange digital loop in the quiet of the mountain valley. "I suppose it is."

"You should answer it. What if it's about… hockey things?"

He still didn't know what that searching thing was about, but he wondered if it had anything to do with the way she'd told him he didn't belong here all those days ago.

Still, she was right. It could be about hockey, and...
he didn't want to think too hard about belonging here
and what Mel might think of that. What *he* might think
of that. So he rolled off her and answered.

"Sharpe."

"Daniel."

He immediately sat a little straighter, the feminine voice crackling through his crappy service shocking the hell out of him. "Mom. Hey, is everything
all right?"

There was a pause, and dread curled in his stomach. Something must be wrong. Mom almost never
called him.

"Everything is fine. I just hadn't heard from you."

"Oh, well, I emailed you when I got here."

"Yes, but..." Another pause. The pauses that had
begun in those weeks after she'd told him her and Dad
were getting a divorce. Silences and watching and
pauses, always so careful with what she said to him.

Because otherwise he might break again.

Because they were a reminder of all the ways he
hadn't handled anything, had caused his mother too
much stress to stay, he couldn't stand the pauses, the
silences. To the point where they almost never talked.
When he'd been a kid, it had been letters. Now, it was
emails and the occasional text.

Calls on holidays only.

But if everything was okay, he didn't understand the
reason for this call. "My service isn't the best, maybe
we can—"

"I'm worried about you."

"Worried about me?" Dan glanced at Mel as she

got to her feet, brushing off her pants, her back to him. "Why?"

"I thought for sure you'd be home by now."

"I told you this was for the summer." Dan got to his feet, trying to decipher the tension in Mel's shoulders.

"I know, but…" He wanted to beat his head against the impenetrable wall of those pauses. Her carefulness with him. Not thirty years between then and now, between acting out as a kindergartner and being a thirty-five-year-old man, had changed the way she approached him.

He watched Mel as she strode away.

What was that about?

"Surely you're tired of that place. I know you didn't agree with me that it was tossing money away, but you see that now. Surely."

Dan tried to make sense of what Mom was saying. She hadn't thought he'd…last this long? Figured he'd screw this up along with everything else? Well, yeah, why should he be surprised? He wasn't the only one who thought hockey was about all he was good at, and he'd never given anyone any reason to believe otherwise.

But, good God, he should be beyond caring if his mommy had any faith in him.

"Actually, I think…" His glance landed on Mel hefting the giant toolbox out of the back of her truck. Mountains in the background, her hat pulled low, and that weird chest-expanding feeling again. "I think this is a good place to be. To build."

Crackling silence. A sigh. More silence. Dan closed his eyes and tried to wait it out, tried to find a way to be a better son. Give her whatever it is she was always quietly wanting from him, to prove she hadn't broken him irrevocably.

But he didn't have it in him. Not the patience or maybe not even the desire. He didn't know, didn't want to know. He wasn't broken. He was just…a person. "I have to go, Mom. But if you have any more questions or financial concerns, email me. I've got my Internet set up and everything."

"Of course."

An agreement that was anything but.

"Bye, Mom," he said, because he honestly didn't know what else to give her.

"Good-bye, Daniel. I…" Pause. Pause. Pause. Silence. "Well, take care of yourself."

"You too, Mom." Though it gave him a lump in his gut to do it, he hit End and shoved his phone back in his pocket.

He took a minute to watch Mel. She was busying herself with things. He had no idea what things. He had no idea…

He needed to shove it out of his brain. There were things he did have ideas about. Llamas. Talking Mel back into his bed.

He forced himself to leisurely stroll to where she stood next to his porch. "Sorry about that interruption."

She shrugged. "Nothing to apologize for. I was thinking we could open up those stalls like we talked about, and then head to town this afternoon to get you a hose."

"I thought I was going to make you breakfast." He reached out for her braid, twirled a loose end around his finger.

But she didn't relax. Didn't loosen. She was coiled tight, no give in her. He couldn't for the life of him figure that out.

"I'm not all that hungry," she said, hefting her tool-box onto his porch.

"Does this have something to do with…" He trailed off because he felt strange about bringing up her outburst about her mother leaving, and because she looked uncomfortable, and he just wanted that moment in the grass again, when he'd been about to kiss her and that was all that mattered.

"She was checking up on you."

"Um, yeah. She thought I'd be back by now, I guess. She never did much like this place." Or believe he could handle anything. *Because you haven't*.

That tension in her shoulders drew tighter, till she looked like a stick that had taken too many slap shots and was about to break. "Your mother lived here?"

"Well, yeah. She got out as soon as she could, from my understanding, but she grew up right here." He gestured toward the house, not quite sure why they were talking about his mother's past.

She still didn't turn to look at him, didn't stop fiddling with the toolbox. Acting like she was supremely busy when it was obvious she was anything but.

"How, um, how old is she?"

"Mom? Um, fifty…eight. Why?"

Mel shook her head. "I don't know. Let's—"

"Oh, you think maybe she knew your family? Like, your dad?" Funny, he hadn't really considered his family knowing Mel's, though it would make sense if hers had been around forever and so had the Paulle side of his.

"No, I, my dad is only fifty-two, they wouldn't have—"

"Your mom?" Shit, he was an idiot. There was a reason she was all tense now, and it started and ended with a mother's phone call. Something she'd probably never had.

"No." Mel was staring hard at the mountains, and Dan wanted nothing more than to reverse time and never tell her who had called. "My mother wasn't from here."

"I bet your dad knew my—"

She turned abruptly. "It doesn't matter. I think we should get to work on the stables. The sooner we get all this done, the sooner you can actually grow your herd... or whatever groups of llamas are called."

"You need to eat something first."

"I've done a lot of work without breakfast, Sharpe."

"Okay, fine, *I* need breakfast." Her calling him by his last name made a matching tension creep into his shoulders. But he didn't have Mel's control, and he'd be damned if he wanted to. "If you want to piss me off some more, keep calling me Sharpe." His irritation, anger, whatever it was—it was a lot more familiar than the feeling of her underneath him, looking at him like he had some kind of answer. He might not understand what it stemmed from, the way she blocked him out, walked away, erected this maze he didn't understand. He might not understand how she—or anyone—could just lock those feelings down and away. But...

Hell, he didn't know. He didn't know a damn thing, and since she was supposed to be the one teaching him what to do, maybe he'd just follow her lead.

Chapter 14

MEL WAS STILL STARING AT THE HAMMER IN HER toolbox when Dan's front door slammed. She wanted to feel angry, but how could she? She'd been...

Hot and cold. Curt for no reason. Unnecessarily bitchy. She didn't mind being bitchy as a rule, but it was the unnecessary part that had guilt lurching in her stomach along with...

Pain. A pain she thought had been buried deep enough it wouldn't get churned up against her will. Listening to Dan talk to his mother, her obvious worry over him, that *was* painful.

She didn't want that ache, and she refused to accept that it was about her mother. It wasn't just that. It was anyone caring about anyone. She was human for wanting someone to care about her, even if she knew the care was a big old pile of horse crap.

Something hot and painful lodged in her throat as she remembered the feel of Dan's finger wrapping around a strand of her hair. She'd had her back to him, but she'd felt the touch, felt the words as if *they* were a touch. *I thought I was going to make you breakfast.*

Like he wanted to. Like he wanted to do something for her.

But there were other words that had dug in, and not just his mother, a staticky female voice in his ear.

I told you it was for the summer.

She didn't like the way him saying being here was temporary had hit her hard. Like a horse kicking her right in the chest. Even though she *knew* he wasn't sticking around; she'd *told* him he wasn't sticking around.

He could build this llama ranch or whatever crazy scheme, but he was still going back to hockey, and if he ever came back here on some permanent basis, well, it'd be years and years from now, when he had nothing else in his life to give.

But she'd felt a little pang, and that was not good at all. Completely not his fault though, so she should probably stop being a jerk to him about it.

She forced herself onto the porch, tried to find apologetic words to say to him, except fear kept her rooted in front of the door, not walking inside.

While she could recognize the feeling of fear, identify it, she was having a harder time figuring out the reason for it. What was she afraid of? All she could work out was that she was afraid of the way he made her feel.

Which was so stupid it actually irritated her. What did it matter how he made her feel? She wasn't under any illusion he was going to stay, so she wouldn't be brokenhearted when he left. She didn't want or need anything more from him than some super-great sex and the occasional not-suffocating company.

And what if he wants more from you?

She wanted to ignore that thought, the way the fear intensified, but how could she? It was right there, flipping in her stomach, urging her to run far, far away, because she didn't need another person needing more from her.

It does not have to be forever. It's not *forever.* So,

there was nothing to get worked up about. No reason for the flutters of fear to mix with the flutters of him looking at her like she was the center of the world.

Please. He'd been trying to get her to have sex with him. Beginning and end of that story. That was all she was after too, all that could ever happen. So.

So. This was all crazy, stupid emotion getting in the way of reason and sense, and that was not acceptable. She would push it away, bury it down, and find a way to get back to where they'd been.

The way he'd tackled her to the ground, his big, hard body on top of hers, popped to mind. Something so foolish and...fun. *And the way he looked at you, was anything but*.

"Okay, brain, I have had enough." She forced herself to turn the knob and open the door and step into Dan's kitchen.

He was standing in front of his stove, still in his sweaty, grimy running clothes. It did not lessen the appeal of him, not when she could so clearly visualize him naked.

"I..." She cleared her throat because something clogged there. "Could I have...an egg?"

He gave her a one-eyebrow-quirked look, like she was crazy. *Yeah, you're definitely crazy*. But he was so hot and he cooked, even if it was just scrambled eggs. There was no reason on the face of the earth not to let this little thing...be a thing. Temporarily.

So she cleared her throat again, and although she was too big of a coward to look directly at him, she forced the uncomfortable words out of her mouth. "I'm sorry. For getting weird. About things."

"Weird. About things." He shook his head. "Yeah, that about covers it."

"I'm not very good with people."

"See, what's funny about that, Mel, is you seem to do pretty damn okay with just about everyone in town."

"I…" She didn't know how to respond to that, mainly because it gave away something she didn't want to be dwelling on too much. He was different. He was special. She wasn't trying to get anything out of him, wasn't trying to rebuild the Shaw name with him. He didn't matter, and in some nonsensical way, that made him matter even more. "God, I'm tired."

His mouth quirked at that as he pushed the eggs around in the pan. "You know why?"

"Not really."

He actually chuckled that time. "You're trying too hard."

"It's all I have," she said quietly, perhaps more seriously than the situation warranted. But it hit home. Because she was trying hard, but what other choice was there?

He didn't say anything to that, and she didn't know what else to say, or what to do, so she stood there still next to the door, hat in her hands.

"As much as I enjoy waiting on you, honey, why don't you make the coffee and maybe we can press reset on this day."

"We seem to have to do that a lot."

He shrugged and she could feel his eyes on her as she moved to the coffeemaker. "Better to start over and try again than walk away and stew over it."

"Is that why you want to play again? To prove you're not…that you didn't?" She swallowed, because she shouldn't care about that, or want to know. But she did.

What was the harm in knowing? In asking? What was the harm in any of this? It was like letting out the pressure valve—all that steam that had built and built and built in her life was about to explode. So instead of exploding, she'd let some steam escape. Have some fun and good sex, and then when he left, she could go back to her life and her responsibilities.

Until the pressure builds again.

Well, she made it through twenty-eight years without needing to let a little loose, which meant after this, she'd probably make it twenty-eight more. By that time, she'd find something else to release the pressure.

So, she could know and ask about Dan. She could be with him, and she could feel things, as long as she didn't feel *permanent* things—and, honestly, what were the chances of that?

Dan blinked at the eggs. It was hard to keep up with her sometimes, the cold, the hot, the lukewarm. But he didn't know what this was, her asking about hockey. He didn't know what he was supposed to say.

Maybe because he didn't know how to answer that question. Of course he wanted to get back into it to prove he wasn't a cheat. Of course he wanted to prove he could handle the pressure. Once, at least once in his life, he could handle it.

But there was more, and he hadn't wrapped his mind around that more. There was an ache, a hole that hockey left. There were parts of his life where he didn't feel it so deeply—doing hard work, planning for the llamas, being with Mel...

It didn't change the uncomfortable fact that being without hockey left a hole, and even if he got back next season...there would be a season he wouldn't be able to go back. Someday.

It scared the hell out of him that the ache might never go away. That in using hockey as an escape, he'd made this temporary thing his whole damn life.

"No one wants to be known as a cheat." He plastered the easygoing, for-the-crowd grin on his face and filled their plates with eggs. When he glanced at her, she was carefully pouring coffee into two mugs.

The moment struck him as something out of a movie or a TV show. Certainly something he'd never witnessed in real life. Two people working together to make a meal. Two people working together to make much of anything.

He'd seen teamwork, he'd seen people help each other out, but not the easy camaraderie of preparing breakfast as a unit. There was a fuzzy memory, dim and not quite fully formed, something to do with his grandparents and that table, but he couldn't put all the pieces together and wasn't sure why it was cropping up now.

"But is it just your reputation?" Mel was saying. "I mean, you said this place meant something to you, or you thought it could because of your grandpa, so... Is it just what people think that makes you want to play again?"

He stood at the counter, two plates in his hand, and she stood next to the table, a mug in each hand. Sunlight streamed through the window across from the table, spotlighting Mel in golden light and dust motes.

Fuck, this day was weird. Had he suffered a concussion last night and forgotten about it?

"Dan."

Well, at least no more Sharpe for the time being. "It's a lot to do with reputation," he said, forcing himself to cross the tiny kitchen. "But it's not just *my* reputation that could suffer."

Her brows drew together. "Who else's would? Your agent's?"

"No." He placed the plates down and studied her. "You don't have a clue about hockey, do you?"

She shrugged. "Sorry, I don't have a lot of leisure time to follow sports."

Dan's mouth quirked. "My dad was kind of a big deal. Hockey player. Like Hall of Fame, did commercials, Olympics, whole nine yards."

"Oh."

"And, anyway, he's a front-office guy now, and there are things he wants to do and…well, having stuff said about me doesn't help him any."

"And it means you couldn't do something in the front office?"

"Oh, I'd never be any good at that shit. Can you imagine me in a suit saying all the right things to smooth people's ridiculous egos?"

She blinked and didn't respond, which almost seemed like she could picture it. Weird. It was just another thing in a long line of things he knew Dad would always be better at doing.

So, no, he couldn't imagine doing that.

"Anyway, we should eat." He gestured to the table, because this was all awkward and not at all what he wanted to talk about. Llamas. Sex. Her. That about completed the list of things he wanted to discuss. "Cold eggs and coffee are less than appetizing."

She gave a little nod and slid the coffee mugs onto the table, but before he could sit, she leaned in and pressed her mouth to his.

He was surprised enough by the move he couldn't do much more than put his hands on her shoulders. Mel didn't do a lot of initiating, but this wasn't exactly sexual. It was more sweet, like an offer of comfort or sympathy.

Why the hell should she feel sorry for him? Offer *him* sympathy? This was all…picnic stuff compared to her life. She should go back to telling him people with money had their problems smoothed away.

But when she stepped back, she only looked at some point behind him, sheepishness wrinkling her nose.

"What was that for?" he demanded, feeling off and wanting to feel something familiar. Irritation would do.

Her eyes were wide, but serious when they met his. Always so damn serious. "I don't know."

It was like that moment in the grass—the overwhelmed feeling again, part sweetness, part the sharp need to bolt. But something pulled them tighter, pulled them close, and though part of him wanted nothing more than to bolt, that instinct was no match for the sweetness, for the pull.

"Cold…eggs," she said, her voice hoarse, the green and brown of her eyes mesmerizing. She cleared her throat. "And work to do."

Work. Right. That had been the main thing that had lifted his spirits this week, so maybe that's what he needed to return focus to. Forget hockey and Mel and all the things that made his nerve endings go haywire.

"I'm going to start emailing breeders. Get a firm date for when we need everything done."

She lifted a bite of eggs to her mouth, but then stopped and set it down. "Maybe you should pause on the breeders. Focus on getting this place ready."

"Why? I have to know when some are going to be available so I can be ready for them by that time. I suppose I could just pick up some more misfits like Mystery, but I'm not sure how I'd go about doing that."

"Speaking as your consultant, I don't think it's a good idea to bring more animals in until you're more certain of your future. If you're going back to play in the fall, there isn't much sense in—"

"I'm not going to back out or screw up. I may not be good at a lot of things, but the things I can do, I don't stop until…" *Until you fuck up two of the biggest games of a hockey player's life and are forced to stop. Forced to try out. Forced to…*

"Dan."

A warm, calloused hand slid over the top of his, which he hadn't realized he'd been clenching into a fist.

"Listen, this isn't about your ability to do something," she said. "This is about the fact that it doesn't make sense to grow a herd if you're going to try to get back into hockey. I mean, how long is a season?"

He took a deep breath at the tightness in his chest. The pressure. The little voice in his head telling him this was a dumb plan that wouldn't erase the real problem. "Start reporting in August, but the season can last until April." If they got to the playoffs, it would be longer.

"It doesn't make any sense to add animals if you won't be here."

He hated that gentle note in her voice, as if she were trying to break bad news to a small child. As if *he* was a small child, too stupid and foolish to understand what he was trying to do. Like Mom, like everyone, thinking this was some dumb thing he was doing to while his time away. "I'll hire a caretaker."

"But…why?"

"Because I'm building something. Like I told you before. I'm building something here because I need something important, and this is going to be it. If my career isn't over, it doesn't matter. I'm building a place to come back to. And if I can't get back into hockey"—he paused to make sure his voice didn't shake, the pain and fear didn't show—"then I've built something for the now."

Mel didn't say anything to that. She went back to eating, and so did he. He couldn't control getting back into the show. That was Scott's domain.

But this ranch, this plan, that was Dan's, and he wouldn't let anyone put any doubts in his head.

Even his own.

Chapter 15

THINGS HAD GOTTEN TENSE, AND DESPITE HER EARLY morning arrival, there had been none of the promised sex. Which Mel was *not* disappointed over. Because she was a camel when it came to sex. She didn't need it. She could last for years on yesterday. *Years*.

So what was the whole itchy, achy, wanty feeling going on in her general…nether regions?

Maybe *she* had the mountain crazies.

They had worked, repairing parts of the stables, running to town to get Dan a hose and have lunch. A lunch where Dan had insisted on sitting at the counter and spending all his time chatting with Georgia and making goofy faces at the Lane girl, who'd been in a booth with her grandpa. Cheerful and chatty…with everyone but her.

Not a meaningful look or conversation for her all day. Flirting, yes, but that light, blank kind that she was pretty sure he'd throw at anyone with the right kind of anatomy.

And certainly none of the "breaks" she had been kind of hoping for.

Now it was her usual quitting time, and she didn't at all know what came next. They'd washed up, were standing next to the llama pen, and…what was she supposed to do?

She wasn't angry at him, and even with his blankness,

she didn't think he was angry at her. He was lost in his personal stuff, and she had plenty of her own personal stuff to be lost in, but quite honestly, she'd rather be lost in Dan.

But how did she initiate that?

Maybe stop being a wimp.

She frowned. She wasn't being a wimp. She was being cautious and sensible and—

Wimp, wimp, wimp.

"Um, hey, if you didn't have anything planned, I could, um, do a cooking lesson for you tonight." She cringed at how stupid she sounded, like a teenage girl desperate to spend a little time with him. *I'll do your homework for you.*

Which made her think of Tyler and how sweet he'd been and how she'd used that to get what she wanted and—

"No need to rush home?"

She looked over at him, standing next to that llama, both of them staring at her. Blankly. Giving nothing away. Ever since that weird moment at breakfast, where he'd been so...angry? Sad? Some mixture of the two. *Because I'm building something.*

Yes, actually, she should go home and make sure Caleb wasn't drinking himself to death, and Dad was okay, and check her email for responses from potential nurses, but she didn't want to do any of those things.

Didn't want to remember or think. She wanted to go back to the other night when he'd made her forget. Over and over again.

So, she did the unthinkable and lied. "No, I don't need to rush home." Caleb had gotten to do whatever he wanted to drown whatever problems he had for twenty-some years. It was long past her turn.

"Let's skip the cooking lesson, then, and do something else."

Oh, thank *God*, she wasn't going to have to say it. His smile wasn't even blank anymore—it was downright mischievous. One of those electric tingles of anticipation wiggled up her spine.

"Let's go ice skating."

"I'm sorry. What?" That wasn't some weird hockey player code for sex, was it?

"There's an indoor rink in Bozeman, according to my Internet research. Let me take you ice skating."

"I…" He actually meant ice skating, and she had no idea what that meant. "I'm not much of a skater. I'm not sure I've ever—"

"Never been ice skating?" He slapped a palm to the side of his head. "That needs to be remedied, ASAP. Come on. Let's go. We can get some McDonald's on the way."

"That's some date." Then she felt stupid, because that's probably not what he meant.

"Well, honey, if you play your cards right, you might just get lucky at the end of this date."

"Dan…" Only she didn't know what to say, if she should agree or argue. She really…didn't know, and since she was tired of having to know, she figured she might as well go along. *And* argue, because that was what she was good at. "I told you not to call me honey."

He wound his arm around her shoulders, walking her toward their vehicles. "But did you ever think to ask why I called you that?"

"There's a why?"

"Of course, *honey*." He fished his keys out of his pocket. "And for the record, we're taking my bike."

"I can't believe your wheels haven't fallen off yet out here. The axel will probably crack right in half just trying to drive out to the main road."

"Ye of little faith in my manly machine."

"Is that a euphemism, or is this where you start talking in third person again?"

"Come on, you know you want to ride it." He waggled his eyebrows. "Both literally and euphemistically."

"It's supposed to rain tonight. I'm not getting drenched on that thing for literal or euphemistic rides."

He frowned, but then shrugged. "Okay, we can take your truck, but I get to drive."

It was her turn to frown. "Why can't I drive?"

"Because this is a date, and when Dan Sharpe takes a lady on a date, he is firmly in the driver's seat."

She wanted to find that irritating, ridiculous. It was her damn truck, but he opened the passenger-side door with a silly flourish, and she just…couldn't resist him.

"One of the most successful NHL hockey players of the past decade is going to show you how to skate, little lady. I hope you're prepared." He made a motion to tip the cap he did not wear, and she rolled her eyes, but he had the effect of making her smile against her will, at the stupidest, goofiest things.

At his gesture, she slid into the seat. He leaned in until she felt the need to pull her head back, press her body to the seat so she wasn't so…

What? Wasn't so what? She wanted to have sex with the guy; usually that involved getting close. But when he focused on her with *something* lurking in his eyes, she felt cornered, pressed down, a kind of fluttering hope without understanding what the hope was for.

"I call you honey, Mel Shaw, because you are sweet and smooth when I kiss you, but the whole of you was made by a million hours of hard work and focus."

It took her a few minutes of staring at him to realize her mouth had dropped open, that she *was* just staring. So, she tried to talk, had to clear her throat. "That's quite a line."

"I can't make you believe me." He said it so seriously, with almost a hint of sadness behind the words, that it made her *want* to believe him. Believe whatever he said about anything.

But that would make her weak, believing, trusting, giving. Even wanting to believe him was borderline weak. It had to be.

He tilted his mouth to hers, but still kept them a breath apart. "But I hope you will believe me at some point, honey."

The sharp inhale of breath she took had to have betrayed her weakness, but she couldn't take it back. Or push him away, or not lean into him.

But he didn't kiss her. He pulled back and buckled her seat belt across her chest. "Buckle up, Cowgirl—you're in for a bumpy ride."

Dan had not sunk his teeth into a Big Mac in a good ten years. Possibly longer. He wasn't sure if it was that good, or he was just that hungry.

It didn't really matter, because tonight he was going to skate. With Mel, which somehow made the prospect even more exciting, if that was possible.

As stupid as eating McDonald's sitting in the back of Mel's truck was, he kind of enjoyed it. Mel seemed relaxed, easy, like she was at Georgia's. Like she hadn't been at the steak place in Bozeman.

And now they were going to skate. Maybe everyone thought he couldn't hack it with the ranch stuff. Maybe they were all quietly—or not always so quietly in Mel's case, waiting for him to fail. It didn't matter. He was good at something. There was something he didn't bail on, or hide from, or was just plain bad at. It wasn't just escape; it was everything.

She would have to see that, and maybe she'd get it.

If she doesn't?

He shook off that question by drowning it in the grease and fat of his last few french fries. "Ready?"

She nodded, rubbing her hands together, likely trying to get some of the salt off them. "Maybe I can just watch you skate."

"Scared?" he teased. He grabbed the skates he'd put in the backseat of the truck before they'd left.

When they met at the front of the truck, Mel was staring at his skates. "No, I just…"

"You're just scared." He took her hand, and she resisted for a second, but only a second. He grinned.

She narrowed her eyes, mouth pressing into a scowl. Christ, she was sexy, and she didn't have a clue. He didn't have a clue, because the heavy work pants and shapeless work shirt did nothing for her, and the braid even less.

But the way she leveled him with one look and carried herself like she could and would fight anything in her path…he could not get over the desire to just worship at the altar of that.

"You're going to be way better at this than me," she grumbled.

"Well, I'm a professional for starters, and it's not like you aren't better than me at everything else."

Her hand twitched in his, a hesitation before she squeezed. "In just about the strangest way, you are too hard on yourself," she grumbled, the words just barely intelligible.

"And in the strangest, grumbly way, you are something of a boost to my ego. Who would have thought?"

She made a grunting sound, but the grip on his hand didn't loosen, even as they walked into the big shack of a building.

The kid behind the counter immediately got to his feet, and there was a crash from behind him, somewhere Dan couldn't see. He turned bright red, scurrying out in front.

"Hi, Mr. Sharpe. I mean, hello. W-welcome to Elkmont Ice Rink. We're really excited about having you skate here." The kid was practically shaking, and it reminded him of the way people used to come up to his dad, in absolute awe.

People had come up to *him* that way too. Not so much in the past year, but they *had*. Still, the way people had done it to his dad when he was a kid stuck with him more.

"Hey, Kevin, right?"

The kid nodded like a bobblehead doll, so Dan tried to be as smiley and friendly as possible. "Thanks for setting this up for me, man." He extended a hand, and the teen shook it with openmouthed awe.

Dan didn't even bother to look at Mel. He could tell

by the way she let his hand go and took a few steps away from him she wasn't comfortable with this.

Well, too bad.

"So, here's the agreed-upon amount." Dan handed over the cash for renting the ice for an hour. The kid stared at it dumbfounded.

"And, hey, if you give me and my friend an hour alone on the ice, I can stick around for a bit after and sign anything you or any buddies want."

"Seriously?"

"Sure. No problem. You guys skate, right?"

Again with the bobblehead nodding.

"Mel, what size do you wear?"

"S-size?" She sounded about as out of sorts as the kid.

"Shoe size. For the skates. Can you get her some skates, Kevin?"

"Yeah, yeah, sure Mr. Sharpe. Thanks so much. My dad and I…we're like, so excited. We've never had anyone famous here before." The kid all but vibrated before turning to Mel. "Um, just follow me, ma'am."

Mel gave him a strange look, but then she followed the kid to the counter and got herself a pair of skates before they were led to the benches outside the ice.

"Give us till eight, then bring out whoever. Sound good, Kevin?"

"Yeah, yeah, that's awesome, sir." The kid slowly backed away from them, clutching his phone to his chest.

Dan slid onto a bench and began untying his shoes. When he looked up, Mel was smiling at him. Innocently, which meant the smile was not innocent in the least.

"He called you sir."

Dan grunted. "So? He called you ma'am."

"That's the polite country thing to do. Sir means you're old. Do you need your glasses to skate?"

"Mel, *honey*, bite me." He shot her a grin as he shucked his shoes and laced up. "And I mean that in a couple different ways."

Her cheeks went pink and she looked down at her feet, carefully pulling off her boots. He tied off his skates and pushed himself into a standing position. Damn, that felt good. Been way too long. Way, way too long.

Mel was pushing her feet gingerly into the figure skates Kevin had given her, so Dan knelt at her feet and began to help her lace up.

"I could probably do this myself," she said. He imagined she was trying to grumble, but her voice came out kind of whispery, and she was looking at him with wide eyes.

So he finished lacing her up, never looking away from her gaze. "Could you?" He tightened the laces, clipped them into the stays, and then tied them off. "Stand up, Ms. 'I Can Tie My Skates.'"

She looked anything but certain as she slowly lurched to her feet, and then she wobbled, grabbing on to his arm. "I don't like this."

"Yeah, that's kind of fun to see. Something you can't handle."

"I can handle it just fine."

"Then let go of my arm."

She straightened her shoulders, steadying herself, and let go of his arm, chin in the air. Until he gestured to the door to the ice and said, "After you."

Then she wrinkled her nose and looked at her feet, but this woman was not ever going to let him think he'd won or had the upper hand, even when he did.

She wobbled and oh so carefully edged her way all the way to the door to the ice, clutching on to it like a life preserver.

"It'd be easier if you let me help."

Something changed in her posture. He wasn't sure if it was a slump or a straighten or what. It just all kind of changed, and he wondered what was going on in that head of hers. Some fear of anyone offering help?

"I'll be all right."

"Of that I have no doubt." She'd find a way to be all right. There was a little pain right at the center of his chest, and he wasn't sure why. Wasn't sure he wanted to know why.

She hobbled all the way to the opening to the ice, and then looked uncertainly back at him. "You go first."

He inhaled, the cold air in his nose, the smell of ice, wet and crisp. Everything he loved in one smell. Everything he loved in the give of the ice under his blade, the way it cut through. He took a few strides, slowly gaining speed as he rounded the curve of the rink.

Everything inside him lightened, floated away. All his problems, all his worries, everything. That whisper he always felt, always remembered. Dad putting him on the ice after Mom had handed him off, needing a "break."

Your troubles don't matter here.

And they hadn't, for nearly thirty years. On the ice, his troubles melted. He gave himself a second in the straightaway to close his eyes, breathe deep, and when he opened them…

Mel was standing there in the opening, holding on to the plexiglass, watching with those wide, serious eyes.

He didn't feel like serious, not in his peace. So he came to a sharp stop in front of her, spraying her with ice.

She scowled. "Not cool. I thought you were going to run into me!"

"Not going to run into you." Instead, he grabbed her by the waist and plopped her onto the ice. She bobbled and held on to him for dear life.

Which was possibly a little bit of what he was going for.

"I can't…"

"Did Mel Shaw, the famous hard-ass rancher, just say she can't?"

"Don't third person me, Sharpe."

"Don't Sharpe me, Shaw." He took her by the hands, possibly getting a little entertainment out of the grave concern on her face. Once an asshole, always an asshole. He placed them on his hips. "Hold on," he instructed, turning around so he could pull her. "Just keep your feet under you and stay balanced. And whatever you do, don't lean too far forward on the blade."

"Why not?"

He started to skate slowly, pulling her behind him. "Toe pick."

She snorted. "Oh my God, you even did it in her voice. Why do you know lines from *The Cutting Edge*? Were you a teenage girl in the nineties?"

"No, I was a hockey player in the nineties, thank you very much."

"Did you secretly want to be a figure skater?"

"I'm going to let you go to fall flat on your ass, or that pretty face of yours."

Her hands gripped his hips tighter. "I'm not going to

fall." But she said it through gritted teeth, all determination, no bravado.

"Hold on now, I'm going to turn around."

"But—"

He didn't let her argue, just turned around carefully so she always had a hand on him for balance, and he could see and critique her form. He skated backwards, giving her a few pointers until she was able to take some slow but steady strides of her own.

She was so focused, brows drawn together. Slow as hell as he all but skated laps around her, but it was amazing. Fun. *Peaceful*.

"How do I stop?" she asked as he was about to pass her again. He swiveled so he was skating parallel to her, but backwards.

"Show-off," she muttered. "How do I stop though?"

She'd built herself up to a steady pace, but every time she didn't stride, she started to wobble.

"You just stop."

"That is not an instruction!"

He chuckled and then positioned himself in front of her and stopped, planting himself in her way so she ended up running into him. But he was braced for it, and wrapped his arms around her, bringing them both to a stop.

She looked up at him, something unrecognizable glinting in her eyes. Something like…mischief or fun. Something he wondered how often she'd had. Something that, *Christ*, it filled him with awe and wonder and just enough damn satisfaction that he wanted to be done skating. Take her home right now.

Home? Really?

"Can you make me go backwards?" she asked, interrupting the weird trajectory of his thoughts.

She was trying so hard not to smile, and it was another moment. He was starting to collect them. Pretty soon they'd be so common they'd turn into breathing. Then what would happen come August?

But he started skating, still holding her close, arms wrapped around her, making her go backwards.

"It makes you happy," she said softly, searching his face for something.

Since he didn't want her to find it, he didn't turn them when he reached the curve—he just skated her right into the boards and covered her mouth with his.

Chapter 16

MEL WATCHED DAN SKATE AROUND WITH THREE teenagers and two of their fathers. The five had shuffled in all but shaking with excitement and nerves. She'd never seen people react to a person that way.

But about half an hour into it, the boys were laughing on the ice, and the dads seemed winded but happy.

And Dan, well, he shone, and he was grinning from ear to ear. He'd raced some of the kids from one end of the ice to the other, looked to be coaching them on their technique, and so far the only thing he'd turned down was an offer to go get some sticks and pucks and goals to pretend to play a game.

He'd declined nicely. In fact, she didn't think the group had even had a chance to be disappointed before they were bringing out all and sundry to have Dan sign, the whole group still in their skates, apparently *not* wobbly even when they were just standing still.

When Dan finally disentangled himself from the group and headed for where he'd left his shoes, the remaining men stood on the ice oohing and aahing over everything Dan had signed.

She met him at the bench, her skates long discarded. He didn't look up even when she moved to stand in front of him.

"You signed a lot of stuff," she offered into the awkward silence, the weird energy pouring off him.

He still didn't look up. "Yeah, Kevin's dad owns the place, so he wanted to put some stuff up on the walls."

"So, Dan Sharpe, you're kind of a big deal."

His lips quirked, but his gaze remained on his shoes as he laced them. "I kind of am."

"Though I did not get to see your stick skills."

Finally, *finally* he glanced at her, but that cocky, "no emotion behind the grin" smile was on his face. "I'll show you plenty of stick skills later, honey."

"All jokes aside, why'd you say no to the..." It dawned on her in that second why he wouldn't want to actually play hockey. She'd been blinded by his joy at skating, forgetting the whole reason he was here in the first place was, well, he'd messed things up with stick and puck.

He got to his feet. "Let's head home, huh?"

Head home. Now she was the one tightening up, feeling weird. *They* did not have a home together. Her home was Shaw. And she was currently shirking all her responsibilities in that department.

It is long past time you had a shirk. This will get you ready to face the next twenty-eight years of no shirking allowed.

She wanted to believe that, believe in it strongly enough the guilt settling in her gut would disappear completely. As it was, she just managed to ignore it now and again.

Dan stood, his skates in one hand, his other hand running through his hair. He looked lost for a second, before the easy, fake veneer clicked back into place. "So, what did you think of your first skating experience?"

"I think I'll leave the skating to you."

"Finally better at something than you, then?"

"Not a contest. Certainly not a fair one."

"A man has his pride. At least there's one thing."

The night had been fun. Even though she really hated that he was better than her at something, even if that was silly. Still, his constant *this is the only thing I'm good at* was getting old. Trying to soothe over men's delicate egos was getting old.

"Do you really, honestly think hockey is all you have? Because it was a pretty stupid move to come here and try to build something if you're going to mope about hockey being the only thing you were ever good at when it's over."

He was silent as they walked to his car—not as if he was angry, but as if he was pondering.

"Do you think I'm going to stay?"

The question, asked in the quiet summer night held a million implications she didn't know what to do with. But not knowing what to do had never stopped her before, and there had been an honesty in this evening. One she would remember anytime she got that stupid, hopeful feeling in her chest.

"I saw the smile on your face when you were on the ice. It would be stupid to stay, Dan. It would be robbing yourself of joy."

He opened the door to the backseat of the truck, carefully placed the skates inside, and then he leaned against the door. He tilted his head back, his eyes on the stars.

She might have looked up too, except she knew exactly what she'd see up there. What was new, what was fascinating, were the hard lines of this man's face, the pensive wrinkle in his forehead, the way his lips pressed together.

He was famous and rich. People had just fawned all over him. He was in magazines and on sports shows, and everything about his life made no sense to her, except that he seemed to be stuck in a very similar space she found herself in.

What do I do next? How do I keep going?

"A guy can't play hockey forever, Mel," he finally said, his gaze dropping to his feet. "No matter how much joy it gives him."

A familiar pain wound its way around her heart, a familiar helplessness. This was not anything she could fix. Luckily, it wasn't her business to fix it.

Unluckily, she found the words spilling out anyway.

"My dad used to ride his horse every day. No matter what. Whether he needed to or not. Boiling heat, freezing cold. At least for a little part of every day he was on that horse. It was a thing he did. He did it because he loved it, and it made him less sad when he was…upset about things. It was everything he had, and when he couldn't have that anymore… Well, you saw. Without it, he has nothing. So, if skating makes you *that* happy, you can't just…hang it up. Even if you can't be a professional hockey player forever, the thing that brings you so much joy is the thing you should be focusing on." Because he was one of the lucky few who had the money and the means to focus on their joy no matter what.

She was one of the unlucky few who had neither of those things, and an unwillingness to go after them at the expense of the people she loved.

"It's not the same," Dan said, shaking his head. For

the first time since they walked out of the rink, he looked at her. "Firstly and most importantly because your father doesn't have nothing. He has you. He has Caleb."

For a moment, she couldn't breathe. Not in, not out. It was as if her lungs were paralyzed—everything seized up inside her with a blinding pain she quite simply could not push away or bury or ignore.

She would very much love for her father to see it that way, but he'd lost his ability to walk, and in that he'd lost whatever pieces in him he'd manage to salvage after her mother left. The pieces she'd clung to so hard, coaxed out of him, begged for. All swept away by one accident…and she'd learned to stop begging.

"Mel?"

His voice sounded thin and cottony. Her vision was wavering with the pain…the memories of all the times she'd begged and succeeded. Begged and failed. Wanting a hug. Never getting it. Until Dan.

"Let's go home, huh?" she said, echoing his words from earlier in a scratchy voice. It wasn't her home, but she didn't care. There were too many other cares clogging up in her chest. She just wanted to be somewhere she didn't have to beg or work or try.

And so far, that was only with Dan.

Dan pulled the truck onto the gravel drive in front of his place. *His place*. And yet, he felt more comfortable back on that ice than he did in the pitch black of night surrounding the cabin, a slight drizzle starting to fall on the windshield.

He glanced at Mel, curled away from him, head

resting on the glass of the window, though he didn't think she was asleep.

He almost wished she was. Or that she'd want to go home, because he couldn't get over or erase the image of her face twisted in a kind of horrified pain when he'd said her father had her.

Those kinds of hurts he couldn't fix, couldn't smooth away. The kind he could see, but she wouldn't really trust him to ease — not that she should. They were things that would always be painful for her, and he didn't know how to make them easier. Distract, that he could do, but actually fix?

He'd never learned how to fix. She needed someone stronger, someone who had any clue what it was to stitch together all the emotional hurts into some kind of healing. How to ask what was wrong and get an answer. He already knew he couldn't do that.

It had been stupid to think otherwise.

"Do you ever get tired of feeling like life keeps beating you over the head?" she asked into the silence of the car.

"Lately, yes."

"Do you want to go have sex and pretend it's not hard?"

God, he wanted to do that. So he went with a joke. "Well, something will be hard."

She snorted. "You're a classy guy, Sharpe."

He grabbed her braid, and while he usually just gave it a tug, this time he didn't let it go. He pulled until she had to look at him, and he was not surprised in the least to be met with a scowl.

"No more Sharpe."

"It's a pet name."

"It's bullshit. I'm not a last name to you." He gave her braid his normal tug, but still didn't let go, keeping it wrapped around his hand. Because he didn't want her to look away or bullshit him again.

Something in her expression changed. Not just a softening, though there was that. The way her lips parted, her gaze drifted to his mouth.

Okay, yeah, something was definitely hard, and he'd kind of forgotten about that whole "wanting her to go home" thing as he leaned across the console and tugged her mouth to his. Pretend life's not hard? Yeah, he liked when they did that.

Because as sharp as her words could be, her mouth was soft, sweet. As much as every cell of her screamed capable and strong, she *melted* into him, and it made *him* feel capable and strong.

Her hand curled around his bicep, but the other one clutched the front of his shirt. He never knew what to do when she did that. When she held on to him for dear life. He wanted to tell her to run at the same time he wanted to not let her go for a second. He wanted to assure her he could be whatever it was she wanted or needed.

You will disappoint her. But she didn't believe he'd stay. She believed so little about him—what could he possibly disappoint?

"D-don't let go."

He didn't know if she was talking about her hair or in general, and he didn't really care. Because he had no intention of letting go. This thing she filled him with, this feeling she gave him, nothing, not hockey, not being here, *nothing* else made him feel that way.

Luckily, her hand moved from his arm to his abdomen,

and then trailed over his erection, and he didn't have to linger on the discomfort that realization caused.

He kept one hand curled in her hair and used his other to slide up her shirt, pull one of the bra cups far enough down that he could touch her nipple, circle it until it was hard, until she groaned, her grip on his cock going tight.

"We have to go inside to get condoms," she said against his mouth, against his lips, not letting him go, not putting any space between them. Those seemed like foreign words. All he could think about was the heated air around them, her grip on him, her breath shallow against his neck.

His eyes met hers, and he refused to get lost in that overwhelming feeling. This was about sex, which was its own kind of escape and distraction. "Well, then let's go."

It took her a minute to release him, and only then did he realize the drizzle had turned to a full-on downpour. He glanced at her, and she flashed him a grin, a grin he'd never seen. Dark, dangerous, like she could light the world on fire. Him on fire. And nothing would survive.

"Better run," was all she said before she pushed her door open and stepped into the night.

He stepped out too, the lash of a cool rain immediately hitting him, soaking him. He thought it might ease the incessant heat in his veins, the tight ache in his groin, but it did nothing. He was all set to jog, but Mel was just standing there in the dimmest of porch lights, head up, eyes closed, the rain surely drenching her.

For a moment, he just watched. The shadow of her in the middle of a storm. Lightning sizzled across the sky, thunder boomed, and he needed to get inside. He needed to be inside her.

She screeched when he bent and managed to leverage her over his shoulder. "Dan!" She pounded a fist on his back, but then her laughter bubbled up, a sound he could not resist if he tried.

He carried her to the porch, water pouring over both of them as thunder rumbled again.

"Put me down."

But there was nothing insistent about her voice in the least, so he carried her all the way inside, and didn't put her on her feet until they were in his kitchen.

He flipped on the light, trying to catch his breath. But the look of her took it away again.

Water was dripping off the strands of hair that had fallen out of her braid. Her T-shirt was plastered to her breasts, her stomach, and she was smiling. *Smiling*. Yeah, that killed him.

It only took one step before she was stepping toward him too, meeting in the middle, and they were kissing each other as if it had been months instead of minutes since they'd had their hands on each other.

He could have sworn the water sizzled between them as their mouths found some kind of solace in each other. Every lick and nip was a desperate need to forget, to have, to *take*.

She unbuckled his belt, undid the snap on his jeans, which were now tight from the rain, but it didn't stop her. Her hands were greedy and determined, and his body strained in response. She pulled him free, her hand cool and wet against his erection.

Without letting go, she leaned in and traced his

bottom lip with her tongue before pulling it between her teeth, not gentle. Not in the least. As she let his lip scrape through her teeth, she fisted her hand up the length of his cock.

A mixture of pleasure and delicious pain arced through him. "Mel. Christ." He pulled her shirt off, which sadly took her hand off him, but gave him access to that beautiful body of hers. So strong, so wet and soft. He scraped his palms over her stomach, leaned in to lick a trail of raindrops from her neck.

She sighed, her breath cooling the rain on his own skin, and if he were a man prone to shivering, he *might* never have stopped.

He pushed her bra down, groaning at the sight of her. Her nipples puckered from the wet and cold, goose bumps rising up across her chest as drops of water from her hair slid down the expanse of pale skin. "I could look at you all damn day," he said, reverent.

He had to back her against the wall, just so he could have something to lean against. Something to keep him upright. She was killing him just by existing, killing him with every stroke of fingertip against skin, a tantalizing design from chest to stomach, stomach to…sweet Christ, finally she grasped him again.

But he wanted more than her hand, needed more. If he was going to be killed, it was damn well going to be inside of her.

He pushed at her pants, trying to get them off. He was so desperate for more, for her, for anything and everything that meant they were together. "Let me fuck you now. Right now. Please, I need to be inside you."

The noise she made, like something between a moan

and a sigh just about buckled his knees, but he used the wall as support while she tried to get her wet pants off. He watched, completely enthralled as more and more of her came into view—those long legs, the muscles in her arms working as she tried to free herself from clothes.

"Condom. Condom. Condom." She chanted it, like she was trying to remind herself as much as tell him. Pushing her panties off, so all that was left on were socks and her bra at her waist.

"Don't. Move."

He didn't pause to see if she would listen. He didn't pause for anything. He got the condom, peeled off his pants and boxers, and was already tearing the packet open when he returned.

She was still standing against the wall, palms resting against it, chest rising and falling, her bra still askew, her hair even more askew, and her eyes wide. There was something wild and desperate in them, matching exactly what he felt.

It pounded through him, some distant beat he didn't recognize. There was a heaviness to the desperation inside of him. There was something more under all this. More than sex. More than sex with Mel.

That was the absolute last thing he wanted to think about right now. He rolled the condom on and she watched, her tongue touching the corner of her mouth. When he just stood there, her gaze finally met his.

"Come here," she said, an order hidden underneath breathlessness.

He was helpless to ignore any order she might give, so he came closer. He reached around to unclasp her bra and let it fall to the ground, and then he trailed his hand down her back, her ass, grabbing her leg and pulling it around his waist.

He might not want to *think* about more, but it permeated the air between them. This thing. Heavy and real.

"Tell me...tell me you need this, Mel."

"I do. I..." Her eyes were squeezed shut, but she braced herself against the wall so he could lift her other leg, slowly push inside of her.

He had to take a breath and a moment to absorb the way things seemed to click into place when they were together like this. It was more than pleasure; it was right.

She locked her legs around him, and he was able to grab her hips, hold her where he needed her to be. Against him, taking him, holding on to his shoulder like he was all there was to hold on to.

"Look at me when you say it."

Her eyes fluttered open, and her mouth opened soundlessly for a moment. He held himself still, eyes locked on hers. He needed the words, the look in her eyes. He needed so much, and he didn't know how to get it all. When she said it, she whispered it.

"I need you, Dan."

Which wasn't what he'd asked, and if he couldn't see her regret at saying it, he might have been frightened enough by that. But she didn't want her need any more than he'd be able to handle it.

"I need you to..." She looked panicked for a second, as if she was trying to take back all the words. As if she didn't understand he wasn't ready for them. "I need you to f-fuck me. Hard, please. Really. Just...rough. Make it...go away."

That was something he could handle. And even if he

didn't know what she wanted him to make go away, he could imagine. This feeling, this desperation, this need. The scary ribbon of connection that seemed to wind its way between them whether they wanted it to or not. Make it go away.

Yes. They both needed this, whether they wanted to or not.

He had to stop and pull himself together. All the strange pieces floating around inside of him with no center, no surety, no belief. He needed to piece them together, for this. For her. To survive.

Then he gave her exactly what she asked for. Hard, rough. Every time he thrust deep and thoughtlessly, she moaned, clutched his shoulders tighter, egged him on.

Her arms wrapped around his neck, her breath panting against him, her body arched and still damp from rain, from exertion, who knew. He didn't care. He wanted her like this always, taking him, wanting more from him. Nothing in the air but the sounds of their heavy breathing and their bodies coming together. Nothing else existed except the feel of her, except being inside of her.

"Come for me, Mel. I can't…" How much longer could he do this and not lose himself in it? Her eyes were closed, arms clamped around his neck, her whole backside pressed against the wall. Every time he pushed deep, she made a sound, but she still held on tight to that last moment, that last give.

He did the only thing he could think of—he reached up and tugged on the braid that was hanging over her shoulder, pushing deep.

"Yes, that's…God." She spasmed against him, her

grip on his neck almost unbearable as she moved her hips. He lost himself in her orgasm, in her, in everything.

He was shaking, not sure how much longer he'd stay upright, about to tell her so, but his mouth didn't work. Nothing worked as the last blasts of pleasure edged through him.

Mel unlocked her legs, her arms. Managed to get to her feet, but she slid down the wall, something like a shaky laugh escaping her lips as her butt hit the floor. He had to lean against the wall to keep upright, Mel sitting at his feet.

"I think I might be dead," he said.

"No deader than me," she replied, sounding out of breath and shaky still.

"Can someone be deader than someone else?"

She only shook her head, pressing a hand to the center of her chest as if trying to catch her breath. He wasn't sure he'd ever catch his again.

She looked up at him, a smile playing on her lips, both pleased and shy and a million other things he couldn't get a hold on. He'd put all those there. He had done that.

He wanted to keep doing it. He reached out his hand. "Come to bed."

Her gaze dropped, and she did the thing where she pressed her tongue to the corner of her mouth, and well, he felt a little stir where he'd just lost himself.

"Or…"

"Or what?" he asked, perhaps a little too eagerly.

"We could take a shower. Together." Slowly, she took his hand and let him help her get to her feet with a kind of grace he'd never seen from her. It was languid, slow, smooth—none of the sharp, determined way of moving she usually had about her.

She pressed her hand to his chest, and he liked the way she did that. As if it cemented them together, as if she needed to. Then she leaned forward, her breasts brushing his chest as she whispered in his ear. "I want to put my mouth on you."

He blinked in surprise.

"If you're interested." Her hand dropped and she sauntered to his bathroom, pulling the band out of her hair before disappearing.

So he did the only reasonable thing a person could do in that situation: he scurried after her.

Chapter 17

MEL HAD NO IDEA WHAT SHE WAS DOING, IF DAN would follow, if this made any sense. But she didn't care. She didn't *care*, and since she didn't, she'd keep on this path for as long as she could.

She'd told him what she wanted. Something hard and rough, and she couldn't believe she had *said it*, and he had *given* it to her. It had been like…it had been like *nothing* she'd ever experienced.

And she wanted more. More of all the things she'd always been too embarrassed or uncomfortable to ask for. To give.

She flicked the shower on. Her hands were shaking—from that orgasm, from adrenaline, from fear, she had no idea. She didn't care.

A laugh bubbled up and out of her mouth. She didn't *care*, and it was the most wonderful damn thing.

"What is so funny?"

She took a deep breath and slowly turned to face him. Naked in his bathroom doorway. She hadn't had a chance to really look at him, hadn't had the bravery to unabashedly stare at his naked body and take it all in.

All. In.

There was a uniformity to the hue of his skin, like he didn't spend a lot of time in the sun. He was like one of those marble statues, every muscle rounded, defined, the only interruption to the smooth look of him the pattern of chest hair that trailed down the center of his abs—like seriously well-defined *abs*—to…

She sucked in a breath. He was hard and thick, and since it had only happened a few minutes ago, it was no trouble remembering what it felt like buried inside her. Against the wall. Unrelenting. Perfect.

Even his legs were things of beauty, sculpted muscle, strong, capable of, well, screwing her against the wall. Capable of shaking her foundation so loose she wasn't sure she had one anymore.

Seriously. That had happened, and it was better than even the lame fantasies she'd had of it. A pleasure so unyielding even *she* had to give into it, get swept away by it. And he was so sure, and so strong, big… He'd held her against the wall as though she weighed nothing, filled her as though she'd always been waiting for exactly that.

A man whose touch could make her feel aglow, whose gaze was so intense and focused on *her* it felt like touch. A man who could fill her with so much excitement and lust and desire, her brain didn't have room to work.

It would be scary if she dwelled on it, so she did the most unbelievable thing she could think of instead. She flashed a grin, crooked a finger, and stepped inside the shower.

It was small, with a little rust, a lot of hard water stains, but when Dan stepped into the small space with her, none of that mattered. She dipped her head into the warm spray. Her hair would be a tangled mess when it was all said and done, but oh well.

Dan's hands rested on her hips, each fingertip a

pressure point against her skin. Each pressure point the start of a delicious trail of heat that all centered at her core. It had been only minutes, but just the simplest touch had her wanting again. Needing again.

She sighed into the spray, until he pressed her against the shower tile, his mouth covering hers. His body covered hers, so much broader and stronger. Against him she felt like she didn't have to be strong or capable. She could just accept his kiss, his touch, let it lightning through her, an electricity she didn't want to fight.

She smiled against his mouth—smiled because this was a moment worth enjoying, worth soaking up without worry or caution or any of the usual things that tightened her into a ball of stress that couldn't ever let go.

His tongue traced her smile, his hands smoothing up her sides before palming her breasts; every time he touched, grasped, held, the trails of heat centered deeper, wanted more. And somehow in wanting more, she wanted to give more.

"Soap?" she said against his mouth.

He reached behind her and produced a bottle of shower gel, the kind you knew was meant for guys, because of course it was blue and had *action* written like three times on the label. When she squirted some on her hand, it smelled like him.

She handed the soap back to him, and then met his gaze as she took his length in her hand, squeezing gently as she stroked, feeling him grow harder as she slid her hand back down to the base. His eyes fluttering closed, water cascading down those unbelievable shoulders. Water droplets collected on his dark eyelashes, in the indentation above his collarbone. They trailed down the expanse of his chest, over the dip above his hips.

She wasn't sure this was real. In fact, she'd go with that. This wasn't real, so she could do whatever she wanted, however she wanted, and there would be no consequences.

So she knelt in front of him, allowing the spray to hit everywhere she'd just soaped up, wash away the lather. She ran her hands over his thighs, coarse hair, ridiculous muscle. The long length of him at eye level. She'd *told* him she wanted her mouth on him. She'd initiated this, because she wanted to give him something, because she wanted this thing he did to her to be mutual.

He raked his fingers through her hair, getting tangled there, stuck, tugging a little. Something about that little shock of pain eradicated the nerves enough that she could take him into her mouth. All the way until he hit the back of her throat and she had to pull back.

The rumble of his groan egged her on, even more so when his fingers tightened in her hair. She wanted him to lead her where he needed her to go, and he did. Her need grew with his. She wanted more than his hands in her hair, but even bigger than that was the need to give him what he wanted. To be what he wanted.

No nerves, no discomfort, no fear of doing it wrong causing her to hold back, to decline. This wasn't complicated. It was elemental. It made everything else from the day fade away into desire, into power, into him. And her. Just this.

She filled her mouth with him again, then pulled back, a delicious, decadent rhythm, but this time he pulled her up to her feet.

His eyes glittered with intensity, and she suddenly

realized the water had grown cool, though she'd barely noticed, not with his hands wrapped around her arms, pushing her back.

"Bedroom."

"But—"

"Now."

Well, sure, okay. She could do that. If he kept ordering her around with that blazing intensity, she could probably do anything. There was something about him taking over, taking charge that made her want to dissolve and go with the flow. As long as the flow led to him on top of her, inside of her, touching her until those lovely waves of pleasure washed over her and made her weak.

Who knew weak could be good? Could be…everything.

He stepped out of the shower, his fingers trailing off her skin, and everything got so much colder even as he flipped off the water.

But then he grabbed a towel from a crooked-hanging cabinet and wrapped it around her shoulders, rubbing the rough fabric into the wet ends of hair that hung down her back.

The heat was back, with his hands rubbing circles on her back, his cock brushing her hip, the memory of it deep inside her mouth, inside of her.

"Come on, Cowgirl." He led her to the hallway, and she let him do it. Because it felt nice to be led. Refreshing. Rejuvenating.

"Please don't make a riding joke," she said.

He flashed that lethal grin. "Not even one?"

"Surely you've got better lines than that."

He nudged her into his room, closer and closer to the bed, his eyes never leaving hers. The light from the hallway poured in, but otherwise the room was dark, his eyes were dark, his face a mix of shadows and light.

He stood there, hands on her shoulders, gaze on hers. They were naked and wet and he was just *staring* at her. She didn't like that look, the "she was the center of the world" look. It felt so much bigger than hot as sin sex. It felt like…everything.

No, she didn't like that at all, so she dropped the towel and stepped to him, pressing against him. Everything. Body. Mouth. Stepped into the fire. Surely he was fire, burning away everything that kept her whole, but she didn't want to be whole anymore. She wanted to be a million shattered pieces, and he could do that.

She pulled him onto the bed, a tangle of limbs, her arms reaching out blindly for the drawer where he kept the condoms. She fumbled and missed, but his arm was longer and more on point. Still something rattled off the nightstand when he jerked the door open, but it didn't stop him from kissing her, from using his other hand to hold her in place underneath him.

She would gladly be held here for eons. That big strong hand making her feel as though it was all that mattered. Him, holding her there. His fingers and palm a vice from which pulls of pleasure wound through her limbs.

Weak. Yes, weak was good. Weak was an amazing contrast to strong.

"I *will* return the favor, but for now, I need to be inside you."

She had no idea how he said those things so easily, so…all sexy growly that made her feel like that was the only possible thing she could ever want. She could do that. She might not know how he did it, but she could be that in the moment. She took the condom packet from him and tore it open. "Say what you said out there."

"What did I say out there?" he asked, hissing out a breath as she worked shaking hands to roll the latex over him.

"That…" No consequences, no embarrassment. She asked for what she wanted, and he gave it. She finished rolling the condom on, determined not to chicken out. "That… That you need to fuck me." Just saying the word with his eyes on her made her pulse jump, the ache between her thighs throb with need. But it would be nothing compared to *him* saying it. To him doing it.

He groaned, but not the kind that made her feel stupid. It was a groan that made her feel powerful. He would give her what she asked for because they wanted the same thing. She might be weak and small compared to him, but that was part of it. He didn't need her to be strong. He simply needed her. She led him to her, but he pulled away.

"Roll over," he instructed.

He groaned again when she did so, his rough hands roaming the curve of her ass. There had never been anything like this, like him, like the recklessness bouncing around like pinballs inside of her.

His hands moved back up to her hips, gripping her there in the way that made her stomach flip, the way that had her arching her back for more. She wanted to be held and grabbed and led. Who knew?

"Tell me if you don't like it," he said in that growly sex voice.

"I-I'm okay," she replied, hearing what sounded like

nerves and knowing it was anything but. It was desperation. She was shaking with it.

He slid inside her, slow, deep, and she had to grasp the rumpled comforter and press her forehead into the bed just to keep from crying out. It was as though where they met was the only thing that existed, that sharp slide of pleasure.

"Still just okay?" he asked, humor lilting the low rumble of his voice, but the pressure on her hips where he held her was *anything* but humorous. It was centering. It was everything.

"Could take it or leave it," she managed, but every tremble of her voice, the way she couldn't help but push her ass against him when he tried to withdraw…yeah, there was no way he didn't know it was a joke.

"Mm. Could you now?" He withdrew and she waited for more, but he didn't move, poised at the entrance, his grip unchanging.

She waited, but she wasn't strong enough to outwait him, to prove she was somehow stronger. She just… didn't care. She didn't have to be strong or play a game, she could just want. She could ask or beg. And he would give. "Dan…"

"Oh, honey, I cannot begin to explain how much I love to hear you say my name like that."

She wanted to argue with that, even though there was nothing to argue. She didn't know what the need to deny his words was, but luckily he pushed inside her, that deep, slow stroke of everything she needed, and the protest and the desire to argue died away. Far, far away.

The orgasm built, higher, teetering on the edge, and for the briefest of seconds she thought she wasn't going to be

able to topple under it. That the sharp edge of needing more
would just stay there until it dulled. But instead of tensing up, letting that worry center itself, she pushed it away.
Because this was Dan. He'd found a way to unlock her, to
make her into something else, and she wanted him to keep
doing that. She focused on his fingers digging into her, the
ragged sound and feel of his breath, the wave of pleasure
when he plunged deep, until it was waving over her, shaking through her. Release. Sharp and sweet and everything.

He withdrew, taking her hips and flipping her onto
her back before pushing her farther onto the bed. Then
he was inside her again, over her, the last jolts of pleasure making her sigh.

"Mel, I need…" He kissed her neck, her jaw, her
mouth. "I need…"

She tangled her fingers in his hair. Even knowing it
was a mistake to look at him, to meet gazes, she did it
anyway. "Me."

He didn't pause, didn't look away, didn't stop pushing into her. "You," he said earnestly.

She should take it back, dial it down, make it stop. She
was losing herself, who she was and what she wanted.
Something about him burned it away until she didn't
know what was left, but his mouth covered hers as he
chased his way to finishing, and she was so tired of doing
what she should, she held on and gave everything she had.

Dan woke up alone, and he wasn't sure what feeling
worked through him when he realized all traces of Mel
were gone.

It was bigger than disappointment, deeper than

wishing she would have stayed, and it scared the shit out of him.

She'd probably gone home to change and get ready for work. This was not something to feel…anything over. Not if he expected…

Well, that was a bit of a problem, wasn't it? He didn't know what he expected. He didn't know what the hell they were doing.

Usually, what he was doing with a woman was pretty clear. It was either only sex, or it was a few dates and sex in the off-season; but hockey had been the calendar of his life, and there had been no waking up hoping to find someone there, because the lines were clear.

There was not a clear line between him and Mel, and he was reluctant to make one. Because if he had to make a line for them, he'd have to make a line for everything. Hockey. This ranch.

If he made lines, he'd falter when he reached them. If he set no lines, only worked toward building something every day…maybe eventually…he could reach something without screwing it all up.

You are so full of shit.

Well, whatever worked. He forced himself out of bed, scratching his fingers through his hair, remembering how Mel had tangled her hands there.

Fuck.

"You're up, I see."

He startled at the female voice, at Mel standing in the doorway of his bedroom. She was completely dressed, and it didn't look like the clothes she had on yesterday, even though he knew they were. No wrinkles, no damp spots. Just ready-to-work Mel.

The relief he felt at the fact that she hadn't gone was...yeah, fuck.

"Um, yeah. I'm up."

"I fed and watered Mystery, and I made you some toast. I was a bit tired of eggs."

"You didn't have to—"

"I...I have to take today off," she said, her hands clasped tightly in front of her. He couldn't read her expression. Part sheepish, part...he didn't know.

Because you don't know jack shit about people.

"The whole day."

"Well, don't look so concerned," he replied, ignoring all the things going on in his head. His chest. He forced a smile. "You should have days off. I never meant for you not to have days off."

"You're paying me an awful lot for days off."

"You're giving me an awful lot." He cringed. "Not—"

"No, I know." She managed a small smile, pushing a few wayward strands of hair off her forehead.

Shit. This was awkward, and he didn't even know why. What had been different about last night? It was just more of that...forgetting thing they were doing.

Minus the part where they'd said they needed each other. Wasn't that more than...escape?

"Anyway. I've got to get the stuff with my dad's nurse situated. I really can't put that off." She chewed on her lip like there was something else she wanted to say, but she didn't.

Because they were not in a relationship. Not the kind where you told each other everything, confided. Wasn't that perfect? He'd suck at that anyway.

You haven't so far. "So far" being the operative

words. Why did his brain have to keep arguing with itself? Maybe he was getting those mountain crazies she'd talked about the other day. Let her go take care of her crap. She'd come back. For fuck's sake, he could probably tell her to jump off a cliff and she'd come back. She was seeing this through, because that was Mel.

And if you asked her to stay? Would she come back, or would she run far, far away?

Yeah, he didn't want to think about that. "It works out. I was going to make a trip out to the llama breeder this week, and I bet I can do it today."

"Isn't that over in Preston?"

"Yeah."

"You can't drive out there on your bike."

"Sure I—"

She slapped her keys to his palm. "Take my truck."

He stared at her keys. "What are you going to do?"

She glanced back at the kitchen thoughtfully, and then she smiled sweetly. "I'll take your bike."

"Noooooo. No."

"Don't be a baby. I'm an excellent driver."

"In your big-ass truck. It's a *motorcycle*. It's a completely different set of skills."

"I've driven a motorcycle before, Dan."

"When?"

She smiled sweetly. "Tyler had one."

"He absolutely did not."

"He did too!" When he only glared at her, she slumped a little.

"Okay, his brother had one and he taught me to ride, but still. I know how to handle a motorcycle. Don't you trust me?" She fluttered her lashes at him, like it was a joke, but it felt bigger. This all felt bigger, and he knew he should get the hell away from bigger before he crashed it all.

But he ran his palm down her braid instead. He stepped closer instead. He did everything he knew was wrong instead, because it didn't feel wrong, and he didn't know how to fight that.

"I trust you." He cupped the back of her neck, pulling her mouth closer to his, though he didn't close the distance completely. "You trust me with your truck?"

Her eyes searched his, all seriousness. So much so he almost told her to forget it, almost released her and changed the subject.

"Yes," she said on little more than a whisper.

They were talking about driving each other's vehicles. Nothing else. So why did he feel all cracked open and not up to the task? "Good."

"Yeah, good," she said on a wavery exhale. "Um, I have to get going, but... If you stop by the ranch when you're done, we can switch."

"Or...you can come back when you're done." He rubbed his hand up and down the back of her neck, some kind of satisfaction working through him that her shoulders relaxed, that she leaned against his hand.

He brushed his mouth against hers, because the curve of her bottom lip, the way her mouth was slightly parted, was irresistible. "And if it's a rough day, I can make you forget all over again."

Her mouth curved just a hint, so he kissed her again, until her arms wrapped around his shoulders and he was ready to make her forget *right now*.

But she eventually pulled away. "I really do have to go, but I'll bring your bike back."

His grip on her neck tightened in spite of himself. "And you'll stay?" *Not supposed to ask that, dipshit.*

"I...I'll stay," she said, her eyes wide and serious again.

So he released her, and forced a smile and a joke and everything that was ten million times lighter than he felt.

"Don't be surprised if my llama herd multiplies on your day off."

She smiled ruefully. "Nothing you could do would surprise me at this point, Dan Sharpe."

He tried to smile back. Considering everything confusing and deep he felt about her surprised the hell out of him, he was pretty sure there were quite a few ways he could surprise her.

Not always the good kind of surprise.

"Be careful, honey."

She gave him a little nod. "Have a good day, Dan." And then she was gone, and he was alone in this tiny bedroom. With nothing but the prospect of llamas to keep him going.

Well, at least it was something.

Chapter 18

MEL PROBABLY SHOULDN'T GET AS MUCH OF A KICK OUT of driving Dan's motorcycle as she did. It had been a long time since her life had been free and easy enough to ride something so impractical. A small piece of machinery that probably cost at least as much as her giant old truck.

It made the amount he was paying her seem like nothing. Which, technically, it would be once she used it to pay off debts.

But it'll put Shaw closer to even ground.

That was supposed to be the only thing she cared about, everything she worked for. Shaw. The thing she could depend on. The life and blood of her.

Why did that fall flat? Why did the hum of a new and impeccable piece of machinery beneath her and this open-aired freedom make her feel like a traitor?

The entire morning had made her feel like a traitor, because she had woken up with her head on Dan's shoulder, her hand curled into his shirt, and she hadn't wanted to move. She hadn't wanted to work or face the day.

She didn't know who she was if she didn't want that. Didn't know who she was if all she wanted was Dan. Waking up with him. Him trusting her with his bike, asking her to come back. That was all she wanted.

It was wrong. She'd spent so long forcing herself to love this place, to work this place, to give everything she had to it in some sort of effort to prove she wasn't the woman she looked so much like.

To be passionless and loveless so she wouldn't want to run away, so she wouldn't be left behind like her father had been. So she could be strong and nothing would ever touch her.

She was failing at that. Failing beyond reason, but it didn't erase the things Dan made her feel, the things he made her forget. It didn't erase the desire to go back to him tonight. A palpable tug back to him.

Her hands shook as she drove up the hill. She was losing herself, and she didn't know how to fight it.

Had Mom lost herself too?

She pushed too hard against the brake and jerked to a stop so she could squeeze her eyes shut. But when she opened them, she didn't have time to indulge in tears.

One of their cows was standing in the gravel between her and the garage. Another was in the yard. She swore and hopped off of the bike, whistling as loudly as she could.

The cow on the gravel lowed at her until she clapped her hands. "Go on. Get back to where you belong."

Slowly, painstakingly, she managed to corral the cows back into the pen. By the time she had the cows in and the fence mended enough to keep them in place, she was sweaty and starving, a headache brewing, probably from dehydration.

Where the living hell was Caleb? She was supposed to be able to trust him. He'd promised he could handle this, but…he couldn't. He wasn't.

She wanted to cry, but the fury took over first. Hot

and uncontrollable. The *one* thing they had left were these few cattle. That was *it*.

And if she hadn't come home… *Or if you'd come home last night*.

Sick realization swept through her. This really was her fault. What idiot had thought she could trust Caleb? Could trust any damn person with the last name Shaw—including herself.

But Caleb had promised. *Promised*. She stalked to the house, blinking back tears, ignoring the futility settling in her bones. It seemed she would always come home to Caleb failing.

And it would be her fault for never pushing hard enough when it came to whatever demons kept driving him. But blaming herself didn't make her any less angry.

"Caleb!" She stomped through the house, making as much noise as possible. When she burst into the living room, Dad was sitting in his wheelchair, watching TV.

"Would you keep it down?" he muttered.

"No, I will not fucking keep it down." She tossed her hat on the ground. For five years she hadn't let her temper loose around him. Hadn't wanted to stress him out. Well, she was *done*.

But he didn't react. Not to her yelling, swearing, anything. He just shrugged. Completely unfazed.

"I suppose you don't care the cattle escaped?"

He didn't break his gaze from the TV, didn't do anything but sit there. "Can't do anything about it, can I?"

"You could care!" Why was she yelling at him? It wouldn't matter. None of it mattered.

"Caring ain't shit."

The tears that stung her eyes were wholly and

completely unwelcome. "It is something to me. You caring would be something to me."

But he didn't. Wouldn't. He sat there and watched some idiot yap on TV while everything inside of her shattered and broke apart.

"Fuck, what is all the noise?" Caleb entered the room, scratching his head. His white T-shirt was dirty with who knew what, his eyes bloodshot, and he hadn't shaved in a few days. This was worse than the night on the porch, so much worse, because she could believe that had been a one off. A little release of steam like she'd needed.

The man in front of her had drunk himself into passing out last night. She knew that the same way she knew her father wouldn't give her anything. Not one ounce of energy, not one drop of affection. They wouldn't share their secrets, their pain; they wanted to drown in it.

Or they'd already drowned. Maybe everything was dead. Her heart felt dead right along with it.

"Why are you looking at me like that?" Caleb asked.

"Do you know what I came home to?"

He rubbed a hand over his face. "Last night?"

It was a sharp pain that he hadn't even noticed her not coming home last night. And a slap of embarrassment that she'd have to explain in front of both of them.

Or she could avoid, pretend. That's what they did. Why not her? "There was a cow. Loose."

"Don't know how."

"The fence, Caleb. You haven't been checking the fences. You haven't been holding your weight. You promised me."

Something ugly flashed in his eyes. "I have done

everything you asked me to do. Maybe I got a little carried away last night and am having a bit of a late start this morning, but I'm carrying my weight just fine."

"No, you're not."

"I am one person and I am doing the best damn work that I can. Don't act like you've never had an animal escape on your watch. That you've never made a mistake. Don't not be around when this place is going to shit and place all the blame on my shoulders. It was *in* shit when you left."

She wished she could argue. He wasn't far off. The place was falling apart when she'd handed over the reins to him. But holding it together didn't feel necessary anymore. Not when she was the only one who seemed to be able to do it. "What am I working so hard for, Caleb? You? Dad?"

Caleb jerked a shoulder. "I thought you were doing it for you. For Shaw. Because you are Shaw. Those are your words."

She was…this was it. The bottom. The breaking point. She didn't have any more fight left, any more armor or bravado. "I don't know who I am."

"I'd say you're walking your way toward being Mom."

The pain was deeper than anything, and there had been a lot of pain. She had spent her life trying not to be a woman who would walk away, but…

All she could see if she stayed was year after year of this. Of this black oppressive pain, of secretly wishing someone would help, of being failed time and time again. If this was what Mom had been up against… maybe she couldn't even blame her anymore.

"Maybe I have to be her to save myself. It's a far

better alternative to drinking myself to death. To sitting in front of a TV all day, pretending like my family means nothing. And I am done being the one trying to keep it all together. I quit." She struggled to say the rest without tears. "I quit both of you."

"You said Shaw was the most important thing." Caleb's voice was rough, hurt. Like she was abandoning him the way everyone always did.

She wished she could bring herself to care.

She looked around the house she used to love like part of herself. Her father sitting there not saying a damn word. Her brother standing there full to brim with a pain she didn't understand, a pain he used to hurt himself, and her. She didn't feel love anymore. She felt it press down on her until nothing was left.

She had sacrificed so much to love this place, these two men, but it wasn't ever going to love her back any more than they were.

"I lied," she whispered, because it had been a lie. To him. To herself. Shaw had been the last thing she could hold on to, but it wasn't her. It was just a fortress she'd built around herself. "If you fail it, so be it. I won't be around to see."

She turned and walked out of the room. The tears stayed at bay, but she was shaking as she walked up to her room. All of her worst fears were coming true. She was her mother, and her father. All mixed up into someone who had nothing left. No family. No home. No life.

Dan.

She squeezed her eyes shut against that thought, leaned against the railing for a second. No, she did not have him. She did not want him. The last thing she was going to do was place all her hopes and needs in another person.

She had trusted every single person in her family. Mom to love her, Dad to comfort her, Caleb to keep Shaw going.

And all of them had failed. She had failed.

So, no, she didn't *have* Dan, but she also had nowhere else to go.

"You're going to have yourself some friends, Mystery." Dan worked on changing out the water in the buckets, doing his normal chatting. Sometimes, in the dusky golden rays of sunset, it didn't feel so stupid. It felt right.

Talking to the llama breeder on his own had felt pretty right too. Like he knew what he was doing. Haggling with the guy over the price of the small group of llamas he wanted to get rid of.

Winning.

Yeah, all in all, a pretty right day. Made even righter by the sound of a motorcycle engine interrupting the quiet. Mel.

They were going to have a talk. A real talk because… because despite all the doubts and whispers in his head, he knew he wanted to be here. Maybe not this year, but eventually. And if he was going to be here, build this, it meant he had to start believing he could.

Not just the llama ranch, not even just hockey. More. He had to believe in more. *In her?* That was the real kicker, he supposed. Screwing up hockey or the ranch was…well, intangible. It might bruise his ego, hurt his pride. It might even be hard.

But it wasn't hurting someone else. He was so afraid he didn't know how not to hurt someone.

He finished watering Mystery, and when Mel still didn't appear, he went in search of her. When his bike came into view, she was still sitting in the seat, though the helmet was hanging off the handlebars. He wasn't sure if it was his appearance or coincidence that she got off then.

She pulled a bag out of the compartment under the seat, then tossed it into the bed of her truck, never once looking at or greeting him.

He stopped halfway to her, uncertain. Something was wrong, and he didn't particularly want to find out what.

Yes, you do. You're building something, and you want her to be a part of it. He swallowed down the fear, because it was true. He wanted her to be a part of it, and he'd have to get over himself to make that happen.

So he forced himself to keep walking. All the way to her. She kept her back to him until he touched her shoulder. "Hey."

She turned slowly, almost reluctantly, and he could immediately see why. Her face was red and blotchy, her eyes bloodshot. She had to clear her throat to speak, but then she didn't speak at all.

He reached out to touch her cheek, warm and damp. "What's wrong? What happened?"

She pulled away from his hand, almost wincing at his touch. She cleared her throat again, stepping around him.

Daniel, please, don't make this any harder on me.

He snatched his hand back, not sure where that

memory came from. Somewhere deep down. He had tried to help Mom, failed.

You're not fucking five anymore.

But he'd been a teen when he'd started distancing himself from his grandparents, and he'd never made amends with anyone or dealt with any of the emotional baggage he'd skated away from. Even at thirty-five.

"Mel?"

"I'm sorry." Her voice was raspy. Everything about her was…even that day she'd cried on his shoulder hadn't been like this. That had been more like a breaking point, a release. This seemed like she was already broken, and there was nothing left.

It made his chest ache hard enough to cover up the fear he didn't know what to do with. "Honey, what is it?"

"I don't…want to talk about it." She stopped, her back to him, her gaze on something, though he wasn't sure what. "But, um, can I stay here? For a bit?"

"Stay here? Well, sure, but…"

Her shoulders slumped. "I don't have anywhere else to go."

She was killing him with this shit. He crossed to her, turned her around so she had to look at him. "Why? What happened at Shaw? What's wrong?"

She didn't meet his gaze, no matter how he tried to get in her line of sight. "I… I don't want to talk about it. Can we… Can we not?" Finally her eyes met his, full of so many things he had to drop his hand, step back.

It was too much like last night. Too much like when he'd told her that her father had her and Caleb, and the pain had been so clearly written all over her face.

He wanted to know what to do for her, how to make

it okay, but he didn't know what to do except what she asked. "Okay, we don't have to talk about it."

Some of the tension in her shoulders relaxed. "Thank you."

So that was the right thing, he guessed. Why did it feel all wrong?

"Did you come home with llamas?"

"Uh. No, but I made a deal with the breeder and he's going to bring them out next week."

"That's great."

"Yeah."

They stood there in awkward silence, the beautiful sunset going eerie as the sun disappeared behind the mountains, as Mel said nothing, didn't move an inch.

Silences used like a shield. Why did that feel so damn familiar? "Do you want me to get your bag?"

That finally got her moving. "No." She grabbed it herself and began striding toward his house. To stay with him. Because something had happened back at Shaw that caused her to pack a bag and cry and leave.

Something she didn't want to talk about. Didn't want his help with. Would this turn into silences and pauses and painful conversations like he and Mom had? Into trying to only tell him the things she thought he could deal with?

She didn't want to talk about it because she didn't trust him with it. With her truck, maybe, but not with her pain.

He let out a breath and followed her to the house, reluctance making his steps feel heavy. He needed a plan. That had helped him with the ranch—maybe he could work that strategy to how to deal with Mel.

She really wasn't anything like Mom, but they both had a tendency to pull in when they were upset. Shut it all down, and while any comparison felt kind of weird, maybe it could help. For everything he had failed at as a kid, he could figure out how to make right with Mel.

He was starting at a slight disadvantage, not knowing why she was upset, not understanding the kind of family dynamics that went on with the Shaws, but he knew she was crying. Sad. So someone had hurt her.

The jolt of anger at that surprised him. The idea of someone hurting her pissed him off. A lot actually. He stomped up the porch stairs and into the kitchen, where Mel was getting herself a glass of water, her duffel bag placed neatly on the window seat next to the kitchen table.

"Was it Caleb?"

Her eyebrows pulled together and she slowly put the glass on the counter. "Was what Caleb?"

"Whatever you're upset about. Caleb hurt you? Because I will kick his ass for you. I know you're capable and all, but since he's not my brother, I'd be less inclined to pull a punch. I'm pretty good at fighting on skates. I'm sure I could do it on my own two feet too."

She blinked at him for a few humming seconds, something he couldn't read in her expression, in her eyes. In her *everything*…and then it was gone. Blank. "It…" Pause. Fucking pause. "Has nothing to do with you, Dan."

The instinct to walk away, to escape, to not push was so deep, so ingrained, he took a step back. Like every time Mom had asked him to leave her alone. He would have kept stepping back, backing away, take the unwanted offer and unwanted comfort and unwanted everything far, far away…

But someone *had* hurt her. "You're hurt."

She shook her head. "That doesn't have anything to do with you either."

Yes, it does! The words were right there, on the tip of his tongue, but they weren't just for her and he knew it. For some reason his brain, his memories, his emotions were all superimposing this with all the divorce stuff from his childhood.

Which was just fucking stupid. He'd learned. Learned to ignore what he felt, hide it with charm and smiles. To escape it with hockey. It had gotten him a very successful life.

Except the emotions were still there, and he still didn't know how to help anyone or make things easier for anyone, and he still fucking wanted to. He wanted to make this easier on Mel, to comfort her, to give her something.

But she wanted nothing from him, except a place to stay, sex to forget, and a job to do. Nothing more.

"I'll make dinner," she said, crossing to the refrigerator. Dismissal. *Just forget about it, Daniel. It's over your head. Everything is fine.* And he'd had to play dumb and pretend like he believed her.

For a second he considered that. Playing dumb and smiling and leaving her to it, forgetting he'd ever wanted to know. She didn't trust him to help, fine. She probably had every right not to trust him with that. No one else in his life did. Why the hell would she?

Except…something about the way she refused to even tell him what happened, even a hint…it made him more angry than anything else. Why couldn't people just trust him, or give him a damn chance? And, while he might fuck every damn thing up, *she* didn't know that. When had he ever disappointed *her*?

Shouldn't she at least trust him until his true colors came bleeding through? Maybe they wouldn't ever bleed through. Maybe this place, Mel, was exactly what he needed. A fresh start. Different from the kid, from the teen who'd skated away from that kid. Different from the twenty-something phenom who'd poured his life into a young man's game.

Maybe he should start demanding to know. Demanding to be trusted. Maybe it was time to man up.

"You know what, fuck dinner."

Her head popped from behind the refrigerator door. "Huh?"

"I said fuck dinner. Because if you don't want to tell me what happened, then you can't stay here." Which was probably all wrong. He was probably messing it up by making this ridiculous ultimatum.

But, hey, it was better than running away.

Chapter 19

MEL TRIED TO MAKE SENSE OF THE WORDS HANGING IN the air, like some sort of line he was drawing between them. *If you don't want to tell me what happened, then you can't stay here.*

So, where was she supposed to go? What was she supposed to do if she couldn't be here? Why…why did that hurt so much? What did it matter if he turned her away? She was more than used to that. Not getting what she'd asked for.

Except, what exactly had she asked for? A place to stay. Him to forget about her being upset. Those weren't the things she really wanted. Why should she be angry at him for not giving them to her?

"It's not asking much to know why you showed up at my door upset. It's not… It should not be this much of a question. Why can't you tell me? What is it? You think I can't handle it?"

He was angry, his hands in fists, his eyes blazing, but underneath it was something more than anger. It was something she hated having put there, was so confused as to how she had. He was hurt. How had she hurt him?

"Handle isn't the right word," she said, doing her best to make her voice sound even. She didn't know the right word. Didn't know the answer to his question. Why couldn't she tell him? Because she damn well didn't want to.

He swore and turned away, as if she'd told him to go to hell.

She didn't want to argue. She didn't want to be mad and confused anymore. She just wanted to lie down. In his bed. With him. "It's just not something I want to talk about." Maybe if she said it calmly, reasonably enough, he'd get it through his thick skull.

"Why not?"

"B-Because." She knew it wasn't an answer, but she didn't have one. Because it would be too hard, too revealing, because it would make her cry and feel weak and stupid all over again.

"Because why, Mel?" he said through gritted teeth, his hands still in fists, everything about him tense and angry, and that damn hurt, she just…she hated it. Hated being at fault for it.

"I don't know!"

"Bull. Shit. Why wouldn't you want to tell me why you're upset, why you're hurt? What possible reason do you have to keep that from me when I'm on your side, when all I'd do is support you in whatever lame way I could? Why wouldn't you want that? Do you think I can't? I can't understand? I can't be there? You think sharing your hurt with me is somehow gonna break me?"

She wanted to laugh. Break him? If she was honest and told him everything that happened, *she* would break. Maybe he would see that she wasn't the person she tried so hard to be. She wasn't the person who stayed, the person who rose above all the hard things life threw at her. She pretended, and when that got to be too much, she walked away.

She turned away from him and his anger and hurt and demands and words and everything. It was too much. "Why does it matter?" Seriously, why *did* it matter? What she'd felt had never mattered before.

"It matters because I care about you!"

He may as well have punched her for the force of those words, and she had to grab on to the countertop to keep upright. She couldn't breathe for a second. Care. *Care*. God, why?

"Why are you surprised by that? What the hell have we been doing the past few weeks if you're surprised by that?"

I'm not worth it. The thought made her sick to her stomach. Was she really this big of a mess she couldn't even handle someone being kind? That's what this was. She had helped him build his ranch, and there was an attraction there, so he thought it was more.

He'd figure it out soon enough. When he went back to hockey and his other life, he'd realize this had just been a nice passing phase. She was never going to be the thing he wanted. She was too cold and brittle to be the thing anyone wanted.

He touched her shoulder, gently, and she had to fight against the ripple of pleasure, the warmth of comfort. The insidious belief maybe he could care, maybe she wasn't untouchable, maybe she could be something someone stayed for or worked for…

She went cold, because she already knew that wasn't the case. "That's very…" Her voice cracked and wouldn't go any further until she cleared her throat, until she dug her fingertips hard into the counter to find some strength. "That's very nice of you."

"Nice? You think I'm being nice? Caring about you is *nice*?"

"Yes."

He laughed, but it was not an amused laugh.

"It's nice that I care about you, but run along, Daniel. You're not needed for the hard stuff."

She puzzled a bit at that. But she couldn't dwell on his hurt when hers was freezing her from the inside out. "I can handle it. And I wouldn't mind having a little space to handle it."

"Space? Space to handle *it* alone? Because you don't need me."

"That is what I said."

"Fuck you, Mel." She didn't turn, but she heard his footsteps, the door wrenched open and slammed shut.

She slumped against the counter. What was happening? Why couldn't she get a handle on anything? Where was she supposed to go now? What was she supposed to do?

I care about you!

Wasn't that what she wanted? Someone to care? Except that hadn't worked with Tyler. He had cared and it had been suffocating, because she hadn't wanted to return it.

That wasn't the problem now. That was the opposite of the problem right now. She wanted so badly to return that caring to Dan. She already had.

Even knowing it would somehow all blow up in her face, she cared. She wanted to confide in him, and maybe that was the worst part. She wanted to give him what he wanted, but she was so afraid that would be the thing that ended it all between them.

But it was going to end anyway, right? This wasn't ever going to be till death do us part, so at least this way…at least if he walked away over who she was, it would be…well, it would be what it always was, and she'd never be able to convince herself it was just distance and different lives.

It was her. The lack in her. Maybe if she stopped forgetting or ignoring that, something would go right. She wouldn't keep getting hurt.

She pushed away from the counter, her limbs shaky, her reasoning even shakier as she forced herself to the door. She would be honest, she would give him what he wanted, and when he turned away…it would be okay.

She knew it was coming. Better to get it over with now.

She stared at the door, trying to ignore the hope inside of her. Trying to ignore the way it multiplied and suffocated the certainty that he would find her lacking.

What if he doesn't? What if he still cares? She couldn't…she couldn't entertain that thought, so she pushed outside.

"Dan?"

She searched the yard, finding him halfway to the stables. He stopped, but he didn't turn around to face her. The moon shone against his back, making his hair edge toward silver before the clouds shrouded it all. He was so tense and hurt. Still that hurt. It was so much worse than hurting Tyler because…because…

Because it's a lie, you asshole.

"I'm afraid." Was that her voice? Wavering in the quiet night, barely more than a whisper, confessing things she never wanted to confess.

He turned, and while his face was still hard, she

knew this was her foothold. If she chose to take it. "Afraid of what?"

Oh, God. How was she going to do this? She swallowed, forcing her legs to take her down the stairs and into the grass. Closer and closer to him.

You want that. You want him. He's just not yours to have. "I'm afraid…that it's not enough. That I'm…" Sadly, even in the truth, she couldn't give the full truth. Because she wasn't afraid of not being enough—she already knew she wasn't. "That what I do is never enough."

"Everything you've done for me is more than enough."

"Those have all been easy things. Little things."

"Not to me." This time he took a step toward her, and then another. "To me they've been everything." He was close enough to touch, and after a moment, he did. His fingers curled around her shoulders, pulling her close enough to kiss.

But he didn't kiss her. He looked her directly in the eye. "Tell me what happened."

She took a deep breath. She'd come this far. There was no going back now. She had to explain no matter how it pained her to do it. "I told them I was leaving, and I wouldn't come back."

"Why?"

"I got home, and the cows were loose, and Dad didn't care, and Caleb was…something is wrong with him, but he won't tell me what. And I knew I'd messed up, because if I'd gone home last night—"

His hands tightened on her shoulders. "Isn't Caleb supposed to be taking care of the ranch? Isn't that his responsibility?"

"Yes, but—"

"But what? You can't do everything. No one can do everything."

"Then he can't exactly do everything, either. I don't have a choice when it comes to—"

"You do have a choice. You told me that in the restaurant in Bozeman. That you wake up every day and make a choice. So Caleb made the shitty choice and your dad has been making a shitty choice and you walked because…"

Because she was her mother. Because she didn't have half the strength she pretended to. Because she was a failure at everything, but she was really good at pretending she wasn't.

This time his fingers didn't just tighten on her shoulders—he gave her a little shake. "Answer me."

"Why?" she said a little too desperately, fearfully, all her cracks getting bigger. She'd already let so much slip out—why did there have to be more? It hurt too much to let out any more.

"Because I want to know when you're hurt, and I want to know what I can do to help, and I hate wanting to know that, because God knows I will screw it all up, but I do want it. I want it, I want you to trust me with it, and I want you and…"

"Why would you screw it up?"

"It is what I *do*. It is what I have always done." He looked so serious, so…something she recognized. Not just fear of getting it wrong, but certainty. As if they weren't really all that different at all.

But. No, that couldn't be. He was successful at everything he did. He had people who cared. He had no debt or failing ranches or withdrawn family members at his feet.

Any sameness was an illusion.

"You haven't screwed this up." She gestured to the ranch, and his gaze followed her gesture. He seemed to take it in, to soak in the surroundings and her words. Then his eyes focused in on her face again.

"What about us?"

"There's…nothing to screw up."

His hands went from her shoulders to her neck, then her face, holding her there with his gaze unrelenting and seeing way too much. He always saw way too much.

"That would break my heart if I didn't think you were just trying to protect yours." He pressed his forehead to hers, his hands on her face making it impossible to move, to run away, to lie.

"I don't think I have any care left in me, Dan."

"I know you don't want to." He brushed his mouth against hers. "But you do. Or you wouldn't be here. You wouldn't be afraid. I only know that because I am just as fucking afraid, Mel. I'm just not as strong as you to pretend to be."

"That isn't strength." It was weakness. It was her biggest weakness. Maybe if she hadn't pretended so hard not to need anyone, Dad would have reengaged, or Caleb would have confided in her, allowed her to help him. Maybe if she didn't pretend so well, the three of them would be able to ask for help.

"Then stop. Stop pretending," he said.

"What do you want me to say to that?"

"I don't want you to— You know what, no. What do I want you to say? That I'm not wrong. That you do care about me, even if I screw it up. You care. That's what I want to know."

If she gave him that, it would be used as a weapon against her. If she gave him that, she'd have to admit it to herself. She'd have to give up her pretense. She'd actually have to be strong instead of perfecting the illusion of strength.

"But don't say it if it's a lie," he said.

"It's not a lie." She closed her eyes, because she knew she would live to regret this. Regret believing this could be anything when nothing ever stayed. But if caring about him wasn't a lie, and if he needed the truth, how could she deny him that?

She swallowed all the doubt away, and it wasn't nearly as hard as it should have been. "I care about you." The words slipped out, truth stronger than any pretense.

His mouth covered hers and she was done thinking, pretending, trying. She was feeling, giving, and taking. Regardless of the outcome.

That overwhelming, chest-filling thing was back, to the point of pain. Dan didn't care. He didn't care because Mel was kissing him and…and she cared about *him*. She did. He was going to do everything, *everything* in his power not to screw that up.

Thunder rumbled in the distance, but he didn't stop kissing her until the random drops of rain became steadier, lightning flashing repeatedly after each low boom. Reluctantly, he pulled away.

"I guess I should make sure Mystery's locked up," he said. A fat drop of rain fell on Mel's nose, traveled the slope down, punctuated by another flash in the sky. "Get inside. It'll only take a minute."

She paused, her gaze never leaving his face. He could only barely make her out in the weak light from the stables.

"I'll come with," she said, her voice rough.

It was such a small thing, a nothing offer, but the way she said it, the way she slipped her hand into his when he offered it, felt a whole hell of a lot bigger than nothing. She wasn't keeping herself locked away where he couldn't reach. She was opening herself up.

They walked to the stables hand in hand, and despite the rain's force increasing, neither of them moved to rush, to hurry. Walking hand in hand in the middle of a storm, he wasn't sure he'd ever been happier.

Well, that probably wasn't true. There was getting drafted, and signing a monster contract, and a million other successes that had to matter more than walking hand in hand with someone. It had just been long enough he'd forgotten.

Or something.

"She must have already gone inside."

"Smart girl, my llama."

Mel's laugh was…he had no words for what that sound did to his chest, to this evening. When he'd walked out with the charming *fuck you* on his lips, he was sure he'd blown it all, but he hadn't been able to suck back in that anger.

It had worked out. For once in his life, expressing the conflict inside of him had turned out okay. Better than. She said she cared, she was holding his hand, and…

"I don't see her." Mel's brows drew together as she looked in each pen. "Maybe I missed her outside in the dark."

"I'll go check." A thorough check of the outside pen had a knot forming in his gut. Nothing. With the dark and the rain, surely they were just…missing a large, furry creature. "She's not out here."

Mel stood in the opening between pasture and stables, holding a flashlight. "She's not here either. Should we switch and look one more time?"

He looked out into the dark storm. They could keep looking here, but how had they both missed her twice? That couldn't be possible. "I guess if she mysteriously got in, she could have mysteriously gotten out."

"You want to do a quick look around the fence line?"

"You go inside. I'll look."

"You'll need help to corral her back. Come on. Let's go." Mel pointed the light into the rain in front of them, but he found himself leading the way. Thus far, Mystery hadn't shown any inclination of trying to escape, but she did like to graze in the southern corner in the afternoons.

So he started there, and even though it was a little stupid, since he wasn't searching for a dog, he called her name out into the steady lull of rain. They fanned out from the pasture, the beam of the flashlight not giving them much to work with.

When Mel's flashlight landed on something white, she immediately jerked the light back to it.

"Christ." Mystery was right up against the barbed wire, and that could not be good.

"Oh, damn," Mel breathed.

Yeah, definitely not good. He stepped forward, but Mystery nipped and then made a truly horrible bleating sound.

"She's stuck in the fence."

Dan tried to get closer again. "What do I do?" Thunder rolled and lightning flashed, and what the hell was he supposed to do? "We have to get her out of there."

"We need wire cutters. Another flashlight. Gloves." Mel pushed a hand through her wet hair.

"You know where all that is, right? You could run back and get it."

She didn't even respond, just started jogging back to the stables. Dan turned back to Mystery. His heart thundered in his ears—or was that the thunder? Dan had no idea.

"Hey, girl. It's all right." He swallowed down the squeaky note in his voice. "We'll get you out. But let's keep still, huh?" He knew it was stupid to talk to a llama like it had any idea what he was saying, but it was the only thing he could think to do.

Mel returned with all the tools bundled in her hands and another flashlight. "I tried to call the vet, but he didn't answer. I left a message. Once we get her free, I'll try his mom. I'm pretty sure I have her number."

"Small towns, huh?" he said, trying to keep calm. "So you cut her out of the fence and I'll try to keep her calm. She's a bit more of a fan of me than you."

"You'll want to keep her steady. Can you hold her still?"

"Let's find out." It was not something he particularly wanted to do, especially with the threat of actually being bitten or kicked, but it was the only option they had. So he did it. He stepped closer, and despite a few nips and horrible noises, he got close enough to touch her, to do his best to find a hold that would keep her from bolting.

Mel worked with the fence, but he could tell she was struggling.

"I can't get a good enough grip to cut it. Everything is too wet. Damn, I wish I had my hat."

Dan moved up Mystery's flank, doing his best to keep his movements smooth, keep her calm. "Let me try."

Mel handed him the wire cutters, and he tried to keep himself close enough to Mystery that she wouldn't try to bolt once she was free. "You just stay put now, all right?" he murmured.

The rain was still falling at a steady pace, and with the gloves Mel handed him, he couldn't get a good enough grip either. So he stripped them off.

"Be careful of the barbed wire. You don't want to get hurt too."

But he couldn't get where he needed to be with the gloves, and if he got a little scraped up, so be it.

Without the gloves, he managed to cut through one side of the fence, but to get the other side that needed to be cut, he was going to have to go around the llama again. "All right, little lady, I'm going to move to the other side, but *you're* not going to move. Got it?"

Mel didn't say anything, but she kept the flashlight trained on the fence so when he got to the other side he could quickly snip it free.

The problem was…now what?

He took a deep breath. They needed a vet. Surely someone who knew anything about animals. What was he doing acting like he had any clue what to do?

"You've got her pretty calm. Should I go try to call the vet again?"

"Shine the light on where she was caught."

Mel trained the flashlight beam on Mystery's leg. It

was matted with blood and a piece of the barbed wire was stuck. Deep and unsettling. Dan had to look away, take a deep breath. "Yeah. I'm not sure what more I can do."

"You've done so much, Dan. Really. I'm going to call him again, and if I can't get a hold of him, I'll find someone who can. Just keep her calm and as immobile as possible."

"Yeah. Just...hurry, I guess." Surely blood and barbed wire couldn't be good. How long would it take to get a vet out here? A while, surely. Dan rubbed a palm down Mystery's wet, shaggy wool. "It'll be okay." Which he didn't believe and she didn't understand, so he wasn't at all sure why he said it.

Mel returned, and then after a while, the vet. All three of them worked in the dark to get Mystery sedated and moved back to the stables, where the vet carefully removed the barbed wire and bandaged her up, saying she was lucky it hadn't caused damage to any bone or tendons. Dan stayed by her side the whole time—this strange creature who'd come into his life and given him a purpose.

A few hours later, Mystery sedated and dry in the stables, Mel and the vet long since gone, Dan finally forced himself to leave her in search of dry clothes.

When he stepped inside the cabin, Mel was in the kitchen, scribbling something on a piece of paper. But she turned to him and smiled. "I was about to come get you. Sit. You're probably starving."

"I don't know what I am," he said. Which was true. He was beyond hungry, beyond exhausted. But Mystery was okay. So said the vet, as long as infection didn't set in, and Dan was sure as hell going to make sure it didn't.

Mel placed a bowl of soup in front of him, and then slid a piece of paper next to it. "What's this?" He frowned down at the paper. There was a stick figure drawn on it, *Rancher Badge* written across the top.

"You've just earned your first rancher badge. Dealing with a hurt animal. Congratulations."

He slumped in the chair, exhaustion settling even deeper. He'd actually handled it. Really well, all in all. Maybe not on his own, but he'd gotten in there and snipped the fence and helped the vet. "I think I'm going to need something a little more official."

She crossed to him and framed his face with her hands—something he wasn't sure she'd ever done. Her calloused palms were rough against his damp skin. She felt warm and dry and perfect, and her smile was like a blanket on a cold day.

"You, Dan Sharpe, did it."

"I had a lot of help."

"You knew just what to do, and you directed it. If I hadn't been there, you'd have done it on your own. It would have been harder, but you would have done it. Because you didn't once back away."

He didn't say anything to that, didn't know what he could say. Beneath the tiredness and the headache and chill of the rain and the night and the fear…satisfaction bloomed, soft and warm.

You didn't once back away.

She brushed a kiss over his mouth. "Now eat."

She went to step away, but he liked having her there more than his stomach rumbled for the soup. So he wrapped his arms around her waist and pulled her to him, resting his cheek against her abdomen.

She chuckled softly, but her hands brushed over his hair, then her fingers trailed through it. He was pretty sure he could fall asleep right here. Sitting in a chair, pressed to Mel.

You didn't once back away. No, he'd handled the whole thing, and there hadn't been time to overthink it or worry he was screwing it up. He'd just done it.

Mel kissed the top of his head. This was the weirdest damn day.

"I'll work on getting you a more official-looking badge."

Dan looked at the sad little drawing and managed to laugh. "Actually, this might be about perfect." He released her and focused on the soup.

Just about perfect. Huh. Wasn't that something?

Chapter 20

Mel woke up to her phone alarm and Dan's clock chiming at the same time. It was like the sound track to the past week. This weird normal that wasn't normal at all.

Sharing a bed with somebody. A shower. A morning routine. Working together to build something.

No, that wasn't normal, and it would be stupid to entertain any thoughts or feelings or fantasies that it ever might be.

She wished the routine, the difference, *Dan* would smooth over everything else, make her forget. But it felt more like limbo, a world that didn't really exist. She was putting off the inevitable, only she didn't know what the inevitability was going to be.

For the seventh day in a row, she woke away from the house she'd grown up in. She had never been away for so long before, and while waking up in Dan's bed wasn't such a bad exchange, it did nothing for the worry that gripped her every morning.

Were they okay? Had Caleb found a nurse for Dad, had he drunk himself to death, had the cows escaped and no one knew or cared? Should she go back? Was that weak? Was being here weak?

Was there some right answer she couldn't find because she wasn't strong enough?

She hated it. Hated this feeling. Hated that she didn't

know what else to do. She tried—she failed. She walked away—she failed. Everything was a failure when it came to Shaw.

And every morning she woke up next to Dan and wondered what the hell she was supposed to do *now*? When nothing she could think of fixed anything, and Dan was so damn careful with her. Like she was delicate, broken. Someone who needed ease and comfort, sweet touches, calming words.

Those things did nothing more than piss her off. Make her snappy and bitchy, but he just kept being so damn sweet and quiet and there. Saving llamas and changing their bandages like…

She didn't know what. And she didn't know what to *do*.

So for the seventh damn day in a row, she had tears in her eyes before she got out of bed, and Dan's arms came around her, a comforting embrace that was anything but.

This wasn't something to treat her like glued-together glass over. It was just life. Life once you gave up the illusion of anyone being able to endure, to give, to rise to the occasion. No one could do that.

Not even her.

Dan kissed the back of her neck. Sweet. Comforting. She wished she didn't lack the ability to be comforted.

"I hate that you wake up upset every morning," he said in a sleep-heavy voice.

The downright concern in that statement had her bristling. "I'm not—" His arms tightened enough that she couldn't finish her sentence.

"If you tell me you're not upset, I'm going to toss you out of this bed, Shaw." The sleep was gone from his voice, but even though it was sharp, that underlying sweet, worrying *care* was there, and she wanted to escape.

His grip didn't loosen, but she managed a breath and tried to change the subject. "Oh, now you're last-naming me?"

"I'm taking all sorts of lessons from you, honey." His arms gentled and he kissed the back of her neck again and, oh, screw him.

"Maybe it's time you talked to them."

"About what?" She pushed Dan's arms off of her because that was some kind of spell. Feeling cared for and comforted and like there were answers. If she hadn't found answers in the five years since Dad's accident, why would Dan's arms around her make her think she could now?

"Talk to them about what happened."

She got into a sitting position, ready to bolt off the bed, but Dan's hand curled around her wrist. She refused to look at the point of contact, even if she felt it everywhere. Even if it mattered despite her not wanting it to. She gritted her teeth. "If I knew how to make it right, I would have done that already."

"I didn't say make it right. I said talk. I mean, don't get me wrong, I'm no expert on this. I haven't really talked about anything…since my parents made me go to counseling, but—"

She whirled to face him. "Why did your parents make you go to counseling?" She could not even imagine.

"Oh, you know, divorce stuff. I was kind of a mess of a kid, didn't take it well. But the point is I started running away instead of…well, the other night. We yelled at each other, but real stuff came out. Maybe that's what you need to do with them too."

She blinked at him, trying to wrap her mind around what that said about him. A mess as a kid. His thing about screwing everything up. It didn't gel with everything she knew about him in the now. Sure, he'd messed up a few hockey games, but even a person who'd started with zero faith in him had to look around and see how much he had accomplished. She might have helped, but the llama ranch—that was all Dan's hard work.

Okay, the money he had helped, but that wasn't the heart of this place. It was the lucky break that got him here—everything else was Dan's sweat and care.

The usual discomfort with that had her pulling her arm out of his grasp. "Look, that's not bad advice, but I've done it. I tell them and they don't care."

"Do you think that's what it is?" He folded his arms behind his head, all shirtless, conversational ease. "Because there are a lot of ways you act like you don't care, and I think you do. But you protect yourself. Same way I run away. To protect myself from the choke. Or the aftermath of the choke."

"I can't believe you're…"

"Making so much sense? I know. I'm surprised myself. Apparently Dan Sharpe is a pretty astute guy."

"You're something that starts with *a-s*."

"Admit it, you love me." He cleared his throat, the ease disappearing as he sat up and scratched a hand through his hair. "Uh, not quite what I meant."

"We should probably…" She gestured toward the door, because this was too weird to deal with. All of it. The neck kissing and the insightful words and the…*that*.

"Get up. Get going. Yeah." He got off the bed and headed for the bathroom. Their normal routine was that he showered while she made breakfast and coffee, then she got ready while he fed and watered Mystery.

It was a nice routine. She liked it. A lot. It was so much more…companionable than the way she'd been existing the past few years. Sure, she worked side by side with Caleb, but it had never felt like working together. Caleb kept so much from her, and she kept so much from him.

Working together felt good. Like before Dad's accident, when she'd been an integral part of Shaw, but so had Dad. Teamwork. A common goal. Respect and…

Crap, there was that *L* word again. Well, that was so not going to be considered, because it was out of the question. Whether it was real or not, she didn't want it, because love did not last. It screwed everything up.

"You could unpack some of that stuff, you know," Dan said, and she suddenly realized he hadn't disappeared into the bathroom. He was standing in the little hallway, watching her. "It's not like I don't have empty drawers sitting around."

"Dan…" No, she could not unpack that bag. It was her last line of defense against heartbreak. She had too much breaking things in her, too little wherewithal for heartbreak. This was the end of the line with them. As far as it could go.

She really hoped that hockey tryout swooped in and saved her from having to do the breaking herself.

"Let me guess," he said. "This is the part where you turn into the douchey guy who doesn't want me getting any ideas."

"Dan—"

"I've been that guy on occasion, so I think I know the signs."

"Dan—"

"Stop saying my name, unpack your damn bag, and get the pained look off your face. What are you so weirded out by? It's not like you can't pack up and go in a hurry if you want."

He stepped into the bathroom, effectively ending the conversation, which was good. Because if he had stayed, she might have been tempted to tell him there were a lot of things to be afraid of. Mainly that if she unpacked, even with her worry over Shaw, she might never want to leave.

Would that really be so bad?

It was a question she didn't know how to break down and answer. She could think of all the ways it would be terrible. Awful. Fights and abandonment and resentment and bitterness. She could picture it all as if it had already happened. All she had to do was conjure up a memory or two of her parents' raucous fights there toward the end.

Mom wanted more. Dad wanted exactly what he had. Secrets had been born and flourished into vines that choked everyone out. And, oh, could she see history repeating itself one way or another.

Because if she hadn't been able to fix it then, what in her now would be able to fix it if it happened with her as a participating party?

No, she had to keep that line of defense. So she left her bag packed. She went to the kitchen to make the coffee and to keep things going as they had been. All she had to do was keep everything as it was and…

Well, she had no idea what followed that, but she'd rather keep her head down and not think about it.

—◦◦◦—

Dan had learned a lot about himself since coming to Blue Valley over a month ago. Firstly, he liked llamas. Not that he'd ever considered his feelings on them one way or another, but now he knew. He liked working with them. They were kind of standoffish and weird at first, but it was all the more rewarding when they treated you with respect.

Maybe llama respect was crazy, but he didn't have to admit it to anyone. It could be his little secret.

So there was that, and then the surprise that hard work didn't necessarily mean forgetting everything else. Sometimes hard work gave him more than ample time to think about hockey, but it was a good kind of thinking. Effective. Decisive.

If Scott got him the tryout, that was great, but he wouldn't drop everything here. He would make sure everything was settled before he went back. He'd spend his summers here, and when the time came—if the time wasn't now—he'd retire here.

This was his present and it was his future, regardless of what opportunities arose. If no opportunities arose, here he was.

He looked around the stables. They were making sure everything was set for his herd delivery tomorrow. Tomorrow, he would have a whole group of llamas living here.

He grinned, couldn't help himself. He had built this, and he would sustain it.

He glanced at Mel, who was working to repair the hinge of the door from the stables to the enclosure. She was bent over, twisting a screwdriver around as she cursed under her breath. The sun from outside haloed her profile, and it reminded him of the third thing he was slowly inching his way toward learning about himself.

He was shitty at holding his tongue when he cared about somebody. With Mel not just working with him but living with him, trying to keep his mouth shut was a daily battle.

This morning had been more of a failure than a battle on all counts. Too much of himself was bleeding all over every moment. He should rein it in, pull back a little. Escape.

But he saw her there, flannel shirt pushed back to her elbows, a few strands of brown hair escaping her braid, and her face lined with sheer determination...and he didn't want to escape. He was drawn to that, to her, to this.

He wanted more. All of it. She had let part of that wall she kept herself hidden behind down, and he kept thinking that next thing would be enough, but she was still holding something back.

There were moments that were comfortable—far more comfortable than that night at the hockey rink, the way she'd said she cared about him as if he was wresting a criminal confession from her.

But the stronger he felt about this place, about what he could do here, the stronger he felt about his ability to make something with Mel. Which meant comfort wasn't what he was after.

He stood from where he'd been organizing the feed, suddenly filled with a kind of purpose. He wanted better than this strange limbo they'd found themselves in.

He wanted more.

Like you're not going to fuck up more.

His phone rang, *Scott* popping up on the caller ID. Dan cringed. He wasn't quite ready for a dose of his other life when he was becoming so good with this one.

But he'd made his decisions, right? Even if he left, he was coming back. Mel's gaze met his as he swiped his finger across the screen.

"Scott?" she called.

He nodded, holding the phone to his ear.

"Good luck," she said before turning back to her work with the gate.

"Sharpe," he answered, Mel's "good luck" ringing in his ears. Because he didn't know what she was wishing good luck for. Getting a tryout? Leaving?

"Hello?"

"Yeah, I'm here."

"You're breaking up."

Dan sighed and stepped out the back entrance of the barn to higher ground and better reception. "Better?"

He didn't answer that question. "I got you the tryout."

For some reason, he hadn't been expecting it to actually be the tryout. He'd expected more *I'm working on it*. But, hell, time was running out, wasn't it? "Tryout?"

"Phoenix. They agreed to take a look at you, man. I'm getting you a flight out tomorrow and the tryout will be Friday."

"Tomorrow?" Any excitement, any burst of adrenaline went cold. "Scott, that's not possible."

"Of course it is. Look, I know you might be a little rusty, but if we get you an early flight tomorrow, you've got all day to prepare."

"That's not the issue."

"Then what the hell is?"

"I have responsibilities here. I have…" Well, he wasn't going to tell Scott about the llamas being delivered tomorrow. "I have responsibilities and I need more than twenty-four-hours' notice."

"You're shitting me right now."

"No, I'm not."

"Dan, I don't know what's going on. I don't need to know. All I need is for you to be on a plane tomorrow morning, and be ready to try out on Friday. This is your shot. I'm not sure I can get you another one."

Dan looked around him. The way the sun blazed on the cabin, the stables, the mountains. Everything was bright and brilliant, too brilliant—too much. Overwhelming, and that wasn't going to change. This was always going to be a big place, bigger and older and steadier than him. Always.

But he wanted it. He needed it. He'd never felt a… *belonging* like this. He felt good on the ice, in control, successful, and that was its own kind of good feeling, but this was more. It would endure, it would be *his*, and for the first time, that didn't scare him—that actually made his place here feel exactly right.

"I can't do it, Scott. If you can't get me another tryout, that's on you. I need at least a week's notice. End of story."

"So you're quitting. You're running away to fucking Idaho?"

Quitting. Running away. *Sucking when it counts.*
"No, I'm not quitting." But he wasn't bending either.
He was after something. Something bigger than just
hockey or just the ranch. Something whole. "You get
me a tryout that gives me enough time to make arrangements and get a few good skates in, I'll take it."

"This is fucking crazy, Dan. You cannot say no."

"I just did." He hit End before Scott could argue with
him anymore. There was nothing to argue. He'd made
up his mind and he wouldn't falter. Not on this.

He stepped back in the barn to find Mel standing next
to Mystery. She gingerly reached out, and for possibly
the first time, Mystery didn't nip at her.

If he needed any more of a sign he'd made the right
choice, he could not for the life of him think of one.

"Making friends?"

She startled and Mystery must have taken her sudden
movement as antagonism because she spat right on
Mel's leg.

"Oh, you fu—"

"Hey, now."

Mel rolled her eyes at him. "So, what did Scott have
to say? Tryout a go?"

He wasn't sure why he hesitated. Maybe it was how
hopeful she sounded, like she wanted to get rid of him.
Maybe it was because he wanted to tell her the whole
thing. Not just saying no to the too-soon tryout, but the
enduring stuff. The making-this-work stuff.

He needed more time to work that out. And some
motherfucking ambience when he told her. Not llama
shit and hay, as much as he'd come to not be bothered
by those things.

"Not yet. Close." A lie was probably wrong, but he needed it for now.

She nodded. "Well, I'm glad it's getting close."

There it was again—hope that he'd leave. It shouldn't bug him, not when he knew she didn't think he'd stay, but… Well, whether it should or not, it bothered the hell out of him. "Why are you glad?"

"Why?" Her eyebrows drew together. "It's what you want, right? You should get what you want."

"And if I said I wanted here and you?" So much for ambience and lack of llama shit.

She froze, like an actual deer caught in headlights. He'd always thought that was just an expression, but her wide-eyed non-movement was exactly like that time he'd hit a deer in college.

And then, of all fucking things, her phone rang. She blinked, pulling the phone out of her pocket.

"Don't answer it."

She swallowed as she looked at the screen. "It's Caleb."

"Ignore it, Mel. We're having an important conversation."

She stared at him, then back down at her phone, and he held his breath, because he needed her to do this. To be willing to talk about this. To be willing to take a chance. On him. On them.

The phone went silent.

Chapter 21

MEL KEPT STARING AT THE PHONE, EVEN THOUGH IT had stopped ringing. *And if I said I wanted here and you?* Yeah, she'd actually much rather talk to her brother than deal with that question.

"Um, I need to call him back. Something could be wrong with Dad and—"

"Mel—"

Whatever he'd been about to say was drowned out by her ringer going off. Caleb again. "It's… It must be important. I have to answer it. It could be…"

"Mel, please."

But she couldn't listen to his "please." She couldn't. *I want you.* This was not what she had signed on for. Him wanting her and wanting this place and that glimmer in his eye like he might stay. No. That was not the deal.

The deal was he leave just like everyone else. And she'd make sure it happened. She would. Once she dealt with Caleb.

"Hello?"

"I need you to come home. Now."

She bristled at the sound of half demand, half desperation in her brother's voice. The twinge of guilt it created in her stomach. "Why? What's wrong?"

"I don't know how to explain this," Caleb said, his voice all creaky and weird. Really weird. "But I need you here. I don't know how to…" His voice broke and trailed off.

"How to what? What's wrong?" She gripped the phone tighter, and even though she could feel Dan behind her, she couldn't think about him and that stuff now. Something was seriously wrong at home, and Caleb needed her.

"There's someone here. I…I don't know what to do with her. I can't let Dad see…"

Mel could have sworn her heart stopped. For the longest, strangest second, she thought he might mean Mom. That she was back. "Who's there?" she asked in little more than a whisper.

"This girl. She says… She says she's our sister."

"Sister." She was swamped by a whole myriad of feelings. There was relief it wasn't Mom, but there were other, more complicated emotions she couldn't wade through. They just sat there, along with the ones Dan had stirred up, a big uncomfortable lump in her gut. "A sister. What, like Mom had other kids? Well, that's not surprising, I guess."

"No, Mel, I mean, she is Mom's but… She says Dad's her father too."

"That can't be." Even though Caleb couldn't see her, she shook her head, because that was ludicrous. How could they have a sibling they didn't know about? "What is this? What is she asking for? Why is she here?" They certainly didn't have anything to give.

"I don't know. I need you to come home. I need your help. She…she's twenty-one. She could be…she *could* be Dad's. What do I do about Dad?"

Mel inhaled sharply. If she knew the answer to that

question, would she be here? But this was new and big and…a sister. It couldn't be.

Twenty-one.

Twenty-one years since Mom had jumped ship. A twenty-one-year-old sister. It really couldn't be possible. This was some kind of mix-up.

"She looks…" His voice lowered, his breath an audible inhale and exhale over the line. "Mel, she looks just like you."

"I'm on my way," she managed. There were some things you could ignore. She didn't look back at Dan, but she could feel him. Whether he liked it or not, she could ignore him. She had to. To survive whatever the hell was happening at home, she needed to ignore him completely.

"I have to go."

"What's wrong?"

"It's complicated." She slid the phone into her pocket, still not turning to face him. She was afraid she'd break if she looked at him and he was being all nice-guy Dan. *What if I wanted here and you?*

Yeah, she didn't have it in her right now to deal with that. She didn't have it in her *ever* to deal with that. So she started walking away. Just keep pushing forward until something works out, right?

And if it never does?

"Okay, it's complicated," he said, following her. "Explain it to me."

"I don't have time."

"Then tell me on the way."

She stopped and turned to him, though she kept her gaze off of him, guarded. "On the way? No." She shook her head and mustered her best no-nonsense tone. "I'm going."

"And I'm going with you."

She waved him off, stomping for the truck. "You have work to do. A ranch to take care of. You can't run away." It was mean of her, but she wanted her words to hit hard enough he'd stop. Anything to make him stop, stop pushing, stop being there, stop…all of it.

He didn't.

"I'm coming with you."

"I don't want you."

"Not what you said last night, sweetheart." She supposed it was an attempt at a joke, but it was too steely. It was too right.

She wanted him, or she wouldn't be here against every rational thought in her brain. Since when was her heart stronger than her brain? When did she let that weakness grow?

Dan plucked her keys from her hand and hopped into the driver's seat of her truck. "You trust me to drive it, remember?" He jammed the key into the ignition, her still standing there staring at him, trying to…

Trying to…

She had no idea.

He took a deep breath, eyes on the dusty windshield. "You can trust me, period, Mel. You don't have to be afraid to need me. I am not going to hurt you. I am not going to let you down. I am going to make this work, and I am here for you. You're *shaking*, honey."

He said it so emphatically, so *sure*, her eyes pricked with tears. She had to rub her unfortunately shaking hands over her face, try to find some source of calm, of strength.

"Stop treating me like..." She didn't know how to finish it, and her voice broke anyway. She just knew he had to stop. He had to stop breaking her apart like this.

"Like what?" It was all gentle and sweet, and she wanted to punch something—him preferably. "Why do you think me offering to help is me hurting you? Whatever's going on with your family is your problem to handle, but that doesn't mean you can't lean on me. It doesn't mean I can't drive you, can't listen."

"I don't deserve any fucking help!" Oh, Jesus, she could not do this. Not now. Pour out all that gross, messed-up stuff inside of her. She had a problem to fix. A more important one than that.

"Why wouldn't you deserve it, honey? Look around you. Everything I've built here is because of you."

"Don't say that."

"Why the fuck not?"

"Because it's bullshit, that's why!" She did not have time for this. She had to get home. To Caleb and Dad and...a sister. They needed her, and she didn't have a choice.

She'd been telling herself she didn't have a choice since she could remember. For the first time in her life, it felt like a lie. She had every choice in the world. She'd left. She could never go back if she wanted to.

Not having a choice was one of those lies she'd told herself so often she'd believed it to be true, like Shaw being *her*.

"Get in the truck. One thing at a time, huh?"

Again with the treating her like she was fragile crap. Did she look fragile? Did she act fragile? She was a motherfucking brick capable of breaking anything.

"If it's them you want to be strong for, I get it. I do. But you don't have to be strong for me. I'm not going anywhere."

"Stop saying shit like that."

"No."

She could only stare at him. "What do you mean 'no'?"

He shrugged. "I'm going to keep saying shit like that till you believe it." He hopped out of the truck, and before she could punch him in the mouth, his mouth brushed hers. His hands grasped her shoulders. "It's going to be okay. No matter what you do or don't do. Everyone will find a way to pick up the pieces. You are not the anchor holding this all together. You're an equal piece like everyone else."

It made no sense, not one ounce of it, but the kiss, the words, bolstered all her flagging strength. They slipped along the edges of all her cracks and helped seal them up.

"Now get in the truck. Tell me what happened. We'll go from there."

She stared at him for a few humming seconds, trying to figure out what had changed in those pretty green depths. When had everything flipped so he was the one who had it all together and she was the mess?

But she didn't have time to figure that out, because whether Dan thought she was the anchor or not, that's exactly what she had to make herself into.

She had to go re-anchor them all. Maybe if she did that, she'd be able to find the old Mel who could handle this. Who knew what to do. Who wasn't bolstered or strengthened by a man's words or kisses.

Who wasn't precariously close to love and all the ruin that came with it.

He had no idea what he was doing, but Dan was pretty sure Mel didn't either.

She was even holding on to his hand like it offered some kind of comfort. A comfort she would actually accept.

He drove up the long, winding drive to the Shaw place, and though there were parts of him that regretted his decision to drive her, to try and be the good, stand-up guy, he wasn't backing down. He wasn't choking. Not when it came to her.

She was so afraid to let her weakness show, and it hurt to watch. She'd buried her emotions in a no-nonsense strength; he'd left his behind. It seemed like opposites, but in the end they were doing the same thing. He was just clawing his way back to some kind of normal and hoping she'd meet him halfway.

So, hopefully, this was right. He was giving her what he would want. Someone to trust with the hurt, the uncertainty. No one shutting anyone out. No one was walking away. He would be here, the rock she needed even if she couldn't admit that need.

As he pulled next to the detached garage, a big... thing came into view. Not quite an RV, not quite *not* an RV. It reminded him of those things the pioneers had supposedly used to go westward in—a covered-wagon thing, only made of wood fixed onto a truck front. Like nothing he'd ever seen.

Dan slowly pulled the car to a stop. He wished he knew something to say, but what could you say to a woman who was finding out she had a long-lost sister? He wasn't sure there was protocol for that.

"I don't know what to do," she said in a whisper, so completely distraught and lost it hurt his heart.

"I'm not sure you're supposed to." Wasn't that a realization? That you didn't always have to know what to do or how to do it. That maybe it was do your best and hope it worked out, and maybe even keep trying if it didn't.

Damn.

Caleb stepped out from in front of the caravan, then a swirl of color moved to stand next to him.

"Holy…"

"Shit," Mel finished before he could.

The woman looked almost exactly like Mel. A little younger, a lot more feminine in her long skirt and fringy top, jewelry dripping from all parts of her.

But the face, the hair—hell, it was even long and in a braid. They had the same sharp nose, the same lush mouth. It was downright eerie.

"I don't believe she's Dad's," Mel whispered. "How could she be?"

"I thought you said the timeline made it possible."

"Possible. But…" Caleb and the woman stood there, and Mel stared at them without making a move to get out of the truck. "How could she have left with her and not…"

Before he could register those words, the absolute pain and betrayal in them, Mel was pushing out of the truck, and he had to scramble to follow.

The relief in Caleb's eyes was short-lived once his gaze traveled from Mel to Dan. "What's *he* doing here?" Caleb demanded.

Dan would *love* to tell Caleb what he was doing here, and it was directly related to Caleb being a grade-A dick to Mel, but he doubted Mel would appreciate it, so he held his tongue.

Mel glanced back at him, but her gaze didn't connect.

Then she turned to face the woman, her face perfectly chiseled control. Painful control. "I'm Mel Shaw." She stuck her hand out to the mirror image of her.

So strong, so determined—how could she ever think she was weak or didn't deserve help? This one-woman wrecking crew, and she didn't even see herself. Not really.

"I'm Summer," the woman said, and for all their physical similarities, at least their voices were nothing alike. Mel's all tough and sharp, Summer's lilting, almost Southern. "Summer Shaw."

Mel twitched a little at the last name, and her hand dropped to her side. "Shaw."

"It seems that comes as a shock," Summer said, and anyone could tell that despite the way she spoke all easy and light, she was not a woman totally at ease or in control.

The direct opposite of Mel.

"I'm sure you can understand our confusion." Mel sounded the same way she did when she'd negotiated a lower price on the lumber for his llama fence. All business with a thin veneer of forced politeness.

It was uncomfortable in this situation. *He* was uncomfortable in this situation. Probably because he didn't *belong* in this situation. But here he was and here he'd stay for as long as necessary.

"Actually…" The young woman glanced at him, then back to Mel. "I don't understand. I thought…" Again her hazel eyes, so much like Mel's, landed on him. "I'm sorry. I'm a little confused myself. Who is that?"

All three pairs of Shaw eyes fell on him. Yeah, he was the odd man out.

"Dan is my...colleague."

"Oh, for fuck's sake," he muttered.

But Mel didn't backtrack or look embarrassed. She glowered. "He was just leaving."

Mel sure knew how to hit him where it hurt. Unexpectedly and out of the blue. Here he was, doing this uncomfortable thing. This thing he had no idea how to handle. He was facing up to all sorts of fears for her, and she wanted him gone.

For a second, he considered it. He even took a step toward the truck. She didn't want him there? Fine. Good, even. He didn't want to be here.

But he couldn't escape the truth laid out to him, the truth she'd given him the other night. She was afraid. Afraid of not knowing what to do, and maybe, just maybe, afraid of needing him and trusting him.

No, he wouldn't stand for that.

"Actually, I think I'll stay put."

Mel's face hardened, if that was possible, but in that hard, determined expression he saw exactly what he'd seen that night in the kitchen where she'd said his care was *nice*. Where she'd finally admitted she was afraid.

Where he had to skate away from his fear of dependence and feelings to deal, Mel had had to push through. She'd had to bury it all, and in doing that, she'd turned strength and determination into its own kind of escape.

He wouldn't fall for it anymore. He wouldn't leave unless he knew it was what she truly wanted, not just what she thought she had to want.

"Dan."

"If it helps, we're more than colleagues," he said to Summer.

"Dan." She grasped his arm, not kindly. It actually kind of hurt, not that he'd ever admit it. She steered him a few paces away from a confused Summer, a mutinous Caleb.

"Go."

"No."

"Why the hell not?"

"Because you need someone here who has your back. Even if this didn't involve your brother or father, I know it wouldn't be them. So it's going to be me."

She released him, pressing fingers to her eyes. "Please, don't…I can't…figure this out while I'm trying to figure you out."

"Look, fuck the colleague bullshit, we can deal with that later. I'm not asking you to figure me out. I'm standing behind you. Period."

"I don't…" Her hands dropped, clenched and unclenched. She looked at him, trying so desperately, he was sure, to hide the fear swirling in her eyes. She failed. "I don't know what to do with that," she said through gritted teeth, dropping her gaze to the ground.

"We can figure it out, honey. I'm not going anywhere." Not any damn where until he knew she would be okay. Hell, maybe not even then.

Chapter 22

I'M NOT GOING ANYWHERE.

Mel supposed it was meant to be comforting and supportive. It felt like a threat, however, him being there, seeing this, seeing her all…vulnerable.

Hadn't they had enough of this? Of him *being there*? What was she supposed to do with all this support? How was she supposed to focus on what needed to be focused on when someone was supporting her?

That weakened everything. Swept away all the strength and conviction and left only shaky, untrustworthy emotion.

Damn.

So she had to ignore it. Had to push him and his steadfast support somewhere else and focus. She turned back to the woman. God, she was barely a woman. She looked like a girl. She looked like *her* as a girl, if she'd ever deigned to play dress up.

She had no idea what to do with this woman. She still wasn't convinced she was Dad's, especially since it was so obvious she was Mom's. Mom could have sent her here. Mom could have…

Dan's hand pressed against the small of her back. Part of her wanted to shake it off, but in this moment, there was a bigger part that wanted to use that as something to hold her up, to keep her going forward. Someone else's warm hand and strong muscle to lean against while she did what she had to do.

"I'm a surprise. I get that," Summer said, looking at her caravan. "Believe me. But…I just wanted to find my family and see…"

"See what?" Mel asked in unison with Caleb, almost feeling sorry for the girl when she flinched.

"I don't know how to explain it. I only wanted to get away. I know you don't owe me anything. I'm not looking for anything." Again she looked at her bizarre vehicle. "Maybe a place to park for a few days, if you're going to send me away. And I'd like to meet…him, first."

"Where's our mother?" She didn't even want to know the answer to the question, but it felt necessary to ask.

Summer's expression was all conflicted pain, and Mel had to look away. This girl needed help and Mel didn't have it in her to help anyone else. Especially a twenty-one-year-old girl searching for some fairy-tale family.

They certainly weren't it.

"As far as I know, she's in California. She doesn't know I'm here. We left on…not great terms."

"Join the club," Caleb muttered.

"You can park on our property as long as you need," Mel said. She wasn't going to turn the girl away, but she did want this over. "As far as…our father…" She took a deep breath and focused on Dan's hand on her back, on the fact that he somehow still thought her strong and capable. "He was injured five years ago, and neither his physical nor emotional health are great. I'm not sure seeing you would be good for him."

Summer's shoulders slumped. Her voice was barely audible. "I see."

"He doesn't know about you."

Summer's gaze met hers, hazel eyes that felt like looking into some bizarre, warped mirror. Her not her. All the times she'd looked in a mirror and wondered what was so wrong with her, what drove everyone away.

"He doesn't," Mel reiterated. Because Dad couldn't possibly know about her and have never told them. Known about her and let her go. Known about her and... no. It wasn't possible.

"Mom claimed he did. That you all did." Her gaze dropped to the ground. "And were very clear you wanted nothing to do with me. With us."

Something in Mel's heart twisted. It wasn't just pity for this poor girl, it was something more like commiseration. "We had no idea, not one, that we had another sibling."

The girl blinked and, oh shit, a few tears fell on her pale cheeks. How could they look so much alike and yet look so different? It was like some sort of feminine, delicate, gauzy filter over herself, and it was fucking freaky.

Summer cleared her throat. "Sorry, it's been...a long few weeks, but yeah, I think I believe it was a surprise for you guys. Mom hasn't always been...honest. I knew I was dropping a bomb. I just... I guess I wanted to find my family, to see if it would be..."

She never finished her sentence. She used her fingers to wipe away tears, the bangles all over her arms tinkling in the quiet of the moment.

She pushed back all the loose strands of hair—the same color, probably even the same average texture, but somehow looking wavy and shiny and perfect on this...person.

Your sister.

Something in her chest kicked at that. There was no denying it. Sure, when she looked at Caleb there were pieces of herself if she looked hard enough. The sharp slant of their nose—though his was slightly crooked from having it broken a time or two—the way their eyes both crinkled into slits when they smiled in pictures.

But in most areas, Caleb had taken after Dad, blond and blue-eyed and sharp, and she had been her mother's. Except not at all. She was a Shaw. Looks be damned.

This poor girl with their last name and the mother they barely remembered and a father she'd never met. A *family.* A history, a place she'd never known.

All the things Mel had been running away from over the past week. It was the kind of reminder that thickened her blood with guilt, even knowing that Caleb and Dad had deserved it. Even knowing it had felt necessary to get out before she crushed to dust under it.

But that looked to be over now. This was not something she could run away from, this lost girl.

Your sister.

She wasn't sure she'd ever be able to truly accept that. Even if she couldn't dispute it, she couldn't just throw her arms around Summer Shaw and welcome her.

"Caleb, why don't you take her down to the old cabin? The clearing next to it will be a good place to park…that." She gestured at the strange vehicle. "Though if you don't mind mice, you're welcome to stay in the cabin."

"The caravan is fine. It's been my home for a while now."

Mel nodded. Perhaps she should treat this as more

than a business interaction, but she didn't know how, and it wasn't as if Caleb was saying anything.

"Do you need anything?" Mel asked.

Summer swallowed. "If you know of any places I might be able to get some work? I've done just about everything—singing and waitressing and answering phones. Before I left Sacramento, I was making and selling jewelry at local fairs and markets and doing pretty okay."

Making jewelry. Singing. Yeah, this girl did not belong at Shaw.

"Have you ever been like a nurse? Not a registered one or anything, just someone who helps—" Caleb began.

Mel stopped him. "Caleb, no." They couldn't bring her into that, even if Dad did know about her or wouldn't figure some kind of connection based on her looks. "I'll take you down. Do you have plumbing in that thing?"

"Oh. No."

"We'll turn the water back on in the cabin. If you want to sleep in your…thing, that's fine, but you'll have somewhere to shower and take care of things."

"That's really amazing. I'm so grateful. I—"

Mel held up a hand to stop the tide of gratitude. It made her feel… She didn't know. Some constricting in her chest and a prick of heat behind her eyes. Uncomfortable.

"Let's get you settled," she said roughly. Before Summer could say anything else, Mel looked pointedly at Dan. "You coming?"

"I'll wait here." He smiled, of all damn things. She glanced at Caleb. Oh, hell. Well, she didn't have time for that. If they wanted to have some idiot macho pissing match, so be it.

"Follow me." She had to force the next syllables out of her mouth. But she was pretty sure this girl deserved something, needed something, and Mel had a bad feeling she knew exactly what it was. Something she really didn't want to give.

Kindness. Welcome. Family.

But knowing how much those things could mean, she had to force the word out. "Summer." Sister. Her sister.

Yeah, she had no idea what to do with that.

———*w*———

Dan probably should have gone with Mel, but despite his determination to stand behind her and help her, he was also sure she needed a few minutes of silence to herself. To wrap her brain around what happened.

And, sure, he had a few things to say to Caleb, which were maybe none of his business, but he couldn't get past the idea that Mel needed someone willing to say something—say out loud that things here were not right. He couldn't imagine convincing her she didn't need to power through it, but that didn't mean he couldn't tell Caleb to get his shit together.

"So it doesn't bug you to pay my sister to have sex with you when she's desperate?" Caleb asked.

Dan didn't move from where he was leaning against the garage. He didn't move, period. Because if he didn't take a few minutes to breathe through the white-hot fury, he'd punch Caleb straight in the mouth.

Mel wouldn't want him to do that, and he was already doing something she wouldn't want him to do. So he took a few breaths and then mustered his best fuck-you smile. "Doesn't it bug you to be so completely useless she breaks under the pressure of carrying your worthless ass?"

Something flickered in Caleb's gaze, dark and violent, and Dan hoped to hell it was some kind of feeling for Mel. Because if he at least cared, there was hope.

He wanted Mel to have hope. "I care about your sister."

Caleb snorted. "Why the hell wouldn't you? I'd bet everything I have that she's ten times the woman than anyone you've ever come into contact with in Chicago. But care doesn't mean shit—you know why?"

"Enlighten me."

"Take a look at those mountains, this house, that fucking truck she's driving. They all belong here. Born here, made here, ground to fucking dust here. Tough. But, more, they've all got nowhere else to go. You've got somewhere to go."

"I see you're an expert on me. I had no idea you'd done so much research."

"I know exactly who you are. Rich and spoiled, and you don't give two shits about anything, or you wouldn't be under suspicion of being a cheating asshole. Maybe you'd stay for a while because it's new and different and you can throw money at any problem you've got. Build a life with *my* sister. Have a kid you barely pay attention to because she's not the image of the perfect baby girl who was in your head, another kid you sneer at like he's a bad seed because…well, hell, maybe he is. Then another you leave with that no one ever knows about."

"I think I have certain anatomy that would make that a kind of impossible."

"This a joke to you?"

"I'm not your mother. And I'm not responsible for

your mommy issues." He pushed off the garage, and though he hadn't been in a brawl in a few years, he relished the thought of one.

But he wouldn't, mainly because he had a feeling that's exactly what Caleb was looking for. Reason for a good fight. Well, he wouldn't be the joker who fell for that shit, especially when Mel wouldn't appreciate it. No matter how angry she might be at her brother, no matter what little Dan knew about sibling dynamics, he doubted he'd be hailed a hero if he bloodied Caleb's big mouth.

"Maybe the reason people leave is because you all go around acting like you're so tough and have it under control when it's obvious to the whole world you don't," Dan said.

"Maybe no one's strong enough to stick."

"Guess we'll see."

"You think I'll let you hurt her?"

"You've done a bang-up job on your own. Don't know why you'd care what anyone else does."

"She deserves better than you."

"Right back at you."

"This isn't about me. She's stuck with me. You're expendable. You should expend yourself away from this place."

"You're an asshole who could do better for your entire family, but you don't see me giving you any unwanted advice."

Caleb shoved hands through hair that looked shaggy and unruly, much like he did as a whole. Dan didn't remember him looking that way when he'd first met him. Sure, a little shaky, but not like a man beyond the edge of what he could handle.

He almost, *almost* felt sympathy for the guy. Caleb was almost a decade younger and had a hell of a lot more on his plate than Dan had ever imagined facing.

"I care very deeply about your sister." Very very deeply. A million verys. Or maybe just the *L* word he was still trying to decide if he could handle. If he could handle, survive, succeed at loving someone so bound and determined to shut him out. "I don't have any beef with you other than she's mad at you, so I'm mad by association. But whether you believe me or not, whether *she* believes me or not, I'm not going anywhere. Not permanently."

Caleb looked hard at where Mel's truck reappeared on the gravel drive. "That better be a promise you're ready to keep...asshole."

Though he muttered the insult, Dan both heard it and wasn't affected by it. If anything, he felt at least moderately better Caleb cared, no matter how poorly he showed it.

When Mel stepped out of the truck, he stepped toward her, because she looked like she needed it. At the same time, Caleb stepped back, as if he couldn't handle the utter confusion and hurt written all over Mel's face.

He wanted to call Caleb an asshole, but he'd been in Caleb's shoes before too. So, instead, he offered Mel what he could. Maybe he could be some kind of an example.

Who would have thought?

"Everything okay?" he asked.

"She's settled. For now." Mel rubbed her temples. "You need to get back." Before he could argue, she pressed on. "Herd of llamas. Friday morning. You need to head back and finish that to-do list. You can..." She trailed off and looked at Caleb, at the way he was all but shrinking into the porch. "You can pick me up at seven. I'll be ready to go home with you then."

Go home. With you. She'd probably never know what those words meant, but someday when they had a moment alone without all their issues crowding together, he'd tell her. And maybe tell her other things too.

"Please don't argue."

He shook his head and held up his hands. "Not making your life harder, remember?" He leaned in and brushed a kiss over her mouth, ignoring the way she didn't reciprocate. Mel had bigger fish to fry at the moment, and hopefully she'd fry Caleb into some action. "I'll be back at seven."

"Thank you."

"Anytime, honey." He offered his best charming smile and walked to her truck, even though it killed him a little bit to do it. Unfortunately, she needed family time, and for this portion, that didn't require him.

He climbed into her truck and looked at her one last time. She offered the tiniest of smiles, the most pathetic of waves, and he wanted to stay. He really did. But she turned to face her brother, and that was not his fight.

As much as he wanted to step in and take that for her.

Instead, he turned around in the drive and headed back to Blue Valley. The sturdiness and longevity no longer haunted him, no longer gave him the heebie-jeebies. It was all a little daunting, but not something he couldn't handle.

Even when his phone rang, his mouth was curved in a smile at that thought. "Sharpe."

"Dan."

At the sound of his father's voice, all that confidence shriveled up. It didn't die, exactly, but it shrunk and went skittering somewhere in the back of his rib cage.

"Scott called," Dad said tonelessly.

Well, shit. "And told you I declined the tryout invitation."

Dad sighed audibly, and Dad was not a sigher. "Yes, that is what he told me."

"My decision on that stands, Dad. I'm sorry if that disappoints you." It was somewhat shocking to realize that he was sorry, but not the guilt-laden, beat-himself-up sorry he would have been years ago. This was a little pang, and one he'd move on from relatively quickly.

Because it was the right fucking choice, and he was old enough and strong enough to know that. To believe it. That belief didn't shake at the sound of his father's voice. Not too much anyway.

"Dan, you know I hesitate to give you advice. I've always wanted you to make your own choices, but... This looks poorly on me. On you. It's throwing away everything you've worked for. If you can't handle the scrutiny, we can work with Scott and maybe a better publicist to—"

"It's not the scrutiny I can't take," he interrupted through gritted teeth. "Both Scott and you wanted me to get away for a bit."

"Yes, a bit. Not forever. Son, you can't give up on hockey right now. There is a team that will take you, and even if it's only for a year, it will erase a lot of the bad press. Then you can still get a job with another team. I can't hire you myself, of course, that'd look bad, but I can pull some strings and—"

"I was never meant for management." He had never had doubts about that, or an interest in changing that. "And since I can't play hockey forever, this…what I'm doing here is something important."

"You could coach. Scout. There are—"

"That's you, Dad. It was… I love that game, but it's different than the way you love it. If I can't play, I don't… Playing is all I ever wanted."

"You could still do that. For at least a year. I played until I was thirty-nine, and you haven't had nearly as many concussions as I have. Your mother and I—"

"Whoa, whoa, whoa, what? Mom and you? You've been in contact?" Dan had to stop the truck, so he pulled into a spot in front of Georgia's.

"We've exchanged a few emails and a phone call in the past few weeks."

Dan blinked at the steering wheel. No contact for years. He or someone who worked for Dad had always, *always* been the intermediary once their divorce had been final. "After twenty-some years of no contact whatsoever."

Dad sighed. "We're worried about you, Dan. For all of the issues your mother and I have, you were always our number one priority."

Well, his mental health, anyway, which he supposed counted.

"Both of us think this ranch idea has gone from… harmless to concerning. Scott's call has me even more concerned. I've reached out to some friends at Phoenix. They should be giving you the week's notice you asked for, and I hope you'll accept that generous offer."

Perhaps if he was eighteen again, he'd feel like he had to do what Dad said. That it was imperative to do whatever his parents asked of him, as long as it involved hockey. Hockey had become the one passion the three of them shared, the glue that held his fragile mess of a mind together.

Shouldn't they be happy he didn't need it anymore?

"I'm happy here. I'm building something here. On my own. Well, mostly on my own. Partially, anyway."

"So it's a woman!" Dad almost sounded relieved, as if he'd solved the mystery of the crazy son and his crazy llama ranch. "Well, that's another story. Is it serious?"

Dan hesitated to answer, not because he didn't know the answer, but because he thought it might undercut Dad's understanding of his reasoning. Mel might be his reason for some things, but not everything. "It's…unrelated."

"Unrelated." Dad sounded puzzled. "You're not easing any of my worries, Son. Are you sure this isn't…"

"Isn't what? Mental breakdown again? Yeah, I'm pretty damn sure. For one, I'm not five. For two, I'm not uncontrollably crying or causing trouble, and I sure as hell don't have night terrors anymore. I'm a grown-ass man."

"I'm not trying to upset you."

Dan wanted to laugh, but he rested his forehead on the steering wheel of Mel's truck instead. "No, heaven forbid we upset each other."

"Come home, Son. Go to the tryout, come home, and we'll talk this all through."

"Talk it all through or skate till we collapse?"

Dad was silent, and Dan straightened. "How about this. You come out here. Mom too. See what I've built. See me here." Meet Mel maybe. "There is nothing you have to worry about. I'm not breaking. I'm not broken, and if anything…I *am* home."

"If I agreed to that, would you take the tryout?"

"No, Dad, this isn't a barter. It's an invitation. You're free to take it or leave it, but it doesn't change my plans. It doesn't change me." The words bubbled out of him all in an excited burst. Because they weren't just words. They weren't just anger.

They were the truth.

"Let me know what you decide, but right now, I need to go." He clicked End on his phone, looked at Georgia's diner, and decided he could really go for a double bacon cheeseburger, calories be damned.

Chapter 23

MEL DIDN'T LOOK DIRECTLY AT CALEB. NOT AT FIRST. She needed a moment. She needed more than a moment. She needed a whole lifetime to wrap her head around this.

"What are we going to do about her?" Caleb asked.

She wished she had any clue. Any glimmer of an idea, but she was blank. Completely and utterly blank, and all the bravado in the world didn't change the fact that she did not know how to handle this.

So she was honest, and it was a strange jolt to realize her honest moments with Caleb were few and far between. "I don't know."

His eyebrows drew together and he stepped gingerly toward her. "What do you mean you don't know?"

"I mean I don't have a fucking clue what we're supposed to do." Her tone was more vicious than was fair, but she couldn't find it in her to care, to rein it in, to promise anyone it would be fine.

This wasn't fine.

"He couldn't possibly know about her," she added. Of all her fears and confusion, that was the one piece that made her feel a little ill. Dad. Knowing. All this time. It wasn't possible. "There's no way Dad knew."

"That girl all but said Mom's a liar."

Mel looked back to where she'd taken Summer, to get her out of the way, to avoid the very off chance Dad looked out the window for once, saw anything, asked questions.

Yeah, that's the reason you're hiding her away.

Mel swallowed down the queasy wave that kept threatening to escape her stomach. Summer had looked so lost. Even more lost than Mel felt. Like she had nowhere to go, and at the very least Mel always had somewhere to go.

"She thinks we knew and didn't care," Mel forced out, her throat tight and words scratchy. "Why would M…" She couldn't say *Mom*, couldn't force her mouth to make those words. "What's the purpose of all this?" Was that the hardest part? Not understanding? Or was it a deeper hurt, a deeper cut she kept trying to ignore?

Throbbing, burning.

Why had she been left behind?

Of all the selfish, childish, foolish things to be focused on. Pointless to feel overlooked. As if she would have wanted to be taken away from Shaw, from Dad.

"Maybe she thought she'd give her a better life."

Every once in a while—though less and less as the years went on—she wondered if Caleb knew more than he let on. She hadn't had that sneaking suspicion in years, too buried under everything bigger than that one betrayal all those years ago.

But in those words, she swore, she *swore* Caleb knew something he'd never told her. "Then why not take us?"

Caleb shrugged, still not meeting her desperate gaze. His eyes were on the house, and the demons and shadows were all over his face.

The thing she missed, the thing she ignored. She wanted to sink into the earth until this all went away, possibly longer, but that was no more an option than it had been five years ago when the doctors had told her Dad was paralyzed.

"Caleb."

His blue eyes met hers then, a million troubles she'd never be able to name haunting that look. He held it only a second before he looked away again. "I think we have to tell Dad."

"How?"

He laughed brittlely. "Hell if I know."

That laugh had nothing on the hollowness she felt. The absolute lack of conviction or knowing what step to take. Which, really, was Dan's fault. *He'd* hollowed her out, made her all vulnerable. Scraped away her coping with all his *being-there* crap, which then made her incapable of being *her*.

Because all she wanted to be right now was far away. Well, not that far, just across town, in a dilapidated cabin much like this one. Surrounded by damn llamas. And one ridiculously painful mistake.

"I'm sorry."

Caleb's words were so unexpected, she couldn't make sense of them. Sorry. *Sorry.* All pained expression, all sincerity.

What on earth?

He cleared his throat. "I know I dropped the ball. I know I'm not what you need. I know it, and I'm sorry. I really am. Please stop punishing me for it."

"How am I punishing you?"

"Leaving? You don't think that's punishment? You're the only thing that keeps this place going, together. You're the only one with any drive, with any hope it can get better. And more…"

There was a part of her that wanted to stop this. To walk away before he gathered whatever words he wanted to use against her, but she also saw this for what it was. An attempt at bridging the gap that had dug deep between them, and she loved him too much to walk away from that.

Even if it hurt.

That scared her more than anything, because if she loved Dan, and she didn't want to walk away when it hurt, good God, what would she have left of herself?

"Mel, you made it seem…maybe not easy, but possible. All the things you did, all the sacrifices you made. You made it look like it was this thing people can do, and then I had to step in your shoes, and I was not prepared. That's on me, I get it, but I was not prepared for the weight you held on your shoulders. I had no fucking clue."

She wanted to blame him. To say he was at fault, but in those words, the lost way he spoke them, the disgust with himself and bafflement with her, she knew this was actually mostly her fault. For taking it all on, for keeping the severity of what they were dealing with and the lack of hope she felt on a daily basis hidden so deep even she didn't always see it.

"Come home." Caleb stepped toward her. He even jerked the hat off his head, grasping it hard between his fingers. "Please, Mel."

"We need the money," she choked out.

"That's not why you're there." He took another step toward her. "Keep doing the work he needs from you, but the rest of the time, we need you here. I need you to show me how you do it. Really. Without the *we've got it covered* act. Maybe then…"

"I'm so tired of working so damn hard, Caleb." She wasn't sure she managed to say it out loud, wasn't sure she managed to say it emphatic enough for him to hear. It was such a scary admission when you had no other choice.

But then his arms wound around her—the hug she was always hoping for and never getting—and, oh, damn it, she couldn't hold back the tears.

She had not cried in front of her brother since he'd sat in that hospital room, promising her he would change. She'd believed him then; it felt foolish to believe him now.

"I need you to step up when shit isn't hitting the fan, too, Caleb. You can't just wait until it's all falling apart."

"It's not falling apart," he said quietly, chin on the top of her head, offering a comfort she'd been wishing for and afraid to ask for for years. "We have a sister. Hell, if she can cook, we just hit the jackpot."

She couldn't believe he was making a joke, couldn't believe she was laughing through her tears, but, really, if Summer *could* cook… "We can't afford her."

"We don't have much of a choice, I'm thinking."

"No. We don't."

"Maybe…maybe this will be the thing that wakes Dad up."

Maybe it would be, and if it was anything else—a moment, a change, instead of a person—she'd be hoping so hard for that. But… "Why couldn't it have been us? Why aren't we ever enough?"

He didn't release her. She tried to step away, but Caleb gripped her harder. "Dad's stuff isn't about you."

"And it's about you?"

"Look." Finally he released his hold, only to go from

hugging her to grabbing her by the shoulders, looking her straight in the eye. "Maybe it won't be all right."

"Caleb."

"I'm trying to be honest here. I think maybe…we've been missing out on that, for a long time. So maybe things won't be perfectly okay. Maybe they keep being fucking hard, but if you promise not to run, and I promise not to drink, and we both promise that girl…she's a part of this if she wants to be…"

Mel waited, but he didn't say anything. Not for the longest time.

"I don't know if we can bring Dad back," he continued. "I don't know if we can save this ranch. But let's at least save ourselves."

"How do we do that?" Because of all the things she'd been trying to do most of her life, saving herself was not one of them. Not until she'd walked off of Shaw property and into Dan's cabin. So how on earth could coming back be the answer?

"I don't know," Caleb said on an exhale, his hands falling off of her arms. He turned away, and it almost appeared as if he was shaking. His eyes were gleaming in a way she'd never seen from him.

Absolutely determined. Absolutely all in. "I think the first step," he said, straightening, "is admitting we need to."

Mel turned away, taking a step away from the garage, away from the house, to where she could see the mountains, the field where their meager herd of cattle grazed. She'd once thought this place was her heart, and then she'd been convinced it wasn't.

Now, she didn't have a clue which version of her was

right. Maybe neither. Maybe there was some answer she was missing, and maybe…admitting was the only way to find it.

"I need saving," she said quietly.

Caleb's hand clamped on her shoulder, squeezed. "You'll come home?"

She took a deep breath of Shaw air, felt her feet sink into Shaw ground. "I'll come back." Home was something she was still figuring out.

Dan sat at his kitchen table, going through his notes, trying to ignore the message on his phone. He still had an hour before he was supposed to go pick up Mel. An hour to dwell and stew in this beautiful summer evening.

He'd thrown all the windows and doors open, attempted to put some lame-ass chicken dish in the oven, tried to make the whole thing homey and inviting and happy, because Lord knew Mel would need that. Hopefully be comforted by it.

He wanted to be, but the voice mail on his phone was looming over him.

"Oh, for fuck's sake," he muttered, poking the screen with more force than necessary to bring up the voice mail.

"All right, Sharpe." Scott's voice rang out into the quiet evening. "I talked with Phoenix and your father talked with Phoenix and you've been given a reprieve. Two weeks from tomorrow. Get in fighting shape. I got you what you wanted, so you better not fucking back out now."

Dan let out a breath. He hadn't promised Scott shit,

and he'd *just* spent a lot of breath telling Caleb he wasn't going anywhere. He hated that suddenly, after that talk with Dad, after an afternoon alone, he felt the itch.

The hockey itch. Skates, cold air, control. He pushed away from the table, scattered with llama books and Mel's notes and his damn phone. The smell of chicken that had about a ten percent chance of turning out.

But the funny thing about the itch, the dissatisfaction, the little niggle of worry and guilt, was it melted away when he stepped out onto the porch. It really did. It wasn't even just escaping, it was breathing in the mountains and realizing this was what he chose.

It was a good choice, and even if the itch popped up now and again, he'd only have to look around to remember that it paled in comparison. That it gave him a satisfaction that was only season-long, game-long, and then he'd have to go back to his loft in Chicago and try to ignore all the ways he didn't add up.

Here, he added up. Here, he stood his ground. Here, he'd found himself, as cheesy as that sounded. This place made him something better, and he wasn't going to ignore that for a few twinges or Dad's reputation.

Dan stalked back inside and dialed Scott's number. Faintly he heard someone driving up the road, a car he didn't recognize. He'd deal with that after.

"You had better be calling to accept," Scott said.

Dan looked away from the window and the stranger's truck and focused on the task at hand. Whoever was showing up at his doorstep would have to wait.

"I know that you and my father would like to see me play another season, and I'm sorry if I led you to believe I'd take a tryout. I only said I'd consider it."

Scott swore, a long and vicious streak of curse after curse, probably imagining money just falling into the toilet. But that wasn't Dan's problem, certainly not when Scott had other clients who made him plenty.

"You can't be this stupid."

"Stupid is as stupid does?"

More cursing, and Dan winced because, fair enough, joking was not the way to go here. "Scott, I'm sorry. I was mostly sure earlier—now I am entirely sure. I'm not coming back. I'm done."

"You're an idiot."

"So be it."

"You know this is it, right? Your last chance. You say no now, I wash my hands of you. No team will touch you."

"I don't want any teams. I don't want hockey. I'm done. I'm going to retire." The words didn't even fill him with dread. Sure, there was a little bittersweet ache, but it was the same ache he'd felt outgrowing anything. He was moving on to bigger and better, sad to leave hockey behind, but not bereft. Not less.

"To play farmer."

"Llama rancher, thank you very much," he said, even knowing joking wasn't going to ease Scott's anger. *He* thought it was rather humorous. Dan Sharpe. Llama rancher in Montana. He liked it.

The line went dead, and Dan couldn't feel bad about it. For starters, Scott was just pissed he was missing out on a paycheck, and Dan couldn't blame him. But he couldn't go play for another year or two just because a few people wanted him to for their own gains.

Dad would survive with a little familial blemish, whether he deserved that blemish or not, and Scott had other clients. He was leaving no one heartbroken or destitute.

The screen door creaked open and Dan turned, surprised, to face Mel.

"Hey, what's…" There was a look on her face he'd never seen, and even as he tried to figure out what it could mean, she let the screen door slam behind her.

"I hope I misheard," she said evenly.

Dan carefully placed the phone on the table, never breaking eye contact. Something was going to happen. He wasn't sure what, but it crackled in the air. "No, I doubt you did."

Pieces of her expression stitched together, and it made no sense to him that she was angry, but fury emanated off of her.

"Call him back immediately and take it back."

"Are you joking right now?"

"Are you?" she demanded, flinging her arms in the air. "You must be. You're throwing away your life. For what?"

He swallowed down the answer he wanted to give, the answer he wanted to shout. *You! I'm giving it all away because none of it compares to you and this.*

Because if he said those words, she'd be gone. He had to find some better way of saying it. Some way of proving himself that navigated all her anger and all the ways she didn't want to believe him. All that fear she kept buried so low she didn't know how to deal with it.

He had to play this right, not choke, because this place gave him the strength to do that. He just had to find the right words.

Where were they?

"You can't not try out," she bit out, each word punctuated with some kind of surety he didn't understand. What the hell was *she* so sure about? "You can't retire."

"Why not?"

"Because!" Again with the hands going up in the air. This should be a reaction for him leaving, not staying.

"What are you so pissed about? I weighed the options and I decided that I like it here better than I like the idea of trying to suck up my way back onto some skates for a year or two. I don't for the life of me understand what you have to be mad about."

"I-I'm not mad." She crossed her arms over her chest. "I'm frustrated with you for giving up on something you love. You…those aren't the options. Hockey and leaving is the *only* option."

Strike when afraid—he wasn't always quick on the uptake, but he saw it now. He escaped his feelings, and she fought them like they didn't exist. "Why do I get the feeling this isn't about me?"

"Of course it's about you! I saw you on the ice, Dan. I saw you skate with those kids and you glowed. I care about you too much to let you just throw that away."

"Well, maybe I fucking glow here too," he grumbled, hating the way she was using her feelings like a weapon.

"You don't."

"Well, so the hell what? This is where I want to be."

"You don't *mean* that."

"What is with you?" He wanted to shake her, and quite honestly, if he thought he could touch her without the *L* word slipping out and over everything, he probably would.

"I don't have the reserves for this, Dan." Weary. "Call Scott back up and take the tryout."

"You don't have the reserves for what? I'm not doing anything to you. I made a choice about my life." She didn't get to do that. Act like she couldn't handle it, say she cared about him and still wanted him gone. She couldn't have it all the ways she wanted, no matter what shit was going on with her family.

"My life is here now," he said. It wasn't the time or the place. It would blow up in his face, but like the time when he'd been a kid and hadn't been able to rein it in— all the emotion and confusion and hurt and love—it took over. It spewed out. So he touched her. He squeezed her shoulders, then cupped her face.

That beautiful, obnoxious face.

"My life is here. I am not giving up anything. I fell in love with this place, and I…" He knew better, every part of his brain was screaming at him to shut the fuck up, but his heart always won when he didn't run. "I fell in love with you."

She looked stricken, as if he'd slapped her across the face instead of admitted the depth of his feelings. "No, you didn't." Her voice was shaky, her head twisting back and forth in his hands as she pulled away. "You did not."

"I see you're set to be perfectly rational about this."

"I can't do this with you right now," she said, still shaking her head, still talking in something little more than a thready whisper. "I have…I have too much on my plate already."

"I wasn't planning on telling you right now, honey. I was saving it for a better time. Maybe a nice dinner, add a little candlelight."

"Candle… Are you crazy?"

"I think I may not be the one you should be asking that question to right now."

"Is it because you know if you try out, you'll choke? Is that it? You're afraid of screwing up hockey? Staying here isn't safe, and it isn't…sticking your ground. This is not your ground. You do not belong on this ground."

"You believe so little of yourself, that I couldn't possibly love you and want to be with you?"

"No, Dan, I believe that little in you."

Chapter 24

MEL COULDN'T CATCH HER BREATH. IT WAS ALL wrong. Everything she'd said since the moment she'd walked in. But she'd heard him talking about retirement and staying, and every piece of solid ground she thought she'd gained on the quiet drive over had disappeared.

No, it had gone up in flames.

He could not stay. Not now. He couldn't ask her for more when she had no more to give.

He'd swept into her life and made everything wrong. She'd run away from her family. She'd been left with only "I don't know what to do" as an answer when a real problem cropped up. Those things had never happened to her before he'd come into her life.

She hated it. She hated him. Yes, that was the feeling twisting up in her chest, around her heart, squeezing until she thought she wouldn't be able to breathe. Hate. All-consuming, heartbreaking hate.

Yeah.

Dan cleared his throat. "I think I'll pretend like *I* misheard *you* this time."

She shook her head. "You didn't." There was no mishearing. There was no going back. She'd said what she needed to say to end this, because ending it was the only way to survive if he actually thought he loved her.

Loved her.

No. She could not allow that.

"Then say it again. Look me in the eye and say it again."

She forced herself to look at him. She couldn't manage eye contact, but maybe if she focused on the dark slash of his angry eyebrows. "I don't—"

"You're not looking at me, Mel." There was a note she'd never heard in his voice. It was something beyond angry or irritated. It felt threatening, whatever it was. It sounded like bleeding, and she had to close her eyes against the thought that she was hurting him like that.

He'd hurt her first. He'd undermined everything she was, crumpled the life she'd always known, just by…just by standing by her. No, she couldn't take that another minute.

She had to do this. She had to get some control back over her life, and getting rid of Dan was the best way. Besides, she was saving him from failure. He wouldn't stay, and this way he could blame her instead of himself.

She ignored everything in the past few weeks that proved the opposite. The way he'd dealt with Mystery getting caught in the fence, the way he had built this place with only the very basics of her help. She *had* to ignore it; she couldn't believe he would stay.

If he did, what would happen? She'd love him and what? Always feel ineffectual and lost? Always run away and not know what to do? No, she had to go back. Back to when she'd been strong. She was saving herself, like Caleb had said they needed to do.

If it felt wrong, if it felt like sacrifice and hurt and cruelty, then that was just the nature of saving herself, she supposed.

Had to be.

"Come on, Mel. If you believe it, if you're so damn

convinced I don't deserve your faith, look me in the eye and tell me."

So she swallowed and forced her gaze to meet those green eyes, dark with the storm of whatever emotions she didn't want from him.

"I don't believe in you." It was similar to ripping off a Band-Aid—actually, a lot more similar to breaking her arm when she was ten. *Snap.* A moment of disbelief, and then a blast of pain. Once the pain hit, it was so over-powering she could say anything. Because nothing could match that initial searing stab. "I don't think you'll make it through the winter. I think you'll run away and leave someone else to clean up your mess. It won't be me."

She wanted to look away, to close her eyes. Well. Really, if she was talking about wanting, she wanted to rewind and tell him she loved him, but the easy thing had never been the right thing in her life. So she couldn't possibly give into it, give into him.

"Huh." His throat worked, but he said nothing else. He didn't need to say anything else—the hurt and pain was all over his face, and the only thing that kept her tears from falling was sheer force of will.

Which meant this was exactly right, because if her sheer force of will was back, then she'd done exactly what needed to be done.

"I'm going to get my things," she said, surprised that her voice was still cracked and shaky. Why should she be any of those things when she knew she was doing the right thing? She knew, she absolutely knew she was.

But her legs were weak as she walked to his room, as were her hands when she grabbed her bag that she'd only minimally unpacked in the past few days. Because this had always been temporary. He had always been temporary. The aching wound in her chest was just…just…disappointment she had to hurt him in the process.

But he'd thank her eventually. He would. He'd see she was right.

I fell in love with you. She could barely breathe through the pain of that. She couldn't think about that. The way his hands, calloused and rough, had held her face in place, like so many times before. The way he'd looked at her and said it as if it were true.

But it wasn't. It wasn't true. She blinked at the tears and grabbed what belongings she could immediately see and pretty much gave up on the rest. She had to get out. Get out before the feelings swamped her and she lost her sense of right. Lost herself.

She stepped out into the kitchen to find it empty and breathed a sigh of relief. She could leave without any more threats to herself.

But when she walked outside, he was on the porch, looking over at the llama stables, the mountains in the distance. For a blinding second of pain and fear, she saw something that was theirs.

But it wasn't. She had Shaw. Not this. Not him.

"Good-bye, Dan," she forced herself to say. Closure would be good. For both of them. Good-bye. And this was the end. The end.

"I won't play the Tyler role in this."

She stopped her quick strides to the stairs, to escape. She didn't want to look back at him, but she glimpsed him out of her peripheral vision: arms crossed over his chest, silhouetted by sun and mountains.

"Regardless of what you think, I'm not going anywhere. I won't run away from you." With every sentence, he took a step toward her, and she could feel his anger and his hurt like it was a living force pushing against her.

And with it came something else. Something he'd misplaced, because he couldn't love her. No one loved her so much she felt it. So this was…not that.

"I will be in this town, in Georgia's diner, in Felicity's store, and when I see you, it won't be a polite hello and a *how are you doing*. I'm not going to fade into the fucking background. You think I'll be like Tyler and give you space? Fuck no. Give up on life like your dad? Not me, Mel Shaw. You will see me in this town, season after season, year after year, and eventually you'll have to face the truth."

She didn't want to hear this. She *wouldn't*. But his words followed her all the way to Caleb's truck.

"You made a mistake. You were wrong. There will be no one to blame—not your family, not this town, not your damn bank account. There will be nothing and no one to blame but yourself."

She climbed into the driver's seat, shaking, the tears starting to fall, but it wasn't just hurt. She might not believe most of what came out of his mouth this evening, but she couldn't dispute that last sentence. Not even a little.

There will be nothing and no one to blame but yourself.

Truer words. She shoved the truck into reverse and peeled out of Dan's gravel drive, ignoring the fact that her truck was still there. It didn't matter.

No, she had no one to blame but herself, but at least

this was her choice and not something thrust upon her. At least it was really hers.

———

Dan hadn't gotten drunk last night, though that's exactly what he'd wanted to do. Instead, he'd made plans. Mostly llama plans, because fuck Mel's lack of faith, but also some hockey plans, because while he was mostly happy with what he'd told Dad and Scott, there'd been a niggling worry.

So he'd plotted and planned, and early this morning he'd called up Buck to help him out for the three days he'd be gone. He felt like shit when the llamas arrived, but even if he'd tried to sleep, he probably would have felt like shit.

He'd never been in love before, never felt loss like this. It was somewhat similar to his grandparents, except they still existed and loved him, when they remembered who he was. He didn't have to accept that they were gone yet. He could pretend all was all right by not visiting or calling. Just send messages through an email with Mom or a card on holidays and birthdays.

That was probably wrong, but he didn't know what else he could do. He took a deep breath and looked away from the new llamas getting settled in the pen, to the mountains, the fields, the cabin.

Maybe there was something he could do. Maybe it would mean nothing if Grandpa wasn't lucid, but...he could try.

Dan pulled out his phone and brought up the number to the nursing home in Florida. After talking with a nurse for a little bit, his grandfather's scratchy voice came through the receiver.

"Hello."

"Hey, Gramps. It's, um, me, Dan."

"Who?"

"Dan. Daniel, y-your grandson." He shouldn't have done this. Why was he purposefully putting himself through more pain? What was this supposed to prove?

"Daniel. Ruth, do you hear that? It's Daniel."

There was a way Grandpa sometimes talked, like he didn't remember but knew he was supposed to, so he pretended, and Dan couldn't get over that feeling now. The way he said *Daniel* like he was some long lost friend, not his grandson.

"How are you?" Grandpa asked politely, clearly having no idea who he was.

"I'm good. Okay. How are you and Grandma?"

"Oh, you know, they keep us all shoved into this room. Won't let me go see the horses. I know there are horses out there."

As nice of a place as it was, there were no horses near the nursing home, and Dan had to close his eyes and lean his forehead against the rough wood of the fence. It was the old part. Grandpa probably built it, and he and Mel had added onto it.

And they were both, for all intents and purposes, gone.

"How do you feel about llamas?"

"Llamas?"

Then Dan felt like a tool for confusing a man with dementia. "Never mind. Sorry. Really. I…" Dan tried to think of something, something that would matter, that would make this stupid phone call worth it.

He looked around him. "You know, I'm, um, in the mountains. Montana. It's, um, late morning and the sun is already really bright. Makes the mountains look like…glass almost."

"Drought?"

"We had some rain last week. It helped."

"That's good. I've missed the mountains for years," he said wistfully. "What else you got out there besides mountains?"

"Well, there's a cabin." A cabin Grandpa had been born in, raised children in, loved with everything he had. "It's small, and old, but I think it was well lived in."

It certainly put some perspective on the whole romantic heartbreak thing. Not that it alleviated the uncomfortable truth that Mel didn't want his love. Didn't trust it or believe in it. That the fence they built together was *not* a symbol. No, that still sucked, because in some half-cocked vision of his future, he'd wanted her there. Kids and all sorts of stupid, stupid shit.

Dan cleared his throat. One heartbreak at a time. "I just wanted to tell you…"

"You know, I know someone else named Daniel. He's going to fix up my place back in Montana, you know? A cabin just like that. That's right. He was going to spend the summer there. I think he'll love it though. He'll stay. He's a good boy. I knew him when he was young, but I don't think he's young anymore."

Even knowing Grandpa wouldn't understand, that he was too lost in some confusing, muffled place, Dan said it anyway. "I'm staying, Gramps. I love it. You're right."

"Maybe you'd like to talk to Ruth? I don't think my hearing aid is working quite right."

"Sure. Yeah. Sure." Dan cleared his throat again, trying to dislodge the tears—the happy and the broken-hearted kind. The words hurt as they healed, and broke as they fixed it all up. He didn't know what to do with it.

Except say "I love you," listen to Grandma talk about some neighbor she didn't like, and then say "I love you" to her too.

Then sit on the damn ground and cry like a damn baby because no one was there to see it.

But once he was done, wrung all the way out, feeling worse and somehow better at the same time, he got up and went to check on the llamas.

Chapter 25

MEL FIDDLED WITH THE END OF HER BRAID. SHE couldn't stop doing that, but having Summer in the Shaw kitchen filled her with a fidgety, itchy kind of dread.

They were going to tell Dad.

Summer pulled something out of the oven that smelled like heaven. For all the ways Mel didn't want her to exist, no matter how harsh that wish was, Summer had breathed a weird kind of fresh air into Shaw.

If it wasn't her youth and the way her jewelry jangled or the way she oohed and aahed over every horse, every chore, every inch of Shaw land and every scrap of attention Mel or Caleb threw her way, it was the fact that she could cook and clean in ways Caleb and Mel had never dreamed of.

They didn't have her in the big house very often yet, wanting to keep her out of Dad's sight. But tonight was the night. She'd been here four days. Mel couldn't admit to feeling sisterly toward her—that seemed fraught with a kind of emotion that was still too raw from everything with Dan—but she did cautiously, carefully, almost like Summer.

If only *feelings* didn't make her think of Dan and then have to deal with the sharp, stabbing pain of being without him. Shouldn't that be going away by now? At least turning dull instead of the sharpness that lingered, seemed to deepen every day. Wasn't heartbreak supposed to get better with time?

"Are you sure you didn't want to invite your boy-friend? I don't mind. I know it's uncomfortable family stuff, but if he's part of your life, I'm okay with it."

It was the third time Summer had asked, but the first time with Caleb in the room. Before, Mel had waved it away, not bothering to explain, but with Caleb there, she…well, she couldn't. Not without a *look*. "He's not my boyfriend."

Summer blinked up from the casserole she was cook-ing. "Oh, but…" She glanced at Caleb then smiled in the brilliant, ridiculously happy way she had that made no sense to Mel. "No worries!"

Mel didn't know what Caleb had done behind her to get Summer not to argue, but she appreciated it. She hadn't told Caleb exactly what happened, and he hadn't asked, but her being here every day was a pretty clear indication.

What was there to talk about?

"Should I go get Dad?" Caleb asked with more gentleness than Mel had heard from him in a long time.

Summer clasped her hands together and pulled her bottom lip between her teeth. She had no poker face, no guile, this girl Mel was somehow related to. It hurt to look at her sometimes, all that emotion just *there*, needing to be dealt with.

Reminding her of all the emotion inside of her she flat-out wasn't dealing with. Because there wasn't time for that.

That was your excuse last time. And the last.

Didn't that make it the right excuse?

"If you guys think this is the right time," Summer said. Even with her nerves written all over her face, she seemed…sure.

Maybe there was some Shaw in there after all.

"All right. I'll bring him in the dining room," Caleb said, disappearing into the hall. Whatever he felt about the whole situation was buried down deep beneath a veneer Mel couldn't breach, and she wondered if they'd made any progress at all.

But they were here, moving forward on the Summer issue, so maybe it was something. Enough of something anyway.

Summer continued to clasp and unclasp her hands, blinking steadily and breathing in short puffs.

"It'll be fine." Which was such a lie. How did Mel know it was going to be fine? "Even if he reacts badly or doesn't react at all, Caleb and I…are…here." Which was a lame promise, but Summer's whole face lit up like it was some kind of offer of riches. "You don't have to be there when we tell him if you don't want," Mel continued.

"I want to be there," Summer said. "I'll never be able to believe if he knew or not if I don't see it."

Mel nodded, all the sick nerves falling over themselves in her stomach.

Summer spoke again. "Can I ask you a quick question though?"

"Sure."

"That guy from the other day…*was* he your boyfriend and something happened, or was he really just your colleague or whatever?"

Mel turned away, hating both answers. They were both wrong and terrible and she hated this feeling. Hate, hate, hate.

"It was nothing," Mel said, wanting this moment to be over. "Just a…thing."

Summer's warm, soft hand slid over hers, and Mel had to fight the urge to pull away. It was another part of the whole weird Summer package. She *touched* people. All the damn time. "I know we don't know each other very well just yet…" Summer began.

Just yet. Like she had every belief they would.

"But if you want to talk about it," she continued, "I'm a good listener." She smiled brightly. "I know you probably have friends and stuff, but—"

"Thanks, I…appreciate the offer, but I'm fine."

"I don't know how you're so strong, Mel. I feel like I'm falling apart every day."

Mel didn't know why her eyes pricked with tears or why she suddenly wanted Summer's hand to stay exactly where it was. Or maybe she did know why. Because wasn't that exactly what she felt? Falling apart. She'd finally found a place where her whole life hadn't felt like that, and she'd been so afraid it wouldn't last, it wasn't real, she'd pushed it away.

You had to. You had to.

Why did that voice in her head sound so desperate?

"You guys ready?" Caleb stood in the doorway between the kitchen and the dining room. He offered a smile for Summer, but it was all frayed at the edges, as jerky as Mel's fiddling and Summer's hand clasping.

"Oh, for fuck's sake, we'll never be ready for this," Mel muttered. And again, admitting that was like that moment in Dan's cabin when she'd said the horrible thing and everything after it was easy. Except those weren't so much painful as they were…freeing. "It's awful and painful and I wish I could just run in the opposite direction."

"I am dreaming about a bottle of Jack Daniel's," Caleb said in a scratchy, grumbly voice.

Summer's laugh was something more like a hysterical giggle. "I want to go home. Only...I don't have one."

She realized Summer was still clutching her hand, so Mel swallowed and held out her free hand for Caleb. It took him a minute, but he finally took the steps necessary and clasped Mel's hand. Then with a throat-clearing sound, offered his other hand to Summer.

They made a circle, the three of them, and Mel knew it was important to make this mean something, no matter what happened when they told Dad. She couldn't control Dad's reaction, she couldn't make the past what she wanted it to be—dear Lord, wasn't *that* a realization—but maybe if the three of them could be honest with each other, they'd somehow resemble some kind of normal sibling relationship.

"This is awful. But, that's not on us." Mel took a slow, deep breath and let it out. "Maybe...somehow we can make it less awful."

"You guys already have. Really." Summer's hand squeezed Mel's. "This is more than I...well, not more than I fantasized, because I fantasized you guys were like royalty and had a spa and stuff, but this is way better than any of my *realistic* fantasies."

"This girl," Caleb said, shaking his head. "Where did she come from?"

They all seemed to look toward the entry to the dining room, where Dad apparently was. Time to face the music.

Dad was parked at the table, somehow managing to look surly and blank at the same time. Mel went first,

Caleb almost next to her, their shoulders nearly pressing together, a human shield.

Shielding their little sister. *Sister*—still a term she wasn't used to, but it was becoming easier to think. It was pretty damn obvious this girl needed some sheltering.

"Dad, we have someone we want you to talk to."

"If this is about the nurse thing, I called up Fiona myself today and did the apology bullshit, and she agreed to come back," he said, not looking at them, his gaze completely focused on the rich wood of the table.

It was a surprise, that was for certain, enough of one that she and Caleb stopped and exchanged a glance.

"*You* called her?"

"Yeah. So?"

"So." Caleb shook his head. "That is something. What we have to talk to you about is something too. Something important."

"We want you to meet someone," Mel said, sounding far more firm and in control than she felt. But she and Caleb parted, and Summer stepped in to be shoulder to shoulder with them.

"Who is that?" Dad demanded, but it obviously took him a few seconds to really look, because he jolted a little, eyes going from Summer to Mel. His hands gripped the armrest of his wheelchair. "What is this?"

"Hi, um, my name is Summer. And…" She looked to Mel, biting her lip. Mel didn't do anything—what could she do? But in some bizarre twist of something, Summer seemed to take strength just from looking at her. "My mother is Linda Shaw, and she says you are my father."

Dad looked surprised, but there was no confusion, no denial in his expression, and that made Mel's stomach tighten and cramp. He couldn't have known. No, this had to be the poker face he'd learned so well.

He didn't say anything for the longest while, and Mel thought Summer and Caleb were holding their breaths just as she was. Silence stretched. Then he looked down at his lap and moved to wheel away.

Mel opened her mouth, but Summer grabbed her hand again. Held on to it for dear life. "Did you know about me?" she asked into the heavy silence.

Mel looked at her, shocked she'd blurted out the question like that. It hadn't been the plan, mainly because Summer said she'd never be able to ask him directly, that she'd chicken out.

But she was standing there, holding on to Mel's hand for dear life, and from the looks of it, Caleb's as well. Holding on to their strength and doing something that just hours before she'd claimed she couldn't.

There was probably a lesson in that, if Mel wanted to look for it, but Dad's answer interrupted any lessons. "Yes."

Summer's grasp loosened, but Mel held on. Held on because…well, she didn't know. For the first time in her life, holding on to someone seemed like the right thing to do, the thing that would get them through the other side.

Yeah, definitely a lesson.

"Dad, you need to explain this to us," Mel said, her voice far more authoritative than she felt.

He'd turned away from them, his wheelchair halfway out the other entrance toward the hallway to his room.

A sigh, silence, his body kind of slumped. "I knew your mother was pregnant when she left." He let that hang in the air. "What more do you want to know?"

"Why?" Caleb demanded, finding words Mel couldn't. "How? How could you have never told us? How could you have let that happen? How could you, when she…"

Dad glanced at Caleb, and the look they shared hinted at all kinds of deeper secrets. Dear God, what on earth was happening with her family? What *had* happened that she'd never known about?

"She told me she was leaving. That she couldn't stand being here for another second, and when I argued…" The first flicker of emotion crossed his profile, his hands tensing on his chair. There was a long pause before he finally spoke again, raspy and uneven. "She said she'd take Mel and disappear if I tried to stop her." Then he shrugged, all hints of emotion gone. "So I didn't."

Take Mel and disappear. Take *her* and disappear. Mel glanced at Caleb, the flicker of an emotion she'd seen many times and never understood on his face. She still didn't understand, but Mom only wanting to take *her* didn't make any sense. Surely Dad misspoke.

"But…that was over twenty years ago," Summer said, her voice small and wavery but there, ringing out. "You had all this time."

"To do what?"

"Find me. Be there for me."

"You had your mother."

"But I could have had this."

Dad looked around like he didn't understand what *this* meant, and Mel thought maybe he didn't. Maybe the paralysis had taken away all his love for this place, or maybe it had been gone long before, only she hadn't wanted to see it.

Or maybe, worst of all, he'd pushed away all the love and good because he was afraid it would break him. Because it had so many times before.

It was hard to breathe past that thought, because it struck a chord so deep it roused all the feeling she was trying to ignore. Push away. Forget.

All to end up like her father? No, no she didn't want that. She didn't want to be the one in a roomful of people begging for her love and pushing it away because it was too much, too hard, too scary.

She'd take that burning lance of pain every time someone left or disappointed her over this...not living. What was the point of being alive, so many years stretching before her, if none of it mattered? Not her family, not Shaw, not...

Love.

She loved Dan. Her heart ached for him. Even when she tried to push thoughts of him away, even when she tried to pretend he didn't exist, he was there. In her heart. She couldn't muscle through that or pretend it away. She just wasn't that strong, and for the first time in her life, she was glad she was weak.

"I did what I thought was right," Dad said, his tone flat and emotionless. "I'm sorry if that hurt you."

"That's...it?"

"I can't move my legs and I can't even take care of myself half the time. I am and have nothing. What else would you want from me?"

"A father."

Summer's answer repeated in Mel's head. It reminded her of all of the things she'd ignored and pushed away for five years. Ever since the accident, she'd just been so glad he was alive, so much so that she'd accepted the emptiness he'd become, because at least he wasn't dead.

It wasn't enough anymore, and being afraid of saying that, of hurting him…it didn't matter anymore.

Better to break and fix than ignore, or lie, or pretend.

"I would like that too," she said, squeezing Summer's hand.

"Same for me," Caleb said.

The three of them, standing in a line, holding hands and asking for their father back. It was like nothing that had ever happened to her, and the hope hurt as much as it lightened the heavy load she'd been carrying.

"He's gone," Dad said, and their breaths seemed to collectively whoosh out as Dad wheeled out of the room.

There was no denying the sting of hurt and betrayal and abandonment, but they had *asked*, and Mel wanted to believe that it was the first step. That they would try again and receive a different answer.

Believing that was so much better than accepting the crap as it was.

"I'm sorry it didn't turn out better," Caleb said, still staring at where Dad had left.

"Me too," Summer returned weakly. "But, it could have been worse."

"We'll keep trying," Mel said firmly.

Summer and Caleb looked at her, and for the first time she saw the resemblance. Something about the way their eyebrows raised to practically the tops of their heads when they were surprised.

"He's still in there," she added. "The man he used to be. He just has to stop being so afraid. We should keep trying, I think. Not right now, but…we should. Don't you think?"

Summer's surprise morphed into a smile, and she flung her arms around Mel's neck. "Yes, I think so," she whispered, squeezing Mel tight.

Mel awkwardly patted her back, offering Caleb a "what am I supposed to do?" look, but he just shrugged, and if she wasn't totally off base, his mouth curled up at the corner just a little bit.

"Let's eat," Summer said, finally releasing Mel. Of course then it was Caleb's turn to awkwardly pat her back when she gave him a hug. "Emotional heartbreak makes me hungry."

She jangled off to the kitchen, and Mel and Caleb stood there, looking at each other.

"You're right," Caleb offered.

"I know."

This time Caleb really did smile. "That mean you're going to go make up with that asshole hockey player?"

Mel pressed a hand to her stomach. *Dan*. Just the mention of him hurt in places that couldn't be reached, couldn't be soothed. Not by anyone but him.

But she had said some truly horrible things in her attempt to push him away. How did she face those? How did he forgive those? She might not be strong enough to deny her love for him, but was it too late? "I don't know."

"For what it's worth"—he shoved a hand through his rumpled hair—"you probably should."

Mel swallowed. "That'll probably be met with the same reaction Dad just gave us."

Caleb shrugged. "You're the one who said we should keep trying."

Right. Keep trying. Because the hope was better than defeat. Because…life with Dan hadn't broken her. It hadn't made everything hard. It had opened her eyes. It had cracked her open, so maybe she could heal instead of soldier on.

Because of him. His strength, his support, his *love*. She'd been cruel, and it hurt that she'd allowed fear the power to make her cruel. But she was still strong. She was still Mel Shaw.

And she was in love. If Dan didn't forgive her the first time, maybe she'd just…keep trying.

Chicago was no longer home. Dan felt it the minute he stepped off the plane. It dug in during his meeting with Scott, as he walked around his apartment, trying to figure out what he needed to do before he could call someone to pack it all up. As he tried to remember why he'd thought he needed three days here. In retrospect, he wished he'd flown in for the press conference and flown out.

This was not his home, and maybe it never had been. Llamas and mountains were home. *Mel was home*.

"Well, fuck that," he muttered. That was… He and Mel were… The word he needed was a word he was having trouble accepting.

Over.

Whether his brain wanted to accept it or not, it was one of those things beyond his control. He had laid his heart on the line, she didn't want it, and there wasn't anything he could do about it except accept it and not let it change the course of his life or the decisions he *could* control.

It was shit, and it did hurt, and maybe it would always hurt, but it wasn't reason enough to run away. If there was something to be taken away from that phone call with Grandpa, it was that hurt and happy sometimes kind of bled all over each other, and the good parts were worth it. Escape didn't change the hurt, but it sure as hell kept a lot of the good at bay too.

That phone call had killed him, but his grandpa thought Dan would stay. Someone believed that Dan Sharpe could be happy *there*. Even if Grandpa hadn't known who he was talking to, he'd…known.

Mel and Blue Valley had changed Dan. He'd grown into someone else, someone who didn't fit into his old life anymore, and that was worth the hurt.

It was all worth it.

If when someone knocked on his door his idiot brain fantasized it was Mel on the other side, it didn't matter. Because it turned out to be his parents. Together.

Surely that had to rank higher on a scale of weird than llamas.

"Mom. Dad. I didn't know you were both in town."

Mom smiled at Dad, but it was one of her pressed-lip smiles, kind of pained—a forced show of politeness. "We thought it might be good if the three of us were in the same place."

He moved out of the doorway so they could step inside. Any random thoughts that perhaps his parents had gotten over their unease with each other disappeared when they immediately separated. Dad going to one side, Mom to the other.

"Daniel…"

"We wanted to talk to you."

Dan took a breath, let it out. He supposed he was about to get double-teamed on the "we're worried about you" talk. At some point he was going to have to accept that neither of them would probably ever understand this.

He plopped on his couch and flashed an old-Dan smile. "Is this where you tell me there's a psychiatrist waiting for me downstairs to talk me out of my cowboy delusions?" He looked at both of them. "A good rancher has to be a little crazy, guys."

"We don't think you're crazy," Mom said, clutching her purse, the pained look softening into something more like hurt.

That was enough for Dan to realize he was handling this all wrong. Pretending it didn't matter, acting like it was a joke. No, that's not what had gotten him this far.

"Look." He pressed his palms together then stood. "Retiring is not a decision I came to lightly. And the llama-ranch thing, I'm sure it seems a little strange on the surface, but there are reasons, and they're both good ones in general and good financial ones as well."

He looked from his mother's still-concerned face to his father's surprised one. "This is not a whim, it's not a joke. It's not even running away from an unpleasant situation. It's something I can see doing for a very long time, and I don't see much point trying to ingratiate myself back into hockey just to prove a point or to help Dad or Scott's career. The thing is, when you find something that…that fits you like a glove, that feels right and like home, you don't let that thing go because it seems a little weird or isn't what you'd planned on."

Mom slid onto the very end of the couch, suddenly looking exhausted. "I think he just effectively undermined all our arguments, Gary," she murmured.

Gingerly, Dad took a seat on the opposite side. "I believe you're right."

Dan stood before them, shocked that was all it took. Just a little honesty. Of course, that hadn't worked with Mel…but he wasn't thinking about her right now.

Of course, his own words haunted him. *When you find something that feels right…you don't just let that thing go…*

Except *he* hadn't let it go. *She'd* walked away. Period. No wishy-washy crap allowed.

"Let me take you guys out to dinner," Dan said eventually. He'd much rather have a dinner with his parents than sit in this apartment, trying to figure out what parts of it would actually belong in his new life. "You can give me some press conference pointers."

Mom and Dad looked at each other, both grimacing a little bit, but they seemed to come to some silent agreement.

"All right," Mom said, getting back to her feet, purse still clutched to her stomach.

They had never been a demonstrative family. Not in all the time he could remember, so pulling Mom into a hug was awkward, but he did it. Because Mom certainly looked like she needed it.

She was stiff for a second before her arms came around him. "My, you have changed," she said quietly.

"It's for the better, I promise."

"Well, you were quite fine before, but if you're happy, then it is better." She kissed his cheek and released him, and it didn't matter that he didn't fit in this place anymore. He had that moment, and like the one with Grandpa on the phone, it would mean something for a very long time.

Chapter 26

MEL CLUTCHED HER KNEES, MAINLY IN AN ATTEMPT TO keep her palms from sweating. And her heart from leaping out of her chest, and her brain from zooming off into the horizon of so many bad outcomes.

"You look like you're going to throw up," Caleb offered, turning onto Dan's property.

Oh, shit, maybe she was. "You're not helping."

"If he doesn't immediately fall at your feet, he's the asshole I always knew he was."

"I messed this up. I really did. He was…" Sweet and perfect, and she'd been mean and awful. Why was she doing this?

Love. Right. She didn't want to live without the cocky bastard. She wanted him in her life. She wanted to help him with his problems and she wanted to wake up each morning, in his bed, in his life—no. *Their* life. She wanted to face every trouble together, holding hands and knowing they would find a way to make it to the other side.

Caleb shrugged. "So what?" He pulled his truck next to hers. She'd half expected it to be gone. That Dan would have gotten rid of it since she'd been too busy to come get it.

And by busy, she meant chickenshit.

Dan's Harley was nowhere to be seen. But Buck Haslow's truck was in the drive on the other side of hers, and something about that made Mel's stomach pitch. "He's not here."

"You gonna wait or come back later?"

Mel swallowed. Buck would only be here if... "I don't know."

Caleb gave her shoulder a little push. "Go. Wait. In fact, I don't want to see your face at Shaw until you've got this sorted. Your heartbreak is getting on my nerves."

"He might be...gone."

"Then he's an asshole and an idiot. And a fucker. And a whole other list of things. Go. Find out. You want me to come with you?"

"No. No. Go home. Summer might cry if you don't get her up on a horse today."

"That girl is going to cry either way. She cries at everything. Happy. Sad. Kittens."

Mel snorted. "She's a mess."

"But I think she might be good for us."

"I have no doubt, actually." Summer showing up felt more and more like serendipity than the catastrophe she'd initially figured it would be. Not that anything good was happening with Dad, but nothing worse than things already were.

In fact, not even worse, because over the past five years she'd slowly come to the conclusion that Dad had never really cared, or loved her nearly as deeply as she'd thought. If he could turn himself off like that because of his accident, then maybe she'd always imagined his affection.

But he'd let Mom walk away with his child because Mom had threatened to take *her*, and she couldn't deny that had to mean something. Couldn't get over the belief that it meant Dad *was* under the shell of a man he'd become. Somewhere.

And maybe they could find it.

But first things first.

"I'll be back as soon as I can," she said to Caleb, pushing the door open and hoping her legs held her up. Her legs felt weak. Everything felt weak.

"Take your time. I've got things covered." He readjusted his hat and made a wry face. "Promise this time."

"I believe you." And she did, which she wasn't sure she could have said a few weeks ago. Caleb had been right about needing to be honest.

Honesty. Trying again. Not shutting off everything in the hopes the pain would shut off too. That was a lot of stuff to change in such a short period of time. Heavy and intimidating, but laced with something she hadn't felt in so long.

Hope.

Laced with something she'd tried to convince herself didn't exist, or couldn't last. But she believed now.

Love did hurt. But it healed and it gave and it supported. It was there, a hand on her back when she was facing something she didn't know how to deal with. Strong arms around her when she broke down or a hand to hold on a starlit night.

On not-quite steady legs, she walked to the cabin. She'd take a peek in the window, maybe the door if it was unlocked, and see if her keys were in there. Then, if she didn't see anything, she'd search for Buck.

She felt like some kind of creepy Peeping Tom, peering into the window next to the door. Everything looked about the same, if dark. Llama books piled on the table, and her truck keys sitting on the counter exactly where she'd left them.

Well, at least he hadn't tossed them into the fields as she'd half expected.

"He's gone."

Mel jumped and turned to see Buck staring at her from below the porch. She swallowed. "Gone?"

"Yup. Chicago."

Even though she'd imagined it, the confirmation was painful. She leaned against the wall of the cabin, trying to stay upright. Trying not to cry. She'd ruined everything. *Everything*. Not just her chances with Dan, but this thing he'd been so excited about. All because she'd pretended not to believe in him to save her own stupid heart.

She slid into a crouch, idiot that she was. She would not cry in front of Buck, of all damn people, but all the strength had been knocked completely out of her. How did she fix *this*?

"He'll be back Wednesday."

"What?" The words made no sense in the midst of all her swirling thoughts.

"Wednesday. He'll be back Wednesday," Buck repeated, looking at her like she'd grown three heads. It was hard to blame him. "Had to go take care of things in Chicago for a few days or somethin'."

"Right. Sure. Yeah." Mel kept nodding, long past the moment she needed to. It took physically putting her hands on her face to stop, to get some semblance of reason back in gear.

Buck muttered something and walked back to the llamas, and Mel sat, trying to breathe through the remaining pangs of panic and heartbreak, and focus on the reality. He wasn't gone for good. If he was taking care of things in Chicago he was, in fact, probably making arrangements to come *back* for good.

Wednesday.

She could wait. She could. Or… No, she couldn't… She'd wait. It would be the sensible thing to wait for him to come back, and then she could lay out her apologies. Her own…love crap.

Or…

Mel stumbled to her feet, swallowing down the jittery flips her stomach seemed to be doing. The idea was *not* sensible. Going to Chicago on a whim, without knowing if there'd be a flight or where he was…it was something she would never, ever do.

Which seemed like reason enough to do it, to prove… something. That she wasn't afraid.

No, that wasn't right. Because she *was* afraid. She was downright terrified, so it wasn't about proving she was strong or brave. It was about laying her heart at his feet because she simply could not wait.

She was really losing her marbles.

One of the llamas bleated, and she had to squeeze her eyes shut, because her first thought was that it was Mystery, and if she was starting to recognize llamas by their bleats…well, she'd *already* lost her marbles.

So…why not go for it?

~~~

Dan didn't mind the suit so much, but all the people were driving him nuts. He'd answered what felt like the same question about thirty times.

No, it's not about the cheating allegations.

Yes, I realize people will think that no matter what happens.

No, I don't care.

It was at least somewhat refreshing to find it was true. Sure, he'd love everyone to think his career was a grand and shining example of how to play the game, but even if he'd done everything right, that was never going to be the case.

He'd just be happy if this official announcement took some of the heat off Dad. Few people had suggested he was an accomplice, but there was no doubt Dad had spent his summer being asked about his son's possible shady dealings. Dan preferred people ask Dad questions about actual hockey, about his actual job. If this took the heat off Dad a bit, so be it.

And if Dan had snuck a little line in there about hoping the NHL considered investigating someday so they could offer a formal apology, well, it was his say, and he got to say it.

The press conference was over, but there was still a room full of people to contend with. But he was ready to be done. Done with reporters, done with a few teammates who'd come to wish him well. Done with Mom's buzzing anxiety in the background.

He supposed that's why Dad had disappeared a few minutes ago. They had enough tension between them, Mom sighing and wringing her hands over the amount of people in the room was probably overwhelming.

"Mom, you can go now. It's over."

Mom managed a paltry smile. "I'm sorry. Is it any wonder your father and I got divorced? I never could stand all this attention."

"Well, it was hardly the only reason."

"Yes. There were a legion." She paused, moving to stand closer. "I'm sorry you ever thought you were one of them," she said quietly, her hand clasping around his arm—a little awkward, but an attempt nonetheless.

"Let's save that for another time."

"Of course, I just… Your father mentioned the possibility of a woman and I hated to think you might be… hesitant because of…things."

Dan thought his head couldn't hurt any more. "Believe it or not, I was not the hesitant party."

Mom's forehead furrowed in confusion. "Oh, how odd."

"I know I'm a rather charming SOB, Mom, but it's not that crazy someone wouldn't be head over heels for me."

"No, it's not that. It's just…" She nodded toward a space by the door. "I thought perhaps she was here to try to convince you."

Dan felt as though he'd just been checked headfirst into the plexiglass. Everything seemed fuzzy and not quite focused, muffled.

The woman Mom nodded toward was tall, brunette. Sharp nose, full mouth. Freckles on her nose and fear in her hazel eyes.

It took at least a minute for all the pieces to align themselves into sense. Probably because Mel being in Chicago was just out of the box enough to make zero sense, but she'd thrown in a dress.

An honest-to-God dress, but her hair was still in a braid, and she wasn't wearing heels. Her makeup wasn't any more jarring than it'd been that night she'd shown up at the cabin demanding sex.

Which he really needed to not think about right

now—except he couldn't think at all. How was she here, standing in a doorway of a Chicago media room, let alone why?

"I have to go," Dan managed, his voice rusty. But he didn't take his eyes off Mel, who was talking to Dad. Awkward discomfort came off her in waves.

Everything inside of him wanted to go over and sweep her away. Back to his apartment. Back to Blue Valley, anywhere where he could...

Yeah, none of that. *I don't believe in you.* He had to focus in on that moment, not the one when her hazel eyes met his across the room, so many emotions swirling under the nerves that he wasn't sure he could say where he was, let alone what day it was.

"Yes, I think that'd be a good idea. Your father will handle anyone else who wants to talk. And, I think we'll assume you'll be busy this evening."

He forced himself to look away from Mel, even though it was physically painful. But he trained his eyes on Mom. "I may not be."

Mom laughed, and he thought how odd it was he couldn't remember the last time she'd sounded so natural. She pushed him toward Mel and, well...

Maybe he would not be busy this evening, but that didn't mean he wasn't going to at least listen to her. She had come all this way.

All this way. What the hell was she doing?

She said something to Dad then stepped toward him. They met in the middle of the room, surrounded by all these people...people he barely cared about outside his parents.

And her.

"Hi," she offered, clutching a colorful purse that seemed so incongruent to Mel he didn't know what was happening. Was that even her? All meek-voiced and in that weird getup?

"That's quite an outfit." He'd wince at the asshole greeting if he didn't so clearly remember the last time he'd seen her. Running away.

"I...borrowed most of this from Summer," she said, waving awkwardly at herself. "Your Dad suggested I come here. I mean, Chicago was my idea, but when I talked to him about how to find you, he said here. That way you could...you know, ignore me if you didn't want to talk to me, and he'd give me a ride back to the airport."

"You talked to my dad?"

"I talked to a lot of people. It wasn't easy figuring out where you'd be and if I'd be able to see you."

He wasn't warmed by that. He wasn't affected by that at all. No, sir. "So. Why'd you do all that?"

Mel looked around the room, and there were a handful of people looking right back. Probably wondering who the strange woman talking to Dan Sharpe was.

"Let's get out of here," he muttered, taking her elbow and immediately regretting it. He wanted to curl his entire hand around her arm, feel the smooth muscle underneath, haul her to him and forget that past week had gotten so fucked up.

But that solved nothing. Certainly not her, and she was the one who needed solving. He'd been right and she'd been...

Scared.

Well, like he wasn't?

Still, he steered her out of the room, out of the

building, to the VIP parking lot and his rental car, if only because as soon as they got to his car, he wouldn't have to lead her. He could let go. Not that he was affected by simply touching her. Not that it made him desperate for her. Not in the least.

Breaking that connection was relief not…pain. The pain had been in her walking away.

"Get in," he instructed, sliding into the driver's seat. He waited almost a full minute, all but holding his breath, before she finally opened the passenger door and slid in. Her dress edged up her thighs.

"You know that's not fair."

"What?"

"Your legs."

She smoothed a hand over her skirt, looking somehow sheepish and pleased. "I…I didn't want to seem out of place."

"You are out of place." *I'm* out of place, he wanted to say, but he kept that in. "Why are you here, Mel?"

She took a deep breath, then shifted in her seat so she was facing him. "I'm here because I'm sorry. And I love you."

He wanted to laugh, because while he hadn't exactly expected her to spit in his face, such a straight answer was beyond him at the moment.

Sorry and I love you? Strangely, as much as he had wanted to hear her say it before, now that she was, it wasn't enough.

Chapter 27

MEL TRIED TO READ HIS EXPRESSION, BUT SHE DIDN'T know what she saw. She didn't know anything. She felt like some other person, and he seemed like some other person, and she didn't know what to *do*. Not beyond what she'd already said.

He didn't look at her, just stared out his windshield—at nothing but concrete and expensive cars. "You're sorry. And you love me."

She blew out a breath. She hadn't let herself imagine he would say *go to hell*, because she never would have been able to get on that plane, call a million people she didn't know, and navigate getting here. But she could see a million ways and reasons he would do that now.

Except she was here, and she had to keep trying. "Yes."

"Have you ever heard the phrase *too little, too late*?"

"Have you ever heard the phrase *better late than never*?" The quip was so unlike her, so like *him*, she surprised even herself, and was rewarded when his lips curled a fraction and he expelled a breath she was going to call a laugh. "It's never too late to fix a mistake. It might be too late for you to forgive me, but…"

"But what, Mel? Because if I remember correctly, you looked me straight in the eye and told me you didn't believe in me."

She squeezed her eyes shut. For as much as it hurt him, the reminder was a painful thing for her as well.

Without the panic supporting that decision, she could feel the ugliness of it. A gross betrayal of trust to lie like that. "I was scared."

"No shit, Sherlock," he muttered.

All the pretty speeches she'd memorized in the airport, on the airplane, in the cab, jumbled in her head. She didn't know how to be honest and open with snarky, angry Dan.

Then maybe you should have been open and honest when he was being all sweet and...loving.

Right. So it was her turn to be sweet and loving in the face of anger and hurt. Something akin to penance. She deserved this. She needed to find the courage to face it. So she pushed a hand to her stomach, took a deep breath, and just spoke whatever truths she could find.

"You don't belong here."

"You have a strange habit of following me around telling me I don't belong where I am. It's getting on my nerves, honey."

Honey. She would not cry at that. She'd hold on to it, though, deep in her heart, and always remember his reason for using that endearment. "I actually mean it this time. Because I'm not scared. Well, I am scared that you're going to tell me I really did mess this up irreparably, but I'm not scared of the truth. Or not scared of it enough to pretend it isn't there."

"Mel."

"You look perfect in that suit," she blurted. He opened his mouth to cut her off again, but she wouldn't let him. "But no matter how perfect you look, no matter how charmingly you smiled at all those idiots asking you those stupid questions when anyone can see you're telling the truth, you don't…it's not you. I've seen the way you light up with an idea, the way you smile after a hard day's work, how much you bizarrely enjoy those demon creatures. That ranch is a part of your soul, and it's where you belong."

"*I* know all that. Why are you telling me? If you thought I was leaving for good, you're an—"

"Buck told me you were coming back Wednesday. I'm saying all this because I want you to see how much of a lie it was when I said I don't believe in you. That saying you wouldn't stay was just reflexive panic because you staying threatened me. And I wouldn't have felt that panic if I actually believed you wouldn't stick. As much as my weird stuff is about, you know, people leaving and people not caring, it's possibly a little deeper than that."

"Possibly."

She was trying to be good and give him his space, wait for him to make the first move, but she found she couldn't keep going if she didn't touch him, even if it was just the scratchy sleeve of his suit. "I have gotten through rough things by pushing through, always moving forward and doing what had to be done. If I ever stopped to think, or reflect, or God forbid feel, I couldn't do that, you know? And then, we told Dad about Summer, and he knew. He knew about her the whole time, and he had his reasons and whatever, but then he walked away. He shut us all out and down, and I don't want to do that. I don't want to shut the good stuff out too because the bad stuff threatens my…ability to get through it."

"It took you this long to figure that out?"

"I'm an incredibly slow learner, if you haven't noticed."

"So you don't want to be your father, shutting everyone out. That doesn't mean you love me, Mel."

Possibly it was the wrong move, but she had to do something, so she slid her hand up his arm, to his neck, fingers brushing the skin above his stiff collar. "You're right. It doesn't mean that, but I do. Dan, I *do* love you, and there is nothing easy about that for me. But you are funny and strong and…you put yourself out there. I love you, I…respect you. I know this doesn't change what I did." She let her fingers glide along the smooth length of his jaw.

She wasn't giving up, but who knew how many opportunities she'd get to touch him if he didn't forgive her.

She swallowed. "I think you had to learn something when you came here, and you did. Well, I had to learn something about…love and life, and I'm sorry it took hurting you to see it. I hope you can forgive me, but even if you say you can't right now, I'm not giving up on you. Because you love me and I love you, and I won't give up on that when I'm finally realizing how important it is."

She swallowed again, and then stopped trying so hard to stem the tide of tears. Because this was about showing her emotions, not being afraid of them, of feeling. She took his chin between her fingers and forced him to look at her.

When his eyes finally met hers, some of that hard tension in his jaw loosened. "Tears are not fair," he said gruffly.

"Nothing is *fair*."

He stared at her for a long time, silent, muscles tense. "You'd really keep trying if I said I can't forgive you and you broke my heart irreparably?"

She swallowed at the slice of pain. "It isn't irreparable if we both want to repair it."

He finally moved—just a slight shift, curling his hand into a fist and then uncurling it, his gaze moving past her. There was a moment she was sure he'd say no, tell her to get out of his car. A band tightened in her chest, somehow choking her breathing but making the tears fall harder.

"Besides, I need you to teach me how...how to change. I taught you how to ranch. You owe me."

His eyes flicked to hers and finally he touched her, thumb wiping tears off of one cheek. "You *are* part of the reason I changed. Your strength. And then you were the thing that made losing my shit seem worth it. Being an emotional wreck who couldn't hack it seemed worth it if it got me you."

Oh, damn him, making her cry harder. "No! That is not right. You can't out-sweet-talk me. It's not fair. I'm apologizing. I should win the sweet talk."

He took her hand, brushed his mouth across her knuckles. "It can be a lifelong contest."

Her breathing hitched, instead of with tears with a sharp intake of breath. "What exactly does that mean?"

He looked down at her hand in his, thoughtfully, then turned it over, pressing a finger to each of the calluses on her palm. "Are you really ready to put all the hard work you put in here"—he brushed a fingertip across a broken piece of skin—"into us?"

"Yes. Absolutely." It was a much scarier prospect

than actual physical labor she could control, but it also offered a better reward. A reward that didn't disappear if her ability to work did. She would have him. What more could she want?

"You make a compelling argument, I suppose. I think I can forgive you." Before she could throw her arms around his neck and just hold on, he held a hand between them. "On three very important conditions."

She nodded, probably too eagerly, but she didn't care. "Anything." And she meant it. She would do anything, and that made anything seem possible.

Dan had no idea what to do with her apologies and declarations of love. He didn't know what to do with her anythings, or if forgiving her was selling himself short. He didn't have a clue if any of this was right, but he'd gotten through the past few weeks doing what felt like the right thing to do.

And that would always be her.

"Anything?" he replied, still holding on to her hand with one of his own and holding her off with the other. "What if I said I wanted the llamas to live inside with us?"

She was leaning over the console, leaning into him. Like she really would do anything. Hell, she even smiled. "I'd take you to a psychiatrist. Lovingly."

He barked out a laugh. The past week felt like some bizarre movie. Had this all really happened to him? Up, down, and up again. But she was sitting there saying she loved him. In Chicago. In a dress. She was telling him she wanted to work hard on them, and wouldn't it be the stupidest thing if he let one mistake be the thing that kept them apart forever?

"Okay, really, three conditions. First, you come live with me. Permanently, unpacked bag and everything."

She bit her lip. "I'd have to make some arrangements with Caleb, but I do want to do that."

"Good. Second, sometime around Christmas, you come to Florida with me to visit my grandparents."

The crying that had finally stopped didn't start again, but her eyes got all watery. She nodded, hand in his, squeezing.

"Third…" He trailed off. Went quiet.

She let out an impatient breath after he was silent for a while. "You're killing me here," she muttered.

"I can't think of anything," he admitted. "But three seemed like such a good number."

"Dan!"

"Okay, serious third condition." He moved so he could have both of her hands in his, so he could look her straight in the eye. If that's how it had ended, that would be how it began again. "When you're afraid or panicked, when you're sad or hurt or ecstatic or …whatever, instead of, oh, I don't know ripping my heart out and stomping on it, or either of us running away, we could go with the easy route. 'I'm scared.' etc."

Her throat moved, but she nodded again. "I will work on that. And just so you know, I didn't relish ripping your heart out, but I was busy ripping out mine, so I may have failed to notice. Maybe we both agree to keep our hearts firmly in place."

"Sure." He brought her hands to his mouth, kissing both. "Except mine belongs to you."

She wrinkled her nose, but there were tears falling over her lashes again. "Gross."

"It can't be that gross—you're crying again."

"I want to go home!" she said with a sniff. "With you." She leaned forward, pressing her mouth to his, briefly. Far too briefly. "Let's go *home*."

Nothing could have sounded better. Well, maybe one thing, but they'd have plenty of opportunity to do that at home too.

"Sharpe."

When he growled, she laughed.

"I just wanted you to know that I fully expect you to be able to use that name on me at some point." She said it so archly, like a challenge.

"That name on y— Oh, no, no, no. *You* are not proposing to *me*. I will be the one proposing when we are ready."

"Of course," she said, all wide-eyed innocence. "Who said anything about proposing?"

He took her face between his hands. "You are a giant pain in my ass, and I love you with everything I have."

She grinned. "Yes. You do." She took a deep breath, the grin softening into something sweeter. "And I love you with all I am."

The kiss was close enough to coming home; he didn't even care that they probably wouldn't be back to Blue Valley before tomorrow. She was here. She was his. And that was more than enough to get them through.

*Read on for an excerpt from the next book in
Nicole Helm's Big Sky Cowboys series:*

OUTLAW COWBOY

CALEB SHAW STARED AT THE BOTTLE OF JACK
Daniel's. It sat, innocently enough, on the table next to
his snoring father.

In his mind's eye, he unscrewed the black plastic cap
and poured himself a double. And then another. The
scorching heat of the amber liquid would dull away all
the sharp edges inside of him.

Next to the bottle was that damn scrapbook Dad
paraded out whenever he was drunk and sad. It was
happening with increasing regularity. Caleb never
wanted anything to do with the scrapbook. In fact, for
an uncountable amount of time, he thought about tossing
the damn thing in the fire.

In fact, he wanted both items gone. Banished forever.
Hell, at this point in his life, he'd as soon use the alcohol
to amp the blaze than drink it.

Liar.

Fair enough. His mouth was watering, and the edgy,
simmering anger threatened to spill over. No amount of
good seemed a match for it. And there had been good
the past few months.

But it seemed like with him, bad always lurked in
the shadows.

What would be the harm in one drink? His older sister would never know he'd broken his promise. She didn't live here anymore. She'd left him with all of this for love.

"Caleb?"

Summer's hesitant voice was enough for him to close his eyes. Christ, Summer. She was a blessing and some kind of curse, this younger sister he'd only found out about last year. Somehow she was managing to fill some of the holes Mel's marriage and move had left in his life.

But, damn, he missed Mel. Sure, it wasn't as if he never saw her. She was only across the valley on her husband's strange little llama ranch, but he'd never felt responsible for Mel, and rarely felt like he needed to soothe her. Summer was in constant need of both.

It's in you.

The voice that had haunted him growing up—the voice he thought he'd erased—had returned with Summer's appearance and Dad's confession. Honestly, it had resurfaced before that, when Mel had trusted him to be in charge when it was the last damn thing she should have done. No one should ever trust him. Hadn't he proven that by now?

"I'm sorry to interrupt," Summer continued, her voice wavering.

Summer was constantly sorry. Sorry to be a burden or distraction. Sorry she didn't know everything. If she wasn't sorry, she was delighted: by the horses, by the mountains, by family.

She cooked and kept the house clean, for him and the father she'd only just met—the father who admitted she was his, but refused to have any interaction with her.

Though, to be fair, Dad didn't interact with much of anybody. Not since he'd been paralyzed six years ago.

It's in you.

Mom's voice. Mom's accusation. *The evil. It's in you.*

"I'd go away. It's just…"

"Just what?" Caleb snapped, immediately wincing. Losing his temper with Summer was like losing his temper with a puppy. Puppies and Summer Shaw could not take harsh words. They cowered.

It was hardly her fault she reminded him of…that.

"I think someone's in the cabin."

He let out a breath. No Jack for him. Which was good. He hadn't had any in nine months. Nine long, sober months living with that boiling anger, a constant presence he had to fight back. But he hadn't broken his promise, so at least there wasn't new guilt to mix in with the old anger. "Someone?"

"I went back to my caravan for lunch—"

"You can eat here, you know." Something about the way she acted like a maid in a house that was very much owed to her always rubbed him the wrong way. She wouldn't take Mel's old room and she wouldn't eat lunch at the main house. She'd only eat dinner with him if she'd cooked it. She slept in a little caravan she'd arrived in last year, parked at the edge of the property.

She was a *Shaw*, and she acted like an employee inside these four walls.

He hated it, and he had no one to tell. Mel was gone, a new focus in her life. Dad was…gone in his own way. And Summer cowered against his temper.

So he kept the anger inside. He tried to freeze it out, muscle it away, but it lingered, in him. *Always.*

"I…" Summer's mouth curved into a smile. She looked so much like Mel, like his fuzzy memories of Mom. "I kind of like being by myself every once in a while. I wasn't allowed to be alone much before…I left."

His estranged mother had disappeared when he was five, pregnant with Summer. Then twenty-some years later, Summer had left Mom to come here and find the rest of her family. And shocked the hell out of them with her appearance, since none of the other Shaws had known about her existence.

Except Dad.

Dad had sacrificed Summer to keep Mel, and all because of him. *It's in you*.

"Are you all right?" Summer asked in a hushed whisper. She reached out to squeeze his arm. She was always so…touchy. Touchy. Smiley. Sorry. She gave him a headache, a guilt he didn't understand, which melded with the anger he figured must be in his blood. *Bad, bad blood*.

He stepped away from her. "Why do you think someone's in the cabin?"

"There was a light inside last night. Real quick, but I know I saw it. And I thought I saw someone in the yard this morning. The snow around the place is all weird. It could be an animal, or just how it's melting I guess, but—"

Caleb strode past her—out of the living room, through the kitchen, and into the mudroom. He plucked the keys to the gun safe from under a tub of rock salt and shoved it into the lock as Summer caught up with him.

Summer released a shocked exhale. "Oh. I don't think you'll need that. I'm pretty sure it's a woman."

He raised an eyebrow at her. "You think women can't be dangerous?"

"Well, of course they can. I am very well aware they can be, but…"

He grabbed the shotgun and locked the safe again. "Show me," he instructed.

Summer blinked at him as she worried her hands together. "Oh, I shouldn't have said anything."

"Someone is prowling around that old cabin, only a few hundred yards from where you currently *sleep*, and you shouldn't have said anything?"

Summer grabbed her coat from the hook and pulled it around her. "I don't think she's—"

"She's—if it's a she—trespassing, and needs to be scared off."

"A gun seems harsh."

"What, you think this is Goldilocks and she's lost and looking for some warm porridge?"

Summer stuck her hands in her coat pockets, her eyebrows furrowed and her mouth pressed into a line. He supposed this was Summer angry. It was like a spring shower compared to the raging thunderstorm of the other Shaws' tempers. Slow and quiet, not one flash of lightning or boom of thunder.

Summer was silent, with none of her normal chatter—nervous or otherwise—as they got in his truck and drove through the slushy spring snow to the other side of the Shaw property where the old cabin was.

The cabin looked the same as it had since Grandpa died fifteen-some years ago. The Shaw men had never lived to a ripe old age, and had never been any good at housekeeping. The windows were dusty, everything slumped and old. The rough-hewn logs supposedly chopped down by some ancestor were weathered by age and harsh winters.

But there was a definite disturbance to the snowpack around the cabin, and while any number of wild animals could be walking around the area, infesting the cabin, wild animals didn't typically attempt to cover their tracks.

And they certainly couldn't open doors. The sagging lump of snow on the left-hand side of the door was unmistakable.

Someone was in there, and that someone didn't want anyone to know.

"Go to the caravan," Caleb ordered, hopping out of the truck. He left the safety on the gun. He doubted whoever was hiding wanted trouble, but he'd been involved in a little too much trouble back in the day to entirely rule it out.

Summer was shadowing him, decidedly not going to the caravan. "You can't go in there alone."

"Why not? I'm a man with a gun."

"You're the one who said she could be dangerous!"

"I repeat, I am a man with a gun." He strode toward the cabin door, but Summer kept following him. He was sure he could yell and she'd stay put, but that seemed like an overreaction. This was probably as simple as someone looking for a warm place to stay.

He tried to peer in the window surreptitiously, but both the grime and the tattered curtains blocked any view of the interior.

"I'm going to ease my way in. You stay outside. Got it?"

She clutched her hands together in front of her, eyes wide and worried, but she nodded. He had to resist rolling his eyes. Lord knew he'd faced a lot more potentially dire situations than some random person in this long vacated cabin.

It's in you.

Every once in a while that was all right, wasn't it? Every once in a while, he got it in his fool head to save somebody, and the not-so-nice pieces of himself came in handy.

Of course, his help rarely really solved anything.

Focus.

He eased the door open, his finger on the gun's safety, his eyes slowly adjusting to the dim light inside. He noticed a long, denim-clad leg dangling over the back of the couch.

A flash of sunlight hit the bottom metal of a boot, and he saw an inscription on the sole.

He lowered his finger away from the safety. He knew that boot and its inscription: *fuck off* in flowing script. He considered keeping the gun up, because Lord knew this woman was dangerous. "Damn it, Delia."

"Hello, handsome," she drawled, not moving off the musty old couch so he could see the rest of her. "Took you a little longer than I expected."

Delia's heart hammered in her chest. It was a lie. She hadn't been expecting Caleb at all. She thought she'd been so careful.

Despite the thunderstorm of fear and nerves inside her, she remained still, except for her foot, tapping absently in the air. She had been bred to weather every unexpected confrontation with a mask of calm and poise.

Besides, she'd known this *could* happen. It wasn't ideal, but she had a backup plan. She wouldn't be trespassing if she didn't have a backup plan. She wouldn't be Delia Rogers if she didn't have a backup plan.

"Who is she?" a voice whispered.

A female voice.

That had Delia moving. A *woman* could put a wrench in her backup plan. She pushed into a sitting position, scooping her hair out of her eyes.

Oh, Caleb. Handsome boys who turned into handsome men simply weren't fair. His hair was still golden and wavy, whiskers glinting almost red in the sun. His shoulders were broader, but his hips were still narrow. Even under the heavy winter coat, she could tell he packed a lot of strength in that lean frame. Adulthood and bad choices had given his face character. The sharp swoop to his square jaw was covered in appealing stubble, his nose was slightly crooked, and she remembered the day that slash had been put in his eyebrow.

He still had a mouth made for sin and muscles made for work. Too bad she knew the history underneath.

And she would use it if it came to that. Use all those feelings she'd denied herself since…well, *since*.

The silence hung between them, glittering with ghosts and secrets, and Caleb made no bones about scowling his distaste.

She'd heard it through the grapevine: Caleb Shaw had gone straight. She hadn't thought much of it at first. The people in their old ne'er-do-well clan ended up one of three ways: getting their act together, dead in a ditch, or where she very well might be headed if she couldn't figure her way out of this mess.

Jail.

Panic welled up in her chest, making it hard to pretend, but panic had been a constant companion since she could remember, so it didn't show. It was her little secret.

"Who's she?" Delia jutted her chin toward the brunette standing halfway behind Caleb, like he was protecting her.

Something uncomfortable twisted in Delia's stomach, but she wouldn't let it lodge there. If Caleb had a woman, that might complicate things, but it certainly wouldn't stand in her way. She wasn't going to jail for what Eddie had done, and she'd use whatever and whoever she had in her arsenal to make sure of it. That's what had kept her from being dead in a ditch for twenty-some years.

That and Caleb's fists one particularly unpleasant night, but that had also caused half of the trouble she was in right now, so it seemed to even itself out.

"She's none of your business," Caleb replied, standing even more in front of the woman.

Delia wanted to sneer. She looked more girl than woman. In fact, she looked like...

Delia couldn't put her finger on it, but it didn't matter. As far as Delia was concerned, the *girl* was a speed bump, and speed bumps were meant to be flown over.

Caleb turned his head to the girl, still keeping her out of Delia's gaze, as though just glancing at Delia would be trouble. His voice was low, nothing more than a rumbled whisper, though Delia could make out the words *go home*. Good. Send the little girl away so they could have an adult conversation.

Now Delia had to figure out what to say. She hadn't expected to have to use the backup plan so quickly, but it was there, fuzzy formed in her brain. Luckily she was used to thinking on the fly.

After a few hushed exchanges, the *girl* finally exited the cabin and Delia was left with Caleb. Alone. She forced her mouth to curl in a languid smile, the kind meant to allure, entice, *remind*.

"What are you doing here?" he demanded in a gravelly voice. That was new. She remembered the barely banked anger in his eyes, but not that steely note to his voice.

"How long's it been, honey? Four years?"

"Not long enough, *sweets*."

He'd never liked pet names, which was why she'd always used them with him. He'd respond sarcastically, but when a woman lived with a dearth of pet names, she didn't care how the men around her said them.

Sweets was like a little bright pop of sugary candy. Delia could pretend for weeks on that sweets.

"Who's the girl?"

Caleb brought the door shut with a loud snap. "She's none of your business."

"A little young for you."

"Jealous?" He flashed a grin that held no happiness behind it, only a grave kind of malice. "How unlike you."

It was the kind of exchange they'd had a million times. Poking at each other, over and over again. She'd always believed there was a magnetic force between them—drawing them together but sparking if they got too close.

Secrets always kept them from acknowledging what hummed in all these exchanges.

Awareness. Attraction.

She was no idiot when it came to those things, but she didn't trust them when it came to Caleb and never had. But she'd use them if she had to. Caleb had gone straight, but he was still a *man*. He was still the man who'd almost killed her father—a fact only the two of them knew. That may have saved her life, but it had also made it far more complicated than it had been before. And it had been plenty complicated before.

Still, she had the upper hand here.

"Why are you *here*?" he demanded. If she hadn't known him for almost her whole life, she might have been offended by the demand. It was harsh, but that was Caleb. When he wanted something, his temper frayed, and she knew he wanted her far away, not tiptoeing on his new straight-and-narrow life.

"I need your..." *Help* wasn't the right word. She didn't need his help. She had this covered—she only needed him to look the other way for a while. "All I need you to do is pretend I'm not here."

His grip on the gun didn't loosen, but she couldn't say she was scared. She'd spent her life at the mercy of a man who used his fists or worse to get what he wanted, or to beat out a bad mood, or simply to lay blame. She'd had guns pointed at her, held to her head. So Caleb didn't scare her in the least.

But jail for a crime she didn't commit? Yeah, she wasn't going down like that. She still had one sister to get out of the hellhole the Rogers called home, and she couldn't do that locked up.

Caleb didn't say anything for long, stretching minutes of silence. He glared at her, and she imagined the wheels inside his head were turning on overdrive.

"Fine," he finally said. "I'll pretend you aren't here… on one condition."

She'd spent too many years living in so many people's conditions. It was foolish that her breath had caught in that pause. Foolish she'd thought he wouldn't have one. Whatever glimmer of connection between them had never been particularly nice.

But there *was* a connection, which made her next move harder. Any stranger, any other man, and the overt flirtation would have been easy, welcome, practiced. But under Caleb's steady blue gaze, she wilted halfway through licking her lips.

She had no power over Caleb, and hadn't since elementary school when he'd caught her dumpster diving.

Caleb Shaw knew all her secrets, but there was one positive to that.

She knew all his too.

Chapter 2

IT HAD BEEN ABOUT FIVE YEARS SINCE HE'D HAD ANY interaction with Delia Rogers, and yet the emotions inside of him were as familiar as if she'd been by his side every day.

Blue Valley, Montana, was not a place where you could be the same age and not know each other. You went to school together, were in the same classes more often than not. Whether you liked each other or not was irrelevant—you *knew* each other.

Delia had been in most of his classes and she had run with the group of trouble makers he'd made the center of his world for the term of his adolescence. She had always, always been there, in the midst of almost everything he did, and he had, for a very long time, suffered the same wariness upon being in the same room with Delia Rogers.

He couldn't remember a time when seeing her, being around her, thinking about her hadn't sent a wave of *feeling* through him. A deep, chest-crushing wave of sympathy. A dark, sharp-edged urge to protect. Painful, unwanted lust.

If she had been just about any other woman, the lust wouldn't be unwanted. It would have been acted on at the hundreds of wild, stupid parties they'd both attended. But long before he'd understood what lust was, one shared moment had always kept him away from Delia.

In the third grade, he'd watched her eat food out of a trash can with the faint mark of what had probably once been an impressive shiner on her cheek. Even at such a young age, he'd known Delia's life was far more complicated and scary than his would ever be, even when he'd thought the devil was all but in him.

He had food to eat, a dad who protected him, and while he was half convinced there was no choice for him but to be bad, he'd known he was *safe*.

Delia was not. Had likely never been.

"What's your condition, Caleb?" Delia asked, her voice edged with exhaustion and…something he didn't want to hear.

Hurt.

Why did he have to see through her? He didn't want to. He wished she were as big of a mystery to him as she had been to the other guys they'd hung around. He *wished* she was an untouchable, wild thing. But instead she was always this clear, complex, *beautiful* woman to him.

He'd watched her have a gun pointed to her head by her own father, and he'd seen that same look on her face: weary acceptance, and determination to be brave.

He'd seen it for a lie too.

Then he'd beaten the ever loving shit out of a man twice his age and left him in a pool of blood.

He was scared to death this was all he had in him—violence and hurting people, even if it was in the name of protecting someone. Protecting Delia.

She'd never thanked him for it either. She'd said he'd ruined her life.

"Caleb," Delia snapped. "Stop tripping down memory lane and tell me what the condition is."

He realized his hands weren't steady and leaned the gun against the wall. She always did this to him. It was why he shunned any and all connection to her in his attempt to be a decent human being ever since Dad's accident. Her effect was more potent than any alcohol he'd downed to ease the anger.

Caleb cleared his throat. He knew she'd see through any attempt to pretend he was unmoved, unaffected by all the secrets that swirled between them, around them, but for his own pride, he pretended anyway.

"The condition is you tell me why you're here." He studied her now, sitting on the old couch like it was a throne. Her long dark hair was pulled back into a ponytail, and the fringe of her bangs was too long, covering half of her eyes.

She crossed long, slender arms across her chest, the leather of her coat stretching at the shoulders. It was old and just a hair too small for her. Something uncomfortable pinged in his chest. "Tell me," he said gently.

He hated the way she yanked gentleness and care out of him without even trying. He didn't trust her with that power.

Her gaze, still half-hidden by fringe, met his. "No." Her nose was sharp, her mouth lush. Her cheeks were too hollow, her shoulders too sharp. She had to be hungry, and from the looks of it, she had to be running.

The wave of sympathy and a fierce urge to protect welled up inside him, but he wouldn't be laid flat by that again. He'd fight it with everything he had. "Then get out."

Her gaze never wavered. "No."

He had to close his eyes and breathe through his

temper, through wanting to run to the house, gather up half the pantry, and shove it at her. She needed someone to take care of her, mess that she was.

Unfortunately, he was no better. He just had a soft place to land time and time again. The ranch. Mel. Hell, even Summer and Dad. He had all these *things* and people he didn't deserve, and Delia had nothing.

She unfolded herself from the couch, all languid ease, but he knew it was an act. Delia used her body and her face like weapons.

He couldn't even blame her for it. It was all she had.

She trailed her fingertip over the back of the couch as she leisurely walked toward him. "I wonder what the statute of limitations on assault is," she said conversationally.

He slowly lifted his gaze from her fingertip to her eyes, but she wouldn't meet it. She kept her head cocked in a way that obscured her eyes with hair, every move she made too casual to be real.

He would not be affected. Or, more apt, he would not let the affected part of himself win. Because he truthfully, had no idea about statute of limitations would be. But surely it'd been too long. He wasn't even sure he cared; all he cared about was that she was willing to try to use it against him. "I wonder what you're running away from," he replied just as casually. "Daddy dearest?"

This time her gaze did snap to his, and for the briefest of seconds, the flashes of anger and hurt and years of *fear* were so evident he almost staggered.

But after a second it was gone, and Delia was smiling the kind of sweet smile that always meant the opposite. "I'd certainly have come to the right place if that were true." Nothing about her syrupy sweet smile changed. "Wouldn't I have?"

"What do you want?" he demanded through gritted teeth, hands clenched into fists so he didn't reach out and grab her by the shoulders. *Too bony shoulders. Too fragile. Too everything.*

Touching Delia in any way, shape, or form could only lead to disaster.

"I want a place to stay. You can pretend I'm not even here. Just don't tell anyone I am. It's simple and easy. Pretend like you never saw me. Tell *her*," she said, jerking her chin toward where Summer had gone, "to do the same. That's it. No biggie."

"I should know what you're hiding from." The minute the words were out of his mouth, he wished them back. Actually, it would be better if he had no idea what she was hiding from. Better if he pretended she'd never existed. *Good luck, buddy.*

"Oh, honey, you don't want to know." Her gaze sized him up in a quick up-and-down glance. "Straight and narrow agrees with you, Caleb. I'd hate to have to mess it up." She raised her hand as if to pat his cheek, but he caught her wrist before she could touch him.

Sadly, that didn't help any. It was still a connection. His fingertips wrapped around her narrow wrist. Her skin was smooth and cool, the pulse slowly bumping into him, a steady *thrum-thrum-thrum*. He wanted to draw his thumb against it. He wanted to do a million things with his hands.

Things he wouldn't do to Delia. Not ever. Maybe he was bad blood, but he didn't prey on weak women, even when they were so convinced they were strong.

"You're too skinny," he bit out, dropping her wrist, willing the feel of her out of his memory as soon as possible.

She barked out a laugh, her arm falling to her side, fingers curling into a fist. "Sorry to disappoint."

"Do you have any supplies?"

"I'll get by just fine." She unclenched her fist, tried to brush the too-long bangs out of her eyes. "I always do."

Not always, he wanted to say, but he didn't want to relive that night any more than she probably did, and if he acknowledged it aloud, they'd both have to face it.

"You have a week," he said instead, trying to exert some form of control.

"Aw, that's cute, trying to tell me what to do. I have as long as I'd like. Just go about your life, being Mr. Upstanding Citizen, and keep that *girl* away from me. End of story."

He wished like hell it would be that easy, but he knew, even as he turned and grabbed his gun and left, it wouldn't be. He'd be back soon enough.

———

Delia blinked at the door. Caleb's hasty departure had been… She tried to analyze it. She thought she'd have to fight at least a little more to convince him to leave her alone.

She had to ignore the disappointment over that not being the case. She needed to be glad he was gone, glad he was going to leave her be. If nothing else, the way he'd held her wrist should send her packing.

Gentle. Gentle would kill her at this point. Still, she had nowhere else to go. Not until she figured out how to get around her current predicament. No one would find her unless Caleb snitched, and she'd ruin him before she let that happen.

She stared at the curtain hanging limply over the window. It looked like there'd been a pattern once, but the sun and age had faded it away. The hem was fraying, but the windows were so dirty, the protection against the sunlight was barely needed.

This place reminded her all too much of home, dark and grimy and old. It reminded her that Steph was still there, only sixteen and under Dad's thumb. Hiding and cowering in the dark and dust and grime and abuse. Would Mom be more protective of her since she was the only one left? Or would it be worse, because his obsession with having a son had never materialized and he thought Steph was a glaring reminder?

Delia swung away from the window. She had to go about figuring out how to keep herself alive here. She had no food left, no means of making a fire, and Montana in March didn't offer much hope for warm weather.

Once it got dark, she could probably sneak down closer to the Shaw house and steal some wood. She'd never been up to the main house, but there had to be a woodpile somewhere outside. And maybe she'd have to put her old Dumpster diving techniques to use.

She'd promised herself she'd never be there again, but what business did she have making any promises to herself—a poor girl with a bad reputation and a dangerous father? There was no promise she'd yet to keep for more than a handful of years.

Except getting her sisters out. She had to get Steph out and then…then maybe there were promises to be made. But before she could rescue Steph, she had to have a plan and she had to be alive.

She had one blanket in her pack. One change of clothes. A tube of lipstick. A pack of gum. A dead flashlight. Two dollars and a handful of pennies. It was all she'd managed to grab while the cops pounded at the door. The only thing that had been in her bag prior to that was a lowly condom.

She'd kept it as a good luck charm. She should have known good luck and sex didn't mix.

A wave of exhaustion and defeat almost knocked her off her feet.

How had it gotten this bad?

Eddie. The bastard. He'd had her fooled. She thought she was using some dumb moron for a warm bed and some food on the table while she used every paycheck to get Billie to Seattle.

Instead, she'd been the one being used as the damned scapegoat when their idiotic drug ring got busted up. He'd been smart enough to fool her, but not smart enough to keep his ass out of trouble.

The only good thing about it was she'd gotten Billie away from Dad first. Elsie, the first sister Delia had whisked out of hell, had settled herself there and was thriving. Now Billie would have that chance too.

All because Delia had spent the past ten years of her life making what she could despite her lack of a high school diploma, and using every penny to get her sisters safe. Thanks to Caleb, because once Dad had realized she had someone protecting her, he'd kicked her out. She couldn't be home to protect the other girls. She'd been forced to stay away for their own safety, sneaking around only when she was sure she could get them free.

For ten years, she'd worked like a dog, using any guy who came along to keep her fed and sheltered so she could afford their escape.

Some guys hadn't been so bad. Some had used their fists like dear old Dad. But none had ever really kept her safe, no matter how often she wished they'd try.

This was a low point—she had to admit that to herself. If she didn't admit it, she'd never get past it. But she had to get Steph out and somewhere where she'd have an opportunity to amount to something—and Delia'd use whatever means possible.

Which meant... She blew out a breath. She had to ask for help. Which meant she had two choices.

First, Caleb. He seemed the most reasonable choice. After all, she had some blackmail material on him. Dad had woken up from being beaten unconscious having no idea who had attacked him. Only Delia knew it had been Caleb.

If Caleb truly was on the straight and narrow, there were quite a few things she'd witnessed him do she doubted he wanted the people of Blue Valley to know about.

She could also go to Rose. No doubt she'd need to let Rose know she was okay sometime soon. But Rose's current location was a mystery. The Rogers women who stayed in Montana knew not to stay one place very long.

Including her. She'd had to stick close until they were all free, but she popped from one town to another to keep Dad off the scent, but close enough to Blue Valley she could get there within an hour or so. Close enough she could keep tabs on the girls. *One more*. She only needed to get Steph out and then *she* was free.

Tears she'd never allow herself to shed started to gather and burn in the backs of her eyes. It was exhaustion, plain and simple, causing all this emotion and fear. She hadn't slept last night as she planned how to sneak her way into the abandoned Shaw cabin. A nap would be the best course of action. Get some rest while waiting for nightfall and her planned prowling for firewood. Plus, if she could fall asleep, she could ignore her growling stomach.

She'd wake up refreshed and ready to take on the next challenge. She sank onto the couch. It was old and squeaky. It smelled of age and dust.

Delia flopped back onto the hard springs of the couch, staring at the cobweb-laden ceiling and trying not to think about her sisters. She didn't want to remember the bruises on Billie's arms, or imagine what other bruises might have been hiding under her clothing.

One more. Only one.

Delia closed her eyes, breathed deep, and started counting backwards—the only way she ever shut her brain up enough to sleep. A harsh slam outside made her eyes fling open, her heart racing as fear clawed through her chest.

Oh God, the police had found her already. They'd somehow tracked her here and she was going to jail and Steph was screwed.

Calm. Down. She took a breath in and slid off the couch, hurrying to the window with purposeful strides. Carefully she pulled the tattered curtains far enough away from the window to glimpse outside.

The window was obscured with grime, but it only took her a few seconds to realize it was Caleb. Relief whooshed through her, top to bottom, and she was suddenly shaky on her feet. Or was that the exhaustion and hunger? It hardly mattered.

The door swung open. Jeez, did the guy understand stealth at *all*? "I don't know why you're back, but I'm trying to take a—"

He dropped a hefty box onto the ground with a loud thump. Her limbs seized up, and she was unable to move, unable to look.

No. Please. Not kindness. Not now.

"Food. Flashlights. Blankets. Water." He spat each word like a curse. "The pump in the back works if you really get it going, but I'm not sure it's drinkable. What else do you need?"

The sob was so sudden, so overwhelming, she didn't have a chance to fight it off. She could only clap her hands over her eyes and hope to hide the overflow of tears.

Chapter 3

CALEB WISHED HE HAD BROUGHT HIS GUN THIS TIME. IF he had it, he could use it to threaten her to stop crying. It was just food, for chrissakes. The woman *needed* food.

She hadn't cried when her father had held a gun to her head when they'd been nineteen, but she was crying now. "You make zero sense, woman," he muttered.

She didn't make any crying noises. The teardrops simply slid from underneath the palms slapped over her eyes, some landing in little dark dots on the grimy gray shirt she wore underneath her jacket.

She took a deep, shuddery breath, slowly let it out, and even more slowly removed her hands from her eyes, wiping most of the tears as she went.

Underneath the fringe of hair, her red-rimmed eyes held his gaze. "I'm exhausted and hungry. Your act of gallantry took me off guard."

"Gallantry?" He raised an eyebrow at her.

She didn't waver. "You've always had it in you."

Only for her. Just another one of the inexplicable ways she affected him. No one else, not even his own damn sister, had ever tugged at his conscience like Delia.

"What else do you *need*?" he repeated, hoping to hurry this along, assuage whatever damn conscious he had, and get the hell away from her. Then he could pretend this little corner of Shaw land didn't exist until she was done hiding from whatever she was running away from.

"I imagine that'll do."

"Do" was not exactly comforting, but she was not his responsibility, no matter how many times he'd felt she was.

"The bathroom works. The water pressure sucks, but we got it going for… Well, anyway, it works and you're the only one using it right now. So." So. That was it. He'd gotten her some food, told her the pertinents, and now it was time to go, oh, anywhere but here.

Anywhere but here or to the living room, where a bottle of Jack stood completely unguarded except for a snoring, paralyzed father.

"Are you waiting for a thank-you?"

Caleb inhaled sharply. He wasn't waiting at all. So why was he standing stupidly so many feet away from the door?

Delia ran a finger over the edge of her bangs, touching her tongue to the corner of her mouth and cocking a hip in one fluid, sensual movement.

It was purposeful, and he *knew* that. It did not change the fact every nerve ending jumped to life, a buzzing static that whispered *beautiful woman* to all the parts of him interested in such a thing.

"I'm sure I could muster one up, but I think I'll grab a bite to eat first." She sauntered toward the box, her eyes never leaving his, the practiced, self-satisfied smile that curved her pretty mouth full of promise and teasing.

She plucked a granola bar out of the box and unwrapped it. Slowly. Watching him through her hair as she brought it to her mouth and placed her lips around the tip.

It was all *designed* to make him think of sex. He saw

it for what it was, for what she was trying to do—control the situation by any means necessary—but his mind was really no match for his dick. At least when it came to reaction. When it came to action, well, his brain was smart enough to keep his hands at his sides.

It helped that her hand shook a little as she took the bite. That everything about her, except that mouth, was too sharp. She needed food, and everything else crackling in the air was secondary to the fact that she was literally *starving*.

Clearly she was running from something, and, sweet Christ, Delia had a legion of things to run from. Things he couldn't allow to touch the ranch right now. So, shelter, food, that was it. The end of what he owed her.

I saved your life.

You ruined *it.*

He wondered if she remembered that exchange, if she still felt that way, because the fury of the aftermath was seared on his brain the way all bad memories branded to it. *It's in you. You ruined it.* All the times he had let people down because even his best wasn't enough.

"Stay out of sight. The last thing I need is someone thinking I've got you shacked up out here." He supposed if any of the Rogers sisters were shrinking violets, the town of Blue Valley might have rallied around them. It was not exactly a secret that Graham Rogers beat his wife and daughters, no secret they'd been poor or hungry.

The way he heard it, before he'd been quite old enough to understand, the town *had* tried to get Delia's mom out, to give the Rogers help, and every door had been shut to them until all anyone could do was pretend the Rogers girls could take care of themselves.

"I keep forgetting. Caleb Shaw. Gone straight."

Didn't he wish? As it was, he was having lunch with Mel to "discuss the state of the ranch." Translation: discuss his continued failure. But that was none of Delia's business.

"Gone straight. Yes, I have. Don't forget it. I won't be sucked into whatever this is. You have what you need to keep you alive. Now, find a way to get back on your own two feet. And the hell away from here."

She had the gall to laugh. All raspy and...sexy, damn it.

"Sweetheart, please don't ever be under the impression that I'm here as anything other than a last resort. But, as you're the one who started this whole mess, it seems very poetic."

Ah, so she did remember the exchange.

"You have a week."

"Oh, Caleb." She said his name with such a weary condescension he didn't need to force himself toward the door anymore. If he stayed he'd be tempted to argue, to snipe, and that would not be productive.

He might be a lousy son of a bitch, but he was no fool. He turned away from her, trying to adjust his fucking erection to a more comfortable position. *Hear that, you piece of shit? Forget any ideas you've got going on down there.*

He went for the door, trying to ignore the fact she was already rummaging around in the box for something else to eat. Against all his better judgements, he dug his wallet out of his pocket and plucked the lone twenty from the crease.

He slapped it down on an old end table by the door, making the whole thing wobble precariously.

"I don't want your money," she said in a thready voice.

"Too fucking bad," he replied, and with that, he flung himself out the door. Away from Delia. Away from memory lane. He'd done his duty, and now he'd wash his hands of her.

And if she wasn't gone in a week, he'd damn well do something about it.

Delia ate her fill of the random conglomeration of food Caleb had brought her. She'd ration later, but this afternoon was all about getting as much food and sleep as possible. How much longer she'd have those things was uncertain.

One week. She could probably twist Caleb's arm for longer, but the bottom line was she didn't want to. Not when he did things like bring her food and money. Not when he all but sneered at her offered thanks.

She could pretend she had the upper hand all she wanted, but if Caleb got a whiff of what was going on, he'd be able to do whatever he wanted. Sure, she could threaten going to the police, but she couldn't actually *do* it, even if the statute of limitations hadn't long run out. Well, as long as he didn't know that.

She rolled over on the uncomfortable, dank-smelling bed. This little room was even darker than the living room, but the bed was barely more tolerable than the couch.

When she awoke later, she had no idea how long she'd slept. Her cell phone had long been pawned for money and there was no possible way the unmoving clocks in this place were right. But it was nighttime and she was freezing.

She pulled one of the blankets Caleb had brought around her shoulders and shuffled into the living room. It was dark enough and the place unfamiliar enough that she had to slowly feel her way to the box, where Caleb had a battery-powered camping lantern.

Before she reached the box, however, she found herself drawn to the faint glow from the window. When she peered outside, she realized it was simply the brilliance of the moon and stars bouncing off that last layer of winter snow and ice. Everything sparkled and dazzled.

For the past decade she had tried not to dream of where she would go once all her sisters were safe. It was a dangerous thing to think about an escape that was so far off, but on the rare occasion she fell into fantasy, it was always somewhere warm and green and lush, far, far away from this crystallized wasteland of rolling grassland and mountains.

Yet it was breathtaking, and in the moment, she had the oddest thought that if she did finally escape Montana, she'd miss this. The vast sky, the bitter cold, the way you could feel perfectly still and alone. Like a star, brilliant and shining and important.

Talk about fantasy.

She shuffled to the door, shoved her feet into her boots, and then stepped outside. If she wanted to stay out of sight, she'd be cooped up in this cabin during daylight hours. So, she'd need to get her fresh air when she could.

The sky looked like a painting: swirls and dots of white against a velvety depth of black. The moon, big and round, hung in the sky, its light gilding snow silver and edging the outline of mountains in an unearthly glow.

She inhaled a frigid breath. The bracing cold seeped through all her threadbare layers, and she hoped spring would come early and fast. Being homeless and on the run was so much easier in the summer.

Oh, if Eddie had only held out a few months before throwing her under the bus, she could be camping out somewhere right now with only the rain as a threat to her well-being.

"Hello."

Delia screeched. She couldn't believe she'd been foolish enough to lower her guard. If this was the end, she fucking deserved it, idiot that she was for ever feeling comfortable.

"Sorry, I didn't mean to scare you," the airy feminine voice said. It surprised Delia that the apology sounded sincere, considering they were in the pitch black at who knew what time of night.

Her heartbeat thundered in her chest, in her neck, so deep and expansive was the surprise and the fear. Still, she did what she always did in the face of imminent threat. She breathed, she held still, and she willed her brain to calm and think.

A flame flickered to light. An honest-to-goodness old fashioned kerosene lamp began to glow, and with it, the owner of the disembodied voice became visible.

The girl from earlier.

Delia was slowly getting a hold of her body's traitorous reaction. She certainly wasn't intimidated by this *girl*. In fact, now that she knew the owner of the voice, she wasn't scared at all. Her instinct was to be cruel and dismissive, but that wasn't the smart choice. That was the instinct that always got her into trouble, and the instinct that idiotically thought Caleb was hers.

"No need to apologize. It's all right. I guess I was lost in thought." She tried to sound casual, friendly even.

"Summer."

Delia puzzled over the word for a few moments before she realized the girl was offering her name.

"Dee," she said in response, her tone only slightly cold. The girl might not pose much of a threat, but Delia didn't feel it necessary to give her any ammunition. That was a motto that had kept her out of a few sketchy situations.

Too bad you didn't give Eddie a fake name.

"Caleb told me to pretend you weren't here, but…" Summer trailed off as if Delia should know what to do with that. She didn't have a clue.

"Anyway, I live in that little caravan over behind that cluster of trees." She gestured vaguely behind her, but in the dark Delia had no idea where she was pointing.

It did mean the girl lived on Shaw property. Delia tried to study her face, but the kerosene lamp didn't give any hints to why she'd seemed familiar earlier. It certainly gave no hints as to who she was to Caleb.

Delia did not have the time to think about Caleb and what his relationship was to this girl. Her thoughts needed to be on how to get Steph out, followed immediately by getting herself out of this situation with the police. Caleb's relationships were irrelevant in every single way.

"Maybe…you should listen to Caleb." Her attempt at gentleness was even less successful than her attempt at friendly.

Summer sighed. "There's always someone I *should* be listening to," she muttered, a strange hint of bitterness to her tone. "Well, anyway," she said, her voice ringing out falsely bright in the quiet evening, "if you need anything, I wanted to let you know you can ask. And I won't ask any questions about…anything. I know what it's like to be…" She paused for so long Delia wondered if she'd ever finish. "On your own," she finally said.

Delia was momentarily stunned. An offer of help that was simply *I know what it's like.* Maybe it was foolish on Delia's part, but she almost wondered if this Summer girl was on the run from something as well.

Thankfully Delia had gotten enough rest that tears didn't rush to the surface, but she did feel a little wobbly, a little warm in the wake of that. So, she offered her best guess at what would constitute a polite response.

"Thank you."

She meant that thank-you far more than any words could ever do justice. She might have an ally, and while she wouldn't trust that easily, it was nice to know she had a possible backup if things got particularly sticky.

"I'll let you be then. But, really, my door is always open." The little old-fashioned lamp she held flickered against her smiling face, and Delia would chalk up the fact it looked genuine to the warmth of the flame.

The girl was a stranger at best, yet…when Delia turned to go inside, she did it with a strange warmth in her chest. It almost fought off the cold.

Acknowledgments

I owe every hockey reference to my hockey-loving husband, even when he despairs of my complete hockey ignorance. Every book I write is made possible by my amazing in-laws, who keep wonderful care of my children while I work. And a multitude of thanks to my wonderful editor, Mary, who did not run in the opposite direction when the llamas showed up.

About the Author

Nicole Helm writes down-to-earth contemporary romance specializing in people who don't live close enough to neighbors for them to be a problem. When she's not writing, she spends her time dreaming about someday owning a barn. Visit her at nicolehelm.wordpress.com.